DECEIVE ME

Boomsong
Publishing

Published in the UK in 2024 by Boomsong Publishing

Paperback ISBN: 978-1-7399452-3-7
eBook ISBN: 978-1-7399452-4-4

Cover design and typeset by Spiffing Publishing
Boomsong Publishing logo by Andrew Summers

To Phil

DECEIVE ME

Enjoy

Greed has few boundaries. Murder has none.

MICHAEL BACON

To Roy and Doreen… thank you x

ALSO BY MICHAEL BACON

38 Sleeps

ONE

THE red Jeep hurtled through the puddles, the storm was closing in.

The rutted dusty road was turning into a pot-holed quagmire. They'd been warned.

'How long to the runway?' His voice was worried. He looked down at his hands as he waited for the response. The blood would wash off.

'Chill out man, we're ten minutes away.' The driver turned to look at him. 'You'll be up in the air 10 minutes after that. Turn east, you'll miss this storm. Is he still out of it?'

He looked in the rear-view mirror as he nodded to the lifeless body and the man with the gold-toothed grin who was sitting alongside. He was still examining his hands, but on hearing the question patted the man's face. 'Yep, he's still out of it.'

A bolt of lightning lit up the sky, a dancing display of light, followed by another, then three, then four. The storm was on track to hit the island, and at exactly the time it said it would. But they couldn't have changed the plan. As the driver put his foot down the journey became more hazardous. Potholes he would have seen during the baking hot days were filled with water, the rusty windscreen wipers struggling to keep up with the deluge as they swished backwards and forwards apace.

'Just round this bend, then about another half mile,' the driver shouted, and grinned again. 'It's all cool.'... Except it wasn't.

Bang! The left wheel of the jeep smashed into a huge rut in the road. The impact sent the three men careering forward, hurtling towards the front windscreen, the jeep thundered to a ferocious halt as it flipped once, twice, landing on its roof, water and dirt flying as another bolt of lightning flashed across the darkened sky. The crash was followed by a deathly hush, aside from the pouring rain.

It was no more than a minute before he scrambled out. He grabbed the lifeless body. He was still breathing. He put the body down and went across to the driver's side of the jeep. 'Ricki, Ricki. Speak to me.' He tried to open the door, but Ricki was out cold, blood seeping from a gaping head wound. He shook him once, shook him twice. It was hopeless, and he couldn't carry two people. He'd leave Ricki. He wasn't in the mood to care.

If he wanted to get the job done, earn his money and get him off the island, he would need to run. And run fast. Time was against him. He had to get him in that plane and away today. He knew the consequences if he didn't. Carrying dead weight was tough. He threw the man over his shoulder, glanced back at Ricki, and started running. His right leg was bleeding at the knee, and he had another cut on his hand. He was lucky, but getting more desperate as he splashed through the puddles. He couldn't be far away. As he continued to thrust his legs with all the strength he could muster, ignoring any pain and the awkwardness of carrying someone, he could see the small landing strip ahead. He could see the plane.

He began to wave as he got closer, frantic waves, his one free hand swinging from side to side above his head. Surely, they could see him. A thousand yards, 750, 500, 100 yards. They could see him now, frantic waves. As he got close to the plane, one of the men stuck his head out of the door.

'Jordan. Hurry up, we've got five minutes to get out of this shit hole. Where's Ricki?' He shook his head. 'Take off. He won't be coming.'

He threw the lifeless body aboard the plane, two men grabbing it. 'Just get him out of here.'

'Is he alive?'

'Yes, he's alive, now go.'

'How are you getting back?'

'Don't worry about me, just get out of here.' He stood back from the plane as the pilot moved to the front of the cockpit and the engines fired up. In any other circumstance none of them would be doing this. But money talks. As the plane taxied towards the grass landing strip, its small engines roared as it took off to the west, the winds tossing it around as the pilot grappled with the controls as they gained height. As soon as he could, he turned east, another 20 minutes and the storm would be behind them.

In the back of the plane, the lifeless body rolled from side to side.

TWO

TWO YEARS EARLIER

'GET your hands off her for a moment, Jack. You want another, I'm going to the bar?'

Looking up from the blond Jack Bianchi was in the grip of kissing, while laying out on one of the long loungers in the VIP area of BBT's nightclub, his expression suggested Jack wasn't amused. 'Bloody hell man, leave us alone for a minute Tony, will ya? On second thoughts, forget that, yep get me another, and my lovely lady here.' She cocked her head towards Tony. 'Make it a double Mr Tony.'

Jack smiled at her. 'You're an expensive babe, not sure I'm looking forward to getting you home tonight, might want caviar.'

'Oh yeah. Getting me home, hey? I'm not quite as easy as the rest of the birds you've had. Don't think for one second, I'm going to drop on my knees for you, Jack. Anyhow, you carry on drinking at this pace, and you will be past useless, even if you were to get me back to your place.' She swung her legs off the lounger and adjusted her skirt.

Jack smiled as the music went up a notch. It was 1am and a standard Sunday morning for Jack Bianchi. A night that had begun seven hours earlier at a swanky Italian restaurant, pizza and Peroni was always a good start to most Friday and Saturday nights. Rarely did it end without a woman on his arm, Jack had the looks and charisma. The bright lights of London had always been appealing to his full-on nature. He rarely missed a beat.

'So, how long are we staying?' she said. 'Just this one? Or are we here 'til it gets messy? Because I'm not one of your cheap birds who will do drunken shit to keep you happy. I've got a bit more class.'

Jack laughed. 'Oh, I see. Are you coming back to my place now? I know you have class, Em. Loads of class. I wouldn't dare attempt anything with you that I couldn't keep going for an hour. I'm at your beckon call.'

She smiled and pulled him close, whispering in his ear. 'Ask your mate Ash over there if he wants to join us. Three would be fun.'

'Piss off. I'm not sharing you with him. He would never share his birds.'

Jack Bianchi was 25, six foot tall, slim with jet black hair, wavy locks, and blue eyes. A City highflier who worked selling pensions and investments, he was enjoying the high life in London. Straight from Durham University and straight into the world of finance, Jack had built up a reputation as a no-nonsense money man, who played hard and worked harder. Living in a £1m apartment which he was renting for £4K a month just a mile from Canary Wharf, he had all the money to go with the swagger. Life was one fast ride for Jack Bianchi, and he wasn't getting off any time soon. His had been a tough road. He'd never known his dad and his mum was now dead, Jack had no family. The only love he had was money – and himself. Life was too short to think about tomorrow, let alone next week, next month, next year. It was the here and now for Jack Bianchi.

'Here you go Jack, I put it on your tab.' Tony returned with the drinks. 'Fuck, Jack, put her down a second. Take this drink, and listen up, I want a favour.'

Jack pulled away from Emma and sat upright. 'What is it with you tonight, Tony?'

Tony held out his arms, he wouldn't be put off by Jack Bianchi, he was too thick-skinned, and he knew him too well. Tony was one of the few close friends Jack had. He pulled Jack close. 'I need a woman tonight. Look at the time and I'm looking at having to pay, I know. Help me out. I've pulled nothing.'

Jack sat up and looked at his friend and his pathetic stare. 'Well, apart from pulling yourself.' Jack laughed out loud as Tony shook his head. 'Not funny. You can get your own drinks from now on.'

'And you can get your own women. What you say to that? Thought that would change your mind.'

Jack and Tony went back a long way and were good pals. They started at the same investment firm before Jack moved on. But they remained friends and spent many nights out in the City. While Jack was spontaneous, Tony had been a steadying influence, and Jack never forgot it. 'Okay, what do you want?' Jack was looking at him, while Emma had got tired of their banter and had gone to the toilet.

'What have you got? I'm not going to be over-fussy, so long as she's a bit of a looker. Come on man, you know more people than I do.'

Jack felt in his coat and got out his wallet. He pulled out a card and handed it to him. 'That's Piotr's number. You know Piotr. Give him a call. I spoke to him yesterday, so I know he's about. Tell him I gave you the number and tell him to put it on my tab. He'll sort you. But it will be £500 at least, that's my deal with Piotr, so no haggling. And don't go pissing off into the sunset with her and leaving me with the bill to pick up.' Jack punched his mate on the arm. 'Or collapse into sleep after a couple of attempts at getting it in! Get your money's worth. You'll get at least four hours for 500 and his Eastern European birds are stunning.'

Tony nodded his head and took the card. 'I owe you buddy.'

'You're right you do. And get some video as well. I want to see what my money is being spent on.'

'Get some video, you serious? The last bird I tried that with smashed my phone.'

'Yeah, but you didn't go to Piotr, did you? His girls will let you do video, all part of the package.'

Tony got up and left as Emma returned. 'Fancy a dance?' said Jack, pointing down to the dance floor.

'Okay,' said Emma. 'I thought you were going to say let's get a cab.'

'Bloody hell. You've changed your tune. No, let's have a dance, work up a sweat.' He took her arm and led her down the stairs.

The dance floor was heaving, the music was loud, whirring around their heads. There was no chance of conversation. Jack was a good mover, so was Emma. On the floor she was moving her hips and moving herself up and down him in erotic fashion. A couple of Jack's friends came closer to join them. They also had women with them, and the group moved seductively across the floor as the music got louder. Sweat was pouring off them, none more so than Jack, who loved the craziness of the music, dance, and drink. This was the life he craved, the one he had dreamed off all those years back at university when he first discovered women, drink, and drugs. He handled it then and, as far as he was concerned, he could handle it now. Only idiots let it get too much for them. Idiots like Tony who was so in Jack's pocket. Poor Tony. He was probably halfway home in the back of an Uber with some bird Piotr had called up from his 'stable'. Hopefully, she was a looker. But then again beggars couldn't be choosers. He'd get the £500 off Tony. Piotr only ever charged Jack £350 for four hours. Tony would have to work it out himself.

She tapped him on the chest, they'd been dancing for 30 minutes. 'Let's go,' she mouthed, as she pointed back to the VIP area and headed towards the stairs framed by the LED lights. Two bouncers were alongside the bottom of the staircase. She flashed them her wristband and went up. Jack wasn't far behind. 'Shall we have another?' she said as they sat on a lounger.

'You want one? Or are you good to go? I'm not fussed, I've got plenty of stuff at my place. If you're coming back of course?' Jack kissed her on the neck as he finished the sentence.

She smiled at him, a sexy smile. She didn't seem remotely drunk. 'I'll get my coat. You call a cab.'

Outside the club, the air was cool, and it had been raining for the first time in days. The weather had been hot for weeks. There were plenty of people milling about, most of them worse for wear. Jack grabbed her hand and began to walk to the corner of Churchman Street, next to the kebab house where the Uber would be arriving in 15 minutes.

'So, what shall we do when we get back to my place?' Jack said with a grin. 'Because I don't have to be up early tomorrow or is it today? Church has been cancelled, I only have evensong and that doesn't start until 6.'

She smiled and raised her eyebrows. 'Is that right? Well, if you play your cards right you might have to miss evensong as well. You can sing me a couple of hymns!'

Back at Jack's flat and after two attempts to press the right number code to gain access, both giggling as Jack's first attempt failed and he smashed the pad with his fist, they wasted no time. She was soon naked despite Jack fumbling with her bra and then making them both laugh as he tried to take his drain-pipe trousers off, before tumbling onto the bed, one leg in, one out. While drunken sex wasn't for everyone, it was for Jack, even more so as he leaned across to his side cabinet and took out a small quantity of cocaine which he laid on his wrist, before taking it down. She shook her head. 'You are a naughty boy, Jack Bianchi. Pass me some of that shit.'

The pair were in worlds of their own. Jack knocked the lamp off the sideboard as he leaned across to get the essentials. However far gone he was, he never forgot protection. 'Shhhhh!' he said as she laughed out loud as the lamp, drawer and condoms all fell with a crash on the wooden floor. 'My gran will wake up, she's in the next room.'

They both burst out laughing again, before stopping and staring at each other. Their lips met as they passionately kissed. Their heads were spinning, their minds were gone as they sexed long into the early morning.

Jack's mouth was dry, and his head felt thick.

He leaned across and picked his watch up off the floor. He looked at it and groaned. It was 1pm. *'Shit,'* he said to himself. Alongside him the bed was empty and as he pulled himself up, he wondered if he was alone in the apartment. What was her name? He sat silent for a moment before it came. 'Emma, you there? You in the bathroom?'

There was silence. He sat on the edge of the bed and took a few deep breaths. From what he remembered it had been a good night. He pulled his pants on, went to the fridge to get some juice, how his mouth needed some liquid. He wandered round the apartment and pulled back the shutters on the main window that looked out towards the City. After telling Alexa to *'play Capital Radio'* and then telling it to play *'volume two,* after it played so loud his head thumped, he sat down and turned the TV on. After flicking through the news channels, he settled down to watch Sky Sports. A double bill of football would see him through. He was going nowhere. It was Sunday and he had one hell of a headache. He got up and cracked a couple of eggs into a frying pan and began piecing together some sort of brunch. He turned his phone on and after a couple of messages from friends talking a load of rubbish about their night out, he noticed a text from Tony… *'Cheers pal, she was a bloody stunner, owe ya 500. I won't forget.'* He smiled to himself, *'quite right you won't',* he text back, before noticing he had another message. He could see who it was from. He opened it… *'Thanks, big boy. Great night, great coke, see you around… Em.'*

He allowed himself another smile. Two satisfied customers in one night, three if you include the broad Tony paid for.

This is exactly why Jack Bianchi loved life.

THREE

SHAUN Walters enjoyed his morning coffee. It was a chance to take stock of his world.

Sitting in the back room of *'Shaun's Books'* he read the local newspaper, not on-line like many of his friends, but a printed copy he could hold in his hands. He liked it that way. Enjoying the printed word was how he had ended up buying his own book shop. A small independent just on the edge of the Cotswolds in the village of Church Masham, within a row of tiny shops opposite the village green. His was on the far end, near the golf course, next to Teresa Sharman's *'Coffee and Cakes on the Green'*. His shop was his pride and joy.

Not that investing in it and running it had been, or still was, easy. He'd been in the right place at the right time when Mr Summerbee wanted to sell. Shaun's dad knew him through the Church, negotiated a price and helped his son with the deposit. The rest was history. That was three years ago, and he hadn't regretted it, even if financially things weren't exactly now running smoothly. Katie, his wife, had wanted Shaun to use his English degree to become a teacher. But classrooms and kids and shouting and telling off and marking books and, well everything to do with school, was not Shaun's thing. And, anyhow, Katie was a teaching assistant herself. It would be classroom pillow talk. Katie was teaching at Solheim Primary in the village. Four days a week, the pay wasn't brilliant, but she was happy. And because she was happy, Shaun was happy. The two of them married four years ago after meeting on a blind date two years previous. Both now mid-20s and childless, life was settling down into the type of structure many young married couples find solace in. Shaun was tall, over six foot with dark brown eyes and not an ounce of fat on him. Katie was shorter, fair, with blond hair. Her friends would comment on her *'hour-glass figure'* and *'English rose'* looks. Katie didn't mind, but neither did she think much about it. Shaun was her world. So long as he loved her, that's all that mattered. And while money-wise, life could be better, so long as they could afford a couple of weeks holiday in the UK each year, a takeaway on a Saturday night and a Netflix subscription, Katie and Shaun didn't want for much.

'Shaun, mate, are you back there?' The bell going off alerted Shaun someone had opened the front door of the shop, Will Marlsford was calling out.

'Hi Will. How are you?' Shaun came through from the back, coffee in hand.

'I'm good my friend. And you? Sold much today, or can I wait for your 20% off clearance sale that you had about 10 years ago to come round again?'

'Ha! Ha! Very good. I've sold plenty thanks,' Shaun lied. 'My next sale will be in about 25 years, I reckon, if you can wait.'

Will was the local publican at The Feathers, in Church Masham. He would often pop in to buy a book or two, supporting local businesses. And it was reciprocal. Shaun and Katie enjoyed many nights in The Feathers, where the welcome was always warm.

'I'm going to a charity event on Saturday, and everyone has been asked to bring a draw prize,' Will said, his bright orange cravat the stand-out feature on his fawn jacket. 'Everyone will bring booze or chocolates or DVDs. There will be bottles of everything, red wine, white wine, cheap whisky, cream sherry. You name it, everyone's unwanted Christmas bottles along with their out-of-date Quality Street. So, I thought, seeing as I'm in the booze trade, I would be different and take a book. A book on drink if you have one.'

Shaun laughed. 'A book on drink? Why not a good crime thriller?'

'Are you kidding me? Crime! Only crimes I know of these days are the ones being committed by supermarkets selling cheap booze. Four cans of lager for £3.99 at one place in Oxford. How can I compete with that? There are too many crime thrillers about mate. Get us a book on drink. I'll tell you what, find me a book on best pubs in the Cotswolds. The Feathers is bound to be in there.'

'I have actually got a book on that, or something similar,' said Shaun cheerily. 'Here you go. *'Pub walks in the Cotswolds'*. I don't think The Feathers is in it though. You'll be promoting the opposition.'

'Don't be a smarty pants, Shaun. Or I'll take my £1.99 and spend it elsewhere. The Feathers has little opposition. We don't need publicity.' Like many publicans, Will wasn't short of a sense of humour.

'Here you go,' Shaun stretched high to reach the book on the top shelf at the back of the shop. Third re-print, so it's up to date. It's among my collection of world's shortest books, *'MPs who don't take expenses'*, *'Hard up Premier League footballers'*, *'Hard up publicans'*, £16.99. Bloody bargain.'

'Very good, I'll take it. Is the banter extra? You take a card?'

'Banter's free. Of course, I take a card.'

Will flicked his card at the machine. 'See you in the pub sometime this week I expect,' Shaun said.

'Hope so, we've got a quiz on Sunday night. Bound to be a section on pub walks in the Cotswolds. But you can't enter seeing as you have probably already read this,' Will held up the book.

'I don't think so. I only drive to pubs. The little Beetle loves a trip out. Can't remember the last time I walked to a pub. I've left the car and staggered home from a few though, so has Katie.'

'I bet Katie hasn't, she doesn't get sloshed like you.'

Shaun smiled. 'You don't know her mate.'

'Maybe not. Anyhow, got to go, see you about.' And with that Will closed the door behind him. The bell ringing again.

Shaun looked at his watch. 10.15am and £16.99 in the till already. Perhaps it was going to be a good day.

FOUR

'MISS, I need to go to the toilet.'

Katie was at Solheim Primary and was standing in for Mrs Ashmore who was on a training course. She had begun to hand out the musical instruments to the Year 4 pupils when Zoe Baker's hand shot up. 'Okay, Zoe, off you go.' Katie continued to pass round the triangles and tambourines as the eager youngsters giggled and began to play them as soon as they got them in their hands.

'Right, children. Now, I want those who have triangles to play them when I say so, and those who have tambourines to play them when I say so. Is that clear? Not all at once, or we won't be able to hear ourselves think. Here we go then. Triangles.' And with that seven boys and girls tapped their triangles all at different times before Katie had time to say 'begin'. It was a din.

Katie put her hand up. 'Stop, stop. I didn't mean you to play them yet. Wait till I say 'begin'. And James if I see you try to hang the triangle from Charlie's ear, I'll take it away, and you can come and sit with me.'

There were giggles among the class and James moved away from Charlie. 'Now, triangles, when I point my finger, you hit your triangle. All at the same time. Now, begin.'

She raised her hand and pointed, bringing her finger up and down as the children got into a rhythm. They were almost in time. Not that Katie could be over-fussed. The likelihood she had a budding Chopin in her midst was nil, so let them enjoy it. 'Right, stop triangles. Now tambourines, I want you to do the same.'

The door burst open. 'Miss, someone's been sick in the toilet!' Zoe had returned to take her place among the group of triangle players, arriving with news she gleefully shared as she shouted above the noise. There was a chorus of urgggghhh as the children stopped playing, heads turning towards Zoe, who was looking pleased with herself.

'Are you sure, Zoe? What, the toilets down the corridor?' Katie knew she would have to go and sort it out now it had been reported.

'Yes, Miss.'

'Is there anyone else down there?'

'No, Miss. I was the only one.'

'Right, children don't play the instruments too loud while I quickly pop down the corridor,' Katie said, knowing full well she might as well have told her eight and nine-year-olds to find out what they knew about The Pythagorean Theorem for all the notice they would take.

Indeed, someone had been sick just as you headed into the girls' toilets. And it smelt terrible. Knowing she couldn't leave her class for long, Katie ran to reception and told receptionist Julie Sweeter to call a cleaner to clear it up.

'Of course, I'll arrange that,' said Julie. 'Oh, Mr Woodward wants to see you at lunchtime. I was going to come down to catch you, but seeing as you are here.'

'Oh, okay. What's that about?' Katie stopped in her tracks.

'No idea. He just told me to ask you. 1pm alright?'

'Yep, sure. I'll pop down.'

Katie ran back to her classroom. She could hear the noise 50 yards away and wasn't surprised to find George Forsell standing on a chair conducting the hastily arranged class orchestra. She had to smile as she watched him jump down as he saw her approach, as the triangles and tambourines silenced. 'Well done everyone, you're not making too much noise,' Katie said as she walked to the front of the class smiling to herself. The children all nodded in agreement with a smattering of giggles.

'It was Clarissa,' shouted Edward No.1.' (There were three

Edwards in Year 4, who had been named, one, two and three, to save confusion). 'She threw up. But she feels better now.'

Clarissa was sitting at the side of the group as Katie looked across at her. She was about to ask her if she was okay, but before she could Clarissa shook her head, pulled a face… And duly threw up again.

Mr Woodward wasn't popular with the teaching staff, which was a tad awkward in a small school of 140 pupils, consisting of five full-time teachers and three teaching assistants.

He appeared smug to his colleagues, whether intentional or not, as though he was too good to be head teacher at a small village primary school. Many thought he was using his current position as a springboard to greater things and while his arrival 18 months ago from Manchester was welcomed at the time because the school had been without a head teacher for four months, it soon became apparent he was not going to adopt the carefree culture Solheim had previously enjoyed under Mr Hall.

Mr Hall had been popular with staff and was all for a laid-back, relaxed school environment. Indeed, it wasn't until he left his wife of 21 years and ran off with Mrs Polstead, the vicar's wife, it became clear the head teacher's job wasn't all Mr Hall was laid back about. What a scandal the pair caused in the village. Certainly, Mr Woodward wasn't Mr Hall, which many parents were more than happy about. Not so the teaching staff. He introduced a stricter dress code, not for the children, but for the teachers. No shorts, no t-shirts. The men were to always wear a collared shirt, the women to wear below-knee dresses. No training shoes were allowed, only for sport. For a man in his early 30s, Mr Woodward's demeanour would have more suited a school in Victorian England rather than a modern-day primary. He had a degree in history and one in business. The teachers gossiped about him constantly. However, only Geraldine Timpson had handed her notice in since Mr Woodward had taken over, citing him as a 'pompous dick', in The Feathers at her leaving do, as she downed JD and Coke like it was going out of fashion.

'Ah, Katie, come in,' said Mr Woodward who, despite having

the first name, James, was always referred to as 'Mr Woodward' at the school, even though he addressed the teachers and assistant teachers by their first names. 'How are you?'

Katie was feeling a degree of trepidation on being called to see him. Their paths didn't cross often. It was as though she was a pupil again and being summoned to the headmaster's study. It was the uncomfortable aura he gave off. The room was bright and airy. Behind his desk Mr Woodward had a couple of certificates on the wall, both with his name on. Katie looked and wondered if they were quite necessary.

'Katie. I see you have been with us three years now,' he began. 'You are very highly thought of.'

Katie didn't know if she was to speak. She felt it a worrying introduction. As it was, she couldn't think of anything to say, so she just nodded. 'So, thanks for all your excellent continued help here. But I have something I need to tell you, well ask you. I hope you'll understand.' The words reverberated in Katie's head.

'We are looking at the school budget for next year and I must be honest, I have been told I need to cut down on staff hours.' Katie wasn't liking the way the conversation was going. 'So, from next term, we will need to halve your days down to two a week from the current four. I don't know how you feel about that. Maybe it suits you, which if it does then good. I'm sorry if it doesn't. But I'm afraid that's the situation.'

Katie had not expected this. She never felt her four days at the school was ever under threat. She was a shy person by nature, especially among people she didn't know, although she was charismatic in the classroom, and with friends. This situation was causing her heart to race, she felt anxious.

'Um, well, no, it doesn't really suit me,' Katie said, surprised at how confident she sounded. 'I don't want to do two days; I enjoy doing four.'

Mr Woodward looked at her and shrugged his shoulders. 'Well, I'm sorry, but that really is the way it is. Please go home tonight and have a think. See how you feel in the morning. We don't want to lose you, but if two days are not going to be enough, there isn't much we can do.'

So far, Katie had kept out of the *'why we can't abide Mr*

Woodward' conversations among the other teachers in the staff room, but she was starting to understand their underlying angst as she heard his tone. It was at times like this she wished she was Geraldine Timpson and was hard-nosed enough to say she couldn't give a stuff about his assistant teacher's job, and he could stick it where the sun doesn't shine. Instead, all she could muster was, 'okay, I'll have a think.'

'Good. It would be great if you could stay with us.' Mr Woodward smiled and held out his hand as much to say, 'so off you go.' Katie got up, pushed her chair back, and walked out of his office.

Julie Sweeter was still on reception. Katie smiled at her but walked on quickly without saying a word. If Katie had been one to use bad language, which she did rarely, she would let out a few expletives right now as she headed back to the classroom.

But that wasn't Katie.

Jack was walking to the office, coffee in one hand, mobile phone attached to his ear in the other.

'I don't give a shit, Piotr. You told me videos were okay by your girls, don't move the goalposts, or I'll change my pimp, pal. And yes, I know how much I owe you. Don't give me that, I pay up. I always do.' He listened as Piotr complained about Tony and the excessive way he'd demanded video off the girl he had set him up with on Saturday night.

'Well, that's tough man. She's hardly in a profession to make demands, is she?' Jack was shaking his head as he spoke. 'You've put the money on my account, so Tony was good for that. Don't fuck me off, Piotr. Video is sanctioned mate as far as I'm concerned, you said so. If you are saying from now on, it isn't, then fine. It will be £250 rather than £350 if the services are less.' Jack smiled to himself and took the phone from his ear as Piotr swore at him and hung up.

He walked into the office. The weather was glorious.

FIVE

'SHAUN'S Books' needed to make around £200 a day to keep safely afloat. But times were tough.

Shaun was breaking even having bought the bookshop for £70K on a 20-year full repairing and insuring lease, costing £20K per annum. It had already had one upward review two years ago. He was dreading the next one. He was the only one taking a wage out of the business and, while in summer months he could make 3K a month profit, with so much footfall in the Cotswolds, most of the rest of the year, he was lucky to make half that. Saving for a rainy day was on the back burner.

So, when university pal Mark Bultitude, a former professional cricketer, turned motivational speaker, popped into the shop asking if he could order 10 hardback copies of both Shakespeare's *'Twelfth Night'*, and Charles Dickens' *'Great Expectations'*, Shaun couldn't have been more delighted.

'Shakespeare. You. What? And why do you want 10 of each?' The pair hugged. It had been a while since they had last seen each other.

Shaun and Mark had been to Bournemouth University together and enjoyed Freshers' Week, before Mark was offered a cricket deal in South Africa. He had only done three months at Bournemouth, packing his course in, only returning to England last year when an Achilles injury forced his retirement from what was turning into a promising cricketing career. He went into motivational speaking after joining a company in London. He had the gift of the gab.

'Well, listen to this, Shauny lad,' Mark said. 'I've only gone and landed a speaking gig with a theatre group at Poole next week. There's 40 of them, £45 a ticket, including a bit of grub. I've heard they may want to make it a monthly thing and this is too good an opportunity to miss. It's going to cost me, but I want to impress. So, I'm going to butter them up the first week with a competition for 10 of them to win a hardback book. And if that goes well, I'll do it again the next time they book me.'

'Yeah, but why do you need 10 of both books? Not that I'm complaining.'

'You're a shit businessman, aren't you?' Mark laughed out loud. 'You're right, why are you complaining? And how's beautiful Katie by the way, or has she seen the light and left you?'

'Very funny. She's fine. Not that I have a clue what that has to do with you buying books. And don't swear in my bookshop. This is a place of peace.' Shaun held out his arms with his palms to the air.

'What are you on about you idiot? And how much discount are you giving me?'

Shaun shook his head and went over to his computer. He and Mark were chalk and cheese, how on earth they had made it through Freshers' Week together, not just in one piece but as friends still to this day, was remarkable.

'It's a decent order, not one hell of an order. 300 quid,' said Shaun.

'What for all 20 books, or for 10 of one set?'

'For all 20 books my friend. That's a good deal.'

'Does that include discount?'

'Yes. Keep your hair on. It includes discount, I've taken quite a bit off seeing as you are such a top bloke and so full of shit.'

Mark stood back and gave it a thought. 'Okay. Can I pay now?'

Shaun handed over the card machine and Mark punched in the PIN of his credit card. 'Top man, Shaun, got to go. Give me a buzz when they're in. Gig isn't for three weeks. Love to that wife of yours. She's a cracker you lucky lad. Might get hitched one day myself but wouldn't want to distress so many women with the news I'm taken.'

Shaun shook his head and smiled. 'Piss off, will you?'

The pair punched fists as Mark shot out of the shop and across the road to his Audi TT. Shaun afforded himself a grin as his friend roared off up the road... *'What sort of businessman am I, Mark?'* he said to himself.... *'One that just gave you sod all discount!'*

Katie was busy piecing together a stir fry when Shaun walked in.

Their small country cottage had one bedroom and faced out onto a road that had little traffic go by. It was a peaceful setting on the edge of the Cotswolds, they could never have afforded a house and business in the heart of it. The back garden was small while the kitchen was a good size, as was the downstairs living/dining room. It comfortably held a three-seater settee and another lounger.

Shaun had parked the car on the road outside. They had no driveway, but there was always space. 'You'll never guess who came into the shop this afternoon?' said Shaun, as he went to the fridge to get a beer. Katie kissed him on the cheek as he greeted her.

'Daniel Craig,' Katie shot back.

Shaun pulled a *'can't you be serious?'* face.

'Boris Johnson, Donald Trump, King Jordan the third of Atlantis. I don't know.'

Shaun shook his head. 'You're right, Donald Trump.' Katie feigned a half-smile. 'Ha! Ha! Who was it?'

'Donald Trump, like I said. Well, like you said. And he ordered 10 copies of *'Twelfth Night'* and 10 copies of *'Great Expectations'*.'

'Who was it, Shaun? Stop lying.'

Shaun put his newspaper down on one of the two kitchen bar stools. 'Okay, it wasn't Donald Trump, it was Mark Bultitude, but he did order 20 books.'

Katie looked at him. 'Mark Bultitude, what our Mark Bultitude? Haven't seen him in ages. Did he? That's great, what did he want them for?'

Shaun relayed the story of Mark and the theatre group while Katie served up the stir fry. It was a while since the shop had enjoyed such a good day, it had taken nearly £500.

'I've got some news, actually.' Katie knew this was going to burst Shaun's bubble. But she had to tell him. 'I spoke to Mr Woodward today. The headmaster. The school want to cut my hours down, by half, starting next term.'

Shaun took a sip of the beer and nodded his head. 'Thought today was too good to be true.'

Katie knew the news would hurt. They both did the finances. Both knew the importance of her steady, if unspectacular, income, while the shop continued to rise and fall in equal measure. Already their luxuries were few. 'I'll look for another job,' she said. 'Two days a week is no good.'

'Yeah, but you like it at Solheim, and it might not be for ever,' Shaun put his hand on hers and looked at her face. 'You might be back at four days again soon. Let's not be hasty. Have a think, have another chat with old whatshisname at school.'

'You mean Woodward,' said Kate. 'No, I'd rather place my arse in hot water than spend any more time than I have to with him.'

'I beg your pardon?' Shaun was taken aback and was half-laughing. It wasn't the kind of comment Katie came out with.

They both smiled. 'Oh, I'm sorry. It's just I've had enough of listening to him today,' said Katie. 'He's so pompous, so far up his own backside. I can't be doing with speaking to him. No-one at the school likes him. If he doesn't want me there, then I'm off.'

'Sell your body.' Shaun pulled a serious face. 'Good money in that. We could probably get a villa in Greece after six months you play your cards right, pretty babe like you.'

'Stop that, Shaun Walters. And why suddenly the smutty talk?'

'You started it. You said arse!'

They both looked at each other, leaned forward, smiled, and kissed across the table. The stir fry was going down well, and Katie had found time to drop into the local stores to grab a cheesecake. They'd enjoy that as well. After washing up, the pair kicked off their shoes and curled up on the sofa, scanning through films on Netflix. Shaun got out a bottle of wine, a cheap Pino Grigio blush. Katie got out a couple of whisky tumblers, they would buy some expensive crystal glasses one day. Both put their phones on silent.

'So, Mrs Walters, forget today's news from school. Here's to things continuing to improve for us both. Which they will.' Shaun raised his glass. 'And you can tell that creep Woodward to stick his job when you are good and ready. You will find something else, smart girl like you.'

Katie smiled at him. 'I do love you. But do you think that is what I should do? I mean we need the money. I know you've had a good day, but Mark Bultitude isn't going to bail us out week after week, is he?'

Shaun hugged her tighter and went to turn the film on, before stopping and taking her hands. 'Okay, we can sleep on it, but I think it's safe to say I know what your thoughts will be tomorrow. You don't want to work at a place that doesn't want you. And as regards the shop, that will be fine. Trust me.'

Katie sat up and turned to him. 'I suppose there is one good thing that could come out of all this, should I have a bit more time on my hands.'

'What's that? Don't tell me you are going to hoover more. Or dust the house? That would be good. Cook more?'

She slapped him on the arm. 'No, it's nothing to do with housework or cooking. I will be able to spend a little more time with Mrs Honeyman, which will be nice. She will love that.'

Shaun smiled at her and nodded.

SIX

KATIE hadn't slept well for a few nights.

She tried to hide it from Shaun, but without success. He knew when she was tossing and turning in bed it was because she was anxious about her work at the school and the decisions that lay ahead. She was a confident enough girl, but also a worrier. At school on Friday, she had confided in her friend Sara, one of the other teaching assistants, about what she had been told by Mr Woodward.

'Tell him to piss off,' Sara had said in her matter-of-fact Yorkshire way when Katie had told her of the predicament Mr Woodward had placed upon her. 'You're too good to be at school for just two days a week. You're too good a teaching assistant for this school, full stop.'

'Sleep well?' Shaun said, as he sat up on his elbow and looked across at her. It was 6am.

'Um, not too bad,' Katie lied. 'Sort of okay. It's warm though. I need to change this duvet to a lighter one. Did you think it was hot last night?'

'Yes, it was hot. And you didn't sleep well. You kept me up half the night. Stop worrying, will you? And before you say you're not, I know you are. Nothing is going to come of worrying. And don't say you're not bothered, either. Look, it's a job. Yes, a job you like, but two days a week is not enough, and you know it. There will be other schools out there. You'll find another job.'

'I know. But I like it at Solheim. Perhaps I could do the two days a week and get another job for the other three? Perhaps I could help you in the bookshop?'

Shaun smiled. They had always said that one day they would like to work together in the shop. Just the two of them, with their business ideas and cups of coffee and pieces of cake, enjoying life as husband and wife with book after book flying off the shelves. The reality today, however, was that books were not flying off any shelves, bills needed paying and all the cups of coffee, hugs, cake and love they may feel for each other wasn't going to pay the bills.

'I can just about take a wage out of the shop myself. I can hardly pay you one as well.' Shaun pulled the covers back on his side and went to get out of bed. 'You want a cup of tea?'

'Yes please. I'll read my book.' Katie threw back the covers on her side. 'Open a window will you. I'm so hot.'

'You're right you are woman! Very hot'.

'Don't start something you can't finish.' She flashed him a smile. The smile that always got him. He dived back across the bed, and they began to cuddle and hug, before starting to kiss.

'No, no, no. Stop,' said Katie.

'Cup of tea please. If I can't work in your shop, then you aren't going to have your way with me whenever you fancy. I'm not a friend with benefits, you know.'

'What? A friend with benefits!' Shaun laughed. 'You're my bloody wife, sex isn't benefits. It's like, well, it's like paying the bills, hanging out the washing. It's part of the gig.'

'Paying the bills.' Katie pushed him away. 'And what sort of bill is us having sex? I mean, I know we have the gas one and the phone one. What's the, us making love one?'

Shaun was on top of her kissing her head and lips. Katie wasn't resisting, she was making a pathetic effort to push him away while at the same time laughing. It was Sunday morning and they had time. He began to kiss her again, going slowly down her neck.

'I said 'no'. Cup of tea first.' Katie pushed him aside. 'And a yoghurt… strawberry. Then we can play.'

Shaun didn't argue. He got up and went to the bathroom where he went to the loo before heading downstairs. The sun was out, and the forecast said it was going to be another glorious day. They would go for a drive somewhere. He pulled back the curtains and looked out onto the street. Mr Tantwell walked past with his two greyhounds, but he didn't see Shaun at the window. Shaun walked down the stairs and went to say something to *Alexa* but at the last minute couldn't be bothered. He put the kettle on and got the yoghurts. As he stood in the kitchen, he picked up the latest bank statement he had alongside the bills and messages next to the cooker. He looked at it, sighed and slid it into his briefcase which was near the bottom of the stairs.

They would have to wait.

Living in the Cotswolds has its advantages; there are beautiful places on your doorstep.

Katie and Shaun had enjoyed breakfast and 'benefits' and were making the short trip to Bourton, a gorgeous village nicknamed the *'Venice of the Cotswolds'* due to the fact it had lots of little low bridges that straddled the river Windrush. With its array of restaurants and coffee shops, as well as independent shops, it was a place they enjoyed visiting. Trouble was, it was a place many enjoyed visiting, especially on a hot, sunny day.

'We should have gone to the coast,' Katie said as they sat in a queue of traffic on the way into the village, the radio playing Dodgy's, *'If it's good enough for you'*, which at least placated their slight frustrations. It was a song they both liked.

'Darling we are almost two hours in any direction away from any coast,' Shaun shook his head. 'We've had this conversation before. If we'd left half-an-hour earlier we would be parked up by now and drinking coffee, whose fault is that?'

'You wanted 'benefits'.' Katie smiled and turned the music up.

Shaun laughed. 'Why are we suddenly a marriage with 'benefits'? You crack me up. You'll be wanting payment soon and then we really are on a slippery slope.' Katie looked out of the window. 'You couldn't afford me.' She turned and flicked him a smile.

'There's a space,' she called out as Shaun turned into the car park on the outskirts of the village. 'Get in there, quick.'

Shaun dutifully did as he was told and, after safely

negotiating a parking payment machine that would have confused many with a degree in maths, let alone the numerous elderly folk who stood alongside pressing buttons with contactless cards in their hands, while shaking their heads, they were soon sitting by the river, cups of coffee in hand. It was a tranquil way to spend a Sunday.

'We do live in a beautiful part of the world,' Katie laid back stretching her legs out and putting her hand out to touch him as he sat upright watching a group of three children paddle in the river, likely sisters by the way they were all dressed alike.

'Yeah, it's nice. We are lucky.' Shaun laid back alongside her. 'Did you bring the sun cream?'

'I always bring the sun cream. It's a bit late asking now we are here, you should remember. It's your nose that glows like a beacon, not mine.' Shaun dabbed the cream on his face.

'Oh, my goodness, don't look behind you,' said Katie as, right on cue, Shaun turned round to see a bloke, possibly late 30s, early 40s with gold chains around his neck, earrings and tan, shirt unbuttoned to the waist, laying out a blanket for himself and his glamorous-looking Botox-lipped partner to lie out on. There were two champagne flutes on the grass and a bottle of bubby in a cool bottle.

'Mutton dressed up as lamb,' Katie whispered, as she took a glance at the woman who was giggling, as the man dropped a strawberry into her mouth with the seductive look of someone who was about to make love to her right there in the middle of Bourton.

'Don't be like that.' Shaun said, although he loved it when his wife got a bit of bitch in her voice. It wasn't her style, but some things triggered it. 'I think she is a very attractive woman, late 20s I'd say. Looks good, nice boobs, and showing them off a bit as well. You should get a dress like that, with a bit of cleavage showing.'

'Get lost. I wouldn't be showing off my cleavage if I looked like her,' Katie laid back down again staring up at the blue sky. 'She's got more wrinkles than your Auntie Edna's forehead and she's 94. Clear boob job.'

Shaun smiled. 'Auntie Edna hasn't had a boob job.'

'Not Auntie Edna, that woman having strawberries stuffed in her mouth.'

Shaun laughed again and laid back alongside her, putting his arm around her as they enjoyed the warmth of a sunny day. Children continued to paddle in the river as more people sat enjoying the views, sights, and sounds, as well as the sun. There was plenty of chatter as one young couple's dog decided to take a dip, chasing a ball. The dog thudded into the water, the spray covering an unsuspecting little girl who was paddling. She looked bemused, not knowing whether to laugh or cry as the water dripped from her hair. The lady who owned the dog was most apologetic, but the girl's parents didn't seem to mind.

'You want me to feed you strawberries?' Shaun was back on one elbow looking at Katie. 'I can go and get some. But seeing as we can't afford whatever posh plonk the Botox twins are enjoying; I can bring us back a couple of cans of Diet Coke. Not sure it will go well with strawberries.'

'The Botox twins! You were saying how great she looked a minute ago, now they're the Botox twins.' It was Katie's turn to sit up on her elbow as she faced her husband, the pair of them looking into each other's eyes, grinning.

'I know. I shouldn't be so nasty. But it's you who started it. I mean look at them. Don't ever let us get as sickly as that.'

'We won't ever get like that,' Katie said nodding her head towards them. 'If she starts to wriggle on top of him, which she isn't far away from doing, I can see someone asking them to cool off in the river, there are kids about.'

'You say that, but I wouldn't say no to us having a little play right now. I mean, it's beautiful and that dress you have on could easily slip off.'

'Don't be so vulgar, you've had your fun for one day, or week if you carry on saying such stuff. Go and get us an ice-cream, a Mr Whippy please, if not one of those orange lollies.'

'Yes madam, your wish is my command.' Shaun kissed her on the cheek and got up to head across the road. He returned to find the couple who had been eating strawberries and drinking plonk, laying side by side fiddling with each other's hair.

'Are you worried about me not bringing in much money if

I leave Solheim?' Katie surprised Shaun with her sudden change of subject as she ate her ice-cream. 'I mean, I will happily stack shelves or get a job anywhere. I can't just do two days a week, can I?'

'Why are you suddenly saying this?' Shaun looked at her. 'We're having a nice day, and you start talking work, don't worry about it. I told you, you'll be fine, we'll be fine, and you'll find something. You always have, we have always got by. Stop thinking about it.'

But Katie couldn't stop thinking about it.

She would speak to Mr Woodward tomorrow.

Mrs Honeyman bent down to pick up the notepad, she was careless sometimes. Her stepdaughters were always telling her off for rushing. Not that they cared. She knew that.

Indeed, her stepdaughters were on her back far too often for her liking, especially as she was now on her own, and had been so since Cecil died seven years ago. They only spoke to her when they wanted something. It was just as well they lived so far away, one in Scotland, the other in Australia. She didn't miss them. She didn't care for them.

Life without Cecil wasn't fun. She was making the best of it and there was still much to keep on top of; sometimes too much.

At least Katie would be over tomorrow, or was it Thursday? Her memory wasn't what it used to be.

Jack looked at the message on his phone. It was another hot day, and he was stripped down to his shorts in his apartment.

He loved a bit of text flirting, even if it was with someone he shouldn't be flirting with, or making love in the bedroom with, come to think of it.

Still, who was complaining? Certainly not him.

Just as well her husband didn't know.

SEVEN

KATIE'S demeanour told Shaun all he needed to know.

She wasn't her usually bubbly self. They had both discussed that morning what she would say to Mr Woodward. He could stick his two days. She'd texted him at the shop earlier, *'done it, now best look for another job'*. He'd replied with a love heart emoji. They both knew it was the right thing to do but Katie enjoyed her work at Solheim, and it hurt for her to be leaving.

'So, have you told any of the other teachers?' Shaun was taking off his coat after brushing past Katie in the kitchen, planting a gentle kiss on her cheek as he did so.

'No. I'll tell some of them tomorrow,' she replied while continuing to stir the chilli she had prepared the pair of them for dinner.

'Do you think they'll be surprised?' Shaun said.

'I don't know. Maybe, but one or two of them knew my predicament.'

'Yeah. You'll miss it, Katie, but there is so much work out there, you'll be fine.'

Katie spun round angrily, slamming the ladle down she was stirring the chilli with on the work surface, sauce splattering everywhere.

'Yes, of course there is,' she said. There are loads of jobs out there aren't there? I'll be just fine, don't worry about me. I'll take it on the chin. Bloody hell, I wish it was all as easy as that. I loved that job. I loved those kids and now it's gone. And while I appreciate your matter-of-fact monologue, I'm sorry but it hacks me off at times to be honest. My life is about to change, trying to find a new job. Where? Who knows? All I do know is that we can't afford for me to sit on my arse and bring nothing into this house because we have a mortgage which even the bloody shop struggles most months to cover. So, if you don't mind, I won't go swinging from the chandeliers about leaving and how glad I am not to have to face bloody Woodward again. You can finish stirring this chilli. I'm going to sit outside.'

Shaun was taken aback by his wife's reaction. He hadn't realised she was going to be this upset about packing her job in. He turned the hob down that was warming the chilli, and went into the garden, sitting next to her on a bench and putting his arm around her.

'I'm sorry, I never meant to be blasé. I thought we spoke last night, and you seemed okay about it.'

Katie looked up to the sky then stood up. She was calmer now. 'It is the right decision,' she said. 'I know that. It's just, well, it's just I don't think you understand how much I worry about money. Worry about paying the bills. You don't seem to worry at all. Well, I do, and I know this is going to impact on us if I don't get a job quickly. Christ, Shaun, we have £1,000 in savings, that's all. £1,000. We're 25 and 26 and that's all we have. How long will that last if I don't get a job? Our mortgage is what? £750 a month. We do live in the middle of a village here you know. This isn't Oxford or Banbury, there's no Lidl's or Asda's here for me to just get a job stacking shelves. The school was perfect. I'm going to have to either bus or take the car if I do get a job in a town. Have you thought about that? I love you Shaun, but sometimes I think you hide away from facts. And that is, the shop needs to do a damn sight better than it is, or we are going to have to think about the future of it.'

Shaun looked up at her. 'We're not selling the shop. Not unless it gets so bad, we have no choice. I took £1,500 last month and £1,300 the month before. I'm not saying it's looking up, but it's not looking down either. Trust me, don't worry.'

Katie crossed her arms. 'Oh, I trust you. But this is my life as well as yours you know. Perhaps I would like my own car, a holiday abroad, a meal out occasionally. Perhaps I would like to take £100 and spend on new clothes like many of my friends do. Perhaps there's a lot I would like.'

With that Shaun stood up. 'I can't believe you have just said that. A few home truths there. How naive was I to think you were happy with our marriage. Clearly not. Clearly, I'm just a waste of space pissing around in my book shop all day. Wow, I never thought you felt like this.'

'No, no, I'm sorry Shaun. I'm sorry.' Katie grabbed hold of him as he began to walk back into the kitchen. 'Please Shaun, I didn't mean it like that.' He turned to look at her as she grabbed his arm.

'Please, no, Shaun. I'm just upset about leaving the school. I'm sorry, I love you; you didn't deserve that, it was just me being dramatic. I know I'll find another job and we'll be fine. I'm sorry.'

He looked blankly at her and took her hand off his arm, walking back into the kitchen. He grabbed his coat and keys and carried on walking towards the front door. He opened it and went out. 'I'm going for a stroll,' he called out.

She didn't try to stop him. He was right to feel sore, but in her mind, she knew she was right to say her piece. The shop was ticking over, nothing more. He would come round, she knew that. Katie looked at the chilli. It would keep and they would eat later.

It was 6pm and she would give Peggy a call now. She had been planning to do it all day.

Peggy Honeyman was in her 70s but was sprightly as a woman 20 years her junior. She had a sharp brain and an even sharper sense of humour.

She had come to terms with the loss of her husband Cecil even though the pair had only enjoyed a few years of retirement together before he collapsed on the golf course. It had been a huge shock, they had so many plans. Cecil had been married before, but for Peggy he had been the only man she had married, the only man she had ever truly loved. Their quaint four-bedroomed cottage and lovely garden was also in Church Masham, at the other end of the village from Shaun and Katie's.

Scampi the cheeky West Highland Terrier was Peggy's love now. He was great company and got her out of the house, not that she needed any persuasion, Peggy was involved in more local clubs and societies than almost anyone in the village. She had only just stepped down as a local councillor.

'Hi, Peggy, how are you, sorry I haven't called lately.' Katie knew Peggy would be glad to hear from her and a cheerful voice is what Katie needed right now. 'Are you well?'

'Oh, Katie dear, I wondered where you were. Yes, I'm fine and how are you and Shaun? Been busy I expect.'

'Yes, we have been a bit busy to be honest and I've had some stuff go on at school which I've had churning round in my mind, so sorry again for not calling.'

'Oh, darling, is everything okay? You sound a little down.'

'No, I'm fine. I'll come over on Thursday and you can make me one of your cups of Earl Grey. You do know yours is the only place I ever drink Earl Grey.'

Peggy laughed. 'You'll have to get that Shaun to get you some. Beautiful girl like you deserves the best tea around.'

'Ah, thanks. So, I'll come round Thursday if that's okay? I'm going into Oxford in the morning, I'm meeting a friend. So, say about 2ish?'

'That will be perfect my darling. Now I've just heard Scampi barking in the garden, so I'll have to go and sort him out or the neighbours will start tutting. Bye darling.'

'See you soon, Peggy.'

Katie hung up and went back to the chilli, turning the cooker on low as it began to heat up.

Shaun would be home soon.

EIGHT

JACK enjoyed his work, and he was on the way up.

His office was almost as big as his ego, high on the sixth floor, with great views over London, leather loungers and expensive paintings on the walls, coffee on tap. His promotion to one of the UK's biggest pension investment providers hadn't been a surprise to him, even if it had been to some of his former colleagues. Apart from the fact he was good at his job, his boss, Angelo Heeson, was also a man he knew socially.

The pair had met in London on a stag night and, while Angelo was ten years older than Jack, he craved the playboy lifestyle of a 20-year-old. He'd hung onto Jack's coattails; sensing Jack could provide him that lifestyle. It was Christmas Eve three years ago they had headed out for drinks, food, women… and drugs. It was Jack who had supplied the drugs. From that moment the pair had kept close, Jack aware there was no way Angelo's drug use was known by anybody else in the company he worked, a firm where Angelo was head of pension investments, a job that guaranteed a cool £450K a year and bonuses up to £1 million. Bonuses he always hit. Jack hadn't wanted to use the drug card over Angelo. However, when things were looking dodgy at his old company, where a new boss wanted to cut bonuses and wages, Jack laid it on the line to Angelo. Either he found him a job within his business, or Jack would shoot his mouth off.

'You wouldn't dare.' Angelo had stood up to him when Jack

had first mooted the idea that he needed a job and would do anything to get it. 'You haven't the balls. You haven't the proof.'

Careless words that Jack was never going to back away from. It was Jack who had Angelo by the balls and, when Jack showed him the phone footage of him snorting cocaine with one of Piotr's prostitutes, Angelo knew he was done for. Jack had his way, and he was given a job at the firm a month later.

'He'll be home at 9, Jack, I'm telling you.'

Jack smiled. 'He won't. That restaurant has some of the slowest service in west London and the people he's with are some of the most boring. He'll be there talking shop way past midnight. Trust me, I know these people.' He winked at her.

'Trust you? I wouldn't trust you as far as I could throw you Jack Bianchi. I mean who would trust you?'

'Well, you don't seem to be doing so bad, you've trusted me to shag you twice tonight. I could go for three, but I may stick for now and save more for another day.'

Jack smiled at her again as she put her finger to his mouth. 'Don't be rude, it doesn't become you.'

Dani Heeson had the most beautiful brown eyes; Jack could see how Angelo had fallen for her. She was gorgeous. Slim figure, hair, and a body to die for, Dani and Angelo had met a year after Jack had got his job with Angelo's firm. But the wedding was a sham, Jack had already had sex with Dani a month before their big day. She didn't care, he didn't care. Angelo had the money and Dani was going to get her hands on as much of it as she could. It was the phone footage Jack had of her husband to be that had tipped her over the edge and got her into bed with him. *'The bastard. And this is after he had proposed to me.'* Jack had never forgotten the conversation. A conversation he and Dani had always kept quiet about since.

'I'd better go,' Jack said, pulling the sheets back, Dani staring at his naked bum as he headed towards the bathroom. 'I've got a meeting first thing tomorrow and I need to prep a bit.'

'You, prep a bit. That's a laugh.' Dani leaned across and grabbed a cigarette.

He went to the loo and returned to sit on the edge of the

bed. 'I knew you couldn't manage three, anyhow.' Dani ran her finger over his nose, across his mouth and down his chest before Jack stopped her.

'I could manage five or six if I wanted Dani. But why should I spoil you?'

He stood up and began to dress. He looked at his watch, it was 8.30pm. He had time to have a quick couple of drinks at the wine bar near his apartment. It wouldn't be a late night, Wednesdays rarely were.

'Make sure you take everything, Jack,' Dani had got out of bed, dressing gown wrapped around herself, to see him out of the apartment she and Angelo shared in London. Their main residence was a million-pound country house in Devon. 'When will I see you again?'

He stood at the door and opened it, before moving towards her and giving her a gentle kiss on the lips.

'Soon, Dani.' He winked and walked out.

Shaun was gone for 30 minutes.

He wanted to walk for longer, but he also wanted to return home to talk to Katie. It was ridiculous them arguing like they had just done. They didn't do arguing. She heard the front door go and went to meet him as he walked into the hall. They hugged and looked at each other.

'I'm sorry, I shouldn't have been so careless about you leaving the school,' he said. 'I know you enjoyed it there.' Shaun was holding her face in his hands; he kissed her gently. 'You are one great girl and I love you so much.'

She smiled. 'I'm sorry as well. And I think I used a swear word, didn't I? That just shows I didn't know what I was saying. I never swear.'

Shaun laughed. 'Maybe. Not only did you swear but you also raised your voice. I don't know why I married such an aggressive girl. I never knew you had such a temper. Your dad's a vicar as well.'

She laughed. 'That doesn't mean I can't let off steam occasionally.'

'I'm not so sure that's right. Come one, let's eat that chilli now. Or is it cold?' Shaun led her into the kitchen.

'It will only take a few seconds to warm.' Katie put her arms around him. 'I'll put a couple of naan bread under the grill. Rice will take too long.'

It was gone 8pm when they sat down to eat, Shaun opening a bottle of red. They were both hungry and the chilli was soon devoured. 'I'm going to see Peggy tomorrow,' said Katie. 'I haven't seen her for two weeks.'

'She will be pleased to see you. Don't go upsetting her about your job, you know how precious you are to her.'

'Why would I do that?'

'No, I know you wouldn't, just wanted to say, that's all. She's protective over you. The daughter she never had.'

'I don't think that's right,' Katie said, getting up from the table to take the plates into the kitchen. 'I think it's just the fact she has never got on with her stepdaughters, so I'm the next best thing to a daughter. Apparently, they feel it was her who split their mum and Cecil up, which of course wasn't the case.'

'How do you know it wasn't the case?' Shaun had joined Katie at the kitchen sink as the pair began to wash up. 'Because Peggy told me, that's why. I know the truth. She wouldn't lie to me.'

Shaun didn't reply. He knew how close Katie and Peggy were. He liked it that way, even if in the beginning he was a bit suspicious of it all after Katie had done some housework for Peggy during the summer holidays a few years ago. They had remained close since.

'Well, it will be nice for you to catch up with her. And get to see her more now you haven't got that rubbish school to worry about.'

Katie turned to look at him. 'It's not a rubbish school. It's a lovely school. It's a rubbish dick of a head teacher.'

Shaun smacked her lightly on the bottom. 'There you go again, language. I'll have to call up your dad to tell him you're dropping your standards!'

'You just try Shaun Walters and I'll make sure he knows about your fetish for pink underwear.'

Shaun frowned. 'I don't have a fetish for pink underwear.'

With that Katie put down the cup she was drying, moved closer to him, undoing the buttons on her blouse as she did so, revealing her pink bra.

He couldn't resist as he pulled her towards him.

'And you call yourself a vicar's daughter.'

NINE

PEGGY Honeyman's life had been full of ups and downs.

Born in one of the rougher parts of east London, her early years had seen plenty of enjoyment at school with her friends, although most of her mischief had come from the fun they used to have away from the classroom, on the recreation grounds that today have been built over with houses and superstores. There were no rich kids among Peggy's friends. They all lived in one of the many rows of terraced houses that swamped the East End at that time. The 'swinging 60s' were still a few years away and, although Peggy was set to enjoy them, her early life was simple. Her parents both worked for the local council, mum administrating in one of the council offices, her father was a dustman. Both were easy-going, kind people and Peggy's early childhood memories were filled with happy days in a happy household. Peggy's dad was a constant source of fun. His job wasn't the most pleasant, but it didn't worry him. Making everyone happy was what he used to enjoy doing, especially his silly impressions; while at Christmas he used to dress up as Santa Claus and say he was one of Santa's helpers. Oh, how they used to giggle as he did impressions of people, animals, and some of his friends at work. They would all laugh until they cried. Drink helped make her dad funnier. She never saw him drunk, he seemed to always have just enough. Their house may have been small, but it was filled with happiness. Until the day Brenda died.

Brenda was Peggy's only sibling. The two were inseparable as young girls, Peggy the older by 18 months, the pair would play happily on the park near their house with the other children. They went to the same school, enjoyed sport together, their favourite being swimming at the local baths, which was a Friday night treat. Both had long blond hair and even though there was an age gap, many often asked if they were twins. Peggy will never forget that Saturday morning it all changed. Her happy family shattered forever.

Brenda was nine years old and had been playing with friends on the park, a park where the swings and slide may have been dilapidated and the grass overgrown, but a place where all the youngsters in that area used to meet and feel safe. It was nearing lunchtime and Brenda knew to be home by midday. Saturday lunch was always fish and chips, before dad would head off to the football in the afternoon. Her friends said she simply didn't look. In her eagerness to get home Brenda ran across the road from the park, the car hit her full on. Flown like a rag doll across the bonnet, her head injuries so severe she died instantly. Peggy can still remember it as if it were yesterday. She'd returned early from the park and had been upstairs reading a book, before hearing the commotion. The screaming, crying, and wailing, the ambulance. Peggy being pushed away from the scene and taken into Mrs Richards' house to sit with her and their son Tom who had been playing on the park with Brenda moments earlier.

The funeral saw the whole neighbourhood turn out. Going back to school without Brenda was so painful. How she ever coped she didn't know to this day, but somehow, she did, somehow, she had, although the hole in her heart Brenda had left had never been filled. Peggy's parents never recovered. Her fun-loving father was no more. The tears flowed again and again, a constant stream of heartache in a house that had been such a beautiful place to be. Peggy was as lost as anyone, and her parents tried so hard... so hard to make things better. The harder they tried the harder it became; Peggy was glad to move out at 18 to rent a house with friends.

It was her dad who passed away first. Peggy was 21 when he died. She remembered getting the call at the library where she was working at the time. The heart attack, a broken heart was how many people saw it, even so many years on after Brenda's death. Mum lived for another 15 years before she too passed away in her sleep one winter's night in January. She hadn't been well and, like Peggy's father, had never recovered from the loss of Brenda. The coughing and wheezing had got worse as the smoking increased after Brenda's passing.

Peggy had felt alone for the first time in her life and, although the first few years after dad died had been difficult, she had already begun to make a life of her own by the time mum went. She had a job in the West End working in the theatres. From ice cream seller to a permanent job in administration, she was made deputy manager of the theatre at 30. She bought her own house and with it came the single woman's social fun and games that saw her rollercoaster life hit new heights. Parties, men, friends, music, holidays, drink and fun, Peggy enjoyed it all, becoming known as the gorgeous woman no man could pin down. Until Cecil came along.

Cecil had been in the army, mostly in Northern Ireland, before leaving to take up a job in a bank. There couldn't have been two more extremes of work if you had tried to find them. But Cecil had seen and experienced enough in the army and, when one his closest friends was killed in Ireland, he wanted out, heading back to London to start over. He was greeted with damning news on his return from that final tour that his wife had been having an affair, something she'd always denied. Cecil knew different. He wouldn't wash his dirty laundry in public, but he knew. And even though the other soldier involved who had been a close friend, was now dead after the result of a training ground accident, Cecil kept what he knew to himself. It seemed most people also knew of the affair. They had divorced two months later...

'We should get married.' Cecil was looking into Peggy's eyes as the pair lay in bed in their home after a Friday night out. They had been seeing each other for a year, after meeting up at a bar in London. 'I love you, Peggy. I've never met anyone like you. I thought I knew love, but I clearly had no idea.'

Peggy smiled. 'I've got this far in life without getting married.

Why now? We can just be together all the time; we practically are already.'

'No, I want to marry you, Peggy. I want us to spend the rest of our lives together, get out of London and move somewhere less busy and more beautiful; the countryside.'

'Can we afford to just give up our jobs and elope like a couple of teenagers?' Peggy asked. Not that she worried about money, and the thought of eloping rather excited her.

'Of course, we can afford it. So, will you marry me?'

Peggy knew the answer even though she had always said she was happy, free, and single. She hugged him. 'Yes, I will. But let's not be too hasty and move out of London yet. We've got a few more years of earning more to make that move and we both like our jobs, don't we?'

Cecil had shaken his head in resigned fashion. The bank was hardly a bundle of laughs, he couldn't wait to tell them where to stick their job. Peggy on the other hand did enjoy her work at the theatre. He leaned across and put his arms around her. He smiled. 'Okay, we won't do anything hasty, apart from get married that is.'

He gave her a gentle kiss, before pulling back and looking into her eyes. 'Before we tie the knot, there are a couple of things I need to tell you. I fear you may change your mind about marrying me. But I hope not.'

TEN

IT had been more than a week since Mark Bultitude ordered the books and Shaun was delighted when they arrived earlier than expected.

It had been a hot week, and the bookshop was enjoying brisk trade, with Shaun able to station books outside the shop on covered stalls he had built from wood in his shed at home. It gave them prominence. Katie was on hand most days. She was doing a bit of cleaning for Peggy, but hadn't found anything permanent since leaving Solheim, and her and Shaun found themselves enjoying each other's company at the shop, even though they knew it couldn't last, unless the business doubled its profits which didn't appear likely.

'I like John Grisham as well.' Katie was talking to a man outside the shop who had picked up a book by the American author. 'He knows his legal stuff.'

The man nodded and turned the book round to read the back before handing it back to her. 'Do you have any more by Grisham?' he said. 'We're down for the week and the wife forgot to pack the book I'm reading at home.'

'Oh, it was your wife who forgot to pack it, was it? Not you?' Katie smiled at him cheekily. The man smiled back. 'Oh, yes, I see. Well, I filled the car up with petrol. You can't expect us men to think of everything!' The two laughed as Katie ushered him into the shop and 20 minutes later, he had walked out with three Grisham hardbacks, £48 safely accrued.

'What did you say to that bloke who bought the Grisham books about forgetting to pack his own book?' Shaun had made them both a coffee and was standing outside the shop next to Katie as the sun beat down.

She grinned. 'Just a sales ploy, my darling, don't worry your little head. He bought three in the end. He'll be all *'Grishamed'* out by the time he gets home.'

'We're having a good week, girl. It's only Tuesday and we've taking £480 already, I can't remember when that last happened.'

'You need more of me!' Katie smiled.

A car roared past at speed and blared its horn as Shaun and Katie sipped their coffees. It went past the shop and turned round at the small roundabout at the end of the road before coming to a stop outside the book shop, music blaring. Mark Bultitude liked to make an entrance. The music shut off and he got out of the car.

'People, how are you? My gorgeous Katie, long time, no see, but still as beautiful and still far too good for my man here.' He waved his hand at Shaun.

'Hi Mark, how are you?' Katie embraced his excessive hug, before giving him a peck on the cheek. 'And don't roar about in that car, this is a quiet village, you'll wake everyone up.'

Mark shook Shaun's hand. 'Hello mate, got the books in earlier than expected then, thanks for that. Do they look good?'

'What do you mean do they look good? Of course, they look good. You got time for a coffee?'

'Always, if my lovely Katie is joining us.' He gave her a wink as the three went into the shop which, for the first time that morning, was empty. Katie made the coffee while Shaun went and got Mark's books. They were packed in boxes and Shaun laid them down just inside the door.

'So, how's life treating you guys?' Katie brought Mark's drink over and the three headed back outside.

'We're okay, aren't we babe?' Shaun looked at Katie. She smiled. 'Yep, we're fine.'

'You still working at the school, Katie? That was the last thing I knew you were doing but it was about six months ago. Been so busy Katie my darling, I can't believe it has been so long.'

'No, I'm sort of in between jobs. So, I'm helping here, but I want to find something else, and I will.'

Mark looked at her. 'You want a job?'

'Why, you got one?' Katie laughed and looked at Shaun.

'Yep, I might do actually,' Mark replied.

She folded her arms. 'Um, what sort of job? I'm suspicious when you say things like that.'

He laughed. 'Why suspicious? I need someone to help me on my speaking engagements, someone to do a bit of organising. I'm finding that trying to do it all myself means I'm missing out on networking with people after the event, or before it. Seriously, if you fancy it. It would only be a few nights here and there, hardly a full-time gig. Tell you what, £100 a pop, there you go, cash in hand.'

Katie looked at Shaun and back at Mark. 'You serious?'

Mark shrugged his shoulders. 'Why wouldn't I be? I need someone to help me. I've been thinking about it for a few weeks, but it's got to be the right person, I reckon you'd be perfect. It's just a case of if your man over here doesn't mind his wife being taken off to secret hotels and flash country mansions with a cool dude like me?' He laughed out loud and punched Shaun on the arm.

Shaun smiled. 'I don't mind, Katie's call. If she wants to do it, why not?'

Katie felt a tad awkward; she didn't know what she was letting herself in for with Mark. He was very different to Shaun. He had a full-on personality, was twice as loud and in your face. It wasn't going to be a quiet evening counting money and handing out leaflets, she suspected.

'Tell you what Katie, have a trial run. This Thursday, I'm in Stratford, 40 minutes from here. Just a small talk with about 30 people. I'll pick you up.'

Katie looked at Shaun again, she wouldn't do it if he gave any indication, he wasn't happy. 'Go for it,' Shaun said.

Katie looked at Mark. 'Okay, I'm in. What time?'

'Brilliant,' said Mark. 'Well, we must be there by six to get everything prepped. Can I pick you up say 5ish? Shaun, text me your postcode and I promise I'll bring her home, unless there's a weather event and we'll have to get a room for the night.' Mark beamed and winked. 'Separate beds of course!'

'Ha! Ha!' said Katie. 'You wish.' Mark flicked his eyebrows. 'Ok, babe, and you make sure you behave, no trying it on with me just because you have me alone for the night.' Katie shook her head.

All three went back into the shop to get the books. 'Right, got to go people. I've got a lunch date with a blond who wants me to do some speaking to her hen party before they head off to Majorca next month. Apparently, they're all businesswomen. Bit of an odd one, but money is money. She's a bit of a looker as well and not married yet.'

'Oh, shut up, Mark, you are a tart.' Katie gave him a peck on the cheek. 'Now get going before I change my mind.'

Shaun moved forward, shook Mark's hand, pointing at Katie. 'Look after her. And thanks mate, for buying the books.'

'I will mate. Love you all.' And with that Mark walked out, flipped the boot of his car, chucked the books in, and roared off, beeping the car's horn as he did so, turning heads in just the manner he would have hoped.

Katie and Shaun looked at each other. 'Well, you okay with that then?' Shaun said. 'I mean £100 isn't anything to be sniffed at and Mark can afford it. Could be fun.'

'We'll see,' said Katie. 'You know what Mark is like. You don't see him for ages and then he thunders back into your life as though he's been there all the time. But I've always liked him, and he seems to attract money.'

'Not like me then?' Shaun put his arm around her.

'Don't say that.' Katie squeezed into him. 'Anyhow, if making money means you have to act as mad and bonkers as Mark does, then I'm glad you don't have that much.'

'Really? But what if I did have money?' Shaun turned and went into the shop before she could answer.

It had been a good night.

Katie and Mark were sitting at the far end of the hotel going through the finances of what had proved to be a successful motivational talking event. There had been 28 businesswomen, at £30 each, which included a small buffet. After the cost of the hire of the hotel room, the food and £100 to Katie, Mark had cleared £400. Not bad for a night's work. Katie hadn't known what to expect, but Mark was certainly inspirational. He'd held the audience in the palm of his hand from the off, and Katie had enjoyed it. After asking her to meet and greet the delegates and offer nibbles, she had then handed out leaflets and chatted to a few of them after the talk. The ladies were all glamorous, loud, and extremely confident, most of them owned their own businesses, some were likely on their way to making their first million if they hadn't already. Katie had been in awe of most of them.

'Did you enjoy that?' The last women had left. It was 10.30pm and Mark had got Katie a drink from the bar.

'It was fun,' Katie said. 'I did enjoy it. All that stuff you come out with, where did you learn all that?'

'Out in South Africa mostly,' Mark said, taking a sip of his drink. 'Plenty of fun banter.' He smiled at her. 'I could see my cricket was doing okay out there, but I was never going to be a top player. When I had time off, I began to investigate motivational speaking, met some guy in a firm over there who loved cricket and he gave me a helping hand. I got quite confident at it and applied to a firm in London as soon as I returned home. Been doing it a while now.'

'Talking to all those confident, brassy women. I couldn't do it.'

'Couldn't do what?' Mark stared into Katie's eyes. Katie was a bit taken aback. 'Well, I couldn't do what you do, or what those women do in their lives, all those businesses they run, the money they earn, the confident chat and full-of-themselves stuff.'

Mark leaned forward and took hold of Katie's hands, looking into her eyes. 'Listen to me. You can achieve whatever you want in life. You are as good as the next person and certainly as good as any of those girls I have talked to tonight. Trust me.'

Katie wasn't sure where this was going as Mark continued to stare at her, his brown eyes piercing. 'Do you think so?' was all she could say, before looking at her watch. 'Look at the time, we better be going.'

He smiled and released her hands, downing his drink, Katie sipped the last dregs of hers. The pair stood up to leave. As they walked towards the car, Mark looked across at her before she could get into the passenger side. He smiled; a charming smile she knew had likely seduced many women over the years.

'Katie. You are one terrific girl, believe in yourself.' He winked and flicked his key fob to open the doors.

She smiled back.

ELEVEN

'HERE you go sleepy head.'

Shaun placed the cup of tea next to Katie and kissed her on the cheek, before jumping back into bed.

'So, how did it go with Mark? Sorry I didn't wait up; I did hear you come in. I was just knackered to be honest.'

'It went fine.' Katie leaned across and picked up her tea.

'You're not cross I didn't wait up, are you?'

'No, I wasn't bothered,' Katie said, although she had thought he would wait up seeing as it was her first time with Mark. 'If you were tired, you were tired.' She took another sip of her tea as Shaun did the same. For a few seconds there was silence.

'We are okay, aren't we, me and you?' Katie turned to him. 'You know I love you.'

Shaun spun round. 'I love you to. Why do you say that?'

'Oh, I don't know. Perhaps it was the other day when you mentioned me not working at the school, and I flew at you. Just ignore me.'

'No, I won't ignore you. Come on, why are you saying this? What happened last night? Was everything okay?'

'I said ignore me, Shaun.' And with that Katie got up and went into the shower. Shaun shook his head and carried on drinking his tea.

He couldn't be doing with this now, he had a busy day ahead.

Peggy hurried to the door. She knew Katie was a good timekeeper, and she was looking forward to seeing her.

'Ah, Katie, my darling, how are you?' She flung her arms around her and hugged her tight. It had been too long for her. Peggy liked to see Katie at least once a week, she hadn't seen her for nearly three.

'Hello Peggy, I'm fine, how are you? You look great, love that shawl, it's so pretty. Were you sitting in the garden?'

'I was my dear, just had a spot of lunch. How was Oxford?'

'Oh, I didn't go in the end, had a late one last night working with a friend of Shaun's, Mark Bultitude. You don't know him; he was at university with Shaun. He's a motivational speaker and needed some help, so I went with him, doing a bit of admin, handing out leaflets, that sort of thing.'

'That sounds interesting my dear, motivational speaking. How's the school? I assume you are still there. Or have you already broken up for the summer?'

Katie smiled. 'Come on, let's talk. I'll tell you all about it.'

The pair went into the garden. It was cottage-style, with wildflowers and a host of perennials. Simple, but pretty, it contained a metal table with two chairs and a hammock in the corner, which Peggy ushered Katie to sit in alongside her. Katie explained to Peggy all that had been going on in recent weeks. Her leaving Solheim, helping Shaun at the shop and how Mark's job came about. She tried to put on a brave face, making it all sound very positive, but Peggy knew her too well.

'Something's wrong, isn't it?' said Peggy. 'Is it leaving the school?'

Katie relaxed herself in the hammock. The sun was beating down, the tea tasted good. 'Oh, it's nothing. I don't know, I feel a bit down at times, it's probably to do with not having the school job anymore if I'm being honest. Shaun and I have had a few little ding-dongs as well, of late. Nothing major, but the sort of little spats that we have never really had. I'm a bit sharp with him, and last night he didn't even wait up for me to come back from that speaking event. It was gone 11 when I got in, but he was in bed. I thought he would stay up and we could chat. He doesn't usually go to bed before 11.'

Peggy smiled. 'And your point is?'

'I know, I know, it's nothing, overthinking things. But you know what Shaun's like? He doesn't get rattled very easily. He's easy-going and here I am feeling we have some sort of issue, which we don't.'

Peggy got up and ushered Katie to pass her the cup and saucer. 'I'll get us another tea. And a few biscuits. I think you are right; you are worrying about nothing.'

When Peggy returned, Katie was looking at her mobile. She'd had a message from Mark asking if she had enjoyed the night and he would contact her for more dates if she fancied it. And she had a message from Shaun which just said, *'love you'*. She looked up at Peggy as she returned with more tea. 'See, what am I worrying about? Shaun's sent me a *'love you'* message. We didn't have much to say to each other this morning. I'll drop him a few love-heart emojis.'

'What are they?' Peggy said.

'Oh, they are sort of, well little symbol shapes on your mobile, like little love hearts. Means I love you as well, type of thing. Look…' Peggy leaned across to look at Katie's phone.

'So, hopefully a lot of fuss about nothing then, my dear,' Peggy took hold of Katie's hand. 'We all have our ups and downs in life, and no-one is perfect. It's been a shock for you leaving the school, I can tell. That hasn't helped things. But your Shaun is a good one, cherish him.'

Katie nodded. 'I know, you're right. Now, changing the subject rather, and I hope you don't mind me asking, how are the grizzle twins?'

Peggy shook her head. 'How do you think? Moaning as usual. I'm glad they only call me once a week, but I know they only do so to make sure I haven't popped my clogs.'

Katie laughed. 'I don't think they call you for that reason, Peggy.'

Peggy raised her eyebrows and took another sip of tea. 'Biscuit, my dear?'

Jenny and Judy were Cecil's daughters, Peggy's stepdaughters. The 'grizzle twins' was how Katie had christened them after listening to Peggy say how negative they were towards her. The first time Peggy had met them she took a dislike to them. It became apparent their real mother was in their ears all the time, chipping on about how their father had been solicited away from, firstly the army, then the family home by Peggy. The girls didn't want to know the truth, they weren't told the truth. When Cecil died, they had expected a windfall. They got little. Almost everything had been left to Peggy. It was up to her what she did with it next, that was why Jenny and Judy kept in touch. Making sure any inheritance was coming their way.

'I won't care if they call me and say they never want to speak to me again,' said Peggy, taking another biscuit. 'When they do call, they ask after me, as if they care, then threaten to visit me some day. My funeral is the next time I'm likely to see them.'

Katie smiled. 'I can't wait to meet them. I bet they are both the most adorable young women.' Katie pulled a face at Peggy and they both laughed out loud.

There was a moment of silence and Katie stared at the small water feature opposite the hammock. It was trickling away as the sun continued to shine. It was still warm; the breeze was gentle. 'Well, let's forget about them,' Katie changed the conversation. 'How about we talk about this new shower room you are having? It's going to be fantastic. A walk-in shower, you are getting posh Mrs Honeyman.'

'I know, it sounds grand and looks grand. I can't believe it myself. But it needs to be done, I'm not going to keep getting in and out of that old bath we have had up there since we moved in.'

The two continued to chat before Katie looked at her watch. It was 5pm. 'I better go. Shaun has promised to take me over to The Feathers tonight and the way we have both been feeling of late, I reckon we may have a glass or three. If he's had a good day at the shop, we may push the boat out and have some chilli nuts as well. We know how to live.'

Peggy smiled and, as she got up, stood still for a second or two to gain her balance.

'Are you okay?' Katie looked concerned.

Peggy nodded, before walking towards her. 'Yes, dear, I'm fine. Got up a bit too quickly. You know how that can affect you sometimes?'

'Well, you take care and I'll see you next week. Probably Thursday. But I'll call you before then.'

The pair hugged as Katie walked out of the door and waved on turning as she got to the gate. Peggy closed the door behind her and walked into the living room. She got hold of an arm of the chair and eased her way round to take a seat on the settee. A little kip would be in order.

She had been busy of late.

Shaun was already home and sitting in the garden when Katie got home. She walked through the kitchen to join him outside. 'Hi. Had a good day.'

He looked up at her and nodded. 'Not bad, £250, not brilliant.'

She went and sat down beside him on the bench. 'Mark is going to get back to me with some more dates. That's good, isn't it?'

Shaun took her hand. 'I'm sorry about this morning. I didn't ask you about last night. I didn't ask you anything. I should have. I should have waited up.'

'That's fine don't worry. It was all good, in fact I really enjoyed it.'

'How was Mark? Did he look after you?'

'He was great, yes. Just as he promised he would.'

'He's a good guy. At university we had so many laughs. He was good to me, bit of a wingman. I used to get so pissed. He could handle his drink, but I was hopeless. The times he bailed me out.'

'Bailed you out?' Katie turned and faced him. 'How pissed did you used to get?'

He laughed. 'Bad enough one night to be slumped in a nightclub asleep near a load of chairs. I'd tucked myself up behind them and it wasn't until Mark and the boys left the club, they noticed I wasn't with them. Some of the boys thought I'd done a runner. Mark had a row with a bouncer. He wanted to get back into the club because he'd convinced himself I was still in there. I was. It was Mark who found me, it was 4.30 in the morning. He got me out of there and took me home. Not that I remember.'

'He's a good sort,' said Katie.

'He is. Come on, let's go down to The Feathers and have something to eat and a few beers. We haven't been out for ages and as much as I love your cooking, you're having a night off.'

Shaun tripped over the mat when he got back from the pub, after he had fumbled to open the door. Katie giggled as he almost went flying. They had enjoyed a nice meal, lasagne for Shaun, prawn salad for Katie. They'd shared a bowl of chips and had more than a few drinks.

'That was fun,' Katie said. 'Not you almost falling over, the meal. Will was in good form as well.'

Shaun patted her on the backside and went into the living room and closed the shutters. He returned to the hallway where Katie was taking off her shoes. He took hold of her hands. The house, like the weather, was warm and both had the lightest of clothes on, Katie a thin blouse and short skirt, Shaun a t-shirt and shorts. He looked at her.

'Come here,' he said. He pulled her close and kissed her on the lips, gently at first, then more demanding, moving her into the living room. 'You are going to have to excuse my language Mrs vicar's daughter, but I'm going to shag you right here on the carpet.'

Katie pushed him away. 'Are you now? You and which pissed army?'

He pulled her back to him. 'I don't need anyone's army, I'm sober enough to have you, right here, right now.'

They were looking into each other's eyes, the passion growing all the time. You could sense it. He put his hands under her blouse and lifted it above her head, revealing her bra, which he unfastened at the back and threw on the floor. She smiled at him, before standing back, reaching out and unzipping his shorts, tugging them and his pants to the floor.

'Come on then,' she leaned forward and whispered in his ear.

TWELVE

THE City was hot, and Jack didn't like the heat.

It made him restless at night and irritable during the day. So, he didn't need Fraser Simmons barging into his office first thing on a Wednesday morning. Fraser worked in the same department and was, in Jack's eyes, Angelo's pet. They didn't like each other or pretend to. Not that Jack cared, he already had one over Fraser, not that Fraser knew… yet. But Jack did care about his own prospects, and in that regard, Fraser was an irritant. A no-nonsense Scot who had joined the company straight from St Andrews University, Fraser had worked there six years and, while socially he could be a party animal, which Jack put up with, in the office he could be an arse. Everyone who worked in pensions and investments had their own office and most liked it that way. It allowed them to get on with their work and rarely were you disturbed. Which made Fraser's intervention even less palatable than it would have been had he at least bothered to knock.

'What the fuck's this Jack?' Fraser stood at the door with a piece of paper in his hand. 'It had better not be what I think it is.'

Jack kicked his feet off the table. He turned to look at him. 'Morning,' he said sarcastically. 'Nice of you to knock. How do I know what, what is? Hopefully, your resignation.' Jack smiled and nodded his head towards the piece of paper Fraser was holding. 'Anyhow, I'm great Fraser, thanks for asking. But not great enough to mind read. So, could you explain why you are annoying me right now?'

Fraser closed the door, walked in, and sat across the table. 'This, Jack, is an e-mail from Thomas Stroud. A Mr Thomas Stroud who I have been working with on how to invest his 800K pension. A Mr Thomas Stroud who I have been in conversation with for the past month about what we, as a business, are going to do with that pension. And a Mr Thomas Stroud who now informs me he will be working with you from now on after the pair of you apparently 'chatted', when I was away last week.' Fraser threw the piece of paper across the table.

Jack picked it up and looked at it. 'So, what's the problem?'

Fraser shook his head and stood up. 'Do you know what, Jack? You really are a fucking moron. I have no idea why this firm employs you. Absolutely no idea. You're an arrogant shit who has no sense of fair play and puts yourself first, second and third. Now, I don't care what you do with your life outside this place, Jack. But in here, we work as a business. We work in the right way with the right ethics. I would say a team, but you wouldn't know what that was.' Jack stared at him and laughed.

'Oh, something funny, is it?' Fraser moved forward and put his hands on the table leaning over him as Jack continued to smile. 'Something funny about nicking someone's client and trying to take their commission. That stinks Jack. And I promise you, I'll be taking this further. It's not the first time you've done something like this. But it will be the last.'

Fraser leaned across and picked up the copy of the e-mail off Jack's desk before heading towards the door. 'You're an arsehole, Jack.'

'Oi, Fraser.' Jack stood up and grinned. 'Close the door before you head off to give Angelo a blow job.' Fraser shook his head and slammed the door shut. Jack smiled to himself. Fraser wouldn't talk to him like that. He needed a lesson. He'd had enough of Fraser Simmons. He went to his drawer and got out the envelope that was buried deep inside. It had been sitting there long enough.

It was lunchtime and Jack would often head into the City for something to eat. He didn't mind the office, but London was so cosmopolitan, he loved the buzz of being out in the open, rather than stuck behind a desk.

The choice of restaurants nearby was plentiful, and he enjoyed the terrace bar at his favourite Italian, a walk of 10 minutes from the office. As he strode along, shirt flapping in the gentle breeze, shades on, he thought of Fraser's outburst that morning. He shouldn't be worried about him speaking to Angelo. Jack had too much on Angelo for him to ever consider giving him the sack. Jack was in safe territory; he had all bases covered. He entered the restaurant and took a table near the far-right window. He took out his phone and began to read his e-mails.

'I say, sunshades on even when sitting at a table in the shade. Very dishy and almost attractive.' Dani placed her handbag on the floor and sat down opposite him. 'Put the phone away. Have you ordered?'

Jack smiled. 'Okay, hang on. I've got one e-mail I need to reply to.' She put her hand on his and ran her tongue round her lips.

'He is definitely in Nottingham, isn't he?' Jack looked up from his phone.

She leaned back. 'I texted him an hour ago, he'd just got off the train. Anyhow, why are we meeting in public if you're bothered word might get back to Angelo? Me and you. We are sort of acquaintances you know; we are allowed to talk. You did come to our wedding, remember?'

Jack grinned. She was right. Who would care if they saw him and Dani Heeson out having a meal? The pair had always got on. They just got on better than most people were aware of. And, of course, it had been Angelo who had handed Jack a job. Most people in the business assumed they were all best of buddies.

'So, you on a long lunch break?' Jack flicked his fingers, and a waiter came over. He ordered a Risotto Alla Milanese; Dani went for Spaghetti Alla Carbonara. They would share a bottle of house red.

'Yep, managed to get an hour off. Carene is covering the boutique while I'm away. We haven't been busy this week to be honest. Too bloody hot for people to shop.'

'You're not wrong. Far too hot.' Jack took his shades off.

He loved Dani's company. She was easy on the eye and easy to talk and listen to. She always dressed simply, but always looked glamorous. Today was no exception, her white blouse and white skirt showing off her tanned legs.

'I hate the heat,' Jack said. 'Makes me so irritable at times, makes me so fucking horny at times.' He flicked his eyebrows at her.

'Shut up Jack, we're about to eat. So, how's business? I hope you're playing your part. Angelo gets his six-monthly bonus in three weeks; well, I assume you all do. And I could do with him getting a large bonus; need a bit of serious retail therapy.'

She laughed. Jack smiled back. 'Yeah, business is good. But we're not here to talk shop. I have a favour to ask.'

'Oh, do you now? And let me guess, it has something to do with sex, money, drugs, or booze?' She leaned across the table and stared at him, her crystal blue eyes piercing, while the shades on top of her head glinted in the sunshine.

'A bit of each to be honest,' Jack smiled. 'I need your help with a little matter. I need you to do me a favour and I know you are just the babe for the job.'

She opened her eyes wide. 'Don't patronise me, Jack Bianchi, *'just the babe for the job'*. What do you think I am?'

'You're a diamond, Dani, that's what you are. You'll love this.'

Dani sat and listened as Jack spoke. She shook her head gently and smiled as he was talking. She was fascinated by Jack Bianchi and always had been. He wasn't husband material; he was a total cad. But he was a great lover, a risk taker, he made her laugh, and she would do anything to please him. She had the best of both worlds with Jack and Angelo and that was just the way she liked it. It was one big game for Dani Heeson.

'I hope you appreciate me,' she said as Jack finished telling her what he wanted her to do. 'You really are a total bastard, Jack. I don't know what I see in you.' She picked up her glass and raised it slightly towards him as she took the envelope.

'You know exactly what you see in me.' Jack winked a return. 'And seeing as your hubby is staying over in Nottingham this evening, likely with a posh lady of the night, I insist you come to my apartment to discuss the latest inflation figures.'

Dani smiled as their lunch arrived. 'Deal. I love inflation figures.'

THIRTEEN

IT was the height of summer, and Church Masham was packed with tourists enjoying the quaint sights of the Cotswolds.

The car park at the end of the village was full before 10am, the coach park was full before midday. Shaun's shop was busy, with people in and out at a rate of knots. Business was brisk and Shaun was grateful to have Katie alongside.

'So, if I buy three books, do I get a discount?' The man had a ruddy complexion and a twinkle in his eye. Mid-60s, his wife nudged him as he spoke to Katie.

'Don't be so cheeky, Eddie. The girl has got to make money. If you want all three, you buy all three.' She smiled at Katie.

'The only discount I can give you is a smile and a cup of tea. Just don't tell everyone, we don't have that many tea bags.' Katie laughed as she took the books out of the man's hand.

'I'm only joking my dear,' he said. 'We'll take all three. It's just that I have always been brought up to do a bit of haggling, haven't I dear?' He turned to his wife.

'Dragged up haggling, more like,' his wife replied. 'And no dear, we're alright for a cup of tea. Just had one at that shop on the corner. Bit expensive mind. I thought we'd get a biscuit with it. But no.'

'Ah well, so long as you have had a cup of tea. Cash or card?'

The man looked at his wife. 'I think we'll do card, my dear.'

'I'll go and get the card machine,' said Katie.

Shaun was busy inside with a young woman and her son.

They were going through the Harry Potter collection; a collection Shaun excelled in always having a good stock of. Harry Potter was one of the shop's best sellers. Katie smiled as she heard the young boy say out loud… 'Haven't read that one.'

She went back into the sunshine where the couple were waiting. It was very hot as Katie walked up to them, card machine in hand. 'That will be £44.97.'

The man leaned forward to tap the machine, before letting out a groan. And what happened next was terrifying. As he leaned forward, he collapsed on the floor, face first. He thudded against the concrete as his wife screamed. Katie dropped the card machine and bent down to turn the man over. His eyes were wide open, and he was panic breathing; he was having a heart attack. His wife began shouting. 'Eddie, Eddie', as more people looked round as Katie, who through the school had done first responder courses, took control. She turned the man onto his back and began to give him CPR, ripping open his shirt slightly so she could apply force onto the middle of his chest. She put her ear to his mouth to feel for any breath, but she wasn't sure she could sense any. The man's eyes were still open. By now a crowd had gathered. 'Someone call an ambulance,' Katie shouted at a man who was standing over them asking if there was anything he could do. Shaun had heard the commotion and had joined Katie outside. Keeping calm, Katie continued to force her hands firmly on the man's chest. One, two, three, four. She didn't stop. She knew she mustn't stop. Eddie was a heavy man and had gone down like a sack of rocks. His face was cut from the impact of him hitting the ground and although his nose was bloodied, there was little time to worry about that. Katie had to keep pushing his chest, pushing, and hoping.

'Anything we can do?' said Shaun as he bent down beside her. But Katie just shook her head. She knew this was all she could do. She was concentrating hard. More and more pressure on the man's chest. She stopped for a moment to take a breath; the sweat was starting to pour off her. The man's wife was keeping remarkably calm. She had her hands clasped close to her chest and was saying to herself, 'come on Eddie. Come on'. A lady had her arm around her. A few people had gathered and John

Barber, from the newsagents opposite, had come over and asked people to move away. Katie looked at Eddie, but there appeared no response. There was nothing more she could do. Five minutes, ten minutes, 15 minutes. *Where the hell was the ambulance?*

Katie continued to work on the man, push, push, push. Still, there was no response, and she was starting to feel overwhelmed. The sound of a siren gave her hope and within a few seconds of the ambulance arriving, two paramedics jumped out and began taking over, thanking Katie as they did so. She was totally drained. Her hands hurt and her head ached. She was sweating profusely as Shaun put his arms around her and led her back into the shop. The few people that had remained had begun to melt away as soon as the ambulance arrived.

'Come and sit down.' Shaun took Katie into the back room and put the kettle on.

'Go and see how his wife is,' Katie pleaded with Shaun, tears starting to well up inside her as her emotions kicked in and the adrenaline subsided. 'Please Shaun, don't worry about me, I'm fine, make sure she has someone with her.'

Shaun went out of the shop just as Eddie was being wheeled on a stretcher into the back of the ambulance, his wife alongside. One of the paramedics called out to Shaun. 'Tell that lady thanks for everything, someone will be in touch to talk to you. Quickly write me down a number we can get you on. We need to get going.'

Shaun ran back into the shop and scribbled down their home number and handed it to the paramedic. And with that, sirens on, the ambulance left.

Eddie never woke up.

Sitting in the garden that night Katie and Shaun had eaten little. They'd closed the shop after the ambulance had left. There had been people milling about and others still arriving in the village, unaware of the drama that had just unfolded. They'd only been home an hour before the phone rang. It was the hospital with the news Eddie hadn't made it.

'You did all you could,' said Shaun, as he sipped his tea. 'You were one brave girl taking that on. You were doing all the right things. In that situation so many people freeze. You didn't. I'm so proud of you. And his wife would have been so proud of you, all you tried to do.'

Katie nodded her head. She knew she had done all she could. But her best hadn't been enough and now a man was dead. A man with a wife, maybe children, maybe grandchildren. 'That poor woman watching her husband die in front of her like that. What was she going through while she was watching me try to save him? I can't get over the look on her face when I caught her eye. She was pleading with me with her eyes. And I failed her Shaun, I failed her. Now she's alone.' And with that Katie burst into tears again, as Shaun cuddled her close.

'You failed no-one. Doing nothing, like the rest of us was failing. You were giving it all you could. And you were doing everything right. You couldn't have done anymore.'

Katie stopped crying but her eyes were red, and her head ached. 'What time is it?' she said.

Shaun looked at his watch. '7.15. Sure, you're not hungry?'

'No, I don't want anything, just perhaps another cup of tea… Oh Shaun….' Katie began crying again.

He held her in his arms once more. 'Come on love, let's go in and sit down. Perhaps have a stronger drink than tea. Let's just relax and then have an early night.'

He rarely left the office till after six. She'd been told that. He was one of those guys who tried to fool the boss by waiting until everyone had left, then sneaking out 10 minutes afterwards to make it look as though he always worked late.

But his boss wasn't there tonight. So, it was well before six and she guessed he'd be gone. She was right. She always had access to her husband's place of work and, using his entrance card, she had easily swiped her way through the various doors, until she was in. The man on reception recognised her. 'Evening madam.' She returned the smile.

She looked at the piece of paper and worked her way around the individual offices. No-one was about, which surprised her. One, two, three, four *('four will have a Chelsea scarf on the outside')* – check. Five, six and finally seven. She turned the handle; all the office doors were still unlocked. The cleaners had yet to come in. As she walked in, she took a quick look round. Yep, this was it, the flag in the corner gave it away.

She put the envelope in front of the laptop.

She picked up the phone and made a call, it was answered on the third ring.

Peggy's voice was stern. 'I got your message. Come over tomorrow night. I'll see what we can come up with. But it's between us, you do understand that? No-one, and I mean no-one, must know. That's the way it must be. You do understand?'

Peggy put the phone down.

FOURTEEN

BUSINESS was booming for Mark. He had three events this week. All at £50 a pop for the delegates who were set to listen, and enjoy, his motivational speeches.

Mark was single. He had enjoyed a long relationship with a girl in South Africa, but on returning to England they had both agreed it should be over. She didn't want to leave South Africa and Mark had little reason, apart from her, to want to stay. Now he lived just outside Oxford in a two-bed semi-detached house. It was nothing flash, he was still sorting himself out financially, South Africa had been okay, but he wasn't back in England chasing down £1m pads just yet. As far as he was concerned, he was on a steady rise. He had texted Katie two days previous. It had been almost three weeks since they last spoke, so he was keen to find out how things were. He enjoyed working with her.

'Hi, Mark, how are you?' Katie was sitting in her kitchen; Shaun was upstairs having a shower. It had been a good day at the shop and, with the weekend on top of them, the pair were going down The Feathers for a few drinks.

'How are you my dear? Long time, no speak. Three weeks, it feels like an age.'

She smiled at the other end of the line. 'Hardly an age, Mark. But I know what you mean. You wanted me to call you, I assume about doing more events. Or am I fired?'

'Fired? I wouldn't fire you. No way Jose. I just wanted to know how you were situated, that's all. You did say call in a few weeks. But if you are busy at the shop, I understand.'

Katie stood up and went into the garden. It was warm inside but there was a lovely breeze outdoors, although the sun was still beating down. 'Well, no, I would like to come and do some more events. I'm sure we can sort something out. I can get time off from the shop. Chuck me some dates.'

'Hang on. Give me a few seconds,' Mark replied. There was a moment of silence as he went through his calendar. Katie bent over and dead-headed a few plants.

'Okay, here we go,' said Mark. 'What's today? Friday; right, next Wednesday I have a talk at Stratford and next Friday I have a talk in Cheltenham. How do you fancy doing one, or both?'

'I think they will both be fine,' said Katie. 'I'll check with Shaun, and I'll see if we have anything on. But I don't think I do. I'll text you later tonight or tomorrow.'

'You're a star. Both start at 7, so we will be home by 11ish. Make sure hubbie is okay with me whisking you off. I don't want to upset my man.'

Katie laughed. 'You won't upset him. He enjoys his own company, gives him a chance to watch a few sensible documentaries on the television, rather than Love Island or Corrie which I like.'

'Love Island?' Mark sounded surprised. 'Didn't think you'd be into something like that.'

'And why not?'

'Well, I don't know. It just doesn't seem your bag, that's all. Then again what do I know?'

Katie smiled to herself and walked back into the kitchen. 'Exactly. You don't know me. I'll text you later.'

Shaun came down the stairs just as Katie was putting the phone down. 'And that was?' he said in a tone that surprised Katie.

She looked at him. '*And that was?* That's a bit abrupt, isn't it?'

'Okay, cool, don't tell me. I'm not bothered. It was a simple question.'

Katie didn't appreciate his manner and it all seemed unnecessary. She took hold of his arm. 'It was Mark if you want to know. And he wants to know if I can do some more events with him. I said yes. You don't have a problem with that do you? Don't be like this. We've had a good day.'

Shaun forced a smile. 'Sorry. Did sound a bit sharp, ignore me. Of course, you should do more events with him. I'll put the kettle on.'

Katie watched him go into the kitchen. She shook her head.

'Do you wish you'd met Cecil when you were teenagers?'

Katie and Peggy were chatting in the garden. It was Sunday afternoon and Shaun had gone off to watch the local cricket team after being at the shop all morning, which meant Katie had a chance to pop to see Peggy.

'Good question, my dear. But I think not.' Peggy took a sip of her tea. 'You see when we met, we were both so worldly-wise if you like, that we knew if our relationship was meant to be or not. He had been so hurt and I was, well quite honestly, I was resigned to never being married, I suppose.'

'But not through the want of other men trying to take your hand,' Katie said.

Peggy laughed. 'Well, yes there were a few. One especially I was close to settling down with. Haven't I told you this?'

Katie shook her head. 'Not sure. You've told me about the man you met who was an actor, who turned out to be gay. And the one who was a rugby player but was already married. Are you telling me there were more?'

Peggy laughed again. 'Gosh, you make me sound like a right good time girl. No, they were flings, this guy, Colin was his name. He was very much single and very rich. He lived in Windsor, in a plush place. I used to go over there at weekends. We were together about a year. I did love him. Loved him dearly, although we never got to the bit about him asking me to marry him. He was a City banker which back in those days was quite a job. But it was a good job, he got good bonuses, but he had to work jolly hard.'

'So, why didn't you marry him?' Katie looked at Peggy. 'He sounds a dream.'

'He was a dream. Sadly, he had cancer. He was just 39.' Peggy took another sip of her tea. Katie held out her hand and put in on Peggy's. 'Oh, gosh, how awful. I'm so sorry.'

'Don't worry darling, that's many years ago now. These things happen. He went downhill very quickly from his diagnosis, just a matter of months. But we had fun. We had laughs. He gave me this ring.' Peggy held out her other hand for Katie to see a beautiful red stone in a diamond cluster.'

'A ruby?' said Katie.

'Yes, a ruby. That's my birthstone. He bought me it a few months before he died. He knew he didn't have long. He asked me to always remember him.'

'Oh, that's so sad, yet so beautiful,' Katie put her arm around her.

Peggy turned to face her. 'And do you know what? When Cecil asked me about the ring, quite a while after we had been courting and I told him all about it, do you know what he said?' Katie shook her head.

'He said, you make sure you always wear that. I never want you to take it off. That man sounds like he made you so happy and you should always remember him. Isn't that lovely?'

'Ah, that brings a tear to my eye, Peggy. What a lovely thing to say, so many men would be jealous, they'd tell you to get rid of it. Or at least not wear it.'

'I know. But that was Cecil all over. You can see why we married and were so happy.' They both gave each other a hug.

'Right, that's enough of all that, look at us both wiping our eyes,' said Peggy. 'How are you my dear, and have you done more of those motivational speaking events?'

'Funny you should say that; I'm doing a couple this week, in Stratford and Cheltenham. So, that should be good, brings in a bit of cash, always nice to have a little extra.'

Peggy smiled. 'Well, you enjoy them. Is it just you and this Mark who does them?'

'Yep, just me and him. Well, mostly him. All I do is hand out some leaflets and chat to the delegates. But he seems to think I do a good job.'

'What's he like?'

'What's he like? Well, I haven't really thought about what he's like. He's Mark, he's okay, loud, and brash, Shaun's friend from university but very different to Shaun.'

'That all sounds nice then. Come on, you can tell me more inside.' And with that she got up to take the teacups in, Katie following her.

The sun had gone in; it had turned chilly.

Jack picked up the bottle of champagne and stood up. The bed clothes falling off him as he did so, his naked body standing proudly over her.

'So, do you want to drink it, or let me tip it all over that sexy body of yours? Personally, I don't care, because if I tip it all over you, I'll lick it off anyhow.'

'Don't you waste it, tipping it all over me.'

'And why not? There are another eight bottles in the fridge.'

She sat up and leaned forward to stretch up, trying to take the bottle out of his hand. 'Now, now, stop that,' Jack said. 'This is my apartment and I'll do what I want and make as much mess as I want. You behave and do as you're told.'

She smiled and laid back down on the bed. 'Come on then, tip it all over me, seeing as you have so much champagne to bloody waste.'

Jack grinned before moving closer, slowly trickling the champagne gently over her naked body, starting at her toes and working up towards her breasts. She arched her body, as the champagne was poured further and further up. When he reached her breasts, he stopped, put the bottle down, bent down and began to kiss and lick her all over.

He sat back up and looked at her. 'Oh, hang on Mrs Heeson, I think I've missed some. One can't let such a good vintage go to waste.'

Jack so loved a good *Veuve Clicquot.*

FIFTEEN

FRASER Simmons had been married 10 months to Claire, the girl who had melted his heart after the pair met in a London nightclub two years ago.

Both were from Scotland, and both had been in London four years when they met. Not that they recognised each other's accents in the madness that was Calipso's Nightclub that first night. Claire had been with her friends, Fraser with his. A few in each group knew each other and so the two groups combined, firstly on the dance floor, then hanging around the bars. Fraser and Claire hit it off immediately. After that, the pair met for drinks and meals, courting carefully. Neither were in a hurry. Claire, petite, pretty, pale skin, wavy brown hair, and brown eyes. She wore glasses rather than contacts. Everyone said glasses suited her.

Fraser utterly adored her, he loved the innocent manner she gave off, the smoothness of her skin, the kindness in her heart, the easiness in her voice. She was strong-willed, but fun-loving. He was a big man, rugged complexion. He had never been a huge hit with girls, his virginity lost in a haze of cider, spliffs, and drunken nights out in Corfu when he was 17. He hadn't enjoyed the sex; he had hardly remembered it. Girlfriends had been few and far between after that, and nobody serious, Fraser preferring to play rugby, and drink with the lads. Girls could wait… until Claire came along. They married in great pomp in Edinburgh, Claire's place of birth. It was a grand occasion, kilts, and all.

They honeymooned in Australia and were now looking ahead to a happy life together, creating their own family, all in good time. Life today was hectic for both. Fraser had his pension and investment work, Claire worked for a bank in the City, dealing with mortgages. They grossed £150K between them a year, with bonuses but, even so, purchasing a house in London wasn't easy, despite Claire getting discount on their mortgage. They lived in a two-bed terrace in Brixton.

Yet, right now, Fraser couldn't have cared less about money, bonuses, or houses. He was angry, hurt and upset. The photographs he'd found in an envelope left on his desk when he came into the office the other morning had horrified him. At first, he thought the envelope was an invite to a function. Or a couple of free tickets to a gig from a client. What he found had been anything but. Claire had looked so young in the photos. But it was her. It didn't matter when they were taken. It was her. He knew that carefree smile. He knew that body. That pale complexion, those glasses.

How? When? Where? Questions that had been spinning through his mind since he had first opened the envelope. And why? Why was it on his desk? How did it get there? It was a dagger to his heart. He hadn't known what to say to Claire. What do you say to your wife when you find photos of her pictured at what appears to be a party with most of the people in them naked, including her, topless? It was eating him up inside. It was her. And it was him. That was what was really killing Fraser. It was fucking *him.* The smug smile, the champagne bottle in hand. Kissing Claire on the neck, his arm around her draped over one of her breasts, as she looked over her shoulder into the lens. And all Fraser could see was her naked body... and him, the smarmy bastard. His now wife, standing with her arms around him and another girl, and three more girls, and more blokes. All no doubt stoned.

He hated Jack Bianchi. He hated him even more now. He could seriously kill him. If he didn't know better, he would have. Knock on the door of Jack's apartment and do him. On the spot. Punch his bloody lights out… And not stop punching. But he couldn't. As much as he wanted to, he wouldn't. Fraser knew the photos came from a time before he ventured into Claire's life. He thought he knew everything about her, but clearly not. She had never mentioned this. Then again, she was not likely to have done. He'd never mentioned his holiday in Corfu. They had only ever looked forward, never back. But this felt different. And all because of one man… Bianchi.

Should he burn them? Forget about them? Confront Claire? Confront Jack? His mind was a whirl and had been for 24 hours. He knew he hadn't been himself last night at home. Claire had asked what was up. He blamed it on the heat and a headache. This was all Jack's doing. He was sure of it. How could he prove it?

He stared in the mirror, photos in hand… *'Fuck you, Jack.'*

SIXTEEN

SHAUN dropped Katie home. It was lunchtime and the shop could close for an hour.

It had been a quiet morning and sales had been disappointing, despite the good weather keeping the tourists flocking in.

'Do you have time for a sandwich, or are you going to go straight back?' Katie was opening the bread bin in anticipation of her husband's request.

'No thanks. I'll nip into Teresa's and get something when I get back. She does a good carrot cake.'

'Carrot cake is hardly lunch,' said Katie. 'You need something more than that. And think of the calories. No, I'm going to quickly make you a salad sandwich, you can take it back with you.'

'Okay, okay.' Shaun turned to go upstairs to the toilet. 'But hurry up, I don't want to close for long.' No sooner had Shaun gone upstairs, than Katie's phone 'pinged' a text. It was Mark telling her what time he was going to pick her up that afternoon.

Katie left Shaun's sandwich wrapped on the kitchen table and took her cup of tea and went and sat in the garden. She looked around at her pretty borders, many of the plants now enjoying the summer heat. As she sat and thought, she began to think... daydream... about her life. Peggy was always telling her to plan, never sit still and wait for things to happen. She missed Solheim school, maybe one day she would be back at another.

But since she had left, Katie hadn't looked anywhere for teacher assistant jobs. Yes, she enjoyed working in the shop, but it wasn't her preferred choice. She loved Shaun, but it was getting too claustrophobic, living, and working together. She hated the thought they may get fed up being in each other's company. As she looked up, Shaun was picking up the sandwich and blowing a kiss through the window, car keys in hand, and mouthing *'Love you'*.

'Love you to,' she mouthed back, with a little wave.

Mark was on time, as he always was. Just before 5pm.

'Hi doll.' He stood on the doorstep having rung the bell once. He looked his usual dapper self, suited, and booted and she could smell the scent of his after-shave. She recognised Sauvage anywhere.

'Ready to go?' said Mark. 'Ready to make ourselves a pretty penny and inspire the next generation of Mark Bultitudes and Katie Walters?'

Katie raised her eyebrows. 'I'm not sure about the next generation of Katie Walters,' she said. 'Mark Bultitudes, yes. Unless, like me, they all want to work in a shop and talk to people flicking through books all day.' Mark ignored the comment as the pair jumped into his car. The roof was already down, perfect for a summer evening. As they went to pull away, he turned to her and smiled. 'You look good.'

It was a 45-minute drive to the hotel. Most of Mark's events were held in hotels, where rooms could be hired with video screen facilities, as well as being able to provide coffees, teas, and biscuits. There were set to be 50 delegates tonight, all at £40 a head. £2K was already in the bank from on-line bookings. It was something Mark had started to do, alongside 'pay on the door'. It was proving successful. After £600 to the hotel and £100 to Katie, Mark was set for another nice little earner.

As they drove along, he turned to Katie. 'I would like to get you more involved tonight, if that's alright with you?' He'd turned the music down on the radio.

'What? What do you mean, more involved?' Katie looked surprised.

'Well, meeting and greeting is fine and chatting to people afterwards is great, but during my talk tonight, I'm going to get you up on stage with me and we are going to have a little fun chat. Let's see where it takes us.'

'Sorry. What?' Katie said, sounding concerned.

Mark ignored her. 'Don't worry. Leave most of the talking to me. I think you are very impressionable, and I don't want you just sitting at the back of the hall for two hours, when you can be an asset on stage.'

Katie looked at him, flabbergasted. 'Hang on, I'm not sure about that. It isn't what I signed up for. I don't want to be embarrassed up there in front of all those people. This is a bit sudden.'

But Mark was having none of it. 'Hey, good looking, what you got cooking?' he sung as he pulled up outside the hotel, flipped the car roof up and got out of the car. 'Just leave it with me. You'll be fine. Do you honestly think I'm going to make you look a fool up on that stage? No way Jose! You'll love it.'

With that, he came round the other side of the car as Katie was getting out, his demeanour changing as he held out his hands to hold hers. 'Listen, superstar. I know a person who is capable of so much when I see them. And you, Katie Walters, are a superstar. You can't see it. I don't expect you to see it. But we've done what, four or five events now. I've been watching you and the way you interact with the delegates. You are popular. All I want you to do tonight is answer my questions, easy questions, in a happy, cheery way. Make me smile as you answer them. There's no tricks to this. You'll make the audience smile; I know you will. I'm not giving you a choice. But I am giving you another £100, as you become part of the event. More interaction, more money.'

'But how do you know I want more interaction?'

'Look, I wouldn't embarrass you for all the tea in Australia. We're friends, your hubby are I are friends. I know you can do this.'

'Tea in Australia? I think you mean China.'

'See there you go, far cleverer than me. Now, let's get this show on the road.'

Mark was 45 minutes into his talk, and he had just finished

his; *'Always challenge the bullshit'* section, a section Katie enjoyed as Mark marched round the stage nodding his head and saying, 'Is that so? Is that so?' The delegates enjoyed it to, there was plenty of laughter.

'Okay, everyone, I want to introduce you now to a young lady who is going to assist me with this next part of the evening,' Mark announced. 'I would like to introduce you all to Katie.' And with that Mark raised his hand in Katie's direction as she began to make her way to the front of the stage, her heart thumping as she climbed the two steps to join him, carefully making sure she didn't trip. As she stood next to him, Mark whispered, 'relax and enjoy'.

'Welcome Katie,' Mark said out loud. She smiled, not knowing what was coming next. She was beginning to think this wasn't a good idea.

'Now, Katie is a business owner,' Mark addressed the delegates. 'She runs a book shop along with her husband, a very successful one I hasten to add. Just outside Woodstock, so if you are nearby call in. There you are Katie; you did say I had to plug the shop.' Mark raised his eyebrows and there was a murmur of laughter from the audience, who all had their eyes fixed on the pair of them.

'Katie.' Mark turned to her. 'I have a question.' Katie stared at him. 'If I had £20 to buy any book in your shop, what type of book would you suggest? Thriller? Autobiography? Fiction?' He smiled at her.

Katie looked at him, remembering what Mark had said about making him laugh. 'A book on how to deliver a professional motivational speech,' Katie replied, impressed with her witty response.

The audience laughed. It was a good one-liner. Even Katie was surprised where that had come from. Mark lapped it up. 'Very good. You are not wrong Katie. That's exactly what I should be doing. Never stand still in your profession. Always much to learn. That you can clearly see, although no need to be so direct, Katie!' The audience laughed again. 'And one more thing,' Mark continued. 'If I asked you to help me with my motivational speaking events, as you are now, and I said I would pay you £25 to a night, what would you say?'

Katie shrugged her shoulders. 'Get lost, probably.' There was more chuckle in the audience. 'It's £300, or forget it,' she added.

Mark nodded. '£300. That's interesting, and thanks Katie.' Mark went over, put his hand out and led her down the steps and off the stage. 'Superb,' he whispered in her ear. He returned to face his audience.

'Folks, Katie is staying with us afterwards, so catch up with her at the end. But… I hear you cry. What has what Katie just said got to do with business, motivation, or anything to do with what we've been talking about tonight? Well, I'll tell you. Because before I came on stage tonight, I told Katie I wanted her to come up here and answer a couple of questions. I didn't tell her what they'd be. I didn't tell her what they were about. This was all off-the-cuff stuff. She could easily have told me to get lost. We'll rehearse it before we do it live; she could have said. But no. That was unrehearsed because ladies and gentlemen life is not a rehearsal. You need to take challenges head on from the off. Don't wait for things to happen. Yes, plan. But over-plan at your peril. Be impulsive. Make it happen. As Charles R Swindoll once said: *'Life is 10% what happens to you and 90% how you react to it.'* As Katie has just proved, you don't need to rehearse, you need to react. Snooze, you lose. Be proactive, never sit still and always front foot. Okay, we'll take a quick 15-minute break.'

There was much nodding of heads and chatter among the delegates as they got up from their seats. As he came off the stage, Mark headed to the back of the room, where Katie was sitting on a chair next to the leaflets and paraphernalia, he liked her to hand out at the end. He looked at her. 'Didn't hurt, did it?'

Katie smiled and nodded. 'It was, I don't know, different. Where I came up with those responses from, I have no idea. They just blurted out. I can't believe I said you should get a book on proper motivational speaking. Sorry, I wasn't trying to be flippant.'

Mark shook his head. 'That was perfect. If you had struggled to think of anything, I'd have asked more questions and then a yes or no leading question, so you would never have fallen flat on your face, I promise you. Your answers were brilliant though, spot on. You made the audience laugh.'

With that, a couple of ladies walked over to where Mark and Katie were talking. They were dressed smart casual, both mid-40s. 'Are you giving her a ticking off for telling you to get a book on motivational speaking?' one of the ladies laughed. 'I thought that was a great answer.'

'Good, wasn't it? Off the cuff. She's so cheeky.' Mark smiled.

Katie raised her eyebrows. 'Need to keep him on his toes ladies, or he'll start to think it's him who everyone has come to listen to.'

The ladies both laughed. 'Well, we enjoyed that. We're enjoying it all, just nice to break it up with something like that,' the second lady said. 'Must go for a wee now though!' Mark smiled at Katie, before heading off to get a coffee and have a chat with some of the delegates. She watched him as he worked the floor, so confident, so in charge.

'Loved that answer about the motivational speaker book.' The man who spoke was in his late 20s. 'James, James Harper.' He held out his hand and Katie shook it. 'So, how long you been doing this?' He had a nice smile.

Katie felt herself blushing. 'Not long. As Mark said, I'm a business owner with a book shop, so Mark and I have just got together in the last few months. Early days but going well.'

James nodded his head. 'Well, good team, I'd say. In fact, had hoped you might stay up on the stage a bit longer to be honest, might suggest that to Mark at the end. Are you getting involved in the second half?'

'No, I'm not,' said Katie. 'I think the saying is, 'that's a wrap from me'.' James laughed. 'Well, quite a little cameo it was to. Oh, our man Mark is back on stage. Better take my seat. Nice to meet you, Katie.'

'Nice to meet you, James.'

It was 11.15pm when Mark pulled up outside Katie's house. The night had been another success and her part in the event had gone down well. Mark was pleased.

'So, you okay for Friday?'

Katie smiled. 'Yep, definitely.'

He returned a smile. 'You done great girl. So proud of you.

That wasn't an easy thing for you to throw yourself into, but you did and look how good you were? I said you had talent Katie. Don't doubt yourself.'

Katie smiled back, leaned across and gave Mark a small peck on the cheek. 'Thanks.' She got out of the car and went to shut the door before Mark spoke again.

'Oh, and make sure you tell hubby you only got £100. Spend the rest on yourself. He doesn't need to know. You deserve it.'

He gave her a wink.

Peggy knew the voice on the other end of the phone as soon as soon as he uttered those dreaded words… *'It's all clear London'*.

She hadn't heard from him for two months and she'd enjoyed the space. But it was only hope that she wasn't going to hear from him again. 'Which accounts do you want them into?', Peggy said, impatiently.

'Cork and Kilkenny. We will want Waterford next week. And hurry.'

'Give me a moment.'

Peggy returned and read out the numbers. She didn't wait for him to say thanks.

SEVENTEEN

THE Feathers was invariably packed on Saturday nights.

Shaun and Katie were having a fun night in the pub. Landlord Will and his wife Angie were being the usual perfect hosts. The pair had laid on a hog roast on the large patio at the back of the pub and many in the village had come out to support. It had been a good couple of weeks at the book shop, and Katie had picked up some more work with Mark. They were sitting outside at a table with Jake and Sue, and Lee and Sandy, the six of them had been friends for many years, but since Sue had presented Jake with a baby boy six months ago, they hadn't been frequent visitors to the pub.

'I was in Oxford last week and you won't guess what happened?' Sue, a police officer on maternity leave, was enjoying the freedom of being out socialising, and her third gin and tonic was causing her to get a little giddy. The rest of group shook their heads. 'Enlighten us Sue,' said Shaun. 'Keep it clean though.'

Sue smiled. 'Well, it is a bit rude. I was getting off the bus near the bus station in the centre of the city, you know where that is in Oxford?' None of them did. 'It doesn't matter,' she continued. 'Anyhow, these two boys, I don't know, about 15/16 are sitting having a vape on one of the seats, when one of them wolf whistles me as I walk past.'

'No,' said Jake. 'You serious? Did they have white sticks?' He nudged Lee, who threatened a smile, not knowing how Sue would take her husband's frivolous remark.

'Shut up, Jake,' said Sandy. 'Your wife is beautiful, too good for you.' She stuck her tongue out at him. Sue ignored them both. 'So, I stopped in my tracks. There were a few people about, so I wasn't bothered about them doing it and I looked at them. Sort of, just stared at them.'

'You shouldn't do that,' said Jake, suddenly getting defensive over his wife's actions.

'Well, I did,' Sue continued. 'And I walked over to them. You should have seen their faces. And you should have seen their faces when I told them I was a copper. They both went pale. But then one gobbed off, *'of course you are love. A horny one at that.''*

Jake looked shocked. 'You never told me this.' Sue ignored him and carried on; the drink was making her chat easily. 'Anyway, the other lad looked at his friend but didn't know what to say. So, I told them both I could nick them for sexual harassment unless they pissed off straightaway. I got my badge out. They both shot up and scarpered.'

'Brilliant,' said Katie. 'Love that. Wow! Oh, to have the power to make people run away. I wish I could do that to some of the fossils who come into the book shop and dawdle around for an hour reading half the books and then buying none. Be nice to tell them to go away.'

Shaun frowned as he looked at his wife. 'Why did you say that?' Katie ignored him.

Jake was even less impressed with his wife. 'You can't go round threatening to nick people. You're on bloody maternity leave.'

'You can nick me Sue.' Lee, the builder, who owned his own company and had built walls, garages, porches, and extensions for almost everyone in Church Masham, was nodding his approval and laughing. 'Handcuff me, take me to your prison cell, interrogate me slowly... very slowly. Good work that, my girl. Getting those lads to shit themselves.' There was much laughter.

Shaun got up to get some more drinks as the music in the pub was cranked up. It was nearly 11, but the pub was open till midnight and the hog roast still had plenty of life in it. It was a sticky night, and only Sandy had a jumper on.

'So, Katie. How's Mr motivational man? What's his name, Mark? You still doing some bits for him?' Sandy stuffed some crisps in her mouth having asked the question.

'Ah, he's brilliant,' Katie said. 'I honestly love it. He's unbelievable. You should see his bit on how to deal with bullshit people. It cracks me up every time. His stuff really is inspirational.'

Shaun returned from the bar with the first of a handful of drinks. 'Have you been to one of these motivational speaking events, Shaun? Sounds fun.' Sandy had finished her crisps.

'What Mark's? No, I haven't. I know him too well. He can talk the hind legs off a donkey. Which is fine if you like listening to someone talk. He can talk alright.'

'Have I met him?' said Jake. 'I can't picture him.'

'He's been in here a few times but many years ago, he has been in South Africa for ages,' Shaun added. 'He was a professional cricketer, well sort of trying to be one. That didn't work out, so he came back here and works for a company in London.'

'Is he dishy?' Sandy was on her fifth glass of Merlot, as she nudged Katie.

'Is who dishy?' Katie looked at her.

'Mark. Is he dishy?'

Katie giggled. 'From some angles, I suppose. Depends on what you call 'dishy'. If you mean does he have a flash car and seem to earn a lot of money, I suppose so. If you expect him to cook dinner every night, iron your knickers and make the beds, doubt it. Bit too cool for that.'

They all laughed… except Shaun who didn't see the funny side. 'So, I'm just good for cooking dinners and making the beds, am I?' His comment was greeted with a degree of laughter, until he went further. 'Maybe I should sell the shop and buy a Jag convertible. That would be good, hey Katie? I'll tell you what, why don't we sell the shop and the house, and we can go and play fucking blackjack in London all weekend and take our chances? Who gives a shit if we're skint afterwards? So long as it makes me look cool, hey love? Would that make you happy, seeing as I'm such a bore?' Shaun's voice raised as he stared at Katie, who looked uncomfortable.

Lee jumped in. 'Hang on, Shaun, come on mate. No need to swear like that. I think Katie was being funny. It was a joke.'

'Was it? What's it got to do with you Lee? You her personal minder?'

'You what?' Lee replied, shocked.

Shaun stood up and headed towards the toilet, looking down at Katie as he did so. Katie looked away. There was an awkward silence before Sandy relieved the tension. 'So, how's Mrs Honeyman, Katie? Do you still see a lot of her?'

Katie had been stung by Shaun's outburst. She had not heard him speak like that in all the years they had been together, and certainly not in front of other people. 'Yes, I still see her,' Katie regained her composure. 'She's fine, I like catching up with her. She's lovely.'

'Do you know what? I'd love a house like Mrs Honeyman's,' said Sue. 'It's beautiful on the outside anyhow. I bet it's lovely on the inside.' Katie nodded her head.

Shaun returned and sat down. 'Sorry, Lee,' he said looking at his friend. 'I was out of order.'

'Don't say sorry to me pal, say sorry to your wife.' Shaun looked at Katie, took her hand and kissed it. But the damage had been done.

'Anyway, what's the best seller at the moment then Shaun?' Lee patted him on the knee trying to get the conversation back on track.

'Oh, I don't know, some good new authors out there you've probably never heard of. If you like Harry Potter though, that never fails.'

'What about Fifty Shades? That still going a bomb?' Jake flicked a smile at Shaun, who was now talking quietly. 'Um, well, not as good as it was doing. But there are still plenty of secret erotica readers out there. Not many in their 70s though, and we seem to attract plenty of people in that age bracket if you believe my wife.'

She shook her head at him, as he took another sip of his beer. He'd had too much to drink.

It was gone midnight when they got home.

'Well, that was fun, wasn't it?' Katie said sarcastically as she hung her coat up and marched into the kitchen where Shaun was pouring himself a whisky. 'Haven't you had enough?' She stood glaring at him as he put the glass to his lips.

'What's it got to do with you?' Shaun's voice was cold as he took a sip. He was drunk and Katie didn't like it. 'Don't speak to me like that.' She moved towards him. 'You misread what I said in the pub about Mark and made a fool of yourself. You were rude to me, and now we're home and you talk to me like a piece of crap. I won't have it, Shaun.'

He looked at her, his eyes half-closing. 'I don't care what you think. I don't care what anyone thinks. I don't care about shit. So, don't keep poking me Katie, or I'll get even more cross and pissed than I already am. Trouble with you is, you have no bloody idea.'

And with that he downed the whisky, brushed past her, and walked up the stairs to bed. 'No idea about what?' she said. But he didn't answer.

Katie let him pass.

'Have you spoken to her lately?'

Judy had at least got her times right. She'd once phoned her sister in Perth at 2am in the morning, thinking it was 10pm at night.

'Nope, have you?' Jenny had her feet up, the television was on, and she was sipping a white wine. It was 9.30pm in Western Australia, it was the middle of the afternoon in Scotland.

'So, are we going to simply turn up on her doorstep? I think we ought to say we're coming.' Judy didn't like the thought of surprising their stepmother.

'I'll have a think on the flight over,' said Jenny. 'We don't need to tell her we're coming. She will probably go out of her way to try and put us off and we don't want that. We need to talk to her face to face. Anyhow, I'm coming to see you mainly sis. We're just tagging her on.'

'Is she still at the same place in the Cotswolds?'

'Yes,' said Judy. 'I did speak to her a couple of months ago. Nice area she lives in.'

'Yeah, nice house, nice place, nice for her to have all of dad's money.'

'Leave it Jen. It's gone. Dad wouldn't want us to fall out or make things awkward.'

Jenny shook her head as she talked into the phone. 'No Judy, you can say it's gone; you can say forget it, but for me, it will never go. I know what that woman did, and I'll never forget, nor forgive. You can if you want. But I don't think that is what mum would want us to do. I was always the harder cow of the two of us, anyway. You were a bit weedy.'

Judy laughed. 'You certainly were tougher than me, but that doesn't say much, I couldn't punch my way out of a paper bag. Little sister syndrome I always reckoned you had. I remember you getting into right scrapes at school discos. Remember that girl, Brenda Bartrum? You punched her for dancing with that boy you had just packed in a few weeks before, what was his name? Jason Toddly, or something.'

'Oh yeah, Jason Toddington. I remember him.' Jenny laughed. 'I know, I always had a temper.'

'And probably still have, so just try and be calm with Peggy. Come on Jen, we are both nearly 50, not kids. And what would Ben say if he knew you harboured such a grudge?'

'He doesn't care sis. He's too busy down the farm. Fine husband he is, hardly see each other at times these days, and it's the middle of winter. Goodness knows how much we will see of each other when the summer gets here.'

'Well, take care Jen and confirm all the flight details next week. I'll pick you up from Edinburgh. Safe trip.'

'Thanks sis. Will do. Can't wait to see you.'

EIGHTEEN

JACK laid back and listened to the rain pelting down on the attic window of his apartment.

It was noise he was happy to hear, the heat had been too much. A change in the weather suited him. It had been a good weekend, although for once he'd been without a girl. It made a change; in fact, it made a nice change. He decided he would do it more often, intentionally, or otherwise. He made himself a shake, with frozen mango, yoghurt, fresh banana, and almond milk. He was soon dressed and heading into the office. He only had two stops on the tube, which was just as well because the rain meant it was packed. He hated the tube. He got off at Canary Wharf and put his umbrella up for the five-minute stroll to the office. He thought about grabbing a coffee, but that would defeat the point of his shake. He liked coffee, but too much often gave him a headache.

There were plenty of people already pottering about as he headed into work. He looked at his watch as he walked into reception. It was 8.02am. As he got out of the lift and headed towards his office, he thought he noticed his door was open, which was unusual if so. The cleaners were always meticulous about closing doors. But the door was ajar. He pushed it open, Fraser was sitting in his chair, feet on the table.

'What the hell are you doing, Fraser?' Jack stood at the door entrance. 'Get out of my chair, will you?'

Fraser sat unmoved. 'Close the door, Jack.'

'Piss off. This my office and get your feet off my table. I won't close the door.'

'Close the door, Jack,' Fraser's tone was menacing.

'Look, Fraser, what the shit is going on? I don't come into your office and sit my second-hand suit all over your chair. Or put my cheap shoes on your table, so you better make this good.'

'I won't tell you again. Close the door.' Fraser, who was much bigger than Jack, stood up and walked towards him.

Jack felt a tad unnerved. Was this what he thought it may be about? He knew being in the office, Fraser wouldn't make a scene. It wasn't his style. Not that Jack feared him. 'Okay. I'll close the door. And when you have said what you want to say, you can then piss off. If not, I'll get security.'

Fraser held up the brown envelope. It was empty. Jack looked at him, unmoved. But he knew what this was about, even if it had been a few weeks ago the photos had been planted.

'What's that?' Jack said. 'An envelope. You're not inviting me to Tottenham for a game, are you? Are there tickets in there? Or is that a bung for me to give you back that client you lost the other week? Just leave it on my desk.'

Fraser moved closer to Jack; his teeth clenched. 'You think you're such a smart arse, Jack. But you're nothing but a lowlife. A total shit, who will do anything to get their own way in whatever way you deem fit. But I'm warning you, what this envelope contained, which you know only too well, was the last straw between you and me. Do you understand? I don't need sordid photographs or cheap stunts to get even with you. I'm now watching your every move. Yeah, every move. Here in the office and outside. Because you'll piss it up Jack. People like you always do. You think you're invincible, you think there is nothing that can bring you down. But you know what? You are nowhere near as big a player, or as big a deal as you like to think. You'll fuck up and I'll be right there, ready to jump all over you. I'll have you, pal.'

Jack stared at him, unflinching, as Fraser continued. 'You think you're laughing now. But forever is a long time. And I have always been one to play the long game. So, go for a drink with who you want, see who you want. Have women over to your pad who you want. Who knows who you are dating, shagging, seeing, and messing about with. Fuck clients over, fuck work colleagues over. But I'll be watching, Bianchi, and not just me. So, just one slip, which I can guarantee you will make, just one slip.' And with that Fraser screwed the envelope up in his fist as he brushed past Jack and headed towards the door.

Jack smiled to himself and nodded. 'Oh, Fraser.' He stopped at the door and turned back to look at Jack. 'Your wife has great little tits by the way.'

Fraser screwed his fist tight and raced back towards Jack, grabbing him by the collar and pinning him on the desk. He pulled his fist back, spit frothing from his mouth. Jack stared up at him, his head having banged hard on the desk. 'Go on, Fraser, do it. Go on, I dare you, fucking do it. In the office, right here, go on.'

Fraser kept him penned down, his fist still back. He wanted to knock the living daylights out of him. But he had to stop. He knew he had to stop. He let go of his collar and stood back, Jack jumping to his feet.

'Knew you didn't have the bottle.' Jack smirked at him. Fraser was struggling to hold himself together. 'You ever speak about my wife like that again, I will hurt you so badly, so very badly, Bianchi. You've crossed a line.'

Jack smirked again, nodding as he spoke. 'She didn't know you when those pictures were taken, Fraser. Grow up. It's you who's crossed a line. Now, piss off.'

'Yeah, you know, don't you Jack? The pictures. You know.' Jack nodded. Fraser had so wanted to hit him. Instead, he turned and opened the door, closing it firmly behind him.

Jack looked around, sat down. He was a bit shook up. Fraser was a strong man. He nodded to himself, straightened his tie, breathed out, picked up the phone... And made a call.

Angelo was in a good mood, which worried Jack.

Then again, business was booming. And if Angelo was happy and Angelo's boss was no doubt happy, then everything in the world was happy, for Angelo at least, and that filtered down to Jack. He'd forgotten about his 2pm meeting with Angelo, especially after his early morning row with Fraser. That had thrown him off-kilter, but if there was one thing Jack Bianchi was good at, it was straightening himself up and getting back on track. Although, he was grateful when Angelo's secretary, Pamela, dropped by later that morning to remind him of the meeting.

'Get in here Jack and sit down,' Angelo was dressed in a blue suit, with a striking red tie and cravat. Jack wasn't sure if he liked the combination. 'So, how's things? Making plenty of money?'

Jack had taken his seat and smiled. 'Yeah. Everything is cool. Seem to be doing well, only missed bonus by one per cent last quarter which was a bummer. But on track to make it this time.'

Angelo was not a tall man. He was thick set, had a dark complexion and while he knew Jack thought he had all the dirt on him he needed to keep Jack in the lifestyle he was accustomed to, Angelo had become more determined as the years had gone on not to let him think that way. 'So, missed it by one per cent, hey. Must be honest, my boss doesn't like anyone missing their bonuses if they can help it. Make sure you hit it next time. I don't want to spend too much of my time defending you. You understand?'

Jack pulled a grin; he didn't like Angelo's manner. 'Um, I think you will probably always spend time defending me, Angelo. I mean, it's not as if I'm shit at this job. So, please don't tell me you've called me in here to give me a talking to about my performances, because if you have, I'll politely leave, get back to work and we will pretend this conversation hasn't taken place.'

Angelo's mood darkened. 'Don't kid yourself, Jack,' Angelo stood up. 'This won't go on forever. You might think it will, but it won't. I don't care about you, but you're rocking boats in other waters and that isn't good. Don't play games with me. I know the score. I heard about your little argument with Fraser today. These walls are thin, and you don't want to be getting a name for yourself, or rumours circulating. I can't, and won't, defend you forever and if you must do what you must do, then you do it, my lad. I'm no friend of yours. We're just inconvenient work colleagues. But if your reputation continues the journey it's on, then even what you have on me won't save you.'

Jack looked at him. So, Fraser had either gobbed off, or

someone had grassed him up. And why suddenly was Angelo growing a bigger pair of balls over their relationship? The rain continued to hammer down outside as Jack looked out of Angelo's office window. For once he decided that discretion was the better part of valour. He got up to leave. 'Is that all?' He looked at Angelo, who nodded his head.

'Jack,' Angelo said, as Jack turned to go. He spun round. 'Just remember, it's a big world out there. And you're not the biggest player.'

Jack shook his head and closed the door.

Claire Simmons would never usually answer a phone call that had 'unknown' on her screen.

But this was the third time in the space of five minutes her phone had rung, and it could be something important. She would chance it. She could soon cut the call dead. 'Hi, who is this?' Claire said.

'Hello, Claire. You don't know me, but I know you.' Claire went to say something but didn't. It was a woman's voice.

'I just wanted to tell you that Fraser is aware. Fully aware of it all, so don't be afraid to ask.'

Claire was going to hang up, but Fraser's name made her stop. 'What about Fraser?' The voice on the other end smiled to herself, if only Claire could see the grin.

'He knows about the photos, Claire. That big bomb sex night you took part in all those years ago when you first came to London. Remember? The one with all those wonderful pictures. They're in circulation, didn't you know? The ones with Jack Bianchi in. The naked ones. Lovely naked ones of you, oh, and Jack. And your husband, who really doesn't like Jack, he now knows. He's seen them.'

The line went dead.

NINETEEN

THE audience were spellbound as Mark continued his conversation with Katie on stage.

'So, you think it's all bullshit do you Katie?' Mark turned and smiled at her. 'What I'm telling you right now is BS? I don't think so.'

Katie turned to the Mark and then the audience as she delivered her final line. 'Well, I do. Because what you don't know is, I'm the one who sent the e-mail in the first place.' And with that the audience let out a big sigh. Many laughed. One or two clapped.

Mark was halfway through another evening, and it was going well. In fact, even Katie was thinking she hadn't heard an audience get as involved as this one was in Birmingham. Again, she had helped Mark with a section of the show, where the two talked about a scenario. It was going down well. There were more than 75 people in the audience and Mark had upped the ticket prices to see if it made any difference or not to the amount who booked online. The fact the extra fiver he was charging had made no difference and the fact he had one of his biggest audiences ever meant his night was again a success before it even started. Katie was loving it. It had been two weeks since she first took to the stage to join him. Her confidence had grown.

'And that my friends, is why you should not bullshit. You will get caught out.' Mark turned to the audience, some who were still clapping, before turning to Katie. 'Thanks Katie.' He then turned back to the audience. 'She's too sharp for me,' as Katie walked off the stage smiling, with many in the audience looking at her and smiling back as she took her seat at the rear of the hall.

Two hours later the last of the delegates had said their goodnights and Mark and Katie were left to put away the chairs and pack away the leaflets. It had been a late one. It would be gone midnight before they got home.

'You were great tonight,' said Mark, as he picked up one of the boxes of leaflets and started to walk to the open double doors where his car sat in the car park, boot open.

'Hang on, I'll bring this box.' Katie picked up a smaller one. 'Good, glad you enjoyed. I'm starting to get quite used to this. In fact, I might ask for a pay rise.'

Mark looked back and raised his eyebrows. 'Might you now?' They continued to work apace to get everything packed.

'Right, we done?' he said, as Katie looked around to see if they had left anything behind in the event hall. They closed the double doors and headed out towards the reception area where a rather large man was sitting, eating a packet of crisps, and looking bored.

'Get in the car, I'll just hand this key back in at reception,' said Mark as he walked one way, while Katie went the other. On returning to the car, he jumped in next to her and looked across. He didn't start the engine. 'Well, how are you feeling about everything? Enjoying it? You're doing a great job.' He looked at her and smiled, nodding his head gently as he did so.

'Why are you smiling at me like that?' she said.

'Like what?'

'Like, that? You know like what, like that sort of smile. That's not a Mark smile, that's a, well I don't know what smile.'

Mark laughed. 'A *'well I don't know what smile'*. What's one of them? I was just smiling at you, that's all.'

'I know, but why?'

'Because I think you're unbelievable, Katie. I think what you are doing is extraordinary. I think you are extraordinary. I don't think you realise it. I don't think you understand how much I think of what you are doing. You're brilliant, Katie. You're helping my business and in doing so, I'm seeing a side to you I never knew existed. I bet it's a side you never knew existed.'

Katie turned her head back to face the windscreen and looked straight ahead. She felt a little awkward. She knew her and Mark had begun to create a chemistry on stage. She'd laid in bed only recently thinking about it. The way they had interacted, the way they had laughed with each other, the way they had gelled. She wasn't happy thinking about other men; she was married.

'Well, that's a nice thing to say,' she said, before turning back to face him. 'You're not so bad yourself.'

The car park was almost empty where Mark had parked up. Most of the hotel guests' cars were around the corner close to the reception area. For a few seconds after Katie spoke, they stared at each other. The silence was deafening, and it was telling a story. Mark ventured forward, moving his lips closer to hers. She didn't pull away. She felt frozen in time. Their lips met and for a few seconds they touched, gently at first, before the kissing became stronger, Mark putting his hand on her neck. The kiss went on for what seemed like an eternity but was no more than a few seconds.

'No, Mark. No.' She pulled away, breathed out, and straightened her blouse. 'I'm sorry,' she continued. 'I shouldn't have done that. We shouldn't have done that. I think we need to go now. Sorry, Mark. Let's go.'

Mark said nothing. He just continued to look at her, her brown eyes, her wavy brown hair, and innocent look. He knew it was wrong, but what could he do? For weeks he had watched this confident and fun girl. For weeks he had admired her more. For weeks he was seeing more in her than he knew existed.

'I'm sorry as well,' Mark eventually said. 'That was wrong of me. Please don't let it affect what we do together. It was just a spur of the moment thing. I'm sorry Katie. I hope I haven't spoiled everything. Please, forgive me.'

She fumbled around in her bag and got her phone out. She was trying to keep calm, but she was trying to get her head round what had just happened. She looked at Mark. 'Let's go, shall we? Let's forget it.'

Mark nodded and started the car up and they drove out of the car park. Katie read some of the texts she had been sent during the evening, trying to pretend everything was normal. *'Hi honey. Hope you having a good night. Just to let you know, I've got to get up early tomorrow, so won't wait up. Love you xx...'* Shaun always signed off with two kisses. Katie put her phone away.

The awkward silence ensued as they headed down the motorway. Mark turned the radio up and looked across at her. 'You can't beat a bit of Bee Gees,' he said.

Katie feigned an awkward smile.

As soon as she felt Shaun get up next morning, Katie did likewise.

'Hey, what are you doing? Shaun said. 'You don't have to get up. It's 6.30. I have some books being delivered, so I'm going in early. You had a late night. Didn't you get my text?'

'I know, I know. Yes, I got it. But I'm coming in with you to the shop.'

'But why? Have a nice day here. I might close the shop up lunchtime and come back for a coffee if we're quiet. You don't have to come in. I won't be that busy.'

'I want to come.' She looked pleadingly at him.

Shaun shrugged his shoulders. 'Okay, if you want to come, come. I'll just pop in the shower first.'

He went through into the bathroom and Katie heard him turn the shower on. She slipped her nightdress off and walked across the landing opening the bathroom door. She knew this would take him by surprise, this was so out of character. But what was *'her style'* these days? Maybe she was changing. More confident, more adventurous, more everything. Last night had triggered something, her love for her husband for one. She realised how much she loved him. She'd always known, but that kiss with Mark had made her think.

'Hang on, what are you doing?' Shaun's tone was one of surprise as a naked Katie opened the door and stepped into the shower, cuddling up close to him. 'Katie.' Shaun put his arms around her. 'What's wrong with you? I've got to go to bloody work.'

She looked at him, lips pursed. 'Shhhh. Don't say anything.'

There were smiles and hugs in the airport as Jenny and Judy embraced.

It had been a long flight from Australia to Scotland and Jenny was dying for a hot bath as soon as they got back to Judy's house in Musselburgh.

'Hi, sis. How are you? Gosh, have you lost weight?' Judy pulled back from Jenny and studied her. 'If you haven't, you look good. And a tan as well. We don't get much chance of tanning weather up here.'

Jenny smiled. The two sisters were similar in height, but Jenny's hair was blond, while Judy had very dark hair, bobbed around her neck. 'The weather has been good lately in Oz,' Jenny said. 'Even for our winter months, the temperature has been in the 20s, so I suppose that's where my tanned face has come from. How are you anyway? And how is John?'

'I'm fine. John is still working at the council, although I think he's hoping voluntary redundancy will come his way. Give him time to play more golf. In saying that, he's been there 30 years, and our mortgage is nothing. That's what you get for having no kids.'

Jenny smiled. Her sister had always played the stiff upper lip when it had come to children. She and John had wanted them, but it had never happened, not that it had seemed to have damaged their relationship. Judy continued. 'Talking of which, how are your two?'

Jenny had two boys, one in the fire service and one who had just left university. 'Sam is well, and Greg is deciding whether to take a gap year. He's just finished university. Got a 2:1 in chemistry. He's happy with that.'

'What's a 2:1? Is that good?'

'Yep, that's pretty good. He's happy, it's just one down from a First. Which is a top pass.' The two smiled and linked arms as Judy pulled one trolley and Jenny the other. They were soon sitting in the car on their way back to Musselburgh.

'So, you say you haven't spoken to Peggy.' Jenny pulled the sun flap down and was adjusting her hair in the mirror.

'No, I haven't', said Judy. 'We can head down to Oxford next week and stay somewhere and call her when we get there. She'll be in, she never goes anywhere.'

'I'm only doing this for dad, you know.' Jenny's voice

hardened. 'I certainly am not doing it for her benefit. And I will demand to know what's in her Will. I'm going to ask, Judy.'

Judy turned to her sister. 'You can't do that. She won't tell you anyway.'

'I don't care,' said Jenny. 'I never get the chance to speak to her face to face and I'm bloody well going to. And if she tells me to piss off then I'll piss off and not come back. Not that I intend to come back anyway. Dad had a bloody lot of money, Jude. You do know that don't you? And he gave mum nothing when they split. Or very little. And I bet it was that cow Peggy's doing. She's a bitch.'

Judy shook her head as she drove towards Musselburgh. She understood her sister's dislike of Peggy, but she didn't let it eat her up as much as it did Jenny.

Judy and John's cottage was a couple of miles outside the town. It was in a beautiful setting and the sun had begun to glint through the clouds which were moving apace. The wind had got up. 'Here we are. Home sweet home.' She smiled at Jenny. 'And it hasn't changed much since you last came.'

'It's good to be here.' Jenny hugged her sister as they sat in the car. 'I'm sorry I go on about Peggy, but I can't help it. Just ignore me.'

'I know,' Judy smiled. 'I understand. Just don't let the situation, or her, get to you.'

Judy held up her two fingers and began to smile. 'Remember, my Aussie sister. We come in peace!'

They both laughed out loud and went inside.

TWENTY

THE break in the hot weather hadn't lasted long.

Jack was hoping it would. The heat had begun to get on his nerves and the recent rain of the last few days had been a blessing as far as he was concerned. Apart from anything else, he'd managed to get out for a jog for the first time in what felt like a while. He never ran in the heat and by the time he was home most nights or, more the truth, back from the pub, jogging wasn't on his agenda, even though he knew it should be. So, today's forecast of 28 degrees didn't appeal, especially as he had a meeting with Toby Ruskin, a man not to be messed with, a man who invested big in the business and was on first-name terms with all the directors. Jack hoped they would sit outside in the shade in Toby Ruskin's back garden.

Jack had not at first appreciated Toby Ruskin's importance to the firm when Angelo had directed him to deal with the former solicitor's investments. As far as Jack was concerned Toby Ruskin, now well into his 70s, was just an overweight, posh-speaking old buffoon with a big house and two flash cars. He had money to play with, and Jack was happy to play with it. But Jack couldn't have been more wrong. Toby Ruskin may have been rich, but he was no fool. He was as sharp as a tack, had been big into property during his lifetime. He and Jack's quarterly meetings could go on for hours if Toby Ruskin so desired, as he fired question after question. Then again, Toby Ruskin did have £2.2m invested with the firm. He had a range of portfolios from the

UK to Asia, Europe to the Americas. He expected his lifetime's savings to be invested wisely and make him plenty of money. It was Jack who had been entrusted to help do so. Not that Jack had ever been allowed to work alone alongside him. Angelo had always cast an eye over proceedings. Yet, Jack and Toby Ruskin had formed a mutual friendship, the old man becoming quite attached to the young city boy he was entrusting his money with. Even Jack had changed his opinions of him from their first meeting.

'Morning Jack, come in have a sit down.' Toby Ruskin lived in a large Victorian house south of the Thames. It must have had six bedrooms, although Jack couldn't be certain, he'd never had a tour. But he'd seen houses this size for sale on property websites in and around the area and they all clocked £4m plus, many with loads of bedrooms. Toby Ruskin lived alone, he had one daughter, Jasmine. His wife had passed away three years previous; she had been almost ten years older than him. Jasmine was the light of his life. Now in her 50s, she lived in North London with partner Peter, and their only daughter, Olivia, who was just finishing university. They were not a big family, but they were tight-knit, and Olivia was the absolute apple of Toby Ruskin's eye.

'Coffee, lad?' Toby Ruskin had taken Jack through the long entrance hall, where they had passed four rooms, two on the left and two on the right, all of which appeared to be big enough to fit Jack's own apartment in, before they ended up in the kitchen which boasted a big table with six chairs. 'Yes please, black, one sugar.' Jack looked round for somewhere to hang his coat. He decided to put it on the back of one of the chairs.

'So, how's things, my boy? Working hard I hope, playing hard I dare say.' Toby Ruskin had got to know Jack well since they were first introduced by Angelo two years previous. And while it was good they did get on, the more important thing for both was that Jack's handlings of Toby Ruskin's portfolio had been impressive. Indeed, in the past 12 months, Jack had managed to put 9% on the old man's pension pot.

'Things are going well, Toby,' Jack said. 'It's tough trading at times out there but you need to know what's what and we're all doing good by the look of things. Certainly, our business is doing well, there are some good portfolios out there, and that is reflecting in your pension pot and investments as well. Hope you are pleased with it.'

'Yes, I am. I must admit I was a trifle concerned when your company handed you to me. Don't get me wrong but I had been used to dealing with more, let's say, 'experienced hands', over the years. You were a bit of a shock. Then again, I've told you all this. Proof would be in the pudding we all agreed. And the pudding is looking, and tasting, delicious.'

Jack smiled. He liked it when someone loved money as much as he did. 'We're nearly at £2.3m in the pot overall.' Jack smiled again as he handed Toby Ruskin his carefully prepared portfolio sheets. He had e-mailed them to him, but he had called out hard copies just in case. It was a wise idea, Toby Ruskin wasn't a regular visitor to his own e-mails, let alone print them off.

'I moved out of one Asia portfolio a couple of months ago, it wasn't doing well, and I didn't think it would move forward anytime soon', said Jack. 'The European one we moved into six months ago has done well. Dare I say those dreaded words, *'green stocks'*? Perhaps not your bag 20 years ago, Toby, but they are worth looking out for now. Many of them are the future.'

Toby Ruskin nodded. 'I'll leave it to you lad. But to be honest the world is changing at such a pace you must go with whatever feels right, it seems to me, although gas and oil I dare say are still important.' He looked up at Jack.

'Oh yes, the large players are still worth being involved in,' said Jack. 'You must look out for the big techs as well. Then it's a case of finding those hidden gems that can move quickly, and in the right direction.'

Jack took a sip of his coffee and waited for any questions. Clearly, they weren't going to sit in the garden. Just as well the kitchen was cool. Toby Ruskin was absorbing the pages of material in front of him and showed no signs of moving outside into the sun. 'What's this German stock stuff here?' he said. 'Is that the European one you were talking about?'

Jack leaned over and looked at the portfolio Toby Ruskin was looking at. 'Yep, that's the one. We have 12% in that and it's up 23% in three months.' Jack looked pleased with himself. 'Not that it's going to keep going up at that rate I have to warn you.'

'Why not boy? Have confidence.' Toby Ruskin laughed out loud. 'I expect my pension to be five million before the end of the year. What are we in now, September? Yep, five mill sounds plausible.'

'I would love to think so. But I'll have to rein you back in a little on that one.' Jack flicked his eyebrows up.

'Only kidding my boy. This all looks excellent and I'm very happy with it. Now, I want to take out more than the 4K a month I'm currently doing, if that's okay?'

Jack looked at him and shrugged his shoulders. 'Depends how much more, but I wouldn't see it as a problem. You'll still make money.'

'An extra 1K a month is what I'd like, Jack. Starting next month. There's plenty in there. I want to spoil the granddaughter a bit.' Jack smiled. 'Lucky her.'

Jack knew an extra 1K a month would hardly scratch the surface of Toby Ruskin's pension pot. An extra 12K a year taken out wouldn't harm Jack and the firm's cut from the pot either. 'I'll draw up the forms when I'm back at work and e-mail them over to you. Just sign them and send them back and we'll start the extra 1K coming out as soon as possible.'

Toby Ruskin stood up and put his coffee cup in the sink. 'E-mail them to Jasmine. She's more into all this e-mail stuff than me. She can help me if I must sign it. I do get your e-mails, but I don't look at them very often. You have her e-mail address, don't you?'

'Yes, I do,' Jack stood up and followed him. 'Doesn't seem we have spoken much about your pension in general, are you all okay with it? Any questions? I don't have to rush off. Chelsea doing well, I see. You still have a season ticket?'

Toby Ruskin turned and put his hands on Jack's shoulders. 'They certainly are and yes, I still have a season ticket, but don't go to every game. And as regards my investments with you guys, my dear boy, as my late aunt always said, *'if it ain't broke, don't fix it'*, and she was right. It all looks good, but don't worry, I keep my eye on things. So, don't get slack on me. And no, I don't have any more questions, I'm at the golf club in 40 minutes for one of my old pal's retirement bashes. He's 70, so left it a bit late to retire you ask me, but he's doing it now. Don't want to be late. Got a taxi, can enjoy a glass or three of Merlot then.'

Jack nodded. 'That sounds fun. I'll get going. And no, I won't slack on you.'

As they headed back down the hallway, Toby Ruskin put his hand into his back pocket and brought out his wallet, delving into the mountain of notes inside. 'Before you open the door, lad. Here you go, treat yourself and your young lady to a night out, and thanks for your hard work.'

Jack smiled. He'd gotten tired of trying to bat this part of their meeting together away. He'd tried to stop this moment over the years, but the old man always wanted to show his appreciation. He put out his hand. 'You know you don't have to Toby. But thanks. Have a good day.' Jack took the £100, the pair shook hands and smiled.

Back in the car, Jack flicked through the £20 notes. He'd have a great Friday night.

Claire's heart was racing.

She knew she would have to front it. The phone call had been playing on her mind for the past week and, although Fraser hadn't said anything, their conversations hadn't been as free flowing as they had been, maybe now she knew why. The fact she'd been on a three-day course in Newark meant she'd had plenty of time to think and, back home now, she knew she had to say something. Fraser knew. That phone call told her he knew.

Fraser walked through the door. 'Hi, good day?' Claire smiled at him and put her arms around him, giving him a little peck on the cheek.

He smiled back. 'Not bad, and how was your course? Exciting, I dare say?'

'What do you think? It was dull to be honest, although at least the trainer had a bit of life about her. The stuff the poor woman was training us on was so boring. But she was fun. Worked through lunch and finished by 4pm. The hotel was nice and there were a couple of fun girls on the course. So, we sat in the bar and chatted.'

Fraser nodded. 'Good, sounds fun. Good journey?'

'Yep, good journey. Got in about 40 minutes ago.'

He went past her and into the kitchen. The weather was still in the mid-20s, and the sun was beating down. Fraser went to the fridge, grabbed a bottle of beer, unscrewed the lid, and headed outside, sitting on one of the chairs the two of them always spread round the garden when it was nice. Claire followed him and sat in a chair opposite. They looked at each other. She took a deep breath. She didn't want to start this conservation, but she felt she had to. 'You know, don't you?'

He looked at her. 'Know what?'

'Please don't make this difficult, Fraser.' He stared at her; the look gave it away.

'The photographs,' Claire continued.

Fraser put his bottle down and stared across at her. His demeanour changed; she could sense the anger. She was regretting bringing the subject up already, but it was too late.

'How the hell do you know about the photographs? And how do you know, I know?' Fraser hadn't been prepared for this. While he had been working out for weeks how to broach the subject, her words had caught him off guard.

'I know because I had a call from someone to say you knew. I'm sorry, Fraser you had to find out like this. You do know this was all before we met, don't you?'

He nodded his head slowly and picked his beer up, taking a swig, planning, and thinking of what to say next. 'Someone called, who called you?' He stood up and walked towards her. She stood up as well. He was much taller than her.

'It was a woman who called, a week ago,' Claire blurted out. 'But I don't know who. She just said you knew, and you were angry. And I'm sorry, Fraser. I'm so sorry. But we weren't together then, you know that. You know I'm telling the truth. I'd only been in London a couple of months. It was a mad party. I'm sorry, just so sorry. I can't change the past. I wanted to let you know about the call as soon as I got it, but I just didn't know how to tell you. I could have said nothing, but... well... but, oh, I don't know.'

Fraser sat back down. He picked up his bottle and took another swig. He stared ahead. 'Jack Bianchi was there, wasn't he?' She nodded.

'Did he fuck you at the party?' The question startled Claire. She hadn't expected that. She began to speak but for a second nothing came out. 'I said, did he fuck you? Did he?'

She was shocked, she wanted to burst into tears. Her heart was beating fast. She had never thought her husband would speak to her like this. But his mood was now dark, and he was looking wide-eyed at her. 'What sort of thing is that to say? What's that got to do with anything?' Claire eventually forced herself to say, as she tried to keep eye contact with him. 'I had partners before you, and you had girls before me. Christ, Fraser what a way to talk to me.'

His voice dropped to almost a whisper as he spoke slowly and precisely. He was nodding his head. 'I said, did he fuck you?' Fraser picked up the bottle and threw it against the brick wall opposite. It smashed into tens of pieces. He was like a man possessed. He grabbed Claire by both arms and shook her hard. 'He did, didn't he? Answer me, Claire, answer me.'

She was shaking now, and the tears began to flow. She had never seen her husband like this, ever, and he was gripping her tight. She was panicking. His eyes were bulging, and she could see the veins on his neck standing out as he grabbed her tighter. She began to shake her head as she went to answer him, but as she did so the shaking turned into a nod.

'Yes,' she cried. 'Yes. He did.'

TWENTY ONE

FRASER released his grip on her.

He stood back and stared into her crying eyes. He was numb. He had thought about the photographs for weeks and, while he knew he couldn't change the past, he had always hoped the party had been flirtatious fun and no more. He was clearly wrong.

'I'm sorry. I'm so sorry.' Claire was rubbing her wrists and had thought of running indoors, but knew this situation had to be faced. Running away was not going to help. 'I promise you I knew nothing about those photographs getting to you. I don't know why anyone would send them to you. I don't know where they came from. Please, you must believe me. And I didn't know you were to end up working with Jack, did I?'

'Was he good?' Fraser's tone was cold. 'Bianchi, was he good?'

Claire shook her head and began to sob gently again. 'Oh, Fraser, please for Christ's sake, don't do this. Please don't keep tormenting yourself, don't keep tormenting me. We can't continue like this.'

But Fraser remained calm and in almost a jocular tone said. 'It's a simple question, Claire. I can't see why you can't just answer. I mean, it's surely not something you have forgotten. It wasn't that many years ago. Did the pair of you do it once, twice, 10 times. You were probably so stoned you can't remember. Perhaps everyone had a go with you.' Fraser was half laughing now, but it was a laugh full of hate and vitriol. 'Come on. I've seen the photos. It looked a brilliant party. And there was me thinking you were a different class of girl to that. How wrong was I? Jack even told me you had nice little tits, sorry, I forgot to mention that. Yeah, Jack and I have spoken. Make you feel good, does it?'

It was the final straw for Claire. 'Shut the fuck up, Fraser, that's enough.' She moved away from him and stared him down. 'Those photos and that night were way before we met. What the hell are we going to do with our lives, spend all the time bringing up the past? I don't question you about your previous girlfriends, parties, and nights out. I don't question you about what certain girls were like. How many you have had sex with. So, Jack works with you. Okay, I know that; you've told me. You've told me he's an arsehole. I don't know, but I get it. You don't like him. But I haven't spoken to him in years. I don't care about him. I hardly remember the night. I was going to tell you I knew him when you've mentioned him in the past, but what was the point? He's a no-one to me. Never has been. Your problem is with him, not me. But if you carry on like this, it will affect us. You have never been bothered about previous boyfriends I've had. You've never mentioned them. Okay, the photographs are what they are. But have you ever thought I'd slept with no-one apart from you? Because I've never thought that about you.'

She stopped and looked at her husband. He was looking away, saying nothing. She mellowed her tone. 'I'm sorry, Fraser. But I love you and only you. You're my husband, my soulmate, we share everything. I love you so much. Please don't let this come between us. It's the past. He's nobody, an absolute nobody.'

Fraser walked over to the garden wall and began to pick up the pieces of the broken bottle he had smashed against it. Claire followed him. 'Fraser, please, say something.'

As he began to pick up the glass, he turned to her, his eyes were watery. 'You have no idea how much this has hurt me,' he said quietly. 'Yes, you're right, I have a real problem with Bianchi. I hate him. I don't think you could have picked anyone worse in the world to have done what you've done. I know, it was before me and all that. Just give me time, Claire. Just give me time.'

He stood up and began to take some of the glass over to the bin, where he dropped the pieces in, before returning to pick up more. The sun was still beating down, but a gentle breeze had picked up, a nice, cooling breeze. Claire remained next to him as he continued to gather up the shreds. She wanted to touch him, bend over, and stroke his head and neck, but she didn't know how he would react.

'Do you want me to go?' she eventually said. 'I can go to my mums or a friend. Libby is at home. We can have some space then.'

Fraser continued to forage in the grass for any small segments of glass. 'I don't know,' he said. 'Just let's see how we feel tonight. I want to say sorry, but I don't know what I'm sorry for. Can you understand that?' He turned his head to look at her. She wanted to hug him, but still wasn't sure.

'It's, I don't know Claire. It's just everything. My worst nightmare. He's an arrogant bastard; you have no idea. And I know he had something to do with sending those photos to me. He's someone I could… I don't know… I could kill. I know that sounds awful, but I honestly could. I could kill him. Why him? Why did you have to do it with him?' He put some of the small fragments he had found back in the grass and put his hands to his face. He began to cry. Quiet sobs, still bending down.

Claire bent down beside him and put her arm around him. 'I love you Fraser. I love you more than anyone in the world. I'm all yours and always will be. Please, don't let this ruin us. It's not worth it. We are so strong, and we have always been so happy. I want us to have a family. That's only something we will share, no-one else. Please, Fraser, I love you.'

He stood up, and so did she. He wiped the tears from his cheeks and nodded, stretching out his arms to hug her. She moved into him, and they hugged tight. 'I'm sorry,' he whispered. 'I'm so sorry. You are my life. I will get over it, don't worry. I will. Please forgive me, I shouldn't have acted like this. I'm sorry if I hurt you.' The pair hugged tight as the gentle breeze swept around them. She eventually pulled back from him and put her hands on his face. 'I love you. More than you will ever know.'

They kissed gently on the lips. They pulled away, then moved into each other again and kissed longer and deeper. They pulled back and he put his hands through her hair. They smiled at each other and turned to walk into the kitchen.

But Fraser knew he could never forget.

TWENTY TWO

ANSON Park was a 15-minute drive from Church Masham

Katie had dropped Shaun off at the shop and returned to pick Peggy up. The pair were going for a stroll round the park to enjoy the beauty that the tall trees, small ponds, and squirrels jumping from tree to tree and running along the ground, afforded. There was a tearoom there. Somewhere they could sit and enjoy a cuppa, likely with a piece of cake. It was another stunning morning; the recent heavy rain hadn't lasted long, and summer was being kind this year. Anson Park was looking its glorious best as Katie and Peggy walked together through one of the many tree-lined paths that criss-crossed the beautiful landscape, the pair occasionally holding hands as they laughed and chatted.

'Did I tell you Jenny and Judy are coming?' Peggy said, as she pulled a face as much as to say, *'oh great!'*. 'Jenny has flown over from Australia. They phoned me yesterday to say they would pop over on Saturday morning if I was about. Apparently, they are spending a couple of days in the Cotswolds before heading off to London. Can't wait to see them.' Peggy pulled another sarcastic face.

Katie smiled. 'Oh, they'll probably be fine. You'll enjoy seeing them for a while. They might even not talk money!'

Peggy laughed. 'No chance. Although, they don't discuss money, just prod round the edges of how I am. Am I coping financially? That sort of thing. Is there anything I need? Can they help me? I remind them I'm in my '70s and living at home, not 100 and in a care home. They don't like me, Katie. I'm not a vindictive person, but I know what those two have been told by their mum, because Cecil used to tell me. She's a nasty piece of work. I've told you, haven't I about the affair she was having with one of Cecil's friends while he was in Northern Ireland?' Katie nodded. 'Well, that's the sort of woman she is, and she denied it all when Cecil confronted her. The girls don't know. If I was a nasty cow, I would tell them. But I wouldn't do that, Cecil never did, so I won't.'

Katie took hold of her hand as they walked past one of three gorgeous ponds in the park. They sat on a seat and looked across at some children who were throwing small petals into the pond on the other side. They were seeing who could throw the furthest and then whose petal took off and moved the fastest downstream. They were giggling and screaming and jumping up and down. Katie and Peggy looked across and smiled.

'Have you thought about having children?' Peggy clocked Katie smiling at them. 'Hope you don't mind me asking.'

Katie shrugged her shoulders. 'I'd love children, I think Shaun would love children, but we can't afford to have them right now. I don't think we have ever really discussed it. Shaun's too busy with the shop and I need to find a job, the thought of children doesn't really come into our world right now. Not that I wouldn't want kids, because I would. It's just that, I don't know, sometimes having them feels so right, sometimes it feels miles away. Shaun and I have had a few ups and downs lately. Nothing major, just silly things. I told you about that stuff in the pub. Then again, I don't know, we've been fine since. Perhaps I'm overthinking things.'

Peggy put her hands on Katie's and there was a moment of silence before Katie spoke again. 'I've got something to tell you, Peggy.'

Peggy looked surprised and turned to face her. 'What, darling?' Peggy smiled, but her face changed to a more serious look as Katie took hold of her hands and looked seriously at her. 'You know I told you I was doing some work for Mark. The one who did motivational speaking and all that.'

Peggy nodded. 'Yes dear, you did. And you said how much you were enjoying it.'

'Yes, I am, well, I was. I haven't done anything with him for a week or so…. Peggy, we kissed. A proper kiss.'

Peggy frowned. 'You kissed. You and Mark. What do you mean passionately? Peck on the cheek?'

Katie sat back feeling embarrassed. 'We just kissed. After one of the shows the other week. We were talking in the car afterwards and it just happened. I don't know what to think, Peggy. In fact, I'm a bit scared. It wasn't a long kiss and nothing else happened, in fact I pulled away and he drove me home and we've not really spoken since. But I can't get over why it happened. It's sort of freaked me out a bit. I've never done anything like that. Shaun would be devastated if he found out. I sound so silly, don't I? Yet, I feel so guilty.'

Peggy gripped Katie's hands. She lifted her head up and looked into her eyes, which she could see were watery. 'Look, dear. We all make mistakes in life. It was only a kiss.' Peggy began to smile as she spoke. She knew she needed the right words. 'Goodness me, if I had a pound for every mistake I've made, I'd be a millionaire.' She continued to smile. 'Katie, it was a kiss. A small thing, nothing more. Probably you were both caught up in the moment of what was going on. Don't blame yourself, don't blame Mark, you are both human. It happens. You are happy with Shaun, aren't you?'

'Yes, yes,' Katie interjected. 'Of course.'

'So, forget it. Forget it happened. It sounds like no more than a moment of passion. It could happen to any of us at any time. As my dear mum used to say, *'let him without sin, cast the first stone'*.' Katie looked confused. 'It's a quote from the bible, dear,' Peggy added. 'You must be honest with yourself though. If you know it was nothing, then deal with it that way and forget about it. If you are going to keep thinking about it, eventually Shaun will notice something. And then what will you do? Tell him? Is it then not making a mountain out of a molehill?'

Katie nodded, as Peggy continued. 'Do you want to still work with Mark? Have you spoken to him?'

'No,' Katie said. 'I haven't spoken to him since. He did say he had a couple of weeks off because he was going golfing in Scotland or somewhere. So, maybe he will contact me when he gets back.'

'And what will you do?'

'I don't know. Should I just forget it and carry on as though nothing has happened? I like working with him and we could do with the money. Oh, I'm so confused.'

Peggy stood up. 'Come on, let's walk and go and have a coffee and I'll buy you a nice piece of cake. Wait till Mark contacts you. I can't tell you what to do, you'll know; as you say, the money is good and I think you enjoy it, don't you?'

Katie smiled and put her arm in Peggy's. 'Yes, I do. He is fun, the work is fun, and the money is so useful. Cash in hand, it pays for the shopping each week and more. And I think Shaun might wonder what's happened if I suddenly do stop, although he won't be bothered, I'm know he won't. But we'll miss the money, that's the main thing.'

'You worry about money, don't you?' Katie nodded.

The tall trees provided shade for the pair as they headed towards the tearoom, passing dog walkers and mums pushing prams. The sun was getting strong now and there wasn't a cloud in the sky. 'I should have put some sun cream on,' Katie said as they sat outside the tearoom, sipping tea and eating cake.

'It is a glorious day,' Peggy agreed. 'We are so lucky to live where we do and have this park so close to us. Cecil and I used to come here. The tearoom wasn't built when we first came but the park has always been beautiful.'

'You miss him, don't you? Katie's voice was sincere as she looked across at Peggy, who nodded. 'I miss him a lot. Far more than you know. We had a lot going on. He especially had a lot going on. Sometimes I wish he was still here. There are things he would know what to do about.'

Katie looked at her. 'What things? Is something wrong?'

'No, no, forget I said anything. The thought of his daughters coming to see me is not filling me with joy.'

'Do you want me to turn up to interrupt things?' Katie said with a twinkle in her eye. 'Tell me what time they are coming, and I'll conveniently call to cut the grass. You can say I'm the gardener. And tell them you pay me £150 an hour. That will make them laugh.'

Peggy smiled. 'You are naughty. No, I'll be fine with them. I ought to talk to them. Cecil wouldn't have liked it if he thought we no longer spoke. He knew they didn't like me, but he was a good man and didn't like to upset the family, despite all his first wife did to him. So, for Cecil, I'll continue to be civil to them. But only for him.'

'Aww, good for you, Peggy. That's nice; you are a decent lady. I don't know if I could cope knowing the two of them weren't bothered about me, only my money.'

'Well, they can bother about my money, house, and everything as much as they like, because they aren't getting a penny of it. Cecil left it all to me and for me to do as I please. Which I have so far, and I will. And I have plenty of spare cash to spend.'

'You're not going to splash out on a motorboat, are you?' Katie laughed. 'Or one of those fast sports cars, a Lamborghini perhaps?'

Peggy almost spat her tea out. 'My dear, the thought. No, I've got a few plans, but not splashing out on boats or cars.'

'Plans, that sounds interesting. Pray, tell!'

Peggy put her cup down and looked across at Katie, taking her hand. 'Forget money, Katie. I'm going to tell you something now that no-one knows. And I mean no-one. You will be the only person alive I've ever told this to.'

Jack was tired when he got home.

It had been a long day at the office and the bloody heat was still killing him. The underground had been hot and heaving. He hadn't even bothered to go for a beer with a couple of the lads in the office when he left off. He'd been playing hard, both at work and socially. Dani had started to become more demanding, which he didn't mind, the sex was great. She'd been at his apartment last night; Angelo was in Ireland on business. They'd drunk plenty, done a couple of lines and made love till early that morning. No wonder he was knackered. He looked at his watch, it was 6.50pm. He took his tie off and went over to the fridge. He pulled out a bottle of Stella, he would enjoy a beer on his own tonight. He'd pop a ready-meal lasagne in the microwave. Just as he flopped in his chair and pointed the remote at his 60-inch TV that adorned one wall, the buzzer in his apartment went off. Someone was calling him from downstairs.

'Oh, shit,' he said under his breath. He pressed the button on the wall and spoke. 'Hello, who's that?'

There was silence. 'Hello, who's that?' Jack spoke again. He was about to take his finger off the button and go and sit back down, thinking it was kids messing about, when a voice said: 'Jack?'

'Yeah', said Jack. 'Who's this?'

'It's Claire. Claire Simmons. Open the door.'

Jack was taken aback. Claire Simmons. What, Fraser's wife? He hadn't seen her for ages. He smiled to himself. 'Hi Claire, long time, no speak, come up. I'm on the second floor, number 25.' He opened the door downstairs to allow her in.

Claire only had to go up one flight of steps to apartment 25. She could see the door was open as she got closer. When she got just a few feet away, Jack stuck his head round to greet her. 'Claire, how are you? Blimey, haven't seen you for… yonks. Come in. How did you know where I lived?'

Claire wasn't in the mood for small talk. 'Don't worry how I found out where you lived, Jack. That wasn't hard. And no, I'm not coming in.'

Jack smiled, but he wasn't stupid. He was sure he knew why Claire was at his apartment. 'So, what can I do for you? I don't have any wild parties on tonight, I'm afraid. You remember the ones? Good, weren't they? Wow, all that booze, all that sex.'

With that Claire marched towards him and slapped him round the face with all the force she could muster. Jack was taken aback. 'What the fuck was that for?' he said. He went to raise his hand, as Claire smirked. 'Yeah, that's right, why don't you hit me, you lowlife? That would sum you up. You know what I'm here for. You know very well what. I'll only say this once. You pull any stunt like you did with those photos and I'll go to the police. I promise. I'll report you. I'll do it Jack. I will.'

Jack regained his composure. 'Report me for what? And what

photos? What are you talking about?'

She went to move forwards and thought about slapping him again but stopped herself. 'Don't do it, Jack. Just don't do anything else, ever, to me and Fraser. Do you understand?'

Jack shrugged his shoulders. 'Does Fraser know you are here? Hope he hasn't sent you to do his dirty work. Sure, you don't want to come in for a drink and a chat, for old time's sake.'

'Piss off Jack. You're a bastard. Every bit the shit everyone tells me you have turned into.'

'Everyone? Are you sure everyone? Don't you mean your jealous husband? He's the one who has put you up to this, the coward. Have you told him we've shagged?' Jack smiled. 'I will if you want.'

Claire was holding herself back, but she pointed her finger. 'Fuck off, Jack and I mean it. I'll find some way of getting at you if you bother Fraser or me again. Any little thing, and I'll get you, I swear. I know people far bigger and better than you. Leave us alone, leave Fraser alone because I wouldn't want to be you if he really got nasty.' She turned and began to walk down the corridor.

'Don't kid yourself,' Jack called out. 'And don't threaten me. You're just a good shag, Claire.'

Claire ran down the stairs. She was shaking with rage and starting to cry. Had this been such a good idea? She was starting to think not.

TWENTY THREE

DRIVING back down the A1 from Scotland, Mark's mind was racing.

The last time he had spoken to Katie was after *that kiss*. He didn't feel good about it, Shaun was his friend; they were both his friends. He shouldn't have done it. But in his heart, he felt something for Katie, and he couldn't shake it off. He'd known her a long time, but he had seen a different side to her during their work together. She had always been attractive physically, but it was her manner, her nature that endured her to him now.

He made the call as he drove, Katie picked it up after three rings. 'Hi Mark, how are you?' He was pleased to hear her voice. 'Golf good?'

'I'm fine thanks and no golf wasn't that good, but the weather was nice. And the beer was nice, and the hotel was nice. But the golf was crap; a good walk spoiled, so they say. How are you?' There was a slight pause. 'I'm fine thanks.'

The conversation felt stiff. Mark knew he had to lighten the chat up. 'So, my gorgeous, how are you feeling? Up for giving me a hand again, now I've lost all my money on pointless golf bets I couldn't cash in because I couldn't putt. I'm working in Oxford next Wednesday night if you fancy it.'

Again, there was a slight pause. Katie was standing in her kitchen; Shaun was at the shop. She was having a day at home and enjoying the sun, working on the garden. The two of them were going shopping when Shaun came home.

'Do you think that's a good idea?' Her voice was quiet.

'Yes, I do,' Mark said confidently. 'Look, let's get this over with. We shouldn't have done what we did. I shouldn't have done what I did more's the point. It was my fault and I'm sorry. But can we not forget it? I love having you on board with me and I hope you like working with me as well. You've made a real difference to my events, Katie. I want you on board. Please, let's not let one silly kiss spoil things.'

The sound of the word *'kiss'* sent a shiver down Katie's spine. Yes, a kiss was all it was, but Katie wasn't a girl who had ever been disloyal, especially not to her husband. 'Can I think about it, Mark?' she said. 'I need to.'

Mark gritted his teeth as he looked at his dashboard in the car, he was doing 78mph. He should slow down. 'Of course. Again, I'm sorry, but let's not throw away the fun we have had, and the money we can earn because of it. Let me know soon though and take care.'

'I will Mark, I promise. Speak soon.' The line went dead, and Katie turned to make herself a coffee. Her mind was a whirl. She had known he would call; he was not the type of bloke who was going to give up on her. She knew they were good as a team, and yes, she liked the money. She would text him in the morning and ask what time he was picking her up on Wednesday.

She thought out loud. That kiss was nothing anyway.

Jenny and Judy pulled up outside Peggy's cottage. It was another beautiful morning.

'Come in ladies.' Peggy was her courteous self as she opened the door. The girls hugged her and went through the hall and into the dining room.

'How are you, Peggy?' Jenny said. Peggy nodded, forcing a smile, 'I'm okay thank you. Shall we go through and sit outside? It's a lovely day. You must have brought this sunshine with you from Australia, Jenny.'

She returned the smile. 'It has been nice recently at home and I didn't know if England would be as good, it's been a long time. It wasn't quite as warm in Scotland, though. Then again, rarely is, so sis tells me.'

It was Judy's turn to speak. 'Don't be so sure Jen. We had four dry days last week, that's almost a drought in Scotland.'

Peggy's cottage smelt nice as they all walked through. She'd tried to make it look and smell as good as she could. Although she wasn't overly bothered what the two girls thought of it, the cottage was her and Cecil's. She was proud of it and wanted his daughters to know that. As they went into the kitchen, Jenny picked up a photograph of her dad and Peggy, which was on a sideboard. She stopped and looked at it. Her dad looked so handsome. Peggy noticed her staring. 'That was taken in Cornwall, about three years before your dad died.' Jenny nodded her head gently and smiled. 'He was a lovely man.'

The three went through and sat in the garden, which was a riot of colour, something that both the sisters noticed as they went round looking at various plants and flowers. 'Do you want a coffee now, or later? Peggy said.

The pair looked at each other. 'We'll have one in a little while,' Judy said.

The conversation was bitty, it was clear neither the sisters nor Peggy were that comfortable in each other's company. They were going through the motions of talking family, friends, work, cooking, and even wine. But Jenny was ready to speak her mind. Peggy had returned with coffee and biscuits after they had agreed to all partake. They'd been chatting for almost an hour. She smiled as she handed the drinks to the sisters and offered the digestives. Jenny had already whispered to Judy when Peggy was in the kitchen that she was going to say something.

'Peggy, I know this is a bit awkward, but I'm sorry, I wanted to speak to you, we both wanted to speak to you.' Jenny's voice was strong and had a slight Australian twang to it. 'Something we think is important.'

Peggy pulled the coffee cup back from her mouth as she was about to take a sip. The mood in the garden felt cold. 'Oh, yes, and what is that then?'

Judy looked a tad embarrassed, but Jenny wasn't backing down. 'We want to know what dad has said about this cottage. About what he said in his Will. We know he obviously left it to you, but you have no children, what happens to it if something was to happen to you? Has he left it all to you to do with as you please? I know you think me a cow for even asking. But I'm sorry, I think we have a right to know. He was our dad and so far, he has left us nothing, just a couple of hundred pounds each when he died. So, what now? Is all this yours?'

Jenny sat back and looked at Peggy, that final sentence sitting uncomfortably in the air. Peggy stared at them. For a few seconds she said nothing. She had known the sisters weren't here for her health. But even Peggy didn't think they would have the front to ask what Jenny had just asked.

Peggy put down her cup. 'I must admit, I did wonder why you would want to come to visit me,' she said, her tone direct and to the point. 'So, I'm not surprised at your question, Jenny. The sad thing for you though is that you have wasted a long journey and many miles because I'm not telling you anything. Not a bean. It's now my Will and I will do with this cottage and my money whatever I see fit. If that is all you have come here to speak to me about and all the fluffy stuff beforehand was just a smokescreen to get to this point, then can I say, you are welcome to leave.'

Judy looked at Jenny, she feared her sister was going to explode. She wasn't wrong. 'You bitch. What an answer to my question.' The Australian twang now more pronounced. 'I can't believe what sort of person you are. But am I surprised? No, you're a family-wrecker, a slag who ruins other people's lives. A bloody gold digger.' Jenny was raging.

'Okay, Jen, that will do,' Judy jumped in. 'Come on, she isn't going to tell us and that's her prerogative. Let's leave it, stop it. You've said enough.'

'Good advice,' Peggy said coldly.

But Jenny wasn't going to leave. 'So, why do you think you have the right to take all our father's money, property, and everything he worked for? Why do you think it's all yours? Why do you think your husband's own children aren't worth a penny? Aren't owed a penny. Are you telling me that before he died you never discussed anything like this? I don't believe you, Peggy Honeyman. You are a nasty piece of work.'

Peggy stood up and walked over to the small water feature

that was alongside where the sisters were seated. She remained calm, but her heart was racing, and she was shocked by Jenny's outburst. 'Your dad dropped dead one day, just like that,' Peggy said. 'We were planning a whole life together. If you think we spent all our time discussing what would happen to this cottage if he, or I, died, you are wrong. Yes, he left it all to me. And now who I leave it to is up to me. Why should I leave you a penny, the way you speak to me? The way you have acted today. Get out of my cottage. Get out of my life. I don't want to hear from either of you again. You're an embarrassment to your lovely father. He would turn in his grave listening to you, Jenny, talking to me like this. Get out.'

The sisters got up to go, but Jenny stopped close to Peggy. Judy went to pull her away, but Jenny was too strong. She took hold of Peggy's arm and squeezed it tight, moving close to her face. 'My mum was right about you, gold digger, gold digger. Bitch.' And with that she let go of Peggy's arm and the sisters headed back into the kitchen, through the hall and out the front door. On the way out, Jenny picked up a vase and threw it at the television. Both the vase and television smashed as Judy took hold of her sister before she did any more damage. 'That's enough Jen,' Judy said.

Peggy remained in the garden but, on hearing the commotion, went indoors just as the sisters slammed the front door. She looked out of the window and watched them drive off, then turned to pick up the shattered pieces of vase alongside the broken television screen. She went over to the photograph on the sideboard, the one of her and Cecil. She hugged it to her chest.

'They don't know what they're doing, Cecil. I'm know that's not the way you brought them up. I miss you so much my darling. I so wish you were here.'

Peggy sat down on a chair and sobbed quietly, before getting on her hands and knees picking up the pieces of vase that lay strewn on the carpet.

It was one her and Cecil had bought together on their honeymoon.

It was lunchtime. Mark looked at the text and smiled… a smile of relief.

It was the answer he was hoping for. He so enjoyed working with Katie. After more meetings in the afternoon, a quick nip to his local for a couple of halves, he arrived home and went into the kitchen where he cracked some eggs into a cup. He made a mean omelette. He turned the music up and went back into the living room where he poured himself a small whisky.

Back in the kitchen the omelette was almost done when his mobile rang. 7pm, couldn't be work-related, surely? He looked at the caller ID. Oh, what did they want?

'Hello, Mark, how are you?' The voice sounded bored, but Mark knew the likely reason for that was his own fault. He didn't like the guy and he didn't like his manner. But he owed him, and Mark hated that.

'I'm okay. What do you want?'

'Don't be so sharp. Keeping off the white stuff, are we? And how's that new lady you are working with? Make a good couple, so I've been told.'

Mark wasn't amused. 'What do you bloody want?'

'Well, seeing as you're in a crappy mood, I've got a quick question I hope you can help me with. It's rather important. In fact, because of recent information we've received, we're sure you know him.'

Mark listened to the name, then shook his head as the caller hung up.

The omelettes were stuck to the pan. 'Shit!' he exclaimed.

TWENTY FOUR

THE forecast was for another warm week.

Even though it was getting almost into autumn there were rumours of an Indian summer on the horizon to add to the glorious July and August. Katie had received a letter from a school just outside Banbury who were looking for a teaching assistant. She'd applied for two jobs, so it was nice to get a response from one almost immediately. They as good as offered her the job. It was three days a week, but with the shop likely to start losing the footfall of the summer, it was an option she had to consider.

'But do you think I should wait to hear from the other school?' Katie said, as Shaun made a cup of coffee at the back of the shop. 'I mean they might want me four days a week, maybe five if they are short. This one at St Jo's is only three days.'

Shaun was in a good mood. He took a sip of his drink and walked towards her. 'No, go for it. Who knows what might come of it. You might get there, and someone leave, and they offer you more hours. Call them and speak to them.'

Katie puffed out her cheeks. Beggars couldn't be choosers. 'Okay, I'll call them. Now, do you want me to sort out that delivery that came in yesterday? Put the books out?'

'Yep, please. I've got a few invoices to sort and I'm not doing them at home, I'll do them here.' They smiled at each other.

'Katie.' She turned round. 'Yes.'

'Do you know, in all the years we've had this shop we've

never made love in it?'

'I beg your pardon? Did you just say what I thought you did Shaun Walters?'

Shaun didn't reply, he just smiled. He'd been in a cheerful mood all morning. He went towards the front door and looked up and down the street before coming back in and closing it. He locked it and turned over the 'CLOSED' sign. 'What are you doing?' Katie was looking shocked. 'You can't close the shop. Someone could come in and spend.'

Shaun smiled. 'Not likely. We've only had one person in all morning.' He walked towards her and in one movement picked her up before carrying her in his arms and placing her on the table at the back of the shop. He began to put his hands up her skirt and started to kiss her. 'What are you doing? No, Shaun, stop. People can see through the front door.' Katie was giggling as she was talking.

'Let them watch then.'

'Bloody hell Shaun, what's got into you?'

He began to feel for her panties as they both kissed, Katie wasn't objecting. She fumbled for his belt as they both giggled away. He undone the buttons on her blouse and slid his hand inside her bra. She squealed out loud, then jumped off and bent down to undo his fly, tugging his trousers down to his knees. They were both giggling. Suddenly, from nowhere, there was a knock at the door. A loud knock, followed by a succession of knocks, louder and louder. Then banging.

'Oi! You two in there? Is that you in there? Why are you closed? I can see you; I think!'

Shaun pulled away from her and spun round. 'Bloody hell', he exclaimed. 'Who the hell is that?' Katie jumped off the table and adjusted herself, doing her buttons up on her blouse. The pair of them pulling their pants and panties up. 'Go to the door, Shaun, whoever it is may have seen us. Shit. How embarrassing.'

'Oh, fuck it, let's carry on,' Shaun said.

'No,' said Katie. 'Open the shop. What's got into you?'

Shaun dusted himself down and headed towards the door. He looked back at Katie who had gone into the back room. As he got closer, he shook his head and smiled. He flicked the

'CLOSED' sign round and opened the door. 'Mark bloody Bultitude. What the hell are you doing here, all that knocking and banging? Didn't you see the closed sign?'

Mark smiled broadly and walked in. 'Yes, I saw the closed sign. But I drove past the bloody shop only two minutes ago. You were open then. I parked outside the bakery up there to get a sandwich. Why the closed sign? And your silly little car is outside, so I knew you were here. What's going on?'

Shaun smiled, but Katie's face was a picture as she came from the back of the shop to say hello. She discretely adjusted her skirt while Mark wasn't looking.

'Hi, Katie, are you okay? Just saying to your man here, the shop was open two minutes ago. What's going on?' Katie just smiled. Mark was his usual cocky self. 'Anyhow, open now. Have you told Shaun about Wednesday night?' He looked at him. 'I'm so glad to have her back on board with me, mate. Ticket sales will double.'

'Yes, she told me,' Shaun said. 'You look after her. Now, what do you want? Don't tell me you've come here, banging the door down just to tell me about Katie helping you on Wednesday.'

'No, I'm not here to tell you about Wednesday. That was just a reminder. I'm here to place an order. A big order.'

Shaun looked at Katie. 'Really?' Well, that's good. When you say big, how big? Let me guess, you want five copies of Ken Follett's latest.' Shaun smiled at him.

'No, I want 200 copies of *'Brave New World'*, by Aldous Huxley – you know it?' Shaun nodded, as Mark continued, looking down at his phone and reading aloud… *'Far in the future, the World Controllers have created the ideal society. Through clever use of genetic engineering, brainwashing and recreational sex and drugs all its members are happy consumers'*… Shall I carry on?'

Shaun laughed; Katie looked confused. 'I know what *'Brave New World'* is', said Shaun. 'And you want 200 copies, why?'

'Because Shaun. It's a masterpiece. A brilliant book. I read it years ago and was transfixed by it. It's always been my dream since I started up my speaking business to give everyone who comes to my talks a book. It was just deciding which book to give them. I started with the Shakespeare books I ordered the other month and now I plan to give every delegate a book at every event. And your Katie has helped make that happen because she has become part of the gig. The audience love her. I'm selling tickets on-line faster than a rat can shag a drainpipe... Or something like that. I'm basically making a bit of money.'

Shaun nodded. 'Good for you. Rat and drainpipe. You're the rat and hell knows who the drainpipe is. But, if 200 copies are what you want, I'll deliver. Come over to the computer and we'll look at when I can get them in.'

Mark followed Shaun, winking at Katie as he walked past. 'Bit quiet, Katie. You look like you've been up to no good.' She half-smiled. 'Nothing you should worry your little head about.' But she could tell he knew. Or suspected that her and Shaun had been up to something. How embarrassing.

Shaun tapped in some numbers and soon found where he could get hold of 200 copies, all hardbacks, but it would take 10 days. With a bit of discount, which he didn't mind giving Mark for such a big order, it was £2,880. The shop was making almost £800 from the sale.

'I'll pay up now,' Mark said. 'Take it off here.' He handed Shaun his American Express card.

'You don't have to pay now,' Shaun replied. 'Pay when they are in.'

'Nope, I'll pay now mate.' He grinned at Katie. She smiled back but wasn't sure what this was all about. Mark had never mentioned to her about giving everyone a book at their events. What was he up to? She shook her head. It wasn't her money.

'Set for Wednesday, then girl,' Mark said as he looked at her. Katie nodded. 'I'll pick you up at 5. Your place or mine.' He winked again and laughed, as Shaun laughed as well. Katie feigned a smile.

'See ya both then.' And with that Mark marched out of the shop, before stopping in the doorway. 'Do you want me to turn the closed sign back over again, so you two can get back to what you were doing? Whatever that was?' Shaun shook his head. 'No thanks.'

Mark grinned. 'By the way Shaun, flies are undone mate. Love you both. Don't do anything I wouldn't do!' He blew them a kiss.

Shaun looked down at his trousers. *Shit.* 'He's an idiot, but that's a nice order he's just handed to us,' he said. Katie wasn't amused. 'He saw us doing it. Doesn't that bother you? It does me. I work with him. That is so embarrassing.'

Shaun laughed. 'He didn't see anything. That was just Mark and his dirty mind thinking that we were up to no good. Probably not helped by the fact you kept adjusting your skirt.'

She shook her head. 'Um, I think your flies being undone didn't help. I'll tell you now, we won't do that again.' He raised his eyebrows at her. 'No, Shaun, I mean it.'

'Of course, you do, dear. We are married. It was just a bit of fun. Harmless fun, would have been great fun if I'd had another five minutes.'

'You mean 15 minutes.' Shaun moved forwards and put his arms around her neck. 'Sometimes I think you think I'm a bit boring,' he said. 'But I'm not you know. I can be as bad as the next man. Sure, you don't want me to turn the closed sign over again?'

'No, I don't.' She looked into his eyes and smiled. 'I can be a bit coy at times, can't I?'

'You weren't in the shower the other morning.'

'No, I wasn't, was I?' They kissed and then hugged. She so trusted him, so loved him for being the man he was. She was glad to see him happy. She loved him like this. A pang of guilt swept over her. Was the thought of that kiss ever going to go away? 'Cup of coffee?' Shaun nodded. 'Please.'

'Actually, do you want me to keep the sign on open?' said Katie, flicking a look at him. Shaun stared up from his computer as she headed to the door, putting her hands on her hips, and wiggling them. 'Leave it as it is please. You behave, Katie.' They both raised their eyes at each other and smiled.

'I need to go to the Premier to get some milk.' And with that she turned and walked out of the shop. Shaun watched her go. She was a great girl. He was lucky. He wanted so much more for her. And she would have it all.

He was now more convinced than ever.

TWENTY FIVE

DANI Heeson walked into the club and clocked Jack. He was in his usual spot, up in VIP.

It was just after midnight and the music was loud, people on the dance floor were oozing sweat and Dani had decided to make a late trip to the club in the hope of catching him. She needed to talk. It had been a bad evening. She and Angelo had a massive row. She wasn't going back. The argument had begun over a night out with Angelo's friends that Dani had said she didn't want to go on. It had manifested into a full-scale shouting match. At one stage she thought he was going to hit her as his temper reached boiling point. He'd been drinking. She should never have mentioned the phone footage of him with the prostitutes. Why had she played such a dumb card? But she'd played it. It just came out. As soon as she said it, she knew she'd messed up. He was so angry. First, he denied it. Then he started questioning her. Eventually, as Dani stood firm, angry and upset at how he was speaking to her and how he had threatened her, she told him she just knew. She knew it was fact. *'How the hell did she know about it?'* he'd screamed. She never said. She'd just picked up her bag, told him that was it, and walked out, catching a taxi to a bar where she'd sat and had a few drinks before heading to BBT's – and Jack.

'Dani, come up, come up.' Jack was waving from high in the gantry to her down below as she chatted to a couple of security guards at the base of the stairs. 'She can come up,' he shouted down to security.

She smiled up to him as the security guards made way for her. But her stomach was full of butterflies. She had to tell him, and he wasn't going to be happy. He gave her a peck on the cheek as she got to the top of the stairs.

'Alright, Dani,' said Tony, who had already pulled for the night and was off home early, the pretty brunette on his arm worse the wear for drink, not that Tony cared, clearly nor the brunette. 'I'm okay, Tony.' She half-smiled. Jack took her hand, and they went to sit down.

Jack loved the VIP area, always had done. It cost, but money was no object, he was happy to pay. And he knew people, plenty of people. It was a great place to entertain, show off the spoils of his work. 'Didn't expect you here,' Jack said. 'This is a bonus. When's the last time you came here? You should have called. We could have met up earlier. Are we on for a night out then?'

He smiled at her. He'd had a bit to drink, but not enough to sense something was wrong. Dani wasn't her usual gregarious self. 'What's the matter?'

She breathed out and stared at him. 'I've left him. Left Angelo. Tonight.'

'Left him? What for? What's happened?'

Dani lent over and picked up a bottle of champagne that was sitting on one of the plush tables. 'Can I have a swig of this?' Jack nodded.

She took a swig and sat back in her chair. 'We had a row, a bloody big row. We've had rows before, but this was different. I thought he was going to hit me. Things haven't been right for a while, and he came on to me in bed this morning and I pushed him away. He took it, but tonight he brought it up and then something about going out with his friends, which I couldn't be bothered with. I said I wasn't going to go. He wasn't happy, wanted to know what's going on. Do I love him and all that? He started shouting, I started shouting and it all kicked off. It's been bubbling, Jack. It was going to happen. And then I said it.' She looked at him. Jack shook his head and shrugged his shoulders. 'Said it, said what?' Dani took another deep breath. 'I told him our marriage had been shit from day one, so what was the point pretending? We weren't going to last.' There was a pause as she looked Jack in the eyes. 'And then I told him I knew about the phone footage. The footage with him and the prostitutes, the drugs.'

Jack took a few seconds to take the sentence in. He shook his head. 'You did what? What did you say that for? Hell, Dani, what have you gone and done? What did he say? Fuck, don't say you mentioned me.'

She shook her head. 'No, he asked me how I knew. I told him I just did. I said he didn't need to know how I found out. As you can imagine he went mad again. He smashed plates in the kitchen, put his fist through a door and told me to 'fuck off'. So, I did. And I'm not going back Jack. No way. Never.'

The music was louder now and some of the group in Jack's party came over to where he and Dani were seated to ask if they were going to dance. Jack shook his head and told them to leave them alone. 'You definitely didn't mention me?' Dani shrugged her shoulders. 'No. I didn't.'

'You better not have done. I told you never to repeat it. He must know it was me who told you. It can only be me. He probably thinks I'm the only one who knows about that video. Shit, what have you done, Dani?'

She took another swig of the champagne and took hold of Jack's hand. 'I'm sorry. I don't know what to say. That's why I came here, to find you. I knew you would want to know. I just want to be with you. Please.'

Jack leaned back, shrugged her hand off, and looked at her. 'Do you know what Dani? I've really enjoyed you. I've really enjoyed the fun we've had. But you have gone and fucked everything right up. The one thing I had on Angelo, and you've gone and shot your mouth off. I thought you liked what we had. What the hell do you think he is going to say to me when he sees me again? I'm shit on, Dani. I should have never trusted you.'

Dani stood up and flew at him. 'Fuck off, Jack. What do you mean, you should never have trusted me? You were happy to tell me about the prostitutes to piss me off and then sleep with me. And now you are saying you shouldn't have trusted me. You're the selfish one. It's not all about you. What about me?

You can piss off, Jack. You knew exactly what you were doing. Told me my husband was a cheat and then bed me. Did you really think Angelo thought no-one, only you, knew about that footage? You're not as bright as I thought you were. You're just an arsehole, like most men I seem to know.' She began to cry.

A waiter came over to see if they wanted more drinks. 'Leave us,' Jack said, waving him away.

Dani sat back down and tried to take hold of his hand again, wiping away the tears. 'Jack. I'm sorry. You know how much I love you. I'll leave Angelo and I'll get a shedload of money. He's worth a fortune. Then you and I could make a go of it. I really think we could. We're good together, Jack.' She sniffed gently and looked into his eyes.

He shook his head. 'Are you serious? Yes, I like you but who said I want to settle down, with anyone? Christ, Dani, you're crazier than I thought. I don't love you. What on earth has ever given you that impression? It's been fun. That's all. And now, that's it. We're over. Your husband finds out it was me, which he will, and I'll be out of London in a heartbeat. He'll make sure of that. He'll make sure every financial firm in the City knows about me, the liar and blackmailer who bedded his wife. I've got no chance. Your big mouth has done me right over.'

She sat back in one of the bright red sofas that adorned the VIP area. It was just her and Jack. She put her hands through her hair. 'You don't mean all that. We're both upset.'

'I do, Dani. Don't call me again. What we had is over.' He stood up, brushed past her, and headed down the steps to the dance floor. She picked up her bag and followed him, but turned left at the bottom of the stairs, and headed for the exit. As she got closer to the doors, she started to run, and cry, at the same time.

Dani felt her life was in tatters.

Angelo began picking up the pieces of the shattered plates that were scattered on his kitchen floor.

Dani had stormed out as soon as he threw the third one against the fridge which she was only standing a few feet from. She must have been petrified. He didn't want her to leave. He loved her. Then again, now she knew about the video, what the hell next? She'd said she'd always known. So, why had she put up with him for so long? Why hadn't she said anything sooner?

He had so many questions going through his mind. The only thing he knew for sure is that the only person who had access to that phone footage, as far as he was aware, was Jack Bianchi. He didn't want to believe Jack would tell her. What would he gain from doing that? He had Angelo by the balls, he had a good job, good money, why would he tell Dani? Angelo continued to clean up as he looked at the hole in door he had punched. He looked down at his fist, his knuckles were bleeding. He sat down and poured another glass of red. It was 1am and Dani had been gone a couple of hours. He'd wait up, but what was the point? His only hope was that she would forgive him. Who knows? She deserved better than him, anyhow. Then again, what if Bianchi had told her? If he had, then at least the prick had no more on him. And with that he could make his life a hell and get him out of the firm. He had to be careful. Jack would deny everything. He took another sip of his drink.

But if it was Jack who had told her, he would throw the bloody works at him.

TWENTY SIX

IT had been a week since Judy and Jenny had left her house.

Would she ever see them again? Peggy cared not. She had contacted John, a friend in the village, to help her sort out a new television. When he asked how she had managed to break the screen, Peggy lied that she had tripped while hoovering and the hoover had banged into the set. John wasn't convinced, but he hadn't asked questions. The new television, a nice one at that, had arrived yesterday. Katie would be over to see her in a few days. She would tell her what had happened. Or should she phone her now? No, she would leave it. Katie had her own life to live. The weather had turned grey and was a tad on the sultry side. It meant although sitting in the garden was nice, it wasn't as appealing as it had been in the warm summer months. Autumn wouldn't be far away. Peggy was making herself a spot of lunch and listening to Radio Two, her favourite station. It had been Cecil's favourite as well. She smiled as she remembered how Cecil used to come home from a game of golf and sit in the kitchen listening to Radio Two's lunchtime programme which was invariably an opportunity for the public to phone in and discuss various topics. He used to get so annoyed with some of the callers. *'Some of these people are so ignorant,'* he used to tell Peggy. *'Why don't they do their homework before they call in?'*

She smiled as she thought of him chortling away. She placed the small slices of cheese on the bread and went over to the cupboard to get some pickle. A Buddy Holly song playing made her smile. Oh, how Cecil loved Buddy Holly. *'Rave On'* was his favourite. She smiled to herself again as she remembered how he would take her by the arm and swing her about on the dance floor, sometimes holding a pretend microphone to his mouth. He was a good dancer. But it hadn't all been perfect. Cecil had baggage from his previous life. There had been many complications. It had been a long time since she had looked at the letter. But after Jenny and Judy's visit, she decided it was time she looked at it again. Why not? She almost knew it word for word. But after what had happened, another read wouldn't hurt. She went upstairs and into her bedroom, opening the wardrobe doors. The safe was tucked away, back left, one of the smallest safes you could imagine. Peggy and Cecil had often laughed at the absurdity of its size. Peggy found the key, well hidden under the carpet, and opened the door of the safe, she put her hand in. It just about fitted! The letter was at the back. She pulled it out and sat on the edge of the bed slowly unfolding it. It wasn't long, a single page, three paragraphs in total. It began, *'My Dearest Peggy, and whoever my dear Peggy feels needs to know this.'*

She remembered the day Cecil had given it to her, two weeks before they were set to marry. After reading it to her, he'd told her he was going to put it in the safe, to remain there, unread by others, until the day he died. Then it was up to Peggy who knew. And when they had both passed… well it was there for all to know. That day, the day Cecil had read it to her before he placed it safely away, will remain with her forever. The look on his face as she digested the contents. The look on Cecil's face when he'd finished. She'd been surprised, but no more. *'You can call the wedding off if you want,'* he had said. *'But I hope not.'* Cecil's happy-go-lucky demeanour replaced with a sadder, more sombre look. He had shrugged his shoulders as he looked at her. But she'd just smiled back. *'I don't care Cecil. I love you and always will. I want to marry you and I will love you forever. Knowing this changes nothing.'*

She remembered saying those words.

Little did she know then, Cecil had even more to tell.

TWENTY SEVEN

JACK wasn't looking forward to work.

Fraser was back from holiday, and it was going to be the first time he had seen Angelo since Dani had left him having told him she knew of the video. Jack's office was always neat and tidy. For someone who lived it up, he was meticulous in the way he not only dressed, but how others perceived him, a tidy office was important. He liked statements. Carol had been his new PA for six months now. Married with three children, she was smart and didn't suffer fools gladly, just what Jack needed. His last PA had been with him a year. Jack had slept with her on numerous occasions. It was a ridiculous working relationship. No-one was more relieved than he was, when she said she was leaving to go work on a cruise ship.

'Morning, Jack.' Carol walked in looking her usual smart self, blue skirt and while blouse. She put down a cup of coffee. 'Angelo wants to see you at 9.15 if that's okay. I said it was. You didn't have anything in the diary.'

Jack smiled. 'Thanks. Yep, I'll pop across.'

'You, okay? You look, well, sort of tired and crappy if you don't mind me saying.'

'I'm okay.'

'Enjoy your coffee.' And with that she walked out.

He leaned back in his chair and looked up at the ceiling. He didn't need this first thing on a Monday morning. This meeting was surely not going to be about work. Angelo wouldn't want a meeting this early on a Monday for work matters. He would have scheduled it last week. There was a knock on his door. Fraser was standing there, looking serious. Jack sighed but waved him in.

'You got that invoice from Mr Chalmers?' Fraser had walked straight up to Jack's desk talking as he did so.

'I think Carol has got it. I signed it late Friday. She will have it. You okay mate?'

Fraser had begun to turn round to head off to Carol's office. 'I'm okay… MATE,' he said with sarcasm. And walked out.

Jack turned his computer on. He looked at the clock on the wall, it was 8.44am. He got his e-mails up and began to read through some of them, deleting most as he went along. He then headed to Angelo's office. His heart was beating fast. He'd never felt like this when speaking to Angelo before. He'd always had his boss on a string. He wasn't so sure he had now. Jack was resigned for a confrontation.

'Come in. Sit down.' Angelo was sitting at his desk, the enormous landscape photograph of the City of London, as pictured from the top of the Shard, adorned the large wall behind him. Angelo appeared mellow, so Jack thought. Bearing in mind what had happened at his house that weekend. In fact, he lit up a smile as Jack sat down. 'How are you then? Everything okay?' If Angelo was trying to make Jack feel uncomfortable, he was doing a good job. Jack had a horrible thought this polite conversation wasn't going to last.

'I'm alright. I didn't know we had a meeting arranged. What's it about? I haven't got any files or prepped anything.'

'No, this is an off-the-cuff chat, Jack. Just wanted to catch up with you on something. Not trying to catch you out, you're right this wasn't planned. Well, not until I got a call yesterday morning.'

The sun was starting to peep through the blinds that weren't pulled far enough across the large window at the side of Angelo's office. The brightness caught Jack in the face, and he adjusted his chair. 'So, what is this all about?' Jack said, as he shrugged his shoulders. Angelo leaned forward on his desk. 'I've got some news.'

Jack shook his head. 'Angelo, I don't like games. I have a busy day, so please let's cut to the chase.'

'I don't like games either,' said Angelo as he looked up as the door opened. Toby Ruskin walked into the office, Angelo's PA guiding him to a seat next to Jack, holding out his hand to shake. 'How are you, Jack? Don't look so surprised.' Jack turned to look at Toby Ruskin, then turned to look at Angelo.

'Hello Toby. What's going on?' Jack said.

Toby Ruskin smiled. 'I'll let Angelo explain, shall I?' Angelo got out a file and put it on his desk. He opened it up. 'Well, Jack. As you know, as we both know, Mr Ruskin is a valued client at the firm and has been for many years.'

'Decades, my dear man,' Toby Ruskin interrupted. 'Decades.'

'Absolutely, decades. Apologies,' Angelo said as he smiled at them both. 'Anyhow, as I was saying, Mr Ruskin is a valued client and has asked the firm for a favour of which I said would be no problem.'

Jack looked at Angelo and back at Toby Ruskin. He said nothing but couldn't help wondering what this had to do with him, as Angelo continued. 'You see, Mr Ruskin's granddaughter, Olivia, is coming to the end of her studies here in London and she wants to make her way in the world of finance. Mr Ruskin has asked me if the business could help her out with a bit of work placement here with us. I've said, most certainly.' Toby Ruskin looked at Jack nodding as Angelo spoke. Clearly the pair had already had a conversation about this.

'So, good news for you Jack is that I'm going to assign Olivia with you for an initial period of a month, but likely it will be longer. I need you to take her under your wing, it's something Mr Ruskin here has also requested. For some reason he's impressed with you. God knows why,' Angelo laughed. Toby Ruskin nudged Jack, who sort of smiled.

'A little more meat on the bone please,' said Jack. 'Does that mean Olivia is working with me all the time? And here in the office? With me. In my office, or will she have her own office?'

'Your office, four days a week, although not Monday afternoons or Wednesdays as she still has studies,' said Angelo. 'There may even be a bit more flexibility than that. And of course, she will be working with others here in the business and other departments.'

Toby Ruskin turned to look at Jack. 'I've been very impressed with you, young man, and I was telling Angelo so. Olivia has been desperate to get into finance. She will learn much off you, I'm sure.' Toby Ruskin looked at Angelo, who was smiling broadly. Clearly, he was delighted one of the firm's best clients thought so highly of one of his team.

'She'll be starting next Monday,' Angelo announced.

'Okay, well, that's fine,' said Jack. 'Um, thank you for trusting me with her. I'm sure she'll learn a great deal.'

Toby Ruskin smiled. 'I think she will. Look after her. Apple of my eye, Jack. And see if you can sprinkle some of that financial magic dust on her.'

Jack smiled and went to get up. 'Oh, one more thing Jack,' said Angelo. Jack went to sit back down.

'No, don't sit down. It's just that Mr Ruskin did have one other thing to say, didn't you Toby?'

'I certainly have,' he said smiling more broadly than Angelo had throughout the meeting. 'The car.' It was Jack's turn to look confused. 'What car?'

'Well,' said Toby Ruskin. 'I've told Angelo here I'm enormously grateful for what you will be doing for Olivia. So, I've given the firm £20K to put towards upgrading your car. Your new Tesla should be waiting in the parking lot below, I believe.' He looked at Angelo. This was becoming a real old pals-fest, as Angelo smiled back at Toby Ruskin. 'Yes, it will be with you this afternoon Jack,' said Angelo. 'Swap the keys over of your current car with the guys who bring the Tesla. That's all.'

Jack turned to Toby Ruskin, shook his hand, and smiled. 'Thank you. You didn't have to do that.'

'I know I didn't. Just look after her.' Jack got up and closed the door as he went out, leaving the two men striking up a conservation about golf. He waited outside and looked back at what had been a bizarre meeting.

The two were laughing aloud.

TWENTY EIGHT

THE event in Oxford had gone well.

Mark had allowed a group of 20 from a company he had worked with previously to turn up on the night and pay, contrary to his 'on-line only' policy. It was all extra income. He had picked Katie up earlier that evening. There had been a little bit of tension in the air between the pair during the journey to Oxford, but Mark had broken the ice. 'Look, if we are going to work together, we must both forget about what happened, Katie.'

Katie hadn't replied before Mark spoke again. 'So, can we forget it? Please. Can we just be little Haribo sweet friends forever,' he mimicked in a high-pitched voice.

It made Katie smile. Mark could be so charming and funny. As much as she was still annoyed about that kiss, she knew she was as much to blame as he was. 'Yes, Haribo sweet friends forever,' she replied. 'Now let's talk about something else.'

The rest of the night went well, with Katie soon back into her stride of helping Mark with the event. They had good chemistry. 'So, what's Shaun up to these days? Shop going well?' Mark was sipping a glass of orange juice, he and Katie sitting in the empty event room after the final delegates had left.

'Yep, he's doing okay. Obviously would like it to be doing better. But it's a funny business, selling books. It's very up and down. I don't know, sometimes I wish he would pack it in and get a steady job, regular income, other days when it does well and he comes home happy, it all seems worth it.'

'Are you happy?' Mark said, catching her by surprise. Katie frowned at him. 'What do you mean, am I happy? With what? The shop? Shaun? Don't say things like that, Mark.'

'No, sorry, I didn't mean anything by that.' He stretched out his hand and touched her arm. 'What I meant was, are you happy here with me, here, doing this?' Katie felt a bit foolish. 'I'm sorry. I didn't mean to snap at you.'

'That's okay. I understand. I've rather messed it up a bit, haven't I? Or haven't we? But we said we aren't going to talk about it.'

Katie sighed, then smiled. 'Yes, we did.' They both took sips of their drinks.

'So, Katie Walters, first things first. Here's your well-earned £200.' Mark passed her an envelope with the cash in. 'Let's drink up and get out of here and, to show what a great bloke I am, you can choose the music in the car on the way home.'

He got up and pulled back her chair as she stood up. They looked at each other for a second, before Katie smiled, brushed past him and the pair headed to the exit.

He was trying hard not to be, but Mark was so taken by her.

It was gone midnight when the buzzer in Jack's flat went off. He had only just gone to bed a short while and wasn't in a deep sleep. It rang twice, and both times for what seemed like ages, as he gathered his Jack Wills dressing gown and headed towards the front door. 'Who's that?' he said as he pressed the intercom.

'It's me, Dani.'

'Dani. Do you know what time it is?'

'Jack, I have no-where to go. I can't keep staying with friends. I need to talk.'

Jack pressed the button to allow her in. She walked up the stairs and Jack opened the door as he saw her approaching. She looked awful, not the Dani he knew. 'Get in here,' he said as he closed the door behind her. 'Where have you been? You look terrible.'

Dani's usual glamorous appearance had been replaced by a face stricken with sadness. Her hair, always so immaculate was a mess. She was wet from the rain that had set in that night. She'd being staying with friends in recent weeks, wandering from one house to another until she could find a permanent place near Clapham. All this in total contrast to the way Angelo had looked and behaved that day with Jack. She went to say something, but the words didn't come out. She just fell towards him and into his arms. The last time they had spoken, Jack had told her he wanted nothing to do with her. But looking at her now, so pitiful, so sad, he felt a huge pang of guilt. Dani had been so loyal to him. Done things with him, and for him other women would not have. He hugged her tight, putting his hands through her hair as she cried on his shoulder.

'Dani. Look. You stay here for the night,' he said. 'You stay here as long as you want. But Angelo will kill me if he ever finds out about us. He knows too much already. Come and go as you please, but you mustn't tell anyone you're here.'

'He won't hurt you, Jack.'

'You think not?' Jack pulled back from her. 'That bloody video was the one thing I had on him. He thinks I'm the only one who knows about it. And now look what you've gone and told him.'

She looked up at him. 'I know, I'm sorry.'

'Who else could have told you? Think about it, Dani? Angelo knows I wouldn't go round telling hundreds of people, does he? That was my hold on him. That was how I had him. Shooting my gob off doesn't make sense.'

Dani took her coat off and threw it over the sofa. 'No, it doesn't make sense. But shooting your gob off is what you sometimes do, Jack. And Angelo knows that. Your best bet is that he will think you couldn't keep it a secret because you're Jack Bianchi. So, you told others, who have then told me.'

Jack stood back and looked at her. 'Maybe, but it's not likely. I'll just have to hope that is his thought process. So long as you never tell him, of course.'

Dani put her hands up to his face and cradled his jaw. 'I will never tell him, don't worry about that. You know what I think of you,' she said staring into his eyes. She kissed him gently on the lips. 'Can I have a drink, then?'

'Help yourself. You know where the drinks are kept.'

Dani walked over to the cabinet and pulled out a bottle of Jack Daniels. 'Coke in the fridge?'

Jack nodded. 'Want one?' He nodded again.

They sat down on the larger of Jack's two light blue sofas, Dani putting her feet up on it and sliding close to him. 'I'm sorry,' she said. 'I know, I've said it ten times.' She waved her hand in the air. 'I would hate us never to have anything to do with each other again. You said you wanted me totally out of your life... do you?'

Jack shook his head gently and put his fingers through her hair. He'd been unfair to her at the nightclub with his angry words, yet now here he was cuddling up to her again. What was it with Dani Heeson? If he believed in true love, he'd think this was it. 'I don't want you totally out of my life, but we can't continue like this,' Jack took a sip of his drink. 'We are going to have to call it a day at some stage. Stay here for a while, but then you need to move on with your life. We both need to move on. It's been fun.'

Dani pulled back. 'I've been thinking to. All that shit about I love you and want to stay with you forever and whatever other crap I came out with the other night, you're right, forget it.'

Jack frowned. 'Oh, okay, if you're sure, Dani? That's cool.' She looked at him. 'Just please tell me, for my own interest. Have you honestly told anyone else about the video?'

'No, I haven't.' She smiled at him and put both hands through her hair raising it in a bun at the top. The drink was relaxing her. She leaned forward and kissed him, moving her hand up his thigh. 'Well, Mr Jack Wills dressing gown man. If I'm moving in for a short while, I really ought to pay some form of keep.' Jack smiled and leaned back. With that Dani moved forward and pulled at the knotted tie of his dressing gown and opened it up. 'Oh, I forgot, you always sleep naked.'

She pushed his chest as he fell gently backwards onto the sofa, drink still in hand.

TWENTY NINE

THE call came at 11.30 that morning.

Katie had been shopping. It was one week before she was set to start her new teaching assistant job. It was unusual for a call to come through on their home phone. The number said 'withheld' but Katie picked it up anyhow. 'Hello,' said Katie.

'Hello, is that Katie Walters?' the voice on the other end said.

'Yes, it is.' Katie didn't recognise who was speaking.

'Hello, Mrs Walters, it's PC Trish Keegan at Thames Valley Police, I wonder if I could speak to you, please.' Katie's heart skipped a beat. 'I'm sorry to disturb, but I need to ask you about Mrs Peggy Honeyman. I believe you know her?' Katie's heart was now beating fast. 'Yes, I do, what about her?' Katie said.

'Well, Mrs Walters, I'm sorry to say there appears to have been an accident, at Mrs Honeyman's home. She's had a fall. A fatal fall, I'm afraid.'

Katie froze. Had she heard right? A fatal fall. No, it couldn't be. Peggy had been fine only a few days ago. 'I've been told by a Mrs Thompson who is a neighbour of Peggy's that you live in the village, know Peggy well, and I was wondering if you could come down to Peggy's house for a chat,' the policewoman continued. 'We are there now. Or I can come and see you.'

'No, I can come down now,' Katie said. 'When you say fatal, are you telling me she's dead? I can't believe this. What's happened?' Katie felt herself beginning to well up.

'I'm afraid so. I'm sorry to break the news like this. Mrs

Thompson has given us your name and number because she said you were close with Mrs Honeyman and, from what we can gather, her stepdaughters live away and Mrs Thompson doesn't know their details. We could do with some help please finding next of kin, Mrs Walters.'

'Okay, I'm coming now. I'll be there as soon as I can.' Katie put the phone down.

She grabbed a coat; the weather was cool, and the sky was grey. There was a cold wind. It was now so different to the long, hot summer they had been enjoying. She thought about phoning Shaun, but she needed to go now. Peggy's house was a 15-minute walk and Katie strode briskly. She was trying to contain herself and her emotions. She started to cry as she walked faster. As she turned the corner, she saw two police cars outside Peggy's house. The tears began to fall again. A nightmare unfolding in front of her. A police officer was standing guard at Peggy's front gate. Katie told him who she was, and she turned to go back towards the house, calling out to another officer inside. A policewoman walked down the garden path to meet Katie. 'Hello Mrs Walters, thanks for coming. I'm PC Keegan, who spoke to you on the phone. Thanks for getting here so quickly. Are you sure you are happy to speak here?' Katie nodded. 'Well, can we just speak outside for a few minutes as we don't want people in the house, as we are still investigating.'

PC Keegan was a small lady with bright blond hair in a bob. She could have been no more than mid to late 20s. She had a nice smile and took hold of Katie's arm as they walked away from the front door. 'I'm sorry to get you here and bring you such awful news,' she said. 'Mrs Honeyman has been taken away by ambulance. Mrs Thompson found her. The two shared keys. Mrs Thompson had let herself in because she was supposed to come round for a coffee at about nine this morning but because there had been no response from her knocking, she had let herself in as the dog was barking which apparently was unusual. Mrs Honeyman was lying at the bottom of the stairs.'

Katie let the words sink in, as she took a deep breath. 'I've told Mrs Thompson to go home. She was shaken up. She said you and Mrs Honeyman were close.' Keegan raised a slight smile, but

Katie didn't notice. 'We need some help on who else to inform. Does she have any children, or brothers, sisters? I assume Mrs Honeyman's parents aren't alive, and we know her husband Cecil has passed because Mrs Thompson told us. She has stepdaughters, I believe.' PC Keegan was firing questions apace, but Katie wasn't taking it in.

'When did this happen?' Katie said. 'How did it happen? Are you sure she fell down the stairs?' It doesn't seem believable.'

'I'm sorry, Mrs Walters, but I do need your help because we do need to speak to family members if Mrs Honeyman had any. We will know more as the day goes on. We have some more specialists coming to the house this afternoon. But from what we saw when we got here it looks as though, yes, she fell down the stairs. There was no sign of forced entry. Mrs Thompson called the ambulance. Mrs Honeyman was not breathing when she found her. They called us just to make sure there was seemingly no foul play. We can't see there has been and her injuries were consistent with a fall from a height. There may be an autopsy. Until then, we must keep a bit of an open mind as well.'

Katie closed her eyes and felt herself welling up again. She looked at the house, looked at Peggy's tidy front garden, she was fastidious with keeping everything neat and tidy. 'She has a couple of stepdaughters, Jenny and Judy,' Katie said, regaining her composure, as PC Keegan got out her notebook. 'They were here recently. Judy lives in Scotland; Jenny lives in Australia. I don't know if she has gone back to Australia. And I don't really care to be honest.'

The policewoman looked quizzical. 'And why is that?'

'Oh, nothing,' Katie said. 'Ignore me. The three of them didn't see eye to eye, that's all. Peggy's only sister died when they were both children and she and Cecil didn't have any children of their own. Jenny and Judy were Cecil's daughters. I can't believe I'm saying all this. She was such a lovely lady. I loved her so much; she was someone I could talk to about anything. Oh, sorry....' Katie bent down and began to cry.

PC Keegan knelt beside her. 'I fully understand,' she said. 'Here, take this.' She passed her a tissue.

Katie wiped her eyes. 'Oh, sorry, yes, I forgot to say,' Katie looked across at PC Keegan.

'Apart from the stepdaughters, Peggy also has a stepson.'

THIRTY

KATIE didn't call Shaun at the bookshop. What difference would it make? He'd only close and come home. And the pair needed the shop's income.

So, it was a surprised Shaun who walked into his house that evening, finding his wife holding back the tears and running to hug him as he walked through the door. 'Hey, hey. What the hell has happened?' It was all he could say as Katie threw her arms around him, crying on his shoulder, the tears falling fast. She had been waiting for this moment to be with her husband for hours. Her pent-up sorrow released.

'Katie, what's wrong? What's happened?' He moved her away from him so he could see her face.

Katie tried to regain her composure. 'It's Peggy. She's dead. She had a fall at home. Fell down the stairs. She's dead, Shaun.'

He just looked at her blankly. 'What? But how? When?' He had questions, but Katie had hugged him again, saying nothing, just tears. Eventually she pulled back and began to tell him what happened. After listening as Katie regained her composure and spoke, Shaun made them both a cup of tea, neither felt hungry, and they sat in the living room talking it through.

'She said to me a few months ago she had felt unsteady on her feet, but you know what Peggy was like, she just batted it away as nothing.' Katie was sitting holding her tea. 'Perhaps she just felt dizzy again and this time she was at the top of the stairs. It's just so tragic. I'll miss her so much. I can't believe it.'

Shaun put his arm around her again and kissed the side of her head. 'Look, you were a wonderful friend. She loved you a great deal and you loved her. It's not as if she hadn't led a life, Katie. I know you don't want to hear that, but she enjoyed her life, she enjoyed Cecil, she enjoyed you, her garden and all the things she did, and that little dog of hers. Oh, what's happened to him, or her?'

Katie stood back and looked at him. 'I don't know. Hardly the first question I thought to ask.' Shaun took his arm away from her and stood up. 'Okay, shall I get some dinner on? We must eat.' He kissed her head again as he stood up. 'I'm not hungry, but there's a lasagne in the fridge,' Katie replied. 'Have you had a good day at the shop?'

Shaun was already in the kitchen and pretended he hadn't heard the question. Hopefully Katie wouldn't repeat it. He hadn't taken a penny.

His mind was whirling.

It wasn't often Claire and Fraser went to the cinema. According to Claire, who has a good memory, it had been 18 months.

Fraser had made good bonus at the firm. It was three weeks since their row over the photographs and things had begun to get back to normal, Fraser was doing his best to forget it all.

'Yes, we are having the large one,' Claire said as she pointed to the giant-sized box that the man behind the counter was about to fill with popcorn.

'Well, you better eat it all then,' Fraser smiled. 'I don't really like the stuff.'

'Yes, you bloody do,' Claire nudged him. 'We had some at Patty's party a few months ago. She had loads of it scattered round the house in bowls and you were stuffing it down. I saw you. Don't give me that you don't like it.'

Fraser laughed. 'I was only being polite then. And I thought it would soak up some of the beer.'

'Rubbish, popcorn doesn't soak up beer. You must think I was born yesterday.'

'Well, if you were, I'd still want to be the one to marry you, my darling. And you have our babies!'

Claire looked at him. 'You had a drink before we left? Is that what's got into you? Babies? Since when?'

'I don't know, perhaps it's thinking of the back row of the cinema, me and you, all romantic. Could be fun.'

'Could be darling. But we're sitting third row back in the middle. So, you keep your hands to yourself, unless you want the whole cinema to see us.'

Fraser followed his wife into the cinema. The adverts were already underway, and it was dark. He'd had some dark moments himself in the past few weeks, but he was feeling better about things now. Claire was his and she was a special girl. He had always been determined, even more so in recent times, that they were going to be together forever, and nothing was going to stop it, stop them.

It was gone 10pm when they left. The film, a thriller based on Victorian London gangsters, had been a bit violent, but Claire had enjoyed it. 'It was good. Did you like it?' Claire had linked her arm in Fraser's, as they made their way to the car, which they had parked in the firm's car park.

'It was okay.' Fraser didn't want to appear to have enjoyed it too much, the cinema would become a regular occurrence had he done so. But inwardly he had. 'Yes, I'll admit. It was better than okay. It was good and you know it.'

'Yes, it was good.' Claire smiled. 'Come on let's go for a drink, make a night of it. There are two pubs over there,' she said pointing. 'Leave the car in the car park and get a cab. We can pick the car up tomorrow.'

'Are you sure? I don't mind driving.'

'No, you're going to have a couple of drinks. I'm going to have a few, get home and who knows?' She winked at him as they walked arm in arm.

The pub was packed. It was a Friday night. Fraser and Claire were on their second drink and had found a table in the corner. They'd ordered some chips and sausage sandwiches, the pub served food until midnight, and it had gone down a treat. Fraser was about to get up to get another drink as he supped up his pint when he noticed someone walk in. Someone he hoped wouldn't clock him and Claire.

Jack Bianchi and two pals were already pretty drunk by the time they arrived at the 'The Brigadier' for a couple more drinks before heading off to the West End clubs. Jack spotted Fraser immediately, as he glanced around the pub. Fraser was getting up to go to the bar. 'Hello, Fraser,' Jack said as he made a beeline for him, slurring a bit. 'What are you doing here? Don't usually see you out in the West End. On your own? Fancy coming to a club with me and the boys? Never know what we might find!'

Jack put his arm on Fraser's shoulder, Jack's two friends smiling at the big man. 'I'm alright Jack, just getting another beer, so if you don't mind.'

Jack smiled and moved aside, but as he did so, he noticed Claire sitting in the corner, Fraser had been blocking the view. She hadn't seen him. 'Oh, you're with Claire.' He smiled at Fraser. 'Brilliant. Having a good night?'

Fraser's mood darkened, but he knew he had to keep it together. His and Jack's paths crossed much at work, but that was work and he dealt with it. This was social and he knew it was a different situation, and both had been drinking. 'Yeah, been to the pictures,' Fraser said, starting to walk to the bar.

'What did you watch?' Jack pulled his arm. Fraser glared. 'Get off Bianchi. And none of your business what we watched.' Fraser shrugged away from him and carried on to the bar.

Jack smiled as Fraser moved on. The sort of *'I'm half-pissed'* smile that meant he heard the answer but couldn't care less. He looked across at Claire. She still hadn't noticed him. 'Hi, Claire,' Jack shouted above the noise of the pub, as he began to walk across to where she was sitting. Wow, she looked good. A short little skirt on, legs crossed, but the skirt was riding well about her knees. She was such a pretty girl, such tanned legs.

Claire looked up, hearing her name. *'Fuck no, not him.'* She adjusted her skirt as Jack approached. 'Alright, then?' He smiled. 'Don't have to fiddle with your skirt, Claire. I've seen it all before.'

'Piss off, Jack.' She said it quietly. 'Fraser is over there.'

'That's not very lady like. And yes, I know he is. I've just spoken to him. He's getting more beers in. Didn't ask me if I wanted one mind you. Bit rude, seeing as I'm a workmate of his.' Claire continued to stare at him. 'What do you want?'

'Nothing. Just being sociable.'

'Well, why don't you be unsociable and piss off?'

Jack laughed. 'I do like you. You're so feisty. Can see what I saw in you all those years ago.'

'Jack, go away, will you? I don't want you anywhere near me.' He smiled at her and went to touch her knee as he sat down next to her, but she recoiled. 'I'm warning you, Jack.'

'What? What have I done?' His silly grin grated on her, before he held his hands up. 'Just trying to be nice. Okay, okay, I'm going. I don't think your husband has seen us chatting, which is good for you. Well, perhaps good for me. Oh, no, I tell a lie, here he comes.'

'Okay, Jack, get lost,' Fraser was at the table putting the drinks down. Claire was steely-eyed. She hoped this situation wasn't going to develop into anything nasty. They'd enjoyed a fun night.

'Bloody hell, Fraser, that's no way to talk to a colleague. Your wife told me to get lost as well. Actually, she said, piss off to be fair.' Jack smiled as he stood up to go.

'Well, you got the message then,' Fraser added.

'Yes, I got the message. I'll go, seeing as I'm not being made to feel that welcome, which is odd seeing as I know you both so well.' Fraser just stared at him. 'Fuck off.'

Jack put his pathetic smile on again and held up his hands. 'Okay, okay. I get it. See you then people. Have a good night the two of you and don't get up to anything I wouldn't get up to. Far too many people running round the world naked, taking pictures. Never know who ends up seeing them.' Jack walked away as Fraser grabbed him and spun him round.

Jack's mood changed quickly. 'Fuck off, Fraser you dippy bastard. Don't make a scene here. I've got two mates over there and your pretty wife won't like how hard they hit. And they will pile in. So, yes, you might get one punch in, but they'll get half-a-dozen on you. Want your wife to see that? I mean it pal. I might have had a few, but nowhere near enough to be worried about you.' Fraser stood still for a moment, looking across at Jack's mates, who were looking at him. A couple of bouncers from outside had come in to see what was going on, but Fraser had taken his hands off Jack who looked at the bouncers, one of whom he knew well.

'No trouble here, Mikey, I promise,' Jack said to the bigger of the two doormen. They both nodded and turned away. Jack and Fraser stood inches from each other. 'One day, Jack,' Fraser said. 'One day.'

'Yeah, of course,' Jack smiled and turned to join his mates who had clocked the scene was over and were now chatting to the three girls they had arranged to meet.

Fraser went and sat down with Claire. 'Come on, drink up, let's go,' he said. Claire wasn't having it. 'No, we're not drinking up. I'm not letting him spoil our night. And you've only just got the drinks. No, way am I drinking up. We're having a good night, don't let it be spoiled.' Fraser nodded. She was right.

'I could seriously hurt him, Claire. You do know that?' She nodded her head.

THIRTY ONE

OLIVIA Ruskin had settled in well and Jack was enjoying showing her the ropes.

He had worried that she was going to be irritating, would cramp his style. He had plenty of work to do and didn't fancy being a chaperone. He had money to make and deals to cut. But he needed not to have worried. Olivia was proving a clever girl with a great sense of humour. For a 21-year-old she was savvy, sassy and streetwise. Tall and slim, she had a great figure that not just Jack, but most of the guys in the office had already clocked. Shapely legs, long dark hair, she loved the social nights out. She was fitting in a treat. Olivia had joined Jack and several others on a Thursday night out in the West End on what was only her third week with the firm. By 11pm they had all been fairly drunk. She was flirty, especially with Jack, taking his tie off at one stage as she jigged around to the nightclub music. He loved it, she was right up his street, but he knew it was a dangerous situation. Toby Ruskin had entrusted him with the *'light of his life'*. Jack made sure after all the frivolities that night she had got a black cab home after he found her outside the club at 1am on her own waiting for one. He stayed until it arrived.

'You want to come back to mine?' she had said slurring a touch. 'There's only me and one of the other girls in our house tonight'. Jack had smiled. 'Not tonight, Olivia, take care.' He'd closed the cab door and bunged the driver £40.

'Get her home safe,' he'd told the cabbie.

'You don't like Fraser, do you?' Olivia said next morning. She had knocked but walked straight into Jack's office on doing so. It had just gone 8.30am and she looked good bearing in the mind the state she had been in just a few hours earlier.

Jack smiled, looking up from his computer as she strolled in, his eyes immediately attracted to her long legs, rather than the three files in her hand. 'I think you mean, good morning, Jack, do you want a coffee?' he smiled. 'And what makes you talk about Fraser?'

'Oh, nothing. Just wanted you to realise how observant I am.' She put the files on his desk. 'I notice you two don't speak much and when you do, you sort of grunt, bearing in mind his office is just two down. Plus, I studied body language one semester at university, something to keep me amused. Found it fascinating to be honest. And you show all the signs of someone who likes to be in control and when you don't like something, you can't help but show it. Like a child, but not a child, if you know what I mean? And when you don't like people, you can't help but show it. A sort of control freak, but a control freak who likes to be liked. Confused enough, yet?' Jack smiled again. 'Have you got nothing to do?' She grinned.

'Get us a coffee Olivia and save the body language psycho crap for a rainy day down the pub when we've all run out of things to talk about.'

'Yes, sir!' she mimicked. 'But I can tell you don't like him – control freak!'

'It's one sugar, Olivia.'

She turned, flicked her eyebrows at him and walked out.

Katie hadn't felt like working with Mark, but she didn't want to let him down. He had been good to her over Peggy's death.

She was supposed to have helped him with an event in Birmingham three days after Peggy had been found dead. Katie couldn't face it and Mark had understood. But it was a week later now and Mark needed her help. It was in Oxford, so wasn't far to travel.

'So, when's the funeral?' Mark said, in what came over to Katie as a rather matter-of-fact question. She glared at him. 'Sorry,

I didn't mean it to sound that way.' He had clocked her stare.

The silence in the car on the way to Oxford was noticeable. Katie was still coming to terms with so much. Judy had been on the phone. She wanted to come down from Scotland, no doubt to pry through her stepmother's house. But Katie had put her off until they knew a funeral date. Thankfully Jenny was back in Australia. She would have been a nightmare if she was still here.

'I don't know when the funeral is,' Katie said to Mark. She imagined she would have to get involved in help organising it seeing as Peggy had no relatives she knew of. 'Sorry, I'm not being very chatty. I still can't believe she's gone, to be honest.'

Mark had never met Peggy and he'd never got round to asking Katie much about her. Now was perhaps a good time. 'You were obviously very close. Tell me if you don't want to talk about her.' Mark leaned across and put his hand on Katie's arm as they drove.

'I don't mind talking about her. She was a wonderful lady, and we were close. She had a couple of stepdaughters, but no children. I suppose I was the closest thing she had to family after her husband died. We used to spend a lot of time together. Funny really. We got close after I took up a job cleaning her house. In the end she asked me to stop the cleaning, as I was doing more teaching, but would I still come round for a coffee? So, I did, that was about three years ago, and I went round nearly every week.'

Mark smiled to himself as he drove along. Perhaps Katie talking about it was doing her good. He hoped so, he wanted her on good form for the speaking engagement. 'Peggy was no doubt very proud of you.' Katie shook her head slowly as she felt a tear in her eye. She was going to miss Peggy.

The event went well. Katie and Mark were packing up and only a dozen people were left in the hall. The bar was still open, and four or five men were enjoying a beer. In fact, they were enjoying more than just the one beer, they'd been drinking most of the night, getting louder as the evening had worn on. Mark had been aware of it and had kept an eye on them. One of them had called out to Katie something about *'you tell him, darling'*, during one of their final sketches on stage. Mark hadn't liked that. Nor had one or two of the audience.

'Went well, didn't it?' Katie was packing up some leaflets. She had enjoyed the night; it had been nice to get back to doing some of the things she had enjoyed before the shock of Peggy's death. It had given her a chance to forget things for a few hours. 'It went very well.' Mark smiled at her. 'I'm glad you decided to come.'

As the pair continued to pack up, the men at the bar were getting noisier. Mark turned to Katie. 'They're getting well pissed.' Katie nodded back as Mark took two boxes to his car. On his return a few minutes later, he noticed three of the men were talking to Katie. He sped up across the hall. 'Everything okay, lads?', Mark said smiling as he approached.

They all nodded, before one of the men, sharp suit and cropped hair going grey, blurted out. 'You two an item then?' Mark looked straight at him; Katie hesitated for a moment. 'No, we're not an item,' Mark replied. 'We're professionals at this and I hope you enjoyed the night.'

A second man jumped in. 'It was good thanks, yes, we did enjoy it. Some great tips.' But the man with the cropped hair going grey hadn't finished. 'So, do you two get a room for the night? If you know what I mean?' He laughed, as did the third guy.

'No, mate, we don't,' Mark replied. 'And if I were you, I'd drink up and watch your tongue, pal.' With that the man moved forward. 'Oh, would you now?'

'Okay, Terry. That will do.' The third man started to pull Terry away. Katie moved aside; she wasn't enjoying this. It was the first time she'd encountered anything like this at their events.

'Don't pull him away, mate. I'm not worried about him. I'm just asking him politely to basically, 'piss off'.' Mark was a big man, and he wasn't put off by the guy's behaviour.

'What is it mate? She turned you down a few times, has she?' Terry wasn't leaving it alone. 'Bit out of your league to be fair.'

Just as Terry turned to pull a smile at Katie, Mark was on him, diving full-length and pinning him to the floor. Terry's drink flew out of his hand as he crashed to the ground, making a thud on the hardwood. Mark had him pinned down. 'You speak about her like that, and I'll punch your fucking lights out. You understand?'

Mark was inches from the man's face, straddled over him with his fist pulled back ready to thump Terry, who hadn't known what had hit him, such was Mark's speed of movement. Mark could only get those few words out before the other men pulled him off. Terry went to get up but fell over, before one of the men grabbed hold of him and took him away as the rest of them put their drinks on the bar and went to go. 'Sorry, Mark,' one of the other men said. 'We'll get him out of here. And sorry, Katie.' You could see the shock in their faces at what had just happened. Katie was shocked as well.

Mark stood up and watched them go, one of them patting him on the shoulder and thanking him again as they left. Terry never turned round to say a word as the two took him by the arm and escorted him out. He was too busy brushing his suit down. 'You, okay?' Katie took hold of Mark's hand. 'Yeah, I'm fine.' Although Mark wasn't feeling fine. Adrenaline was rushing through his body and he felt a bit light-headed. It was gone 11pm and he hadn't eaten much during the day. He sat on a chair and smiled at Katie. 'Don't know why I act the hard man,' he said. 'Bloke could have been a black belt in karate for all I know.'

Katie looked him up and down. 'You've cut your hand,' she said as she noticed blood coming off his knuckles where he had hit the deck with Terry.

'I'm okay. Feeling better already. Let's go.' He picked up the last box of leaflets, the barman coming over to check everything was alright with them both. Katie re-arranged the chairs, one or two that had scattered after the men hit the floor.

'Dickheads,' the barman said. 'You, okay?'

Mark nodded his head. 'Is everything okay here?'

'Yeah, leave it with me.' The barman began to mop up Terry's spilt drink as Katie and Mark headed towards the car park. It was a quiet drive home, Katie keeping the conversation going as much as she could with the radio on in the background. Mark was still feeling uneasy.

'You should have seen his face when his mates got him up.' She tried to break the ice with a bit of humour. 'He fell back over, made himself look a right idiot.' Mark smiled. 'Yeah, he did look a dick.'

As they pulled up outside Katie's house, she took hold of her handbag from the footwell and opened the door. She looked at him, he'd been quiet on the way home. She leaned across and kissed him on the cheek. 'Thank you.'

He smiled and nodded as he watched her get out of the car and walk towards her front door.

John Ashcroft had done more autopsies in his 30 years' service than he could remember. He'd seen many things, good and bad. He enjoyed his work.

His job wasn't everyone's cup of tea but, as a pathologist, he knew he had, on many occasions, come up with causes of death the coroner, police and emergency services had never thought might be the case. It was satisfying to know he played important parts in the justice system when called upon. And he knew he had found something odd that may prove that while the lady in his morgue, a Mrs Peggy Honeyman, had no doubt fallen down some stairs and cracked her head, the authorities had been right to suggest an autopsy.

Because he was beginning to suspect the fall alone hadn't necessarily been the cause of her death.

THIRTY TWO

'WE need to do a toxicology report on this lady, and we need to do it fast.'

John Ashcroft was standing with a file in his hand and a pen in the other, PC Keegan and detectives Steve Jacobs and Pete Hally listening intently. While it was assumed Peggy Honeyman had died after a fall, it had been decided an autopsy would be in order seeing as she had always seemingly been in good health. Ashcroft had carried it out. 'Yes, there are lots of broken bones, cracked skull and bruises that would suggest the fall killed her,' Ashcroft said. 'Indeed, I imagine she hit her head four or five times on the way down, that alone could have been enough, she's suffered severe head trauma. Four of her buttons on her blouse were ripped as well, her bra was exposed, which seems strange. A fall wouldn't have done that. May have been a sexual motive?' The police officers looked on shocked as Ashcroft continued. 'However, I found something that I'm not happy about and a toxicology report will confirm my thoughts or suggest she likely did just fall.'

Jacobs was the first to speak. 'Okay, John, so you're saying we do a toxicology report because, what? You think there is something in her system?'

Ashcroft looked the officers square in the face. 'I found a hole just under her chin, above her windpipe. A pin prick, nothing more, but a pin prick that was far too deep to just be a spot or mole or something on her skin that had come away. I think it could have been a needle. And I don't know why it's there. Could be a good reason, but I'm not sure enough just to wave this through as an accident.'

'But what would a pin prick prove?' Keegan said.

Ashcroft raised his eyebrows. 'It could prove that something was injected into her. A drug, even a poison, I don't know. And while yes, she fell down the stairs, that's not in doubt. It's a case of did she fall, or was she pushed? Maybe even thrown?' Silence fell in the room as Ashcroft's words sank in.

'So, what you're saying is she could have been drugged or poisoned and then it was all staged to make it look like an accident?' Hally said.

'I'm not saying anything, DC Hally. I'm just saying I want this toxicology report done because I don't often see a hole under a person's chin without a reason. I'm uneasy about it to be honest.' He flicked them all a smile. 'I'll get this toxicology report moving.' Ashcroft left the room, leaving the officers to work out their next move.

'So, you were on the scene first,' Jacobs looked at Keegan. 'What did you find? Did you think anything suspicious?'

'No,' said Keegan. 'I just found her at the bottom of the stairs, lots of blood. Pictures were taken at the scene so you can look at them. But quite honestly, the first thing I thought was that she'd fallen. There was nothing to suggest otherwise. No forced entry, no broken windows, doors, anything. The house hadn't been trashed. You wouldn't know if anything had been taken because everything was immaculate. We were called because a neighbour couldn't rouse her. I didn't notice the buttons on her blouse were open. I'm surprised what he has said, but then again, I suppose we are never surprised by anything in this job.'

'Exactly,' said Hally. 'Has she got family?'

Keegan puffed out her cheeks. 'Not from what I can tell. A couple of stepdaughters, one lives in Australia, one in Scotland, they are both aware what has happened. Her husband is dead. 'Apparently there is a stepson. But I don't know anything about him. Bit of a mystery.'

The two detectives looked at her. 'What do you mean bit of a mystery?' Keegan shrugged her shoulders. 'I haven't got round to chasing him down to be honest, that's all. In fact, I haven't even got a name. Apparently, Peggy told a friend of hers, Katie Walters, who I've spoken to, about her having a stepson. But she never told Katie his name or much about him. I did ask.'

Hally was next to puff out his cheeks. What on the outside had appeared to be an accident of a lady falling down the stairs, was now potentially a murder case. He could do without this, especially four months from retirement. 'Well, let's hope the toxicology report comes back negative and old Ashcroft is satisfied nothing is wrong, then we can put this one to bed,' he said. 'Not sure I fancy trying to track down a murderer who injects their victims. I'd rather just have a punch-up in the street, and everyone knows who threw the punch.'

Jacobs smiled. 'Pete, you're already demob happy, that's your problem. Why don't you go to the Chief Constable and tell him you want to go now? Go tell your doctor you've got flat feet or something. Start retirement early.' Hally and Keegan laughed.

'I'm off,' said Keegan.

'Alright Keegan, see you later,' Hally said. She smiled and left.

'What you reckon Steve?' Hally looked at Jacobs.

'Don't know mate,' Jacobs said. 'Thing is, you know Ashcroft is bloody good at his job. If he suspects something, there is often something in it. I once worked on a case in Sheffield involving the death of a three-year-old girl. Horrible case, horrible circumstances. Everyone was convinced it was the girl's stepdad. The locals were up in arms, he and the family had to move house, rumours flying everywhere. Ashcroft was working in Yorkshire at the time. He was on the case, autopsy, and all that. The girl had some bruises on her arms and legs, I don't think the mum and stepdad, both druggies, were especially gentle with her, and the stepdad was a rough neck. Anyhow, turns out some of the bruising was caused by the stepdad shaking her and trying to bring her round after she collapsed in the garden. She'd had anaphylaxis, an allergic reaction to tree nuts of all things. They had this tree in their garden with these nuts she was allergic to. No-one knew until she ate one. The stepdad was arrested on suspicion of her murder; old Ashcroft proved it was the allergic reaction that caused her death. Nothing to do with the bruising or shaking. Blew the case wide open. If he hadn't done his job properly some poor bloke could have spent years in prison for something he didn't do.'

'Maybe he does know his stuff Steve, but I still retire in four months,' said Hally.

'You retired years ago you old git. Come on, let's get a coffee.'

The club had been hot, the music had been loud, and the drinks had flowed and now he was back in his apartment. Summer was turning into autumn, but the weekends were still lively for Jack Bianchi. And it had been another intense one.

Work was ticking along better than he'd hoped. Angelo appeared more chilled, helped by the fact he and Dani had made up after their recent bust up. She had moved out of Jack's and back in with Angelo, not for the love, but for the convenience of her rich husband. The video hadn't been mentioned again. The elephant in the room it may have been, but neither Angelo nor Dani were loyal partners. And anyhow, they both enjoyed the high life. They needed each other, for all the wrong reasons.

'That's twice now you've mentioned her name.' Dani was fiddling with the hair on Jack's chest. They'd made love twice, the second time Dani scratching so hard into Jack's shoulders, she'd made them bleed.

'You just keep stroking my chest and make me feel better after all that unnecessary scratching and hurting, you hussy bitch you.'

Dani laughed. 'Sorry, but it was good and especially for you to manage it twice on a Sunday morning.' He smiled back at her. She was always there for him. Angelo away, Dani back at Jack's pad after a night out.

'But you still haven't told me why you mentioned Claire Simmons' name twice in the last 15 minutes. You saw her in the pub the other week. So what? I don't care.'

'I know you don't Dani, darling. Just thought I'd relay the story. Then again, perhaps I was thinking of her while I was shagging you. I've had her as well you know.' He turned his head and smiled. She pulled at his chest hair. 'You are a bastard, Jack.'

'Ouch! That hurt. I'll tell Angelo.'

'Ha, Ha, he won't believe you. And while we're at it, I'm not interested in Claire fucking Simmons, so stop talking about her.

Jack smiled. 'No, me neither. That ship's sailed.'

THIRTY THREE

HALLY and Jacobs stood outside the police station, file in hand. 'Let's go for a coffee and make some plans,' Hally said. 'We need to get moving.'

John Ashcroft had delivered the bombshell news to the detectives and PC Keegan 30 minutes previous. He'd travelled to the station with the file. He'd had his suspicions and had got the toxicology report done *'on urgent request'*. His suspicions had been proved right. Peggy Honeyman had been poisoned, injected with Arsenic, of which there was a *'plus 5000%'* in her system, the small hole under her chin the point of entry. She had likely died instantly or within 10 minutes at least. Had she managed to stagger to the stairs and fallen? Or been pushed? That was up to the detectives to work out. All Ashcroft would say is that it would take some strength by Peggy to get up after being injected, let alone either walk up some stairs, then fall back down them.

Hally, Jacobs, and Keegan had called a meeting with their superior who had told them to get cracking. This was now a murder inquiry, and more resource would be forthcoming. Keegan had been sent back to Peggy's house. She had taken the key when she had last been there and was planning to give it to a next of kin, so they could start making funeral plans. That was out of the question now. The house was now a murder scene and already another PC had been posted and was standing outside the front gate when Keegan arrived.

'Hi, Jane, how are you?' Keegan said to the young officer.

'You're here quick.' Jane smiled. The pair knew each other well. 'I was told to get here immediately and stop anyone touching anything. What's happened?'

'Looks like a murder,' Keegan said. 'Thought it was an accident, but pathologist says he's found poison in her body. Poor woman, what a way to die. Anyhow, I've got a key, so will take another quick look round, but SOCS will be back here soon, I reckon.'

Meanwhile, Hally and Jacobs supped up their drinks. They needed to crack on. Scenes of Crime Officers were on their way to the house. They had few leads and Peggy seemed to have little family, only a few friends. One person they did want to speak to, Katie Walters, was at home. She let the two detectives in after they knocked. 'No,' Katie exclaimed. 'How? What? Oh, no, this is just awful. Murdered? Are you serious? No, that can't be true.'

Katie had so many questions, but it was Hally and Jacobs who wanted to do the questioning. 'Look, Katie, relax if you can, we need to move quickly on this, and we need you to think of anyone and I mean anyone who Peggy may have spoken to you about in recent weeks, or even months, even years,' said Jacobs. 'Anything you know about her maybe crucial. Her friends, her family. Is there anything you can think of, or anyone you can think of you are not sure about, you think we need to talk to? You were close to her. Possibly as close as anyone.'

Katie sat there and felt like crying. She'd just been getting over the fact Peggy had died and now she was finding out she had been killed. 'I really don't know what to say,' she said. 'I mean Peggy had friends, but not much family. I told the lady policewoman all this.'

Hally looked at his notes. 'You mentioned Peggy had two stepdaughters, one in Scotland, one in Australia, and a stepson. Cecil's son, who you'd never met and as far as Peggy had told you, she'd never met. Is that right?'

Katie nodded her head. 'Cecil had two daughters, Judy and Jenny, both from his first marriage. He also had a son from another relationship, apparently it was all a mistake, and the woman was a nightmare. Her name was Teresa and she'd run off to Scotland with the child when he was only an infant, and for years Cecil couldn't track them down. She was half Italian and was scared stiff of her

Italian parents. They came from Naples, or somewhere like that. This is what Peggy told me. But Cecil did find out who his son was because he found the birth records, even though he hadn't been named on the certificate. Cecil had told Peggy he knew he was the father. Teresa had told him she was pregnant. He'd been trying to find his son for years. When he found out he was in Scotland, he wouldn't go and meet him because he didn't want to disrupt his life. So, apparently, he found out the boy's name and left it at that. Peggy said there was something else, but she wouldn't say what. Apparently, I'm the only one she ever talked to about Cecil's son.'

'What's the son's name?' said Jacobs. 'I have no idea,' replied Katie. 'Peggy never told me his name. Just said Cecil had put the story in writing in a letter that she kept in her safe in her bedroom at the cottage. I didn't pry more. It wasn't my business.'

Hally picked up his phone and called Keegan. 'Trish, hi, it's Pete. I need you to do something. I assume you're still at the house.'

'Yep, I'm here.'

'I'm with Katie Walters. I want you to go into Peggy's bedroom and try and find a safe which is hidden there somewhere. I need you to get into it and if you can't, get a locksmith, or someone who can. We're looking for a letter inside the safe, and possibly a name. It's urgent.'

Katie sat at the kitchen table as Hally made the call. She could hardly believe what she was hearing. How had it all blown up into this? She had been on the phone to Judy at the weekend. Although she despised the sisters as much as Peggy, she had to keep them in the loop. What the hell they would make of this now Peggy had been murdered, she couldn't imagine.

'Anything else you can think of Katie?' Jacobs said. 'You've been really helpful, and it seems Peggy confided in you, so if you think of anything, anything at all, call us.' The pair left their calling cards as Katie showed them out.

She put her hands in her head and began crying.

Keegan had called a locksmith. She had found the safe which was tucked away in the bottom corner of the wardrobe.

In fact, it was only on a second look, she'd discovered it. But she couldn't unlock it and she certainly didn't have time to wander around the house looking for a key. It had taken the locksmith 30 minutes to open and, after Keegan had seen him off the premises, she put her hand inside to take out the contents. The safe was small. There was a watch inside and some jewellery. A blank envelope with a letter inside. And not only a letter, but a Will. Peggy and Cecil's Will. She sat back on the bed and began to read it.

Keegan called up Hally. 'I've got it here. There's a letter and a Will. I won't read it all out, but yep, the stepson, Cecil's son, is called Jack Bianchi, it says it in the letter. And from the date of birth, it looks like he's 25 years old. Apparently born at St Mary's Hospital, Paddington. There's a piece about Cecil feeling guilty about him not ever being in his life. But get this. The Will leaves half the house and half their money to him should they both die.'

'Let's get checking on his records,' said Jacobs. 'Get back here Keegan and start finding out who this guy is and where he comes from, where he works and all about him. Half the house, hey? Who is the other half left to, Trish, does it say?'

Keegan nodded to herself as she read the Will. 'Yes, it does.'

THIRTY FOUR

THE taxi pulled up outside the restaurant and Fraser got out.

It was 8pm and it wasn't usually his bag to meet up with Angelo for dinner. It had been Angelo's idea. He was supposed to be going to the Spurs game, but Angelo had insisted they met tonight. Why the urgency, Fraser had no idea. He would rather have gone to the football. He paid the taxi driver with the company credit card – he was one of three trusted employees to have one – Angelo being another. There was rain in the air, and he looked up to the skies before entering the swanky establishment his boss had decided would be a good place to meet up. Angelo was sitting at the far end of the restaurant. *Bangkok Heights* was one of the best Thai restaurants in the West End, many celebrities from all genres frequented it and getting a table wasn't easy, but it was a Tuesday night, and the restaurant was less busy.

Angelo got up as Fraser approached. 'Hello Fraser, how are you?' Angelo was all smiles and dressed down, not even a tie, which was something Fraser wasn't used to seeing. 'Thanks for coming.'

Fraser smiled as they shook hands. Meeting his boss socially wasn't something he did often, indeed he couldn't remember the last time. 'Enjoying work?' Angelo smiled again as he passed Fraser a menu and called over a waiter. 'Beer?'

'Yep, please, and yeah, everything's fine, thanks. Couldn't be much better, hit bonus last week for the month, as you know, business seems good. Me and Claire have got a holiday to the Maldives coming up.' Fraser smiled. But it all felt a little awkward. What was this about?

'Excellent,' said Angelo, as the waiter put down the two beers on the table and looked as if to say are they ready to order? Angelo clocked it. 'Give us 10 minutes please, then we'll order'. The waiter scurried off.

'So, what have I called you here for tonight, then Fraser?' Angelo took a sip of his beer and looked more serious. Fraser shrugged his shoulders. 'I must admit, I've been thinking that all day.'

'Jack Bianchi.' Angelo let the name drop and settle for a few seconds. He watched Fraser's reaction, and he got the one he knew he would. Fraser sighed and sat back in his chair. 'What about him?' Fraser stared blankly at Angelo. 'Please don't tell me you have called me all the way across London to talk to me about that prick.'

Angelo smiled. 'Prick. Why do you say that?' Fraser shook his head. 'Is this a wind-up, Angelo? Have you got something serious to say, because Bianchi is the last person I want to talk about tonight, last night, tomorrow night, or any night. So, unless you're about to tell me you're firing him or he has some terminal illness that he's confided in you, then I don't want to know. Cheers!' Fraser held up his beer and took a sip.

Angelo laughed out loud. 'I knew you'd say that. I knew what your reaction would be. Oh, my goodness for two work colleagues, you really do hate each other, don't you?'

Fraser half-smiled back. 'Well, there you go, you've had your fun. Now can we look at the menu, or tell me what you really want?'

Angelo put his hand on the menu as Fraser went to pick it up. 'Now, listen. I know what you think of Bianchi and if you think you're alone, then you are very much mistaken. He thinks he's a big shot and he thinks he's indestructible. Well, don't believe it. He's taking on far more than he can handle right now and most of it away from the office from what I've been told.' Fraser remained silent.

Angelo was more serious now. 'Last Friday night, about 7pm

when most of you had gone home, I had a couple of detectives come to the office wanting to speak to Jack. Well, I say they wanted to speak to Jack, they didn't know if Jack was *the* Jack Bianchi they were looking for. It all seemed a bit bizarre, anyway Jack wasn't there, so I gave them his number. But how many people called Jack Bianchi do you know?' Fraser shook his head. 'Me, neither. These cops were the real deal, suited and booted detectives and I'll bet you a million dollars, it will be our Jack they want to speak to.' Angelo smiled and raised his eyebrows.

Fraser stared at him. 'I don't get it. Just because a couple of cops want to talk to a Jack Bianchi, it's not necessarily the prick we know, so what? I don't understand.'

'He's in trouble.' Angelo smiled at Fraser. 'People like Jack always get caught in the end. Of course, it's him.'

Fraser looked bemused. 'But why are you so bothered? Why do you think that's the case? I still don't understand. How do you know it's him? I hate the bloke, but I don't see where this is all going.'

Angelo picked up the menu and began to scan the dishes on it. 'Well, you wouldn't do, in fairness,' Angelo carried on with a smirk on his face. 'But you see the two cops left their card with me and I saw what station they were working out of, which was one near Oxford. A station where my cousin happens to work. My cousin who is also a detective. What's the chances?' Angelo smiled. 'So, I called him up to see what was going on.' Fraser half-smiled. Was this a wind-up?

Angelo noticed his look, then continued. 'Apparently the two who called into the office are working on a murder case. Some old dear was pushed down some stairs, or something like that. And they want to speak to a certain Jack Bianchi, who they said is 25 years old and was born in London. My cousin said he's a suspect.' Fraser looked again at his boss. 'You serious?'

Angelo grinned again. 'Don't tell me you know hundreds of 25-year-olds called Jack Bianchi. I'll wager he's in the shit. Might be nothing, but people like Jack do stupid things. I just thought you'd like to know that's all. God moves in mysterious ways, and all that, Fraser. Anyhow, order up, there's a couple of other things I want to discuss with you, including a new bonus scheme.'

Angelo tapped Fraser on the arm. 'Oh, and how are Spurs getting on?'

The bang on the front door came at 5.30am.

'Open up, police. Open now.' Two booming voices and two more loud bangs on the door and even Jack, after a heavy night of drinking at home, couldn't sleep through that. He was shaken by the noise and jumped out of bed, looking at his mobile phone to see what the time was. More banging, more shouting. Jack was wide awake. *What the hell was going on?*

He got to the door, just as another bang on it ensued. 'Alright, alright,' he called back, as he looked through the peep hole to see police officers outside. He opened the door, as Hally pushed it open, showing his badge to Jack as he did so.

'Jack Bianchi.' It was a statement not a question.

'Yes, what the hell is this all about? Bloody hell man, what's going on?'

Hally kept deadpan as Jacobs saddled up alongside him. 'Jack Bianchi. We need you to come with us to the station at Chelsea. We want to speak to you in connection with the murder of Peggy Honeyman. You are not being arrested at this point, but you are a person of interest we want to talk to. So, get dressed, we're going now.'

'Peggy who? What the fuck are you talking about?' Jack looked at Hally then Jacobs, half shaking his head. 'What's going on? You crazy?'

'Just get dressed,' Hally said. 'We'll talk down the station.'

Ten minutes later Jack was in the back of the car, Jacobs alongside him, Hally driving, two other officers had stayed behind, they had a search warrant. What they were looking for, Jack had no idea. Down at the station, his personal information was taken, before he was placed in a cell.

Jack had been in a cell once before, after he abused a copper who had been called to a restaurant, he and his mates were in down the West End. They were so pissed; they had played around refusing to the pay the bill. The owner didn't mess about, called the police and an argument saw Jack spend a night sobering up. That was two years ago. He didn't enjoy it then; he wasn't enjoying it now. He'd been given a cup of coffee and told he would be seen within a couple of hours. Fortunately, it was a Saturday, so he wasn't at work.

He racked his brains. *Peggy Honeyman, who the hell was she?*

Katie had pushed Shaun's advances away as they lay in bed. He didn't complain, just shook his head, got out of bed, and went downstairs to make a cup of tea.

It wasn't the first time of late she had said 'no', and she knew Shaun would be hurt by it. But she had no appetite for sex. All she could think of was Peggy. It would pass, things would get back to normal. 'Here you are,' Shaun said, passing her the tea. He half-smiled.

'I'm sorry,' she said. 'Please don't think it's anything to do with you. I just can't stop thinking about Peggy and I'm all over the place. Sorry.' She leaned across and kissed him.

Shaun said nothing. He turned away and picked his phone up off the floor.

Angelo looked at the WhatsApp message and photo.

'Is this him? He's helping with enquiries, big suspect… a murder most foul my dear man. Delete this message when done. Just thought you might like to know.'

Angelo smiled to himself.

THIRTY FIVE

JACK had been left for more than an hour when Hally and Jacobs eventually entered his cell and asked him to come with them. They wanted to speak to him *'under caution'*.

He'd been asked if he wanted a solicitor, but Jack had said no. He'd done nothing wrong as far as he was concerned. They weren't going to pin anything on him.

'So,' Hally said. 'Jack Bianchi, the tape is on with DC Hally, that's me talking, and DC Jacobs present. You are being interviewed under caution and have declined any legal help currently, is that right?'

Jack nodded. 'Please, say yes for the tape, Jack,' Hally said. 'Yes,' said Jack.

'Okay, so Jack, we've brought you in to ask what you know about a Mrs Peggy Honeyman, a lady who lived in Church Masham, a village in the Cotswolds.' The detectives stared at him. 'You know her?'

Jack stared back. 'Where the fuck is Church Masham? And who the hell is Peggy Honeyman?' Jack sat back shaking his head.

'No need for the language, Jack,' Hally said. 'Just answer the questions. Do you know a Mrs Peggy Honeyman, yes or no?' Jack shook his head again. 'No, I don't know a Mrs Peggy Honeyman.'

'How about a Cecil Honeyman then?' Hally leaned forward. 'Ring any bells?'

Jack shook his head. 'Honestly, I don't know what you are talking about. I don't know any of these people and I don't know what the hell this is about and quite honestly, I would prefer it if you would just say sorry for wasting my time and let me out of here. You sure you're speaking to the right person?'

It was Jacobs turn to take over. 'Okay, Jack. How about this question. Where were you born?'

Jack locked eyes with Jacobs. 'Is that a serious question?'

'Just answer it.'

'London', Jack replied. 'A hospital in London. Can't remember which one.'

'And your parents are?' Jacobs raised his eyebrows. Jack again, stared back, saying nothing. Jacobs looked at him again. 'I said, and your parents are called? Well, what's their names? Where do they live?'

Still Jack said nothing. He felt frozen in time. He didn't want to give the answer. All his life he had coped, all his life he had dug deep, all his life he had put his childhood out of his memory and now he was being confronted with questions he didn't want to address. He sat upright and glared back at the officers. 'My mum was called Teresa. She has passed away. I didn't know my dad.'

Jacobs looked serious. 'You didn't know your dad?'

'That's what I said.' Jack's left leg was starting to twitch, it often did when he was tense or under pressure and he knew he would be giving off signs that he didn't like this line of conversation.

'Okay, so your mum was called Teresa, what, Bianchi? But you didn't know your dad.' Jack didn't reply.

'For the tape, is that correct, Jack', Jacobs added.

'Yep, that's correct,' Jack replied.

Hally and Jacobs sensed their chance. He wasn't so cocky now. 'So, you never knew your dad?'

'You want me to repeat it? No, I don't know my dad, I never knew my dad, that okay with you two?'

'Okay, Jack, appreciate it's a sensitive subject, but we're asking questions because we are investigating the death of a lady who we are almost certain was murdered. Her name was Peggy Honeyman.' Jack shrugged his shoulders.

'And,' said Hally. 'Mrs Peggy Honeyman was married to a Mr

Cecil Honeyman who, we think, in fact we are pretty sure, was your dad. Sadly, he is no longer alive either.'

Jack sat there, motionless. Never had he heard anyone tell him who his dad was. He knew nothing of this. How he had tried to find out in his teenage years. How he had begged his mother to tell him, how he tried, but failed to find his father. His birth certificate had no name of his father on it. He'd seen it. And when his mother died three years ago of cancer, he'd never found out the truth. He'd asked, oh how he'd asked, but she had never said a thing, his dad was a taboo subject, simple as that. He had asked so many times, but he loved his mother so much and she refused to tell him, even on the last night before he headed to London to start work, he had one more try. He wanted to get angry with her, but he couldn't. No-one in his family appeared to know, either. Or wanted to tell. He'd just had to deal with the lack of knowledge. The big hole in his life. Now he was facing this possibly uncomfortable truth he had tried to bury.

'How do you know this?' Jack said quietly.

Jacobs smiled. 'Come on Jack, we're police officers. Our job is to investigate, find out things. Find out where people come from, relationships, jobs, careers, debts.... It's not hard. Didn't you know about your old man, then? Strange.'

Jack stood up and went to throw a punch at Jacobs. Hally was up in a flash as Jacobs moved back too fast for Jack to connect. 'Sit down Jack,' said Hally. 'Don't be an idiot. You could be in big enough trouble as it, assaulting a police officer would be the least of your worries, but you don't want more hassle, do you?'

Jack sat back down, but he was shaking. 'Okay, so you reckon you know my family history more than I do. Big deal. But don't tell me you want to talk to me because you reckon my dad, who I've never met, was married to some dead woman I've never heard of. Because if you are, then I'm getting out of here. I'm done. I don't understand why I'm here.'

'Done? You're not done, Jack.' Jacobs stood up and walked round the room, before turning to look at him. 'I'll say again, did you know Peggy Honeyman? You must have, don't give us crap that you had no idea where your dad was, or who he was with.

You got someone to help you find the birth certificate, surely. You're not a fool, Jack. You must have found out about Cecil and Peggy.'

Jack shook his head. 'I have no idea about any of this. Who Peggy is or was. I didn't know my dad, who you're now telling me is dead, let alone this other woman.' Jack banged the table.

Hally stood up, turned the tape off, and pointed to Jacobs to go out of the room with him. Once outside, they looked at each other. The line of questioning was going nowhere, and they had no evidence Jack had anything to do with Peggy's murder, only the circumstantial stuff in the letter that could give him a reason to kill her to get half the house. They could throw that at him later.

'I believe him on one count,' said Jacobs. 'The lad did look shocked when we mentioned his dad. I believe he didn't know who he was. Not so sure about Peggy, though. I reckon he knew her. But we need evidence, because he'll play the, *'I don't know Peggy Honeyman'* card all day long. We can't just say he had good reason to want her dead. There's no proof. We need evidence, DNA from the scene, anything. He's off the hook for now.'

The pair went back into the interview room. They looked at the clock. It was gone 2pm. 'You can go,' Hally said. 'We'll just take some more details at reception. If we need to speak to you, we'll catch up again.'

Jack stood up and shook his head. 'You do my head in, coppers.'

'Just get out, before you say something that will keep you here longer,' Hally replied.

Jacobs escorted Jack to reception, then out of the front door.

Jack needed a drink.

It had been a shit of a day, but he was beginning to unwind as he enjoyed what was about his ninth JD and Coke, at BBT's. Tony was there, as were a few more of Jack's mates and their groupies. The VIP area was packed and theirs for the night and, while it had taken Jack time to get into the swing of things after his time at the police station, he was in the groove now. On the dance floor, he was in his element as the stresses of the day began to vanish. This was his world. As he left the dance floor and made his way up the stairs, he looked at his watch. It was 1.30am and he decided he was going back to the VIP area for one last drink and get a taxi home. 'Oi, Mr Jack Bianchi. Can I come up? I'm a VIP, you know.'

Jack was four stairs up when he heard the call. He turned round to see Olivia Ruskin standing at the bottom next to the two bouncers who checked on people going up to the VIP area. 'Hey, yeah, sure.' Jack came down a couple of rungs and grabbed her hand as the bouncers moved aside. 'She's good to come up,' Jack said to them. 'How long have you been here?' Jack looked at Olivia as they reached the top step.

'Since about midnight,' she giggled. 'Hell, I'm pissed.'

Jack laughed and put his arm around her. She was so bloody attractive, her short skirt almost showing off her knickers. Jack smiled to himself. Her low-cut top showed her perfect cleavage. He looked at her. 'I'm going home soon to be honest, been a bit of a shit day. I'm just drinking up, but you're welcome to stay with my friends up here. You know Rick and Tony; Rick works with us.'

'Yeah, I know Rick – Rick the prick with the little dick,' she giggled. Jack shook his head. 'Well, I'm not staying if you're going, Jack.' She looked at him and smiled. 'And you're not packing me off in a cab like a naughty little girl, like you did last time.' She leaned on his shoulder and kissed his ear. 'I'm coming home with you. And don't say you don't want me to, because if you say that, you're a liar.'

Jack smiled at her. 'You're one funny girl, Olivia. I'll give you that.' She raised her eyebrows and downed her glass of wine, putting her arms around his neck. 'Not just funny. But funny, sexy. And I'm not joking. Just hope you haven't had too much to drink.'

He smiled and downed his JD and Coke. She was so attractive; he wasn't going to palm her away this time. He took her hand and walked her down the stairs and out of the club, where he hailed a cab.

They started kissing in the back of the taxi.

THIRTY SIX

SHAUN hated Mondays.

Especially now autumn was just around the corner and the footfall would go south. The kids were back at school. At least Katie was earning again. The previous week had been good at the shop. He'd taken £600, not bad for the middle of September. He made himself a coffee and turned the 'OPEN' sign round. Not that he was likely to get too many customers at nine in the morning. But you never knew. He felt shit. Outside, around the green, more shops were coming to life. He took his coffee outside and watched as they busied themselves. He took in a large gulp of the Cotswolds air and looked at his phone. No messages. Newsagent, John Barber, was putting out his 'A-board' with the local newspaper headlines on.

MURDER LATEST – LOCAL SHOCK

Shaun looked across at it and took another swig of his coffee. It had been a shock. A huge shock to the village after the news had somehow leaked out on a social media post that Peggy Honeyman was the lady who had been murdered.

'Morning Shaun,' came the familiar voice of John.

'Morning John.'

'Going to be a nice day, I think. And on a Monday as well. Can't stand Mondays, but at least when the sun is shining, things seem better.'

Shaun smiled back. 'I hate Mondays as well, mate. Like that Boomtown Rats song, *'I don't like Mondays'*. That should be played at my funeral.'

John laughed. 'You are joking.'

'No. I told Katie. Not that she was happy with me talking about being dead.'

'I'm not surprised,' John said. 'My wife, well she might have a different take on it. She's always telling me she would be better off without me. Trouble is, I think she means it. Anyway, got to go. Have a good day.'

John waved his hand as he went back into the shop. Shaun turned and walked back into his shop. His phone beeped, a text from Katie. *'LOVE YOU XXX'*

He took a deep breath, thought about not replying. Then sent a love heart emoji.

Katie smiled at his reply.

It was morning break at Driffing Park School and Katie was in the staff canteen eating a sandwich and chatting to other members of staff. She had settled in well at the school and had sent Shaun the text while Mrs Catley had got up to go to the loo. The pair had been talking dogs! Mrs Catley had one, Katie had spoken of the idea of her and Shaun getting one. She looked again at his love heart emoji. Should she send something else back? Perhaps something a bit risqué. No, she didn't bother. She only had 10 minutes until break was over and she was back with the Year 7s – and it was PE, so she had to get her trainers on.

'What are you smiling at?' Mrs Catley had returned and sat down next to Katie.

'Oh, nothing. I just sent hubbie a text and he replied. I was thinking of keeping the conversation going with something a bit naughty.' Katie laughed.

'Yes, go on, do it,' Mrs Catley laughed back. 'Make his day.'

'No, I mustn't. He owns a bookshop. He might be in the middle of a conversation with a professor of history who wants to order 100 Russian Revolution books.'

'Oh, how nice. Do people order that many from your husband's bookshop?' Katie raised her eyebrows. 'If only.'

Mrs Catley got up to go. 'Well, I like a good book, but for now, it's year eight drama class for me. Best get ready. There are enough drama queens in that class for us to all have a ball. See ya!'

Katie looked at her watch. It was almost time for her to get ready for the next lesson. Her phone beeped. She smiled to herself. Now what did Shaun want? She looked at her phone, but it wasn't Shaun who was texting, but Mark. *'Hi, Katie. Hope all well. You'll be pleased to know I'm still in one piece after the fight at the OK Hotel the other week. Up for another event next weekend? It's in London. Might be an overnight stay.'*

She looked at the text. She hadn't forgotten the way Mark stuck up for her at the hotel that night. She enjoyed working with him, but that kiss still haunted her. She didn't fancy Mark. But she did feel vulnerable right now. Did she really want a night away in London working with him? She thought hard as she tied up the shoelaces of her trainers.

'What's the date?' she texted back.

THIRTY SEVEN

JACK'S PA was waiting for him as he returned from lunch.

'Angelo wants to see you. ASAP. You been a naughty boy again?' Carol smiled.

'I'm naughty with everyone, or so it seems, what does he want now?' Jack said, as he got up and brushed past her.

Angelo was sitting at his desk. He didn't get up. 'Come in Jack, sit down.' The sun was streaming through the large windows that overlooked the City and Angelo had a grin on his face that concerned Jack.

'So, how's things?' Angelo got up and walked over to his coffee machine. 'Coffee?'

'Yeah, please,' said Jack. 'Things are okay.'

'Good. Can I ask you something?

'Of course.'

Angelo turned to face him. 'I had a couple of coppers in here a few nights back. And they were asking after you.'

Jack remained poker-faced. 'Oh, yeah.' He tried to make light of it but knew Angelo would have clocked his awkwardness. 'Yeah. Just came in all very calm and asked after you, well after a Jack Bianchi, and if one worked here. Obviously, I told them you did. Assume it was you. Not too many Jack Bianchi's work here, I don't reckon, do you?'

Jack looked at him. 'And your point?'

Angelo smirked and moved towards Jack. 'My point is this, Jack. I don't like coppers crawling round the office looking for my employees. Not good for business. I'm sure you understand that. So, if there is something you need to tell me, then let's have it. It might not be any of my business, but if it impacts on this place, then it does become my business. You understand?'

Jack took the coffee off Angelo, who sat back down. 'It's nothing for you to worry your head about. I haven't spoken to any coppers and no coppers have called me. But if I do, I'll make sure they don't come here to the office. Don't want them asking questions about stuff, do we? Like videos with prostitutes, stuff like that. It could get uncomfortable.'

Angelo glared at him. 'You're a smart arse, aren't you?' Jack shrugged his shoulders. 'It was you who told Dani, wasn't it? You really are a tosser.' Jack shook his head. 'Told her what?'

Angelo glared at him. 'You know what. The video.'

But Jack was unmoved. 'It was only drugs and prostitutes, Angelo. I won't say anything. I promised you that. The likes of Toby Ruskin and his pals don't need to know.'

Angelo pointed across the table. 'You blurt your mouth off to anyone, and I promise you, I'll fucking finish you.'

Jack frowned. 'Why all the threats suddenly, Angelo? We had a solid arrangement. You got something else to hide? Come on, I'm not going to tell anyone about your secrets, and I never have done. So, why do you keep poking me? Cut it out. I'm not the man you should worry about. You keep on about me being an arsehole, look in the mirror Angelo. You don't trust me and I certainly don't trust you.'

Jack took another sip of his coffee, got up and left the office.

The event in London was on the South Bank and Mark was delighted to get such a grand place to stage it. Katie had enjoyed the evening and was glad she had decided to go.

It finished at 10pm and after they had packed up, Mark suggested they headed into the City, find a restaurant and enjoy a meal.

'Did you see that bloke with the red suit?' Katie laughed as she enjoyed her second glass of wine. 'He was so over the top it was incredible. But he loved it. Left me his card. Apparently, he's an artist who works in Chelsea. Told me to pop over and see his studio.' Katie laughed. 'Not sure if that's an offer I can refuse.'

Mark smiled. 'We've made nearly two grand tonight.' Katie flicked her eyebrows. 'You're getting £300 quid my girl. Think of all the pens and pencils you can buy your school with that!' They both laughed. The ambience in the restaurant was perfect, and the restaurant's pianist was playing chilled-out music.

'Tell you what. Let's go to a club after this.' Mark looked at Katie, they had both finished desserts. 'Come on, it will be fun.'

'Oh, I'm not so sure,' she said. 'I'm a bit tired and I don't really do clubs.'

'I don't expect you do. Not many in Church Masham are there?'

'No. We have bingo at the village hall on Thursdays.' Katie laughed; she was feeling giggly.

'Come on then, just for an hour or two. We won't be too late. I know a club near here.'

Katie looked across at him. Her defences were beginning to rise. It was all well and good working with Mark but going to restaurants and then nightclubs. What would Shaun say? 'Oh, what the hell. Come on, let's go,' she said.

Mark smiled as they finished up their drinks. 'This is all on me, by the way, so keep your purse well hidden.'

'I should hope it is. You're the money man.'

Outside the restaurant, Mark hailed a taxi. 'BBT's nightclub, please,' he said to the driver.

For a Thursday night, the club was packed. It was years since Katie had been in a nightclub. The peace and quiet of the Cotswolds seemed miles away as the pair made their way to the bar.

'What do you want?' Mark, leaned into Katie's ear to make himself heard. 'Fancy trying a cocktail? They do great ones here. I'm having one.'

'Go on then,' she said. 'But if I don't like it, you can drink it.' Mark nodded. 'I'll drink anything!'

They found some seats a good distance from the dance floor so they could at least make themselves heard as they looked up at the VIP area. It was packed. 'I haven't been to a London club before, used to enjoy them back in the day,' Katie said as she enjoyed her mojito. 'It's good though. I like it. I didn't realise they played so many older tracks. I thought it would be all the latest stuff.'

Mark shook his head. 'No, I've been here before, and the music was one of the things I used to love about it. I can't stand too much modern stuff. Everyone loves a bit of Abba.' He laughed out loud as *'Dancing Queen'* was being played, the dance floor packed with people who were too young to remember the Swedish group in their heyday. 'So, how are you and Shaun? All good?'

Katie looked at him. 'Fine, you've asked that before.'

'Just wondered, that's all. He's a good man for letting you out with me for the night, that's all.'

'He is a good man,' Katie said. 'I love him a lot and it's been tough lately. The shop is getting quieter this time of the year. But that's why you get married isn't it? For better or worse.'

'Don't ask me.' Mark sat back in his chair. 'Marriage, no thanks. I was too close to that in South Africa, just managed to avoid it.'

'You'd make a great husband,' Katie leaned forward. 'There will be a woman out there for you. And imagine if you had kids? You'd make a great dad.'

Mark shook his head and leaned forward, the two of them now just a few inches apart, the music beating fast, the drink taking hold, their eyes glazed and fixed on each other. 'Perhaps there is someone out there.' He looked into Katie's eyes. 'But maybe I can't have her, maybe she doesn't want me. Maybe I just don't know, maybe I do know.'

Katie stared at him, saying nothing as her eyes fixed on his, her head dizzy, the music, the drink. They moved closer and went to kiss… but at the last second, she pulled away. 'Come on,' she said, starting to get up. 'Let's have a dance, another drink and then go.' Mark shook his head and pulled away.

She took hold of his hand and smiled. 'Let's not spoil things.'

Jack looked at his phone.

'Don't get tight on me Jack. I'm starting to get pissed off. And not just me. You owe.'

He went to reply but decided not to. He would sort it out. Anyhow there was drinking and dancing to be had and he'd spotted a gorgeous bird on the dancefloor… Trouble was, the tall guy with the looks appeared to be with her, they looked an item.

Ah, forget her. There were plenty of others.

THIRTY EIGHT

MRS Henshaw didn't know Peggy Honeyman especially well.

They lived opposite each other for 10 years, but their paths rarely crossed. The shock of her death hit Sheila Henshaw though, like it had all the people in Church Masham. The police had called round to see if she remembered anything. She hadn't at the time, but she had now. It was just a small thing. Her son had told her she should contact the police after she told him what she'd remembered. Sheila had seen a man leave Peggy's house. It was a couple of days ago, the day before Peggy was found dead. She was sure she'd seen the man at Peggy's house before. She didn't know him. So, when PC Keegan called to see her, Mrs Henshaw began to tell what she'd seen. It had been 6.30pm or round about that time, two nights ago. Mrs Henshaw had been out in the front garden putting some grass cuttings in her compost heap at the side of the house.

'He was moving so fast, I suppose that is why I noticed him,' Mrs Henshaw told PC Keegan. 'He turned right out of her gate and headed towards Pope Road and went up there. As I said, he was walking fast. He was soon out of sight. And yet I thought I'd seen him before, but my memory isn't that great.'

'Any description, Sheila? Anything at all that you can remember?' Keegan was hoping for a little more.

'He had a hat on, like one of those, what are they called? Beanie hats. It was black. Dark coat, oh and white shoes. He was quite tall, oh this is so boring, I am sorry. He looked just so ordinary, I mean I didn't see his face, he was looking at the ground. But as I said, I'm sure he'd been round to Peggy's before.'

'That's alright, Sheila,' Keegan smiled. 'When you say quite tall, what do you mean? Alot taller than me?'

'Yes, much taller than both of us. Oh, and I think he had gloves on which is the only thing I did think odd because it wasn't that cold an evening.'

'And you say you think you have seen him before?'

'Yes, I think so. I don't know why, it was the way he walked, I'm sure I'd seen him leave Peggy's on another occasion. But I could be wrong.'

'And he went down Pope Road?' Keegan said. Sheila nodded. 'Well, look, thank you Sheila and if you remember anything else, any little thing at all, let me know. Here is my card, call me.'

Keegan put her notepad away and went to get up, Sheila's son, David, escorting her to the door. 'I'll keep asking her if she remembers anything else,' he said. 'She's 81 now and sharp, but as I'm sure you appreciate, she's not going to remember everything. Do you think this is a one-off? This murder I mean. I don't know whether mum should come and stay with me and the wife for a while until someone is caught. She doesn't seem worried, but I am.'

Keegan raised her eyebrows. 'I really couldn't say. A stranger, or maybe someone Peggy knew. It's all very open right now. I would say, tell your mum not to let anyone in the house she doesn't know, or to call you if she's concerned, but don't over-worry her. We often find these things are one-offs, not serial stuff.' He opened the door and let Keegan out.

Keegan went down Mrs Henshaw's front path, closed the gate behind her, crossed the road and headed towards Pope Road. Pope Road wasn't very long. No more than 30 houses, mostly small cottages, each side of the road. She had called in to the station to say she was going to start house-to-house there, see if anyone saw the man Sheila Henshaw had mentioned, walking down the road at that time. Any clue, any tip, was being taken seriously. Keegan had been knocking on doors for 30 minutes and was surprised how many people were in considering it was a midweek lunchtime. By the time she knocked on No.36, *'Bramble*

Cottage', it was past 2pm. After she went through the formalities of introduction again and was waiting for the customary, *'no, sorry dear, I didn't see anything'*, or *'no-one in the house was in'*, a large, bearded man, grey hair, looked mid-60s she guessed, stood in front of her.

'Tuesday, 6.30ish, you say? A couple of nights ago.' He stroked his beard. Keegan nodded. 'Well, funny you should say that, because I was putting my lawnmower away in the side garage here.' He pointed left to the side of his house. 'About that time this young kid comes past on his bicycle, on the bloody pavement and clips the wing mirror of some damned car that had been parked outside my house for half-an-hour. Hadn't blocked me in, but I hate that sort of thing. Looking out your window and seeing a car you don't recognise. Don't appreciate it, to be honest.'

Keegan was scribbling down his words apace, even though she had no idea where this was going.

'Anyhow, the young kid stops and looks at the mirror and tries to put it back in position. The harder he pushes the mirror, it makes no difference, and it won't go back. Suddenly, this guy comes up behind him and nods at him, asking what he's doing. The boy starts to say something, I couldn't hear what, but the bloke sort of waves him off as much as to say, just go, don't worry. And with that the boy bikes off and the bloke gets in the car and drives off. About time he moved the car I remember thinking.'

Keegan looked up. 'Can you describe this man?'

'Pretty tall, average everything else really. White guy. He had a hat on. Black, I think. Oh, and gloves.'

Keegan shot a look towards him and turned over a page in her notepad. 'Definitely had gloves on?'

'Um, yes, he did. I think they were black, could have been grey.'

'I don't suppose you remember the car, do you? Possibly the registration? I know that's a big ask.'

'Didn't get the registration. But it was blue, and I know the make of the car. Used to have one like it myself.'

'Hi Jack.' Olivia walked into his office, coffee in hand. 'Want this? I just made a pot.'

Jack looked up as she put the cup down on the table. Hell, she looked good even at this time of the morning! They'd spent the night together after going to the club, it had been some of the best sex he could remember in a long time. It had released all his tension after his day with the police. He was treading on dangerous territory with Olivia, and he knew it, but that was the way he rolled, and he wasn't going to change any time soon.

'So, when are we going out again?' Olivia sat on the edge of his desk, her skirt riding up to show off one of her long, tanned legs.

'Olivia. Don't. And you know what I'm talking about before you say anything. Keep things quiet, please. It was a great night, but let's not get carried away. Yep, we can go out again, but don't shout your mouth off about us. Certainly not here in the office. You understand?'

She smiled at him. 'Oh, look, Mr Bashful. I thought Jack Bianchi was Mr Stud, Mr Go-Getter. Shag 'em and ask questions later. What's the matter, am I too much for you?'

Jack shook his head. 'It's bloody 9.15 in the morning and you're talking like this. Shit, Olivia.'

She slid herself off the table and walked towards the door. 'I'm only in today and tomorrow this week,' she called back as she got to the door. 'Got uni exams I must study for. But I'm free both nights if you fancy doing anything, or fancy any of this.' She led her finger up the side of her thigh to reveal a bit more leg.

Jack shook his head and smiled. 'Get out'.

THIRTY NINE

JACOBS and Hally twice walked round the car.

It wasn't until Hally looked closer a second time that he noticed the small dent on the wing mirror. He looked at his partner and nodded at him to come and look. 'What do you think?' Hally said as the pair of them walked up to the front door of the cottage. It's where Keegan said a mark may be.

'Let's get reactions first,' Jacobs said. 'Poacher turned gamekeeper; I doubt.'

Hally looked at him. 'What the hell does that mean; poacher turned gamekeeper?'

Jacobs shrugged his shoulders. 'Well, she's been helpful, there's not likely much in it, but you never know. She might be poacher, turned gamekeeper. Isn't that what they call it?'

'What are you on about? Christ Pete, you still pissed from last night?' Hally shook his head. 'In saying that, there aren't many cars like this around.'

It was 9am on a Sunday morning and Hally rang the bell, he didn't have to wait long. Katie answered the door. She looked surprised. 'Hi.' Katie had a long red dress on. Her and Shaun were going out for a drive into the countryside. It was set to be a sunny day. Hally and Jacobs held out their badges. 'Detectives Hally and Jacobs, Thames Valley Police,' Hally said. 'Can we come in?'

Katie looked bemused. 'Um, hang on, yes of course. What do you want? Is this to do with Peggy because I told the policewoman everything I know and said I'd call her if I remembered anything else?'

Jacobs smiled. 'Can we just come in? And is your husband about?' Katie nodded as the two detectives walked into the hallway and stood silent for a while as they took in their surroundings. Shaun came down the stairs, he had a blue dressing gown on. He looked at Katie, before looking at the detectives.

'Mr Walters?' said Hally. 'As I told your wife, we are police officers from Thames Valley. Do you mind me asking, is that your car outside, the VW Beetle?'

Shaun looked at Katie, then the officers. 'Yes.'

'Can we sit down and have a chat, please?' Hally smiled at them both. Katie looked worried. 'Is something wrong?'

'Let's just sit down,' Jacobs said.

Katie led them all into the living room where the detectives sat on two single chairs, while Katie and Shaun sat on the two-seater. Katie was beginning not to like this. It didn't take much to make her anxious. 'Okay, so what is it?' she said. 'And what about the car?' She looked at Shaun, who was staring blankly. She looked again at him.

'Shaun. Are you listening?' But something was wrong with him. And Katie could sense it.

Hally looked at her husband. 'Shaun, can I ask you first. A car was seen last Tuesday night round the corner from Peggy Honeyman's cottage, in Pope Road. We have someone who saw a blue VW Beetle like yours. It had just been damaged by a lad on a bike, a slight nick on the wing mirror, like the damage on yours outside. Maybe it is nothing, but we need to clear it up, as I'm sure you understand. Tuesday was the day we are sure Peggy was murdered. Is it just coincidence that your car could have been in the vicinity, round about 6pm. Were you there? Or, was Katie there?'

'What?' said Katie. 'I wasn't there. I was still at school on a teacher training evening. Shaun, you picked me up at 7, didn't you?'

She looked at Shaun who looked at her back, still saying nothing. 'Shaun, you picked me up, remember. Shaun, say something please. Is this some sort of joke? I wasn't there on

Tuesday. Nor were you, were you?' Still Shaun said nothing.

Katie looked at the two detectives. 'Are you suggesting we had something to do with Peggy's murder? Are you mad? She was my best friend. Shaun, tell them.' The room, which had been warm and cosy, now felt cold as ice, and still Shaun looked blankly ahead. He began shaking his head.

'Shaun,' said Jacobs. 'Answer our questions, please. Were you at Peggy's house on Tuesday?'

Shaun looked at Katie and then back at the detectives. His eyes started to well and he began to shake his head again. Katie hadn't seen him like this before. She put her hands on his. They were freezing.

'Shaun, you're scaring me, what's wrong? You weren't there on Tuesday night, you picked me up. Just tell them.' He turned away from her.

Shaun looked at Hally and Jacobs… 'I've got nothing to say.'

Jack had some days owing and he needed time to himself. He needed time to find out something, anything, about his dad.

For too long he had placed his dad out of his thoughts. He was never going to know who he was; he had convinced himself of that. For too long he hadn't chased it down. For too long his mother had made sure he never knew, and he'd always thought that was the way it was going to stay. But his mum had passed away long enough, and the fact police officers seemed to know that Cecil Honeyman was his father, meant Jack knew it was time he tried to find out. Jack and his mother had lived in Kirkcudbright, a harbour town on the Solway coast, in Dumfries and Galloway. It was a peaceful place and Jack had enjoyed his school years there after his mum moved them both to Scotland when he was five. It was a long shot. But he hoped his mum may have confided in someone in the town. While he had moved back to London, his mum had remained in the house he was brought up in until her death. His dad's name never mentioned. It was time to chase his past.

The Tesla was good at cruising, not that Jack had used it much since Toby Ruskin had gifted it to him. He hadn't heard anymore from the police, and he smiled to himself as he drove up the M1, thinking of Olivia. What a girl she was. Jack stopped at a hotel near Scotch Corner for the night and fired off a few e-mails to people in the office. He may be having a few days off, but work was never far away. Fraser had sent him a text about a client Jack was looking to get onside and away from Fraser. He'd done it before, and while he knew Angelo didn't like the two of them getting pissed off with each other, he didn't give a shit.

'I know you've spoken to John Sedgley because he told me. Why don't you give it a rest, get your own clients, and stop dicking around with mine. Anyhow, you'll be pleased to know me and John have come to an agreement, today actually, seeing as you are away. Don't rush back. Oh, and careful how you drive'. Jack smiled at the text. There was something about getting under Fraser's skin that was quite satisfying. He thought about sending some cute reply but decided against it.

Next morning, Jack was up early. The hotel did a hearty full English and he headed across the A66 and onto the M6, continuing north and turning off at Gretna Green. Jack followed the A75 as the signs for Kirkcudbright began to come into view. He did love Scotland and even though he hadn't lived there long, he only had good memories. It always appeared so bleak, yet so beautiful. The roads the higher north you went seemed to mould into the countryside and were never as busy. Dumfries and Galloway looked beautiful, the sun shining bright, the sky jet blue. He put his shades on and continued the drive. Quite where he would start when he got to Kirkcudbright, he had no idea. He knew the location of his old house in the High Street, almost opposite the golf course. He remembered some of the shops and wondered if they were still there. He knew he was a like a kite flying in a strong breeze. Where he would end up, he had no idea. But he needed to try and find out the truth about his dad. Surely someone would have known his mum. She hadn't died that long ago and there were many people at her funeral. Yet, Jack also knew he could be leaving Scotland in the days to come with no answers to any of his questions.

And what would he do then?

FORTY

KATIE'S world had been turned upside down.

Shaun had been taken to a police station in Oxford leaving Katie staring vacantly around the house. It was a nightmare. Shaun had just got up and walked to the car with the officers. He said nothing, hardly looked back at her. She had gone to hold him, touch him, but Shaun had walked on. She had watched as the car drove off, Shaun in the back seat. The tears had begun as soon as she went back into the house. Sobbing uncontrollably, Katie had seen none of this coming. Why did he go so easily with the police and not sat and talked to them, to tell them of his innocence, this nonsense? She had as many questions as the police had. She thought she knew her husband. It must be a mistake. Who could she call? Who could she speak to? There was no-one. Not now Peggy was gone. She couldn't tell her parents, or Shaun's; none of them would handle it well. Then again, there was nothing to tell yet, was there?

It was just after 5pm when the doorbell went. Katie had called the station three times, but each time she was told her husband was being questioned. Katie rushed to the door. Oh, to see his face and hug him. But it was PC Trish Keegan who stood there. 'Hi Katie, can I come in?' Katie nodded, as Keegan walked through. 'Can we sit down?'

'What's going on?' said Katie. 'Tell me, what the hell's happening? Surely, this is just routine or something. Shaun wouldn't hurt anyone. He hardly knew Peggy. And why has no-one bothered to tell me what's going on. Bloody hell, I've called the station three times, and no-one has bothered to speak to me. I am his wife.'

Keegan leaned forward. 'Katie, I'm sorry. I won't beat around the bush; your husband has confessed to killing Peggy.'

The words hung heavy in the air as Katie looked at her in disbelief, then looking out of the window, her eyes focussing on nothing, as though she hadn't heard what had been said. She turned back to look at Keegan, shaking her head. 'I'm sorry Katie. I really am,' Keegan added.

'This is ridiculous. You're not serious, are you?' Katie began to speak as her eyes welled. Her heart was racing. She didn't know where to begin. She hardly knew what to say.

'Your husband has confessed, Katie. He's told us you knew nothing of what has been going on in his world, in his life. His money problems. He told us he's been living a lie. And he's committed an awful crime. You can't speak to him now. That time will come.'

Katie stared at her. 'Are you crazy? What money problems? What lies? What has he told you? This can't be right. What has he said? Tell me. I need to know.' Katie stood up and walked towards Keegan. The tears were falling. She was sad, yet angry, shocked. A nightmare unfolding in front of her. The life she knew about to be shattered. It couldn't be true.

Keegan stood up and took hold of her, but Katie shrugged her off. 'Get away. You're not telling me my husband has killed Peggy, killed anyone. Has he got a lawyer down there? He's talking rubbish. It's impossible, you have no proof. It's just not true. Why would he say it? Why? You can't be telling me this. Have you any idea about Shaun? No, I don't know why you think it, or what he's said. But it's lies. He's lying. He hardly knows her. I've told you.'

Katie began screaming as she threw herself on the couch. She picked up a cushion and cried into it. Shock and anger had turned to despair. Keegan sat next to her, putting her arm around her. Katie was crying too much to shrug her away. Her tears were getting stronger as her body gave way, and she rested her head on Keegan's shoulders. 'Tell me this isn't true,' she said as she looked at Keegan through eyes that were full of hurt, full of sorrow.

'Look, Katie. There's another officer in the car outside. I'm just going to tell her to leave us for a while and we can talk. I'll tell you all I know. I'm so sorry, but this is happening. So, let's sit and talk.'

Keegan got up and went to the front door. She spoke to the other officer and told her to come back in an hour. She walked back into the house; Katie was sitting staring out of the window. 'Do you want a cup of tea?' Keegan said on her return. 'Let's have a cup and talk.'

'I don't want anything,' Katie said. 'I feel sick. Just tell me what is going on.'

Keegan sat beside her. 'Shaun's car – your car, the VW Beetle – was seen near Peggy's on the day of her death. That's why we came round here to speak to you about why it was there. Neither of you were suspects. We just had to clear it up. But you saw how Shaun reacted. And down at the station, he told us everything. And yes, he has a lawyer with him.'

'Everything? What's everything?'

'Your husband has a lot of debt, Katie, or so he's told us. We are looking into it. He says you had no idea the mess he was in. He has told us you have no idea about what he has done. Shaun has known Peggy far longer than you are aware of, apparently.'

Katie shook her head. 'He didn't know her. We never spoke about Peggy unless I mentioned it. Peggy never mentioned Shaun to me. What is all this? It's rubbish. Peggy would have told me if she'd seen him. He's making it up. Why is he doing this?'

Keegan took a deep breath. 'Peggy was good at keeping secrets, obviously. And one of them was him visiting. Another was she loaned him money – money to keep the shop afloat – thousands apparently. He also knew something he thinks even you didn't know. That Peggy had left half her house and savings in her Will to you.'

Keegan looked at her. Katie stared back. 'What? Half her house in her Will. Shaun told you that, how the hell does he know? This is rubbish. I didn't know that, and I spoke to Peggy all the time. She would have said something. What has Shaun been saying? What have you got him to say?' Katie was shaking her head as she pulled away from Keegan.

'Look, Katie. These are the lies and deceit he has been keeping from you. We have no reason to think he's making it up. Why would he? He told us that if Peggy died, you would inherit half the house. He says he went round Peggy's, poisoned her, and threw her down the stairs. We have no reason not to believe him. We are at the bookshop now. He's told us everything, Katie. We found a bottle of Arsenic at the shop. Arsenic was what poisoned her. We have toxicology reports. He told us where to find it. He said he was going to dispose of it soon. I'm so sorry.' PC Keegan put her arm around her.

'And we suspect there's probably more he's not telling us.'

FORTY ONE

SHAUN sat in his cell. He knew what he'd done was set to trigger hell.

Someone put a cup of tea next to him, but he wasn't thirsty. He wasn't hungry. He didn't want anything. He sat staring at the metal door. Sitting on the bed knowing this was going to be his life for years to come. He knew people wouldn't believe what he'd done. Not Shaun, the easy-going bookshop owner. What would they say now? He couldn't believe himself what he had done it. But he was muddled, and far more than anyone knew. Life for Shaun Walters had been going off the rails for a while, and he'd had no-one to turn to… only Peggy.

He'd re-mortgaged the house to keep the shop going, not that Katie knew. He'd borrowed money off a lender he should never have got involved in. The threats that followed. He should have told Mark. He could have helped make sense of the mess he was in. Mark was sensible. He'd have thought of a better idea out of the mess, rather than the deranged, sick one he'd come up with on his own. And what about Katie? The tears began to flow down his cheeks as he thought of her innocent smile, her fun laugh. How she went out of her way to please him, while he chased his dreams, yet all the time they were lies. All he wanted was for her to have money, them to have money. Now she would have nothing but sad memories and hurt. He hadn't thought of anything, only himself. And it was all too late. Peggy had offered help. She'd been giving him money for the past 14 months. Her secret, his secret. Their secret. It started with one short visit one January evening. He'll never forget it. Katie asked him to drop off some second-hand books she'd read and that Peggy she thought would enjoy. It was only the second time they'd met. The conversation he had with Peggy that night changed his life forever. A conversation that began so easily and ended with him pouring out his heart to her.

Peggy so loved Katie; she didn't want to see her life drift while he got them in more and more debt. She was annoyed with him for getting his finances in a mess and, over the next few months, she was happy to ply him with funds and tell him some of her utmost secrets, so long as neither of them said a word. And he never did but he so wished she hadn't told him – especially about her Will. Now, look how he'd repaid her. He replayed the terrible afternoon back in his mind. Peggy had opened the door and welcomed him in, just as she always had. Why he did what he did he will never know. She didn't stand a chance against his strength. Once in the kitchen he'd overpowered her and injected the poison. It hadn't taken long for her to pass out and he watched as she took her last breath. Carrying her up the stairs, sweat pouring from him, his mind was frazzled, a mass of hysteria and cruel determination. Yet underneath it he was strong and focused. He disgusted himself as he remembered holding her upright, staring into her blank eyes, his forceful actions ripping open her blouse, before hurling her down the stairs, a final disgusting act he knew he would never erase among all the horrors of that day. What the hell had he turned into? He stood up in his cell and kicked his mug of tea across the floor, screaming out loud.

He laid down on the bed and put his head in his pillow as the tears continued to flow.

Jack spent three days in Kirkcudbright and two nights in the local pub.

He spoke to plenty of people, asked lots of questions but only one man, John Kingsley, had the news he craved. Jack met John having put up a post on a local Facebook group, *'Kirkcudbright Friends'* asking for any information about his parents, Teresa Bianchi, and Cecil Honeyman. It was a long shot, and he hadn't expected to hear anything. But to his surprise he'd been messaged by John. They'd arranged to meet. John was in his late 70s, he looked younger. He was tall at over six foot, with greying hair. He had known Cecil – not well – but well enough. His wife Diane had known Teresa far better. The pair agreed to meet in The Bull on Jack's last night in the town. Jack said he would be standing at the bar, all a bit secretive like a spy movie. Not Jack's style, but he had no choice. Luckily, the pub wasn't busy.

'Jack?' He turned round. John stood alongside him and held out his hand. 'John Kingsley.'

Jack shook hands and got him a drink as the pair sat down at one of the numerous free tables and, after pleasantries about the weather and how long John had lived in the town, the pair got down to business.

'Cecil Honeyman, hey? I knew him. Not wonderfully well, but I knew him enough,' said John.

Jack was on edge, although why he didn't' know. He wasn't by nature a worrier, but he was feeling anxious. Unsure what he was about to hear. 'You and your wife apparently knew them both? How come?' Jack's question lacked pleasantries. His demeanour cold. John smiled at him. 'You don't trust me do you Jack?'

'I don't trust anyone. So, entertain me with your stories of my dad, if indeed Cecil Honeyman is my dad.'

John grinned. 'Just like your old man. Smart and confident. He trusted few people, playing the hard man. He didn't have to; he was better than that.' Jack stared at him but said nothing.

John took a sip of his beer. 'I was in the army, lad. Irish Guards, 1st Battalion. Your dad was with me.' Jack listened. 'Your mum, Teresa, and my wife, Diane, were good friends. And your mum used to talk a lot to my wife about Cecil, and about you. It was the army connection that got them talking, they had husbands who had been there, done that. Your mum told my wife everything but asked her to say nothing, which we always felt strange, but understood in time. It was just coincidence that I knew your dad and our wives ended up at the same school gates.

We weren't old buddies or anything. We played a bit of sport against each other, socially saw each other out; all this in the army. I knew him. Anyhow, it's my wife who knows more. She's on her way.'

Jack looked at John, not sure what to make of it all. 'Well, where is she?' Jack got his first words out for a while.

'She will be here soon. Your message said you only had tonight to meet because you were going back to London tomorrow. Is that right? Diane is at WI tonight. I told her I would go ahead and have a chat with you and if you seemed quite normal, which you just about seem, she will join us, unless I call to say otherwise.' John half laughed, but it broke little ice.

Jack picked up his drink. 'Yeah, you bloody well make sure she does join us. I'd like to speak to her.'

John leaned across the table and pointed his finger. 'You speak to me like that my boy, and I'll get up and walk out, you hear me. I don't have to be here, nor does my wife. Your choice. You swear in front of her or are rude to her, and we're off.' John leaned back.

Jack nodded. He'd got the message. 'I'm sorry. You must understand this is all very crazy for me. I didn't for a second expect to hear from anyone about my dad and now you're sitting here talking about him. A bloke I never knew, never met. Someone I tried to ask mum about, but she wouldn't tell me. Why I don't know. I'm struggling to take it all in to be honest. I've had a shit few weeks, and now I'm here and you've turned up talking about things I never expected to find out. It's just, oh I don't know, just crazy.' The two men looked at each other and a moment of silence followed.

Diane arrived a few minutes later and, like her husband, looked good for her age. She was slim, attractive and Jack rose to his feet, smiling to greet her when she came into the pub. 'So, Jack Bianchi, I assume.' Diane was forthright, confident and had a nice smile. Jack took to her straightaway.

'Nice to meet you, Diane. Thanks for coming.'

Diane had a relaxing demeanour as her husband went to the bar to get drinks. 'So, you want me to tell you how I knew your mum?' She smiled at him. 'Gosh, it's a long time since I've seen you. You don't remember me, obviously. You were just a little lad in shorts.'

'Don't embarrass me Diane,' Jack smiled. 'I would say it's nice to see you again, but I don't remember the last time. So, tell me about mum and dad.'

John returned and Diane took a sip of her drink and began to tell Jack about his mum. How they had met, how friendly they became, the secrets Teresa told her. 'It's a long story, Jack. And a bit complicated.'

Teresa Bianchi had made friends with Diane within a couple of weeks of her moving to Kirkcudbright. Jack had gone to school with one of Diane and John's three children. Teresa had few friends, but Diane was one, and the two became very close. They used to spend a lot of time in each other's company and Teresa had told Diane about her fling with a Cecil Honeyman, when she lived in London. Cecil Honeyman was Jack's father; 'I will never forget a surname like Honeyman,' Diane smiled.

'He was recovering from the break-up of his own marriage,' continued Diane. 'Your mum was five years younger and single. She told me it was a fling, but then told me it was nearer five months they knew each other, which is hardly a fling. Cecil wanted them to marry.' Jack listened intently.

'But your mum didn't want that. I don't know why, Jack. Perhaps she just didn't know him enough for that degree of commitment. She wouldn't say. I always felt she loved your dad. She also told me it felt a hopeless situation for her. When she found out she was pregnant she told your dad by letter, then told him to stay away. Told him her parents had said stay away, although that wasn't strictly true. Time moved on and she had you. Your dad kept trying to make contact during the pregnancy, while your mum told her parents she didn't know who the father was. Your mum's parents, your grandparents, were a big issue. They were old fashioned and were furious with the situation. They wanted to know who the father was. Your mum wouldn't say, there were lots of rows. You were just a nipper, and one day there was some violence towards your mum. I think her dad went to hit her. So, she upped sticks and headed to Scotland. Why Scotland, I have no idea. Cecil didn't know for years where you'd gone. He wouldn't dare contact your mum's parents.'

Diane continued. 'It was an unhappy time for her. She was young and knew no-one up here. Her family wanted little to do with her. Having a child out of wedlock had been a big problem for her family. I don't think they spoke again after she left London. Yes, things got better, and you had a good life up here, but not before your mum did something she shouldn't have been proud of. And you need to know this, Jack.'

John looked sternly at his wife. 'Yes, he needs to know, John,' Diane said firmly. 'It's the full picture and he deserves to know.' Jack looked from John to Diane. 'What is it?'

Diane leaned forward and touched Jack's hand, looking into his eyes. 'I'm telling you the truth Jack, I'm telling you what your mum told me, and I'm telling you this because you should know and, as much as I loved your mum, what she did was cruel. I never said anything to anyone while she was alive as I didn't agree with what she did, and she had sworn me to tell no-one. Today, with her not here, you should know.' Jack looked worried. 'Go on.'

Diane took a deep breath. 'Well, your mum would never let your dad see you, even though he tried. Oh, he tried. But she simply wouldn't have it. Apparently, your dad was involved with some dubious characters in Ireland where he was stationed in the army. She almost told me the full story one night but backtracked. But she told me that when they returned to England, Cecil and some of his friends were storing cash, guns, and ammunition in exchange for big money. It sounded all wrong. These people sounded like they could be terrorists. Those were your mum's words. It sounded as though Cecil mixed with the wrong crowd and your mum became more determined he wouldn't see you. One day she let slip to me it was for your safety your dad never had anything to do with you. I never pushed her for more. But I know when he once again tried to see you, she threatened him.'

'Threatened him?' Jack repeated.

'Apparently, he had been in trouble with the police in Ireland,' said Diane. 'Nothing to do with the arms and ammunition, that was later. But while he was over there his first wife, who he had two children with, two girls, had an affair with another soldier, a friend of his in England, and your dad found out. He didn't take it well, as you can imagine. One night he'd gone out drinking in Ireland and got into a fight. A young lad was killed. Run over by a car after a group of men chased him into the road. Three men, including your dad, were accused of manslaughter for chasing the lad, but found not guilty. But it was a huge stain on your dad's character even though he was found not guilty. He left the army. On leaving, Cecil tried to contact your mum again, but she didn't want him anywhere near you. She'd heard the story of the lad getting killed.'

Jack was taking it all in. 'Your mum told me that when he did try to make contact once again, she told him she would call the police and tell them she wanted him to stay away because he had attacked her previously. She told him she would say she hadn't reported it, but she would stand by the accusation. It was a lie of course. It was wrong of her. He had never attacked her. But she knew they would investigate your dad's past, and present. Cecil knew this. He knew your mum could cause him a great deal of harm. So, apparently, he kept away. And that was the way it stayed.'

Jack puffed out his cheeks. 'That's crazy. I can't believe it. My dad was involved in guns, manslaughter trials. My mum wouldn't let him see me. Hell, what a background story.'

'I'm sorry Jack. But your mum was adamant he wasn't to see you. I tried to talk to her, but it was useless. She developed a very tough skin. If it's any consolation, your dad was desperate to find and see you. He didn't abandon you.'

Jack took a deep breath. 'That's all just incredible, I don't know what to say. There's a lot to take in.'

Diane took hold of both Jack's hands and lifted his chin up, staring into his eyes. 'Your mum adored you, Jack. You were the apple of her eye. You went without nothing. I'm sorry to have to tell you all this, but in some ways I'm glad you know. You should know. But you should also know your parents loved you. It was they who had the issues with each other, not with you. Your dad wasn't squeaky clean. And your mum was a very determined woman, half Italian if you didn't know, hence Bianchi.'

Diane smiled, but Jack was shaking his head. 'I don't know if I feel happier or more upset knowing all this,' he said. 'Why did mum treat dad so badly? It seems so cruel.' He shook his head again.

Jack looked at his watch. It was almost 11pm and the pub would be closing soon. He wanted to carry on talking but he knew time would run out. He still had so many questions. 'I go back to London tomorrow, Diane. But please can we stay in touch. I need to talk to you.'

She smiled. 'Of course. Anytime. Come on, drink up. We're the last three in here.'

Back in his hotel room, Jack was exhausted. He lay on his bed and got out his phone.

Fuck, a message he could have done without.

'Jack boy. Where are you? You know what today is. You're late again, well late. What are you trying to do to us? By the way. Have you met Marcin?'

FORTY TWO

IT was 6pm when Jack opened the door of his apartment.

It had been a long drive from Scotland with just the one stop on the M1 where he grabbed some over-expensive food and filled his car up with even more over-expensive fuel. He threw his keys on a chair and went to the fridge to grab a beer. He had thought endlessly about his mum and dad on the drive home. About the lies, deceit, the love, the confusion of it all. Looking at his phone, he'd had three messages since he left the motorway services. One from Angelo confirming he was back in the office tomorrow. One from Tony, talking a load of rubbish – drunk again. And another one from some healthcare scheme he knew nothing about. He went to reply to Angelo to tell him, yes, he was back in the office, when his phone rang.

He looked at the number – *'shit'*.

'Alright Piotr?' Jack tried to sound confident as he answered.

The voice on the other end sounded surprised. 'Well, well, Jack. You've answered. I can't believe it. You must have a guilty conscience. Got my message then.' Jack remained silent.

'So, you know what's happened. Your mate Tony has been a stupid boy. He hasn't paid his dues. And his dues are starting to spiral out of control; you are the man who guarantees he pays. Am I right? Yes, I'm right. On top of what you owe Marcin as well, I'm in no mood to compromise. Marcin is in no mood to compromise. You know Marcin? No, don't think you do. Anyhow, you're the one who told me Tony is a sound lad.

Well, he's not Jack. And you know it. And you aren't acting too smart either. I don't have time to play around. I want £15K by Wednesday. Or I will make sure the right people know about you. Marcin is well unhappy, I'll warn you, he's on the prowl. He's calling money in all over the place, Jack. You aren't alone.'

Jack didn't have that sort of money to hand. And he didn't need this conversation after the past few days. 'Give us a little while. I'll have the money. Don't push me Piotr, or…'

… 'Or what Jack? Shut the fuck up will you. You are sailing close now, far too close. Marcin and Tomasz called me an hour ago. I said I would get back to them. So, what's the answer? I'm warning you…'

'I'll get you the money as soon as.'

'Wrong answer.' The line went dead.

Jack hurled his phone across the room.

Katie's parents had come and gone by the time Mark phoned.

Katie had been told she could visit Shaun who was being held in a prison near Reading having been refused bail after his court hearing. But she couldn't bring herself to. It looked like he was going to plead guilty. Her world was in turmoil and her parents had been little help. Her dad spent much of the weekend saying nothing, while her mum flapped around like a headless chicken.

'So, how are you?' Mark's voice was the cheeriest one she had heard for a few days. Clearly, he didn't know, why should he? 'Looking forward to Friday?' Katie was supposed to be working with Mark in Shrewsbury. She took a breath and told him the shocking news about Shaun. Mark was as good a listener as he was a talker.

'No, Mark, you don't have to come over, I'm fine.'

'I don't care if you say you are. I'm coming over now. Bloody hell, Katie, this is horrendous.'

'I know. I know.' She began to cry. 'I've just had my parents over. I'm up to my eyes in it. I've been told I can go see him in prison, but I don't want to. I've had enough. I feel sick. I can't sleep, eat. I don't know what to do. I have no marriage. He's totally betrayed me, lied to me, deceived me. The shop, when do

I open that? How do I do stuff? What debt has he got? I could go on and on. I don't know what to do.'

'That's it. I'm coming over. I'm only in Oxford. I'll be there in 30 minutes.'

Katie cried as she hugged Mark tightly. It poured out as she told him of how it had all unfolded.

They sat on the sofa, and she let all her feelings out. Her desperation, her fear, her anger. 'No-one will ever know why, Katie,' Mark said. 'Some things are almost impossible to try and understand. Only Shaun will be able to tell you. And he will only be able to tell you when, or if, you want to see him again. You will want to talk to him. But I get now why you don't, take your time. I must admit, I'm totally stunned as well.'

'But I'm so scared,' Katie's hand was resting on Mark's. 'He did everything in this house, the finances and now I find out he – we – are in a financial mess. How badly, I haven't a clue. What do I do? I don't know where to start. And I'm married to a murderer Mark. A bloody murderer. I thought I knew him. What will people think? I can't stay here. Oh, what the hell is happening?'

'You can stay here, and people know this isn't about you. This is horrific for you, but no way is this your fault. Who knew what Shaun had been up to? Never blame yourself. I'll help you as much as I can. I'm here Katie.' He lifted her chin up. 'I will give you all the help you want. I promise.'

Katie looked at him, her eyes still full of tears. She leaned forward, kissing him on the cheek and hugged him tight.

'Please, help me, Mark.'

FORTY THREE

SUMMER felt over as the rain came lashing down out of dark skies.

Angelo and Fraser were in Angelo's office and had been since 7am. Jack headed to his own office where he arrived just after eight. He'd not taken an umbrella from home and needed to dry off after his short walk from the Tube had left him suitably wet. Olivia appeared at his door. It brightened his mood. Jack had spent many nights with her since that first encounter.

'Angelo wants to see you,' Olivia said. 'He's been looking for Carol, but I told him she wasn't in today, so he passed the message onto me. And he wants to see you now.' Jack smiled at her but kept the pleasantries simple. It had been a difficult week.

'Morning Jack, sit down,' Angelo said as Jack entered Angelo's office. He wasn't smiling. Fraser was sitting alongside.

'Morning', Fraser said. Jack didn't reply.

'What is this about?' Jack sounded as impatient as he felt. His head was still spinning. The last thing he needed was a rambling lecture from Angelo.

'Well, I was going to ask if you had a good few days off. But clearly not if that's your tone.' Angelo glared at him as Fraser pulled a sly grin.

'I've had a great time,' Jack said. 'Been nice getting away from some people.' He looked across at Fraser.

'Okay,' said Angelo. 'I'll get to the point. What's with you and the police, Jack?'

'What?' said Jack. 'What are you talking about?'

'Don't play games. I know the police have been sniffing about and as your boss I need to know what's going on. They came here a few weeks ago as I told you and they called again on Friday, so the business is now involved, don't fob me off.'

Jack looked at Angelo and then nodded at Fraser. 'What the fuck has this got to do with him?'

Fraser shuffled in his seat. 'He's here because I asked him to be here,' said Angelo. 'The police were here on Friday wanting to find you and Fraser was in. I wasn't. If you don't want Fraser here, I suppose I have to say that's your choice.'

'Get lost Fraser.' Jack stared at him. 'None of your business, this.' Fraser got up shaking his head, half smiling but without saying a word. He closed the door behind him.

'So, Jack, what's going on? No more bullshit.'

He'd been charged with nothing and as far as he was concerned done nothing. So, Jack told Angelo about being questioned over a murder that he had no idea about. Told him he'd heard nothing more from the police and expected nothing to come of it. They were likely here on Friday just to check up on him or even tell him there was nothing doing. He certainly had nothing to hide.

'Alright, so you keep me in the loop on this, you understand.' Angelo was far from impressed. 'And if anything changes, you make sure I know. And I'm watching your numbers okay. If your work starts to go downhill, I'll be on you like a ton of bricks.'

Jack started to get up, but Angelo told him to sit down. 'Sometimes Jack, as I've told you before, you sail close to the wind. Your time will come my boy. Don't think you can continue to be the guy you like to think you are. Just a warning.'

'Yeah, you're right Angelo.' Jack got back up. 'I've got to get on though. Oh, by the way, how's Dani?'

Angelo looked up at him. 'She's fine, fine. Wouldn't hurt you to settle down with a woman like her, get a grip of your life. You're not a kid anymore.'

Jack smiled. 'Thanks for the advice.'

Mark had spent the night on the sofa.

He had insisted on staying at Katie's, even though he had to be in London by lunchtime. He'd cooked up some breakfast and was sitting at the kitchen table when Katie came down the stairs. She looked exhausted. 'You, okay?' he said.

'What do you think? I've had to text school to say I won't be in again. I will need to have to tell people why, soon. How the hell am I going to do that? What am I going to say? *'My husband's on a murder charge, so I won't be in today.'* Hell Mark, how does that sound?'

Mark put his arm around her and gave her a hug. 'Look, I'll be about as much as I can. We'll sort things. But you are going to have to want me to help. I won't help if you don't want me to. Have you any other friends you can confide in?'

'I have Alice, she's a good friend. I have other friends, of course, but I can't face them yet.'

'You do know his name is going to get out there soon, don't you?' Mark said. 'I'm surprised it hasn't yet. As soon as someone is charged, the police will likely name them.'

'Oh, don't worry, it's already out there.' Katie took her phone out of her handbag. She went to the *Oxford Mail* website; it didn't take her long to find it. *'Man arrested over murder of woman.'* She held up her phone to Mark.

'A man has been arrested over the murder of a woman in Church Masham last week. Shaun Walters, 26, was arrested on Thursday night after the body of a woman was found at an address in the village. The police were quick to say while they are treating the death as murder, there is no danger to the general public, despite the obvious concerns a case like this causes.'

Mark read it and handed it back. 'We'll have to take it a day at a time, Katie. I'll come back this evening.'

Katie put her head in her hands and began to cry again. 'Why, Mark? Why? I thought I knew him. What lies has he been telling me? I just want to go, leave this house, and go. Just go away and not come back.' Mark continued to keep his arms around her.

'I know,' he said. 'I know.'

Toby Ruskin wasn't in the best of moods. He didn't like gossip and he didn't like gossip when it concerned a member of his family.

Olivia had seemingly been getting on well at the firm in London. Angelo had said she was doing well and, while he didn't speak to Olivia much, he worried little about how she was getting on. Angelo's word was enough. But things had changed. One of Toby Ruskin's golfing partners' sons had seen Olivia on a night out in London. Apparently not only was she the worse for drink, but looked as *'high as a kite'*, according to the man who had grassed her up to his dad. While he knew it wasn't his business, he wasn't going to let it pass. He would speak to her mum, and he would tell him what he'd heard about Olivia. She wouldn't like it, but Toby Ruskin had never done things in his life to be popular. A spade was a spade as far as he was concerned. And his daughter would have to listen to his concerns.

Olivia wouldn't get into drugs – of that, he was sure.

FORTY FOUR

SHAUN Walters was charged with the murder of Peggy Honeyman and appeared in court only answering his name after pleading guilty to the charge. It was all over in five minutes. He would be sentenced later.

Katie got the news from PC Keegan, who called the day before Shaun was set to go to court. She called again after the hearing. Katie didn't know what to say. Didn't know what to think. Keegan had asked her if she wanted to go and see Shaun, who was being held at Full Sutton prison, near York, a category A. It was a long drive from Oxford, but Keegan said she would arrange visiting.

Katie called up Mark. 'Of course, I will take you.' Katie had thought long and hard about whether she wanted to go, but she needed to look her husband in the eye – even if it was for one last time.

'I'll book a hotel; we can stay overnight. No need to drive there and back in a day.' Mark was forever the gentleman. She went along with it even though the thought of staying overnight didn't appeal.

The trip to Full Sutton took just over three hours. There was conversation on the way between the pair of them, but mostly small talk. Katie was getting butterflies as they neared the prison for her 2pm visit.

'Shall I see if I can come in with you,' Mark looked at her as they parked in the visitors' car park.

Katie smiled back. 'No, it's okay. PC Keegan only booked me in. But I appreciate all you are doing.'

As she got out of the car and headed to the entrance, Mark watched in his rear-view mirror. She looked so sad. He felt so sorry for her. He wanted to put his arms around her, make everything right. Katie arrived at the entrance, showed her ID, went through all the various security checks, and was led into a room with about 20 other people. There were eight prison guards, most of the visitors in the room were women. At 2pm they were led into a bigger room with tables and chairs. Katie's hands were sweating, and her heart was pounding. What if Shaun didn't turn up? He didn't have to see her. The first prisoner walked in, then a second, third, fourth, five, six, seven. Still no Shaun. Almost all the chairs were taken, and people were starting to chatter and then he walked in. Katie hardly recognised him. Shaun was led to the seat opposite Katie. He'd lost weight, clearly hadn't shaved for a while and he had a cut on his cheek. His eyes were bloodshot. He sat opposite her.

'Hello, Katie.' She stared at him, feeling herself welling up. 'Hi. You, okay?' she replied.

He half-smiled. 'Oh, I'm great, thanks. Just looking at about 35 years, I reckon. Life over, but hey, who cares? Sure, you don't.' She went to get up, but he put his hand out. 'Sorry, stay, I'm sorry, I didn't want to start the conversation like that.'

Katie sat down and looked him. She knew she had to be strong even though she was feeling anything but. 'Why did you do it Shaun? You've broken us, broke me. And I have no idea why.'

He shrugged. A look of resignation, a look of guilt. 'I can't even start to tell you why. I can't even tell you what I did. I'm Jekyll and Hyde, Katie. Can you not tell, now? You don't know me. We've been married, what four years. And you don't know me, you don't know me one jot. Isn't it obvious?'

'That's not true.'

'Oh, but it is. You have absolutely no idea. In your ideal little world, our life was idyllic. Perfect. We were happy. Yeah, we had issues, but nothing more than anyone else. I bet you used to tell our friends about how happy we were. All our plans, our future, kids, bigger house, holidays. They were all coming, weren't they Katie?' Her eyes began to well as Shaun leaned back in his chair and continued. 'And for the first couple of years, you were perhaps right. But you see, your world was never the one I was living in. I've been living so many lies. I've been telling you so many lies. I'm not the only one.' He looked down, before looking back up at her. 'I love you Katie and always will, but inside I have demons so terrible, you don't want to know. I have cost myself everything. Us, everything.'

Katie continued to stare at him, determined to hold back tears, but desperate to hear more, even though it hurt. She needed to know more. 'Please tell me Peggy was some sort of accident. You didn't mean to kill her.'

He took a deep breath. 'Peggy thought she could help, could help us, financially. She knew I had debts. We used to meet. You never knew. She gave me money. She trusted me, Katie. She took to me because she loved you and look what I did. Killed her. Drugged her and threw her down the stairs. I'm not going to lie about what I've done. I could try, but I can't go through with any more lies. I'm too tired of it all.' His eyes stared blankly. 'You have no idea. No idea at all what is going on in my head. What was going on with me and with Peggy. I'm a very sick person. Get over me, Katie. It's all too complicated. Peggy was complicated.'

'What do you mean Peggy was complicated?' Katie glared. 'How the hell is she anything but an innocent. Don't blame her for anything. And why was she giving you money? Hell, Shaun what have you been up to?'

He raised a slight smile. 'Peggy wasn't all you think she was. Peggy and Cecil were anything but an innocent couple. She told me how she had such large amounts of money. It wasn't all 'clean money'. Her and Cecil had been laundering money for Irish drug dealers, terrorists. Why she told me that I have no idea. But she did. Wanted to get it off her chest, I reckon and since Cecil died it all worried her.' He stared at her. 'Didn't you know? Of course, you didn't. Just like you didn't know how much debt I'm in. We're in.'

'Great. Debt we're in. I've heard enough,' Katie said. And went to get up, before Shaun stood up to stop her. 'No, sit down, please, Katie. Surely you want to know the truth, as hard as it is to take.' A guard moved towards them. Katie sat down.

'Everything alright?' the guard said as he came up to the table.

'It's fine,' Shaun said glaring at him. He turned back to speak to her. She sat in silence looking down at the table, then back up at him.

'I won't go into all the details on how they came into so much money, Katie. I don't know everything myself. But their money wasn't squeaky-clean. I have no reason to lie to you. Peggy told me plenty. And don't worry about debt, their house was always going to be half yours when she died, their savings half yours,' Shaun went to put his hand on hers, but she pulled her hand away. 'Did you know that? Peggy thought that much of you. That's a lot of money. It would have solved everything for us. It will solve much for you. I'd have been a different person, I'm sure I would. I know I would. All my worries, our worries, taken away; debts paid. I'd be the man you always loved once more. No more demons, no more thoughts. But I couldn't wait, I just couldn't wait.' He put his hands to his face and breathed in deeply.

Katie just stared. Her disgust evident. 'Killing a defenceless old lady to get her money. You lowlife. You would never have been a different person. I've heard enough. I'm done. I don't love you and I don't care what happens to you. But at least I now know. I've heard it from you. Rot in hell. You're sick.'

Shaun shook his head. 'You don't mean that.'

She stood up… 'Oh, I do, Shaun. You bet I do.' And with that she got up, turned, and walked out apace, as she heard him calling out… 'I love you, Katie.' She kept walking.

Outside, she took a few breathes and tried to regain her composure, before heading towards the car. She felt sick. Mark was looking at his phone, he looked up, surprised to see her so soon. 'You okay, you haven't been that long?' he said.

'No, let's go. Please, let's just go. I'll tell you about it later. I need a bit of time, Mark. Sorry.'

They got into the car. He looked at her, although she didn't make eye contact, looking ahead as she spoke. 'I don't want to stay anywhere tonight; can we just go home. I'll refund the cost of that hotel you booked.'

Mark leaned across and put his hand on hers. 'You don't have to refund me anything, don't be silly. Let's go get a coffee, have a bit of break before we drive home. Talk to me when you want.' She looked at him, nodded and sighed.

He kissed her head as she leaned on his shoulder.

Olivia had left the pub early.

It was 10pm when the taxi dropped her off. She made her way up the stairs to her flat in Clapham. It was a nice area, a bit chic, a bit lively. Plenty to do, plenty to see. She put the key in the lock and opened the door, flicking a light on and throwing her Gucci handbag on the bright orange chair she had bought in a retro shop in Chelsea. £300, but well worth it. Startling her, she saw the man leaning on the kitchen door in front of her. She let out a scream and turned to run to the front door, but she ran straight into the other man, who grabbed her tight.

'Olivia, now, now, calm down, shall we?' the first man said, walking towards her. Both men had ski masks on covering their faces. They were dressed in black and wore gloves. Olivia began shaking. She went to scream again, but the second man put his hands over her mouth. 'Quiet, Olivia. Quiet,' he said. 'Now listen, I'm going to release my hands, so don't scream.'

'What do you want? Leave me alone. A friend is coming up the stairs behind me. He'll be here soon,' she lied.

'Of course, he will,' the first man said. He laughed.

Olivia went to scream again, but the second man was too quick and grabbed her once more, before throwing her Gucci handbag on the floor and sitting her on the orange chair, wrapping a gag around her mouth, standing her up, flicking her around and tying her hands behind her back, before pushing her round again to look at her. The two men stood back. All Olivia could do was stare, wide-eyed, unable to speak, tears beginning to fill her eyes. She was petrified.

'Olivia,' the first man said. 'I've always been taught to keep the right company. It's a life skill. Weeding out the good eggs from the bad ones. Not always easy, many fail and mix with the wrong people. You are one of them.' His voice had a twang of eastern European in it. 'It's not your fault. You're a bit naïve perhaps, a bit young. Perhaps good in bed. I don't know about that bit, but I'll wager the first two are correct. Sex, drugs and rock and roll. Or just sex and drugs.' He looked at the second man, who nodded his head.

Olivia's head began to shake as she sat looking up at them. 'Sometimes,' the man continued. 'Sometimes you must learn, or the company you keep must learn, that you can't just do what you want in life. You can't have, what is it they say in this country… your cake and eat it. Do you understand?'

Olivia nodded. She didn't understand but would do as she was told. 'I'm sorry it's come to this,' the first man added. 'It really isn't your fault.' He bent down and got hold of her arms, lifting her up out of the chair. She began to shake her head again and tried to speak but the gag had silenced her. 'I say again, you keep the wrong company, Olivia.'

The second man moved towards her. He produced a small knife from his pocket and held it towards her cheek. With that he moved it down her body, looking back up at her. 'Keep still, Olivia, or my friend here will use that knife on you. I promise.' The first man continued staring at her, even though he'd taken a step back. Olivia had a black leather pleated short skirt on above the knee, with small, high-heeled boots, her tanned legs showing off. The second man had bent down and was lifting one of her feet, taking the first boot off. She went to kick out. It was foolish, the second man stood back up and slapped her around the face as she fell back down into the chair.

'Don't piss us about,' the first man said, his mood changing. And with that he moved forward and leaned over her and slapped her as well. Blood trickled from her lip. The tears were flowing as the second man pulled her second boot off, then stood her up. He was face to face with her, a few centimetres taller than she was. She could smell cigarettes.

'Don't move,' the second man said, speaking for the first time, a more pronounced eastern European accent, this time. 'Or my knife will cut you.'

He moved his hands down her hips and was touching her

knees. With that he put his hands up her skirt to her thighs. She shook her legs, but fear got the better of her and she froze. He got hold of her panties and in two pulls ripped them down to her ankles. With that he bent down to her ankles and slit the panties in half with his knife, pulling them off, looking at them and putting them in his pocket. He laughed. Standing back up he got hold of Olivia's blouse, a simple white one with five buttons. He untucked it from her skirt and ripped it open, revealing her delicate white bra. The man stared at her and snickered again, looking round at the other man. Olivia was swallowing hard and shaking her head. He got out his knife and moved it towards her bra, getting hold of the right-hand strap and in one motion, snicking it with the knife as the strap broke in two. He moved across and did the same to the other strap, standing back, before moving forward and pulling the straps and the bra cups down to reveal her breasts. He stood looking, holding the knife ever closer to her nipples, moving it around, teasing it around. The other man moved forward, pushing the second man aside. He stood in front of Olivia and began to unzip his trousers. Olivia began shaking even more. He undid his flies and began to unbuckle his belt, before stopping. He stared at her, then laughed, as he zipped his trousers back up, and got hold of her chin.

'Look at you Olivia. Look at you,' he said. 'What could we do with you now? So much fun, just the three of us. But we aren't here for that. This is a warning for you and the people you mix with. And one person, especially. He knows what he and his friends have done, what they owe, and he knows what we will do next time. Not us, we are gone tomorrow, for good. But there are others who will take our place. Next time it will be messier. A lot messier.'

He got out his phone. 'Look at me, smile for the camera.' He snickered as Olivia raised her head looking straight at him as he took photos. 'Now, you listen Olivia. You see, this is Jack Bianchi's fault. Not just him, but mostly him… You know him I've been told.' Her eyes widened. 'Yes, you see you fuck Jack Bianchi, he fucks us because his mates fuck him. All that adds up to us being here. We don't want a next time.'

He stepped back, but the second man walked up to her, took

off his glove and went to touch her breasts. He stopped just short, put his glove back on, smiled underneath his mask. 'I hope there is a next time,' he said. 'Or why not now?' He kissed Olivia on the cheek, his gloved hands on her waist.

'No,' the first man said, pulling him away. 'You know the rules.' The second man stopped, looked at the other man and nodded. They picked her up and moved her into the bedroom, where they tied one of her hands above her head onto a bed post.

'Don't try to move until we're long gone. You will be able to undo the tie. Do you understand?' She nodded. The first man bent down looking in her face, kissing her cheek before moving his hands back down her body, getting hold of her skirt slitting it with the knife and ripping it down to her ankles before throwing it aside, laughing as he did so. He got off the bed, both men looking at her nakedness.

They nodded and headed out of the apartment.

'He's a loser, Dani. And you know he is.'

Jack had just come out of the shower, as Dani walked past him to go in. 'Whether he is or not, he's still my husband.' Dani moved her finger across Jack's face as she walked past him, dropping her towel as she looked back at him, closing the en-suite shower door.

Jack smiled to himself as he heard her turn the shower on. A shower before bedtime was something he enjoyed. Clean themselves up and start again in the morning. What a day. Angelo pissing him off in the morning, Jack getting his own back on Angelo in the evening, without his boss even knowing. He smiled to himself. He went to the fridge and got out a bottle of Louis Roederer. He looked at it, flicked it round a few times. A gift from a customer. He couldn't remember who gave it to him, gifts were perks of his trade. But he did remember seeing a bottle like it in a shop in Fulham recently, £360. Why not? Dani deserved a nice glass of champers. His phone bleeped. A message, and photo attachment.

Jack's face dropped as he stared at the image and read the message... *'Smile for the camera. Time's up Jack'*

'Oh, shit,' he said to himself. *'No, no, no, no.'*

FORTY FIVE

JACK stood outside Olivia's apartment door.

He'd knocked twice, the second time as loud as he dare. It was gone midnight. 'Olivia, Olivia. It's me, Jack. Are you in there? I'm outside. I'm here. I promise it's me. Olivia, please let me in.' He banged the door again. 'Olivia. It's me, Jack.'

'Jack, is that you? Jack, help me.' Olivia's voice sounded scared.

'Yes, Olivia it's me. Now let me in. Let me in.'

The latch turned slowly, and Olivia opened the door slightly looking through the slit she had created. Jack stood there. She opened it up, he burst in. She fell into his arms, crying hysterically. Jack pulled her back and looked at her bloodied face. She had a dressing gown on, but she was shaking. She had managed to undo the tie on the bed post but had waited just in case the men were still there. It had taken 30 minutes before she'd dare move.

'Olivia. Shit, are you okay? What has happened?'

It took her another minute or more to calm down as through tears of hurt she told him what had taken place. He cuddled her tight and put his hands through her hair. He thought of the photo. He knew what this was all about. How could they? *The bastards.* This was spiralling out of control.

'Did they hurt you? You said they used a knife.'

'They didn't cut me, one of them hit me. Oh, Jack, they just humiliated me.'

He went and made her a drink. She was still shaking and confused. 'I was going to call my mum, but she's in France,' Olivia had stopped the tears, but looked desperate as she spoke. 'I was going to call the police. I don't know what to do. They spoke about you, Jack. The men who were here. They spoke about you. They mentioned you. You should have seen what they did to me.'

'I know, I know. I'm so sorry. This is my fault and I'm sorry.'

She pulled away from him. 'Why is this your fault? How do you know these people?' She stared again. 'What is this about?'

Jack pulled her close again. 'I don't know them as such. I don't know how they know you. If it's who I think it is, it's me they are trying to get at. I'm so sorry they were here. I don't know what else to say.'

'I thought they were going to rape me, Jack,' she said as tears flowed again. 'They took photographs. I must go to the police but what do I say? I don't know who these people are.' Jack pulled away from her, touching her lips… *'quiet now, quiet'*.

'Don't go to the police. It will cause you so much hassle. You won't find these people, Olivia.'

She looked at him, regaining a bit of composure. 'Won't find them? How do you know that? They're not getting away with this, Jack.' She looked at him again, moving forward. 'You do know these people, don't you? So, why are you hiding them?'

'I'm not hiding them, don't be stupid. I want nothing more than to see them caught. But these are dangerous people, and I don't know them. The thing is, they won't get caught. They are long gone. They have other people who will replace them. It's a sordid world. I'm so sorry you've been dragged into it.' He sat down on the chair and looked up at her, taking her hand. 'Olivia. I owe money. A lot of money. A lot of money to the wrong people. And they know you know me. So, they came after you to get to me. I had no idea this was going to happen. Of course, I had no idea, or I would have paid them. I can't stop you going to the police. But I'm just saying it will get you nowhere; and even make things more dangerous for both of us. And yes, I know that sounds selfish.'

Her mood darkened; her face contorted. She moved towards

him and struck her hand across his face. 'You owe money? For what? Let me guess. And because you owe money, I've been attacked here tonight. I'm calling the police.'

'No, Olivia, don't. Seriously, it will make things worse, not better. Trust me.'

'Trust you? Make things worse. Worse for who. For you? For me? How much worse can it get for me?' She was getting hysterical. 'You can fuck off Jack; I'm calling the police. I'm not having them get away with this. And you can tell them what it has to do with you. And if it drops you in it, tough. I'm done with you.'

She flailed her hands at him, screaming, throwing punches at any part of his body, before she gave in as he grabbed both her hands as they fell onto the sofa, and the tears flowed again. 'It was so horrible, Jack. I feel so sick.'

He held her tight. 'I know. I will find out who did this, I promise.'

He stroked her hair, but the anger was building inside him now. Towards Piotr and his pieces of filth, and to the man he knew had something to do with this – a man who gladly would have dropped Olivia in it to get at him. Jack knew if the police were involved, he would be involved. If he was involved, so would others get dragged in. He had to keep Olivia onside and convince her not to speak to them. It would be difficult. 'Please, do not tell the police.' Jack was almost pleading. 'I know this has been awful and I can't stop you going to them. But unless you know who these people are, which you don't, what can the police do?'

Olivia sat up looking at him. 'You're scared, aren't you? Scared I will tell the police, scared they'll come to speak to you. Scared of the people who did this will find you. I should never have trusted you. Never believed in you.'

He stood up, looked around and breathed out. 'Look, Olivia. I will pay what I owe and that will be the end of it, I promise you. They want my money, nothing else. They won't hurt you again. They won't come anywhere near you again. I promise. Please, Olivia.'

She looked up at him. 'Just go.' He got up and started to walk to the door. 'Don't go to the police. Please.'

'Don't tell me what I should or shouldn't do. Who do you think you are? You're the trouble here. I will drop you right in it if I must.'

'I'm sorry what's happened, but please don't threaten me, Olivia. There's a lot to lose – for both of us.'

'Really? Me, me, me, that's all you care about – Jack Bianchi. I thought we had something. What a fool I have been. Well, you just might lose whatever it is you have to lose… Every bit of it.' Jack felt anger rising and not towards Olivia.

He turned and slammed the apartment door behind him.

Mark was always late going to bed. So, it wasn't unusual for his phone to be on after midnight. He would flick through social media, lay down a few bets on sport. Yet he rarely got messages at this hour.

And the photograph shocked him. The picture of a girl with a gag round her bloodied mouth, topless and looking like she was crying, or had been. He didn't recognise her, but the message he understood.

'Pretty little thing, don't you think Mark, the boys flew over and had a play and enjoyed. It's what can happen to those close to you if you don't settle your scores… Oh, BTW, how is your little bookshop lady? Lonely, so we hear…'

FORTY SIX

HE knew exactly where he was heading, and Jack wasted little time.

He looked at his watch, 12.39am. He would still be up, or if he wasn't he was about to be awoken. He caught a taxi, the 20-minute drive across London didn't take long, the rain keeping plenty of people from venturing out at this late hour. His heart was racing, his head full of the images of Olivia. Her face, the story she had told him, her tears, her anger. There had been no need for them to do what they did. They'd been tipped off, and he knew by who. Jack was no saint, but he would never stoop so low. And he knew what he was about to do was going to be the end of so much. His life was going to take a turn right here, right now. There was still time to stop. But he was in no mood to weigh up the options. Her ordeal had changed everything. The rain had stopped by the time the taxi pulled up outside the apartment block. He threw a £50 note to the driver and jumped out. He knew the guy would be here; so predictable, no doubt flashing his money with the tart he tried to keep hidden from view. But everyone knew where he went. He was a shit liar. Jack took the lift to the third floor, there were five, and the views over the city improved the higher you went. He buzzed the apartment. Once, twice, three times, keeping his finger on the buzzer until eventually he heard his voice. 'Who the hell is it?'

Jack said nothing. He knew he would open the door, especially when he looked through the peephole to see him there. The door opened a fraction. 'Jack, what the hell are you...'

But before he could get out any more words, Jack was in. He kicked the door open and flung himself full on him, catching him off guard as the pair thudded to the floor. The girl shot out of the bedroom, Jack shouting at her to 'get out, get out now'. She picked up her handbag and fled, pulling her high heels on as she left. Punch, punch, punch. Jack was letting it all out, pummelling the man's face. He didn't stop. He felt bone crack, as blood splattered on his knuckles. The adrenaline in his body was full on. He was holding nothing back. Pent up fury, disgust and sheer violence flowing through him. He stopped only to lift the man's face up and stare into his bloodied eyes. Punch, punch, punch. More, more, more, he couldn't stop himself. He was out of control. He stood up over him, and stood back, breathing heavily, before laying two fierce kicks into his testicles. The man groaned out loud. Jack looked behind him to see the door still open. He walked back and pushed it closed, before coming back again, leaning over the man, and punching him one more time. And then there was nothing. Just silence, the sound of Jack's heavy breathing. He looked down at him, wiping the spit from his mouth. He leaned beside him and turned his bloody face to face his own. He hardly recognised him such was the damage inflicted, and he didn't know if he could hear him. He didn't care. It had taken no more than two minutes. The most ferocious minutes of Jack's life.

'You bastard. You bastard,' he said as he stared at him. 'Olivia's just a kid and you set her up. It wasn't her fight, it was mine, it was yours, it was everyone's except hers. We're the ones who owe money, not her.'

He sat over him, disgust welling again. The man continued to moan, trying to shake his head. Jack dragged himself up and stared at him. He put his mouth to the man's bloodied ear. 'I fucking hate you Angelo. Inside, I always have done. I'm smiling at the state of you now.'

Angelo spat out a defiant line of blood and spit in Jack's direction. But it was a weak effort, Angelo's face was bloodied, Jack had knocked two front teeth out, his nose was broken. Jack thought about hitting him again but decided against it. 'Don't worry. I'll fire myself, you motherfucker Angelo. And don't think of bringing the cops into this because I know you set Olivia up. You've grassed her up to save yourself. You should have told them where I lived, not her. I would have dealt with them. You've crossed a line tonight, Angelo. You have no idea what they did to her. You shit.'

Angelo coughed up blood as he turned his bloodied head towards Jack and spat out…. 'Fuck you, Jack.'

Jack smirked and looked down at him, kicked him one more time, then headed for the door.

FORTY SEVEN

THE next morning Jack headed into the office and took all his personal possessions. He had to move on.

Fraser clocked him and came to see what was going on. Jack told him he'd had enough and was leaving. Might do a bit of travelling. He knew it would make the big man smile, getting Jack out of his hair. But Jack wasn't in the mood for conversation or scoring points off Fraser. He couldn't stay at the firm and, so long as Angelo kept quiet, which he would if he had half an ounce of sense, Jack was a free man. Angelo was in hospital. A security guard at the apartment complex had answered Angelo's late-night call and called an ambulance. Battered and bruised, Angelo was never getting the police involved. So many questions would need answering and Angelo's position in the business would be cut to shreds.

'He's in a terrible state, Jack. He could have been killed. They could have had a knife, anything.' Jack was sitting in a pub in the West End enjoying an orange juice and Mac and Cheese. He always took Dani's calls. 'He's no angel, but he doesn't deserve this. Jack, are you still there? And where did you shoot off to last night by the way? I had to let myself out.'

'Yeah, I'm here. It sounds terrible, poor Angelo. How bad is it? What did he say happened?'

'Well, that's just it, he can hardly speak. All I got out of him is that someone attacked him after knocking on an apartment door where he was seeing a client. Says the client fled, mistaken identity Angelo reckons. He's a right mess Jack. Broken nose, broken ribs, black eyes, three teeth knocked out. Something isn't right. Can you go and speak to him. He'll speak to you.'

'He won't speak to me. Anyhow, I'm leaving the business, Dani. Likely leaving London as well. I'm out of here. Going for good. I've cleared my desk.'

It caught her by surprise. 'When? Why are you leaving?'

Jack took a sip of his juice. 'I need a change. I need to get out of here and spread my wings. I've had enough of all this. Fucked up people, drink, drugs, work, repeat, repeat. I need something different. Perhaps I'm getting old, Dani. Need to grow up.'

'That will be the day. Does Angelo know you're going?'

'I'll let him know, don't worry. But I won't disturb him for a few days. Let him recover.'

Dani had stopped walking as she was talking, but she continued to walk once more. 'Well, I suppose that's us over with, is it? After all our ups and downs. Can I come with you?'

'Well, unless you want to wander around the globe with me, getting pissed, ducking and diving for cash and sleeping on beaches, I guess it is.'

'Doesn't sound that bad. I've slept in rougher places.'

He smiled to himself. 'Look Dani, we've had fun, but you get Angelo back to full fitness. You two were starting to piece it together. You have the oddest marriage in the world, but it works. Doll, I'd take you in a heartbeat if I thought the lifestyle I'm gunning for would be the one you would crave. But you'd get bored. And anyhow, you deserve someone better than me.'

She stopped walking again and looked around. 'I love you, Jack.' She felt her eyes welling up. 'I always have. You know that. You say you'd take me in a heartbeat, but you don't mean it. You won't settle down. Not with me, likely not with anyone. You go, have fun.'

He nodded. 'Ah, we'll see. Maybe I'll change my mind, not leave London, and end up walking over Tower Bridge another thousand times, still being that old City trader into my 50s. You're going to say we could meet up again for one last hurrah. But I'd like to leave it the way we ended last night. Prosecco all over you, me running off to goodness knows where and leaving you alone, just a standard, confused, night of Dani and Jack.' He smiled down the phone.

She smiled to. 'Behave Jack. No, I wasn't going to say meet up one more time. Don't flatter yourself. I'm a stronger woman now than when we first me. I've had to be. I don't do drama as much. And I don't stroke egos. Especially men with ones as big as yours. We've had loads of fun. It was always going to end sometime. If it is to be, now is as good a time as any, I suppose.'

Jack smiled again. 'Ah, Dani, Dani, Dani. What could have been, hey? Do me a favour and look after the old man. He's going to need you.'

'I will, Jack. See you around.'... She hung up.

Back in his apartment, Jack looked at all his worldly goods. Not much to show for a young life that had paid well. At least the fridge was full of beer and wine!

So, where to now? He picked up the post and noticed a letter that looked formal. He opened it and was surprised by the contents; the name of the woman took him aback.

He checked his calendar. He'd stay in London for a couple more weeks at least.

FORTY EIGHT

THE solicitor's office was modern and bright, and Katie made herself known to the receptionist, who had just finished filing her nails as Katie approached.

It was a beautiful sunny morning, a week after Peggy's funeral which, in contrast, had been a dull and wet afternoon. There had been more in attendance that Katie thought, with many from Church Masham turning out. Not that Jenny nor Judy bothered to come. The bookshop was on the market to be sold. Mark had contacted people he knew to help with the sale, as well as looking into the debts Shaun had accrued. It appeared that if the book shop sale went through, it would eat into the debt. But Mark had warned Katie there would likely still be more money needed.

'Good morning, Mrs Walters, please come through.' Jonathan White was a partner in White & Marshall Solicitors, in Banbury. He was a tall, thin man, with a strong handshake and a serious demeanour. The letter from the solicitors advising her of attending Peggy Honeyman's Will reading had arrived two weeks ago. She had kept the news to herself and pencilled in the date.

'So, Mrs Walters, did you bring your passport or driving licence?' Mr White smiled.

'Both.'

'Excellent, well give me your passport here so I can take a copy. Have you been to a Will reading before?'

Katie shook her head. 'No, never.'

Mr White was all smiles as he returned from the photocopier. 'Well, we'll be ready to go. Just waiting for one other person.'

Katie looked around at the splendour of the office. Like the reception area, it was modern, with a large television mounted on the wall and classy decorations on white shelves. There was a large green plant on a stand next to a huge portrait window that overlooked the town's square. The two continued to make small talk, before there was a knock on the door. 'Ah, come in, you must be Jack.' Mr White got up from his desk and took hold of Jack's hand.

Jack smiled. 'Yeah, that's right.'

'Well, let me introduce you to Mrs Walters, Katie Walters.'

Katie went to stand, but Jack put his hand up. 'Don't get up, nice to meet you. I'm Jack Bianchi.' She shook his hand, a firm shake. The pair smiled at each other, as Jack sat beside her. Mr White asked for Jack's passport and took a copy.

'Right, Katie and Jack.' Mr White spoke as he sat down, passing Jack his passport. 'Do you know each other?' They both shook their heads.

'Okay, well, all friends now.' He had a small chuckle to himself. 'I don't know if you've been to a Will reading before. Katie said she hadn't. What about you Jack?'

'Ah, no. I really have no idea why I'm here at all to be quite honest,' he said. 'I got the letter and, well, here I am.' He smiled again at Katie. She smiled back – *she liked his smile.*

'Okay,' said Mr White. 'So, we don't usually do things this way, not in the 21st century – read Wills – bit old fashioned to be honest, but, in the circumstances, we felt it best if we could meet with you both as we, as a law firm, are the executors of Mrs Peggy Honeyman's Will. And we want to read it out to you. The pair of you being the main recipients.'

Jack looked surprised, Katie less so. 'The main recipients? Can I ask something?' Jack said.

'Of course, you can,' Mr White replied.

'I know this sounds crazy. But I don't think I've ever met Peggy Honeyman, certainly not to my knowledge. I have heard of her. I don't really want to say why I've heard of her. If it is her this Will is about. Does that make sense? Are you sure I'm in the right place?' Katie looked at him quizzically. *He dressed cool.*

'Trust me, you are in the right place Mr Bianchi. Your passport confirms what we know and what Peggy wanted in her Will. The letter you received was sent after due diligence was done to confirm it was you who was the intended recipient. Does that make you feel at ease?'

'Well, sort of, I suppose.'

'Perhaps when I read the Will, more will make sense, Jack.' He smiled at him.

Mr White opened the envelope and began to read, getting to the saliant points after a long intro… *'I wish for my estate and all my savings to be left equally to Mrs Katie Walters, a loving friend who has been like a daughter to me over the years, and Mr Jack Bianchi – my late, dear husband Cecil's son. A son he never got to meet, but who he cared for deeply and always loved. If Cecil could have changed one thing in his life, I know it would have been to have a relationship with his only son.'*

Katie looked at Jack, but he was emotionless.

'The 50/50 split is after £2,000 has been left to the RSPB, £2,000 to the Village Hall at Church Masham and £1,500 to the local primary school at Church Masham.'

Mr White continued to read more formalities as Jack and Katie sat in silence. At the end he looked at them both. 'Any questions?'

More silence, before Jack said; 'I've never met my dad. This is very strange for me.'

Mr White looked perplexed. 'Well, that's what the Will implies, I think. But Cecil was indeed your dad, Jack. Peggy has told us and there is all the paperwork here. She has been into this office on many occasions in the past. We knew her well. We knew Cecil well; he's your father.'

Jack shook his head. 'I've been told that. It's all rather complicated, sorry. This is a lot to take in.'

Katie looked at Jack, then back at Mr White. 'Well, I sort of understand it all,' she said. 'I assume you will look after much of what happens next?'

'Yes, Katie, we will.'

'I don't suppose we know how much money we are looking

at here, do we?' said Jack. Katie flicked a look at him. Clearly, he'd regained his composure.

Mr White smiled. 'Well, I have no idea how much Mrs Honeyman's house is worth, I'm not an estate agent.' He laughed at his own joke. 'But I can tell you how much she currently has in four savings accounts that we have in our keeping. They will become yours.'

Jack and Katie looked at each other, as Mr White began reading from a sheet of paper. 'In one, Mrs Honeyman had £4,456, in another she had £6,023, in another she had £45,090. And in her final one, which appears to be based in Ireland, approximately £480,000.'

Katie and Jack turned their heads to each other, neither saying a word.

Mr White continued. 'Of course, we must take out the money Mrs Honeyman gifted to her three causes. As well as our fees and any sundries. There may be inheritance tax. We can discuss all that at a later point if you wish to appoint us to help with your affairs. He looked at them both. 'And all that money is without the sale of the house,' Katie said quietly.

'Yes. As you heard the house has been left to you both equally. What you do with it is up to you. I shouldn't say this. Bit unprofessional, but quite a nice gift.'

A few signatures later Katie and Jack were sitting on a bench outside the solicitor's office, both stunned by what they had just heard. 'Well,' said Jack. 'That's a bonus. I don't know what to say. It's all rather unbelievable. That's like £250K each or something and we still haven't sold the house. It's like winning the lottery.'

She smiled back at him. 'I know. It's ridiculous, isn't it?'

He turned to face her. 'Don't suppose you fancy getting rat-arsed and partying all night, do you? Only kidding. Not all night. Just till say 4am. I still can't believe what I've just heard.'

Katie smiled. *She had a lovely smile.* 'Me neither. I'm a bit overcome to be honest. Could do with a coffee, though. Not really into partying in the middle of the afternoon, I'm afraid.' They both laughed. They got up and walked over to a coffee shop in the square. Jack ordered, latte for her, flat white for himself. He put the drinks down on the table.

'Did you know Peggy Honeyman? I have heard of her if that makes sense, which it probably doesn't. I think it best I tell you how and why. We could be here all night.'

Katie looked at him. 'Yes, I knew her well. It seems we both have stories to tell.' She took a sip of her coffee and breathed out. 'Okay, I'll go first, but it isn't an especially nice tale, even though Peggy was a lovely lady. I guess you don't know... Peggy was murdered.'

Jack looked shocked. 'Murdered. Oh, shit. A few things are starting to make sense now.'

Katie looked at him. 'Really? Well, Jack, make sense of this. She was murdered by my husband... soon to be my ex-husband.'

Olivia sat with her mum, who had flown back to London as soon as she called her, pouring out the story of her ordeal.

The tears flowed as she relayed what had happened. Her mum wanted to her to go, firstly to the hospital for a check over, and then the police. Olivia wanted none of it. 'You cannot let people do this to you and you do nothing,' her mum Jasmine said, her anger welling up inside at the horrors her daughter had gone through. 'Someone is responsible. You can't just say, 'they've long gone'. What does that mean? They haven't vanished, Olivia.'

'Mum. Please. I can't do anything about it. It's happened. They didn't physically hurt me. I just needed to tell you. I need you to hug me. I need you to help me through. I'll be fine in time, going to the police will just prolong it, drag more and more people into it. I can't do it.'

But her mum wasn't having it.

Mark looked at the text.

He couldn't believe it, but he knew it was likely true. The man was 100% legit. He'd worked with him before. He shook his head and prayed the man was wrong for once. He made a call.

Explaining this was not going to be easy.

FORTY NINE

IT was an old and dirty industrial unit in east London; Mark had been there before.

The rain was coming down hard as he pulled up outside Unit 65. There was no-one else about, or if they were, they were working indoors. Piotr didn't like people about. As he got out of his car and headed in, Mark felt his coat pocket once more. The envelope was there. When he got closer, the large door cranked open and two of Piotr's thugs nodded him in. There were four large circular lights on the ceiling, but little else inside, apart from a few chairs and a long table that Piotr was sitting at, with another man.

'Come in Mark. Take a seat.' Piotr waved him over, as the two who had guided him in walked alongside. Three more men appeared, one holding a gun. 'So, how are you?' Piotr smiled. 'This is Marcin,' he said pointing to the man alongside him. 'You don't know Marcin, do you?'

Mark wasn't amused. 'Cut the shit, Piotr and let's get down to business.'

Piotr laughed. 'Ah, listen to him boys. Cut the shit, he says. Oh, how I love a tough guy trying to call the tune. He owes me and my friend Marcin here money and yet he wants to get down to business. Whose business, Mark? My business, Mark. The fucking business you and your stupid friend have pissed right up.' Piotr's mood turned dark. Mark said nothing. He needed to be careful.

'So, Mark. Where shall we start? Money was due from you for the cocaine, and Shaun for the loan, four months ago and my bosses have been more than patient. Don't worry, you are not the only one. But now we are calling all our debts in. And there are a lot of them. England is not seemingly such a trustworthy place anymore. 40K is not a fortune in our world, Mark. But lots of £40Ks is starting to become – let's say – irritating. Understand me?'

Mark said nothing. He just stared at Piotr, as Marcin sat motionless. 'In your case, £42K, I believe. The interest seems to build up so quickly.'

Still Mark said nothing. He sealed this fate five years ago in South Africa with the woman who almost became his wife. The drugs had been rife, the pair of them and their friends lived a life they couldn't afford. Then again, never did he think the network who supplied him had links back to London. He thought he'd escaped. How wrong he'd been. Mark threw the envelope on the table. Piotr picked it up, opened it and began counting. The notes were all in 50s and it took him a few minutes to count it all out. £42K, on the nail. Piotr looked up and smiled.

'Nice, Mark. Very nice.' He smiled, as he nodded. 'So, tell me, how is Katie, the wife of that idiot who killed our Mrs Honeyman and has messed us right up. Why did he do that?' Piotr looked at Marcin. 'Peggy still has our money. We hope it is safe. We assume it is. Perhaps we should pay a trip to this Katie girl and see if she knows anything.'

Mark went to move forward, but two of the men jumped at him, holding him back. 'You leave her alone. She has nothing to do with this. You blame Shaun, you blame me. But you touch her and....'

'... And you'll what, Mark?' Piotr smiled. 'You'll what?'

'I will kill you, Piotr. I promise. I will kill you.'

Piotr stood up laughing loudly. 'Look at him boys. What a hard man our Mark is. Clearly, in love, perhaps?'

The men joined in the laughter, the one with the gun coming forward and pressing it into Mark's chest, grinning and threatening. Piotr jumped over the table and went face to face with Mark, as two men held his arms. Marcin lit up a cigarette but remained seated.

'Don't threaten me my friend,' Piotr said. 'You got yourself into this. If you can't play with the big boys, then you shouldn't have taken a seat at the table. You and your pal Shaun have taken a seat. We own you, because you owe us – and even after this money today, you still owe us – remember that. We will take back what is ours and we will get what is ours.'

'Piss off.' Mark spat in Piotr's face, as Piotr returned with a punch to Mark's jaw, sending him to the floor. He stood over him. 'Listen to me and listen good, Mark. Your friend has made a bad move. You should have known what he was set to do. You should have stopped him. We trusted you. And now look what has happened. Money, we invested with the old couple has been blown apart. Our money, Mark. You know as well as anyone, Peggy's old man had been laundering our money as good as a prostitute takes dicks. Cecil had it all sorted. For years it's been fine. I knew when he died this thing could go tits up. We should have done something about it then. Too late now isn't it, Mark? You said you and Shaun would keep an eye. And now she's gone. What the hell was Shaun playing at? Why? Well, I'll tell you something. You will get us our money. That money is ours. How you get it, is up to you, but you will. Shaun has done us over, but we'll sort him from the inside. You on the other hand had better find out what's happened. Where it is and who's got it, and how you're getting hold of it. And quick.'

They released Mark's arms. He stood staring at Piotr. 'I'll find out what's happened. Even if I have to speak to Shaun.' Piotr looked at him. 'You're right you will.'

They'd been on the phone for almost an hour. It was the third time that week. 'Look at the time. I'm supposed to be meeting my friend at eight. It's nearly 7.30. I must go.'

'Don't leave me hanging after, what, 50 minutes.'

She laughed. '50 minutes is a long time chatting. But it has been nice.'

'Let's go for a drink on Friday. I'll come and pick you up. Drop me your postcode and a time.'

Katie smiled to herself. 'I do live near Oxford you know.

It's not like just round the corner from you, Jack. You okay with that?'

'I'll be there, I promise.'

FIFTY

JACK picked Katie up at 8pm. It had been a two-hour drive from London.

He thought she looked stunning in her short green polka dot dress; he kissed her on the cheek as he entered the house. He looked around; simple, tidy surroundings. Katie offered him a drink, but Jack said no, so she ushered them both out of the door, laughing as he tripped on the step.

'So, where shall we go?' Jack said. 'You better guide me, I'm not familiar with the Cotswolds and I've been driving for hours, so don't tell me you like Wales, because I am not driving all that way.' He looked at her and smiled.

Katie smiled back. 'I know a pub about a couple of miles from here, go left at the junction at the top of the road.'

Jack had been away from the office for three days and was enjoying the freedom and the lack of stress. He looked at her as they headed through the country lanes. He felt so relaxed. He was never going back to work with Angelo and that creep Fraser. Katie hadn't gone back to the school for almost a month and had called the headmaster that day with the news she wasn't returning. Their chilled moods aided conversation.

'I know we shouldn't talk money, because I like to think we might have more in common than just Peggy's inheritance.' Jack looked across at her as they drove through fields of golden wheat, the sun beginning to set. 'Well, don't then,' Katie said.

'Ah, but I was just wondering what's the first thing you will treat yourself to. Something special, something nice.'

Katie thought for a moment. 'I'm not telling you even if I knew, which I don't.' She smiled. 'I've never had much money and I'm not the sort of person who would know what to do with a lot of it. And anyhow, in one breath you say I know we shouldn't talk money, then you talk about money. Let's forget it. There's more to life than money.' He turned the music up and smiled at her. 'You're right. I like your vibe. Very chilled.'

'That's me!', she smiled…

The pub was half full, and had a comfortable ambience that made for a pleasant meal, Jack had the steak, no dessert, while Katie had salmon and the homemade cheesecake.

'You don't drink much.' Jack was looking at Katie's wine glass which was still a third full. They'd been sitting there an hour.

'I'm not a big drinker. Can't handle my drink to be honest, get a bit giggly.' She smiled.

'And you? Do you like a drink?'

'Well. Obviously driving tonight, so no can do. But yeah, I like the odd drink, in moderation.' He nodded as he spoke, hoping Katie couldn't tell he was lying.

'I'm sure you only like the odd one,' she flicked her eyebrows. 'Working in London, I can imagine you only go out what, once a fortnight? And didn't you say we should get, what was it? Rat-arsed, when we spoke outside the solicitors' office.'

He laughed. 'Now, in fairness, I didn't say we should get rat-arsed outside the solicitors' office. I said, shall we get rat-arsed? Where, I didn't say. We just happened to be outside the solicitors' office at the time.' She shook her head and smiled back.

'Okay, cards on the table. Yes, Katie. I like a drink and a good time, I'll be honest. But then again, I've been doing it for so long now, I'm starting to get a bit fatigued with it. Perhaps I'm getting old. I can't be, I'm only 25. But London makes you feel about 10 years older, it can be full on.'

'I imagine it can. Not that London would appeal to me. I prefer the countryside, quieter, less stress. Bit boring really.'

'I bet you're not boring. I reckon you can be great fun. In fact, I bet you're one of those quiet types who goes bonkers on a night out. The one who drinks the least but dances the most.'

She flicked him a smile. 'Maybe. And maybe one day you might find out.'

They stayed until last orders were called, Katie having another glass of wine, while Jack continued with his non-alcoholic lager. The conversation remained easy; the chemistry pleasant.

'So, where are you staying tonight?' Katie said, as they drove back through the Cotswolds lanes.

'I'll go back to London. I'll get back quicker than I got here, traffic will be lighter. Took me 30 minutes just to get out of the West End this evening.'

'You can stay at mine if you like. I've got space. Seems daft you are driving all that way home. It's nearly midnight now.'

He looked across at here. 'You sure? I don't mind if you don't want me to. I won't be offended. It takes a lot to offend me.' He winked as he turned to her.

'I wouldn't have offered.'

They stood in the kitchen, both with cups of hot chocolates in hand chatting away. It was almost 2am.

'I'll be honest, I haven't felt this relaxed for a long time,' Katie said. 'It's been difficult. So much has happened. Worries, more worries, money worries, my bloody idiot of a husband.'

'Well, you don't have money worries anymore,' Jack said. 'And you can forget your husband, he won't be coming home anytime soon. I hope you don't mind me saying that.'

She shook her head. 'I know he won't. I feel totally cold to him. It's as though I don't know him. Never knew him. He's not the man I married. No way. I don't know what happened to him, but I hate him. I don't want to ever see him again. It's only been a few months, but it's all changed. I'm in another world. Can you understand that?'

Jack put his arm around her. 'I can. Don't worry. My world has been topsy-turvy recently. The police questioning me. It's all been so weird, and for both of us. Now here we both are, a couple of rich kids.'

'Yes, but for me the problem is Shaun had plenty of debt. I won't get all the money from Peggy. Well, I will, but loads must be paid off, I reckon.'

'Paid off to who?' Jack said.

'I don't know. Apparently, he owed people money, debt collectors. I've got a friend working on it. He's a good bloke, he'll sort it for me. I was going to ask him to arrange the house sale as well. He doesn't know I've come into all this money. I'll tell him. You mind if he does get involved with the sale of Peggy's house? You said you wanted to sell it. He'll sort it all and I trust him 100%.'

Jack shrugged his shoulders. 'Yep, as I told you, sell it. So long as we get our money. So long as you can trust him, as you say. And, if you need a hand, I can help. I've got a few debts myself to pay off, but nowhere near the sums that Peggy's money won't clear. It feels like a new life to be honest. A new start. And it will be for you as well, I'm sure it will.'

Katie put her cup in the dishwasher. He followed her, took her arm, and gently moved her towards him. She looked into his eyes. They were so very blue. She put her hands in his wavy black hair and played with the locks. 'I don't think. In fact, I know, in all the years I've been on this earth, which is not many I'll admit, I don't think I've felt so happy to be with someone, as I feel right now with you, Jack. It's a strange but nice feeling.' He smiled, not wishing to give away he felt the same. 'Sorry, if that comes over all wrong,' she added.

Jack took hold of her face and stared at her. 'It doesn't come over wrong because I don't know what it is, but something is making me feel the same. And I really am not someone who does emotions. Perhaps my life has been so complicated, I've tried to be hard about things. But now, I feel… I feel almost helpless. It's odd, but I'm loving it, yet it's very strange for me. I don't give this much away normally.'

They were close now as their heads moved forward to meet each other's lips. They kissed, gently at first and then more passionately. He put his hand on her waist and moved his arms up and down her side, before moving up to her neck and caressing her gently around the back of her head, toying with her hair. She moved her hands up and down his back, digging gently into him. She pulled back. She found him so attractive, the light stubble growth on his tanned face. Those eyes. She'd thought from the first day she'd met him how handsome he was.

'I want to stop, but I don't want to stop. Does that make sense?' she said.

'I just don't want to stop,' he said jokingly. 'Does that make sense?' He smiled. She smiled back.

'If you want to stop, we stop, right here,' Jack said. 'I'll make up the sofa, chuck a couple of coats down, wash up the cups of chocolate, turn the lights out, put the cat out, if you have a cat, and see you for breakfast in the morning.'

She laughed. He made her feel so at ease. She kissed him again on the lips, then pulled back, looking at him once more. She took his hand and flicked him a smile. 'I don't have a cat and you can leave those cups till the morning.

'But yes, if you're okay with it, I'll see you for breakfast.'

FIFTY ONE

'OH, hell Alice, I should have slept with him.'

Katie was on the phone to her friend. It was Saturday lunchtime and Jack had just left having enjoyed eggs benedict, orange juice and more conversation. 'I really should have done. It took all my willpower. I find it hard to be impulsive.'

Alice laughed out loud. 'Took all your willpower. Oooh, you brave girl, you. Jump into bed with him if he's that hot. What harm would it have done? You could do with a bloody good shag after all you've been through!'

'Alice, you are a cow. I should have expected that from you.'

'Besties always tell it as it is. You're too much of a prude for your own good sometimes. Seriously though, darling. If you like him that much, don't hold back. You can't be celibate forever. A woman has needs. Be honest. I can hear it in your voice, you would have straddled him quite happily.'

'Alice. Don't be so rude. Celibate forever, bloody hell, I'm still married! You haven't even met Jack. But yes, I could have shagged him.' They both laughed.

Alice changed the subject. 'Hope you don't mind me asking, but what's happening with all this money you've come into?' Alice was one of the few people Katie had confided in.

'I'm leaving it with the solicitors for now,' Katie replied. 'They will tell me how much I'm going to get and will sort it out. It won't be for a few months, and we, well I, have some debts. I'm going to ask Mark to help with the sale of the house. Jack seems cool about that, so long as he gets half of it. Jack does make me laugh. I asked if he wanted anything out of Peggy's house, like a TV or any stuff. Do you know what he said?'

'Shock me,' said Alice. I can't imagine.'

'He asked me if Peggy had a hot tub or any blow-up dolls. I told him she was 70 not 17.'

'You really like him, don't you, babe? He sounds fun.'

'He is. We've talked on the phone for hours. Last night we went out to a pub. We just get on, everything feels easy. I don't know though, is it just me having a reaction to what's happened? Wanting to find something different, someone different, and quick? Am I grabbing at the first good thing that seems to have come along?'

'Crikey, listen to yourself, Katie. I've said shag him, not marry him and have five kids. You do make me laugh, you're so dramatic. But you do have one big thing in common.'

'What?' said Katie.

'You're both bloody rich.'

The girls laughed out loud. So loud in fact, Katie didn't hear the doorbell go. It wasn't until she'd stopped laughing, she heard it. 'Someone's at the door. Got to go darling, speak soon.'

'Call me soon darling. And send me a photo of Mr Hunk.'

'Will do, love you.'

'Love you to.'

Katie put the phone down and opened the front door. 'Mark. How are you? Wasn't expecting you.'

'Hello, my gorgeous girl, how are you? Good to see you smiling and looking good.'

Mark was, as usual, suited and booted, even on a Saturday lunchtime, although he'd given up on the tie for a day. He kissed her on the cheek. 'Can I come in?'

Katie stepped aside. 'Of course, you can. Cup of tea? Two sugars?'

'You know me well.'

The pair sat down in the living room. The sun was streaming through the front window, Mark's car was parked outside.

'I'm glad you've come,' said Katie. 'I was going to call you. I need to ask you something.' She looked into his eyes and took a deep breath. 'You know you're sorting out my debts. I've never actually asked, which seems crazy, but are they bad?'

Mark shrugged. 'Not great, but I'll get it sorted. We may have to think about selling your house I'm sorry to say, and any finance we can generate from it. Any savings you have, the bookshop will raise something. I'll sort it, we'll sort it. You'll be fine. You'll still have money, don't worry.'

'Mark, I'm not worried, it's sorted. I've come into money.'

He smiled. 'Come into money. Okay.'

'A lot of money. It's private. I'm trusting you because I know I can.' He nodded.

'It's Peggy. She left me half her house in her Will, also half her savings. It's a huge amount, Mark.'

He looked at her and then out of the window. What had he just heard? Seriously? Peggy had gone and done it. She'd changed the bloody Will. His information had been right.

Katie continued: 'I don't know how much, please you mustn't say anything. I can trust you. But we are talking hundreds of thousands. She's left me half of everything, Mark. I'm going to be financially fine. I won't have to worry about selling this house. I won't have to worry about money again. I can just pay off Shaun's debts.'

Mark stared at her, not knowing what to say. He tried to stay upbeat. 'That's great. I'm a bit speechless to be honest. Hope you don't mind me asking, you said half the house, who has the other half?'

Katie looked at him. 'What of the money? Does that matter?'

'Um, well no, I suppose it doesn't. Just interested that's all.'

'Well, you don't know him. He's called Jack, he's Cecil's son. We've been talking a lot. He's a great guy. I like him, you'd like him. You'll help me, won't you? I'll tell you what's happened.'

Mark swallowed hard and nodded. 'Yep, sure.'

'I'll make the tea,' Katie said.

FIFTY TWO

OLIVIA sat opposite Jack outside the coffee shop.

She looked terrible, pale, and gaunt. Her life was not the same. Her spark had gone. That night, that awful attack, had destroyed her.

'My mum knows. I could hardly keep it a secret, look at me.' She stared at Jack, waiting for his reaction. 'She wants me to go to the police.'

'Nice,' said Jack. He looked up as the words sank in. 'And what do you want, Olivia?'

'I don't know. I feel shit,' she said as she pulled out a cigarette. 'Sometimes I don't get up till the afternoon. I feel like hurting myself. I'm drinking too much, smoking too much, erasing the memories. The scars will never heal, Jack.' She pulled a sarcastic face. 'I could drop you in it of course.'

Jack stared at her. 'What's the point of that? It wasn't me who did it. I will just be in a lot of shit with the coppers for a while until they realise they won't get anything out of me.'

Olivia sipped her coffee and looked at him, dragging hard on her cigarette. 'You're an arsehole. Look at me. I'm nothing to how I was. I hardly go out. I have no job. I drive my mum crazy. I think I'm going crazy. I hate myself, my friends have gone, my mum's worried sick. You know I won't go to the police right now. But I promise you if I ever feel threatened again, your name will be with them straightaway. God help me, I will drop you from such a height.'

'That won't happen,' Jack said. 'I promise.' She laughed, her head flying back. 'You fuck with my head Jack; you do know that don't you? I thought we had something. I really liked you. Now look what you've done to me.'

Jack went to protest, 'I didn't do….'

'Why did I ever trust you?' Olivia's feet were tapping the floor as she stared in his face. 'I'm going. Don't contact me again.'

She swung her bag over her shoulder, got up and walked out. Jack sat there his mind whirling. He felt so guilty as he saw her walk away. He'd have to move on. He'd paid up his dues to Piotr. Angelo was another who had squared up his debt. The Eastern European boys were calling in their monies all over the show. But Jack was twitchy, the state of Olivia worried him. He needed to get out of all this, he needed to get out of London.

He'd had enough. It was time to go.

Mark left Katie after talking for much of the morning. Paying off her debts was her main concern. Not that she had a clue how much those debts were. Who the hell was this, Jack? If he didn't cough up some of Marcin and Tomasz's money, Katie would have to pay the lot. It was going to eat into much of her inheritance. And more worryingly, they would come for her if she didn't have enough cash, no matter what he tried to do. That was for sure.

It was a bloody mess. Why the hell did Peggy put the two of them in such a position? She must have known.

Katie and Jack had been on the phone for more than an hour.

'Why don't you come over tonight?' she said. 'You can be here by 10 and I'll make that sofa up again. You're not working tomorrow; you're not working ever! I know I shouldn't say this, letting my guard down and all that Mr Bianchi, but I sort of miss you.'

'Sort of, miss me,' Jack replied. 'What, sort of? Not much, or sort of a little, or sort of a lot.'

'A lot,' she said quietly. 'So, there you go, I've said it now.'

Jack smiled to himself. 'I'll call you tomorrow and we'll make plans.' He was walking round his apartment which was adorned with boxes. He'd begun to pack. The boxes would follow him later.

'Well, come soon. I might even not make up the sofa for you next time.' Katie smiled to herself.

He imagined her pretty face as she said it. He imagined her innocent smile. He imagined her bubbly ways. How he would love to spend nights with her. How he would love to make love to her. But he'd caused too much damage to others, and Katie wasn't going to be the next. She was so beautiful. Different to any girl he'd met. If he was being real with himself, he would drive the two hours to her house and ask her to spend the rest of her life with him. She made him feel that way. That is how he felt. But Jack didn't want real. It was too complicated. Olivia's story haunted him. Angelo and Fraser, he despised. Work he could do without. At least he knew more about his parents. But Jack was in no mood for real. It felt too complicated to do the simple things. He had the chance for a new life.

'I'll call you soon, Katie'...

Tomasz and Marcin were counting their cash.

The money had been rolling in, stepped up by Tomasz who had flown over to England to beef up the operation. His presence had made a big difference. 'I see Bianchi has paid up.' Tomasz smiled.

It was Tomasz's father who had known Cecil. They had worked together in Ireland, and both had struck up a friendship. It was a bad time, terrorism was rife, bribes easy to take, money laundering even easier. Cecil had gone along with it, until he was in too deep. And then he couldn't get out. They'd trusted Cecil with the money. They'd trusted Peggy knew the full picture.

Either she hadn't, or she couldn't have cared less.

The flight from Heathrow left at 10.50pm. It would be another 12 hours before he would set foot on land again. Everything had been arranged. It hadn't taken long. It was one of the advantages of working in finance in a big city and knowing many people.

Already Jack had a job sorted with Dartwood Investments. It had taken two days to organise. Robert Dartwood was an old friend from university days who was making a name for himself on the West Indies islands of St Kitts and Nevis. He was always looking for good staff and Jack calling fitted the bill, even a small house thrown in for good measure, rent free for six months. Not that Jack was desperate for the money, just a new life.

He looked at his watch as he boarded. He had a thousand thoughts, only one of them sad.

Katie smiled to herself as she made herself a water bottle, before walking up the stairs to bed. She was feeling quite giddy, in a lovely way.

It was a chilly evening.

FIFTY THREE

JACK'S plane landed on time. His new boss had laid on a car to pick him up from the airport. The weather was hot.

'Welcome to St Kitts and Nevis, Mr Bianchi.' The chauffeur beamed a big gold toothy smile. 'I'm Jordan. Pleased to be of service.' Jack smiled and handed him his two cases. The rest of his stuff would follow in the coming weeks.

'Would you like to go straight to the office? Or would you like to go home to freshen up. I don't mind, either way.' Jordan was very attentive.

'I'll go straight to the office. I assume Robert is there.'

'He is.' Jordan smiled again.

It was just after lunchtime when they arrived at Jack's soon to be place of work. A new life in a new country. Robert Dartwood came down to reception to greet him. 'Jack, my man. How are you? Great to see you, good trip?'

'Yep, it was good. Bit tiring, but I'm here now. Look, thanks Bob for all this. You sure everything is good about me working? I don't know all the rules, visas, etc. I guess you do.'

Robert laughed. 'No, I don't know them all,' he joked. 'Of course, I bloody do Jack. It's a six-month working visa. You want to make it permanent; we can arrange. Not only do I employ nearly 200 people here and on Nevis, but I know the Governor like the back of my hand. We're good friends. He's a good guy, we play golf. Sometimes turns the other cheek. You know what I mean?' Jack nodded. 'I know what you mean.'

'So, I'll take you for a quick look round, then Jordan can take you back to your new home. It's about a 15-minute drive. We'll meet up tonight for drinks at my place. Jordan will pick you up.'

It was 8pm when Jack arrived at Robert's huge mansion overlooking the Caribbean Sea. It was a glorious setting.

Two large electronic gates secured the property at the front, as a palm tree-lined drive took them up to a small roundabout with a fountain making a beautiful feature. Robert and his wife, Ellis, were there to greet him as Jordan took the car round the back of the property. After dinner and, with the drinks flowing, the three got talking.

'So, how's the house we have put you up in?' Robert smiled.

'It's really cool, I'll be honest.' Jack had been impressed. A hammock on the front porch, decent-sized back garden, two bedrooms and a modern kitchen. The sea just a short walk away. 'How much would something like that cost?'

'Not a lot,' Robert said. 'Easy for you to afford on the wage you'll be on. And the money you will have come your way. Hope you don't mind, but I told Ellis your story, the inheritance and all that. But why the sudden move?' Robert lit up a cigar and was pointing it in Jack's direction. 'I thought London and you were lovers. You could buy a one bed flat in Chelsea with all that money. Or, I suppose, a ten-bed house over here.' He laughed.

Jack nodded. 'Not wrong. Yep, we were lovers. But things have happened. Let's just say I decided a break would be a good idea. I told you about the money. So, next it was a case of where in the world to go with it. I want to keep working. Thought of the Caribbean, thought you could help me. Here I am.'

Ellis smiled at him. 'Well, Robert tells me you and him were great pals at university.'

'We had our laughs,' Jack smiled and winked at Robert. 'There was a good crew of us. I think we have all done well for ourselves. Well, apart from Keenan Driffield, remember him? He's gone a bit rogue apparently. One of those eco-protestors.'

'He was always a strange one,' Robert said. 'But what about you, rich kid? You could lay around in the sun all day now. Why still work?'

'Yeah, suppose I could. But I want to keep my hand in. Can't see myself swinging from a hammock for the next 50 years. I'm not work-shy, Bob, although I'll be honest, I'm not a great lover of the heat either. Makes me a bit crazy at times.'

Robert and Ellis both laughed. 'You're not a lover of the heat. Christ man, it's bloody 30 degrees about 10 months of the year here. You could have chosen somewhere a bit cooler if you'd wanted.'

'Yeah, but it's a different kind of heat, isn't it? And you have good air conditioning.' Jack smiled and raised his glass. 'Cheers. I assume I start tomorrow.'

Katie picked up the phone and dialled the number. The line was still dead.

It was the fourth time she had tried to call. She had sent four texts, she sent another, and then looked at her watch. She should go to bed; it was almost midnight. She'd ring one more time... But again nothing.

She sat on her bed and looked in the small mirror and combed her hair.

FIFTY FOUR

THE total amount came to £275K. Tomasz smiled as he wrote out the number on a piece of paper for Mark to digest.

'I don't care. No, I'll rephrase that, we don't care how you get that, my friend. Just be sure you do. Because that, is our money.' Tomasz looked at Piotr, who smiled at Marcin as they delivered the news.

'Jack Bianchi, hey? Well, well, well,' Marcin stood up and walked towards Mark. 'He struck gold, didn't he? No wonder he squared up his dues. We thought it was because we threatened his little lass, but obviously he knew more. Got out nicely. You know him?'

Mark shook his head. 'No. And I don't want to. But you will have to get some of that 275 off him. He's not my problem.'

Piotr laughed. 'Oh, no Mark. Bianchi is your problem. Especially as we have it on good authority he's no longer in the country. That means getting hold of him if you want him to cough any of the rest up. Katie on the other hand is here and ready to go… if you get my drift. She can pay the lot, especially as 40K of that is her husband's debt. We don't care how you get it.'

'Why should she pay you the whole fucking lot?' Mark stared at Marcin. 'It's not all her problem. So, you're saying minus Shaun's debt, 235K is the amount of laundered money, I'll sort her to get you half of that, you can go do your own dirty work and get someone else to get Bianchi's half.'

Marcin shook his head, then banged the desk. 'No, no. I

don't think you understand, Mark. We are not planning to hang around for much longer. You get us our money and you get us the whole lot. If you can find Bianchi, all the better. But this is not negotiable. We want £275K ... and soon, very soon. We're not scared to put the frighteners on people. And before you jump up and down about your precious Katie, let me tell you, it won't make a bit of difference. If we need to visit her, we will. Just as we visited Bianchi's bit of stuff, Olivia. Unless you have 24-hour guards on her.'

'You're arseholes.' Mark so wanted to do something to the three bastards in front of him, but it would have been pointless. 'She doesn't have that money yet. You'll have to wait.'

Piotr smiled. 'We will wait a while, but you will keep us informed what's happening. Or we will make our own arrangements.'

Katie and Alice met up for coffee and cake, but Katie's demeanour was very different to the last time they had talked on the phone.

She had spent the week trying to get hold of Jack. She'd given up. Mark had put Peggy's cottage on the market and, within three days they had a buyer. The solicitors had told her Peggy's savings could be released as early as next month. She should have been so happy, a rich girl, but she was anything but.

'I don't believe for one minute he's simply gone off you,' Alice said. 'Something has happened. Why should he just stop contacting you? You were chatting away having a great time. And anyway, if he doesn't want anything to do with you, that's his loss. Katie don't chase him. I know it sounds hard but forget him.'

Katie took a sip of her drink. 'I honestly, can't believe it. We were getting on so well. He stayed the night. We kissed. It was just lovely, so natural, there was a spark. And now nothing. Not a word. Perhaps it's just me. Just when I thought things were turning. I shouldn't have been so stupid. Perhaps I appeared too easy. Oh, listen to me. I'm pathetic.'

Alice leaned across the table and took her hand. 'Pathetic is one thing you are not. So much has happened to you in the last few months, how on earth you are keeping sane, I have no idea. You are a brave girl coping with what you have had to put up with. Now come on, enjoy that drink. There's likely a good explanation and if there isn't… sod him!'

'I know, you're right. I just liked him so much.' She looked at Alice. 'Are you as hard as this with your Jeff?'

'Yep, I am. Serves him right for marrying me.'

They both smiled… but Katie was so hurting.

That evening Mark met at Katie's house to tell her the uncomfortable truth.

He'd made some calls to Jack Bianchi's place of work or, what was now former place of work, but no-one knew where he'd gone. Apparently, he'd left a note with his boss to say he was quitting, left his car keys on his desk. His apartment keys had been handed in. Where he'd gone, no-one knew.

'£275,000. Are you serious? Shaun owed that. Bloody hell Mark, what was he doing?'

'I don't know.' But that's what we are looking at. That's what we must settle. At least you have it.'

'With whom?'

'What?'

'I said, with whom? You have been going on about his debts. Who are they payable to? I want to know. I want to speak to these people. It's not I don't trust you, but I'm set to get a fortune and already a huge chunk of it is going… where and to who? If they are just debt collectors, I want to know who they are.'

Mark looked at her. He was weaving a web of half-truths. She needed to know. 'Okay, Katie, here's what's happened. Shaun got involved in drugs. He wasn't taking drugs, but he was involved with some guys who he helped launder drug money in return for cash that kept the shop afloat. Peggy and Cecil were laundering the money as well. That's why they had money to give to Shaun. Now those guys want their money back. Jack Bianchi owes half, but he's nowhere to be found.'

Katie was shocked hearing Jack's name. 'How do you know he's gone missing? And told by who?'

Mark shook his head. 'I can't say who told me. And why are

you so bothered? Hell, Katie, he's left you right in it. He likely doesn't know Peggy's money is dirty money. If we could find him, he pays half. That would be the best result for you.'

She looked at him, not knowing what to say. She wasn't going to tell Mark about how she felt about Jack – not that she was starting to care anymore. 'Trust me, Katie. I'm telling you the truth. I know you don't believe it, but you must pay this money, or… I don't know. You are in danger from these people. I know it sounds mad, crazy. But trust me. What I'm telling you is right. 100%.'

She stared at him. 'You're serious, aren't you? Jack owes half but he's gone. Why don't we go to the police?'

Mark shook his head. 'Don't even think about the police. Why would I make this stuff up? Why would I want you to pay this amount of money? It's you I'm protecting. There is no negotiation here Katie. Peggy wasn't the person you thought she was. Shaun wasn't the person you thought he was. These are dangerous people we are dealing with. At least you have the money, and more besides. It's not perfect, but it's a deal you can afford, and any danger is then over.'

Katie shook her head. Her hurt was turning to anger. 'What danger? If you say pay up, I'll pay up, but I want to know what the hell this is about, Mark. Be honest with me.'

As Mark drove away from the house, Katie walked back into the kitchen and looked out over her garden. She'd listened to what Mark had said. It felt like another bad dream.

She folded her arms and stared blankly. Shaun had let her down; Peggy had let her down; Now Jack had let her down. What had she done to deserve all this? The rain was starting to hit hard on the windows and her tears began to fall. Yes, she would still have money, but her life felt like it was in pieces, and not for the first time. As the tears fell, she thought of her and Shaun having fun by the river at Bourton, laughing at the couple with their champagne and strawberries. She thought of the fun they had when they first met. Shaun, her first and only true love. Their first time away together in a little hotel at Scarborough, the excitement. The way they worked together in the shop, how he supported her through her teacher training. How she supported him and his dreams to own that shop. Their wedding day, a glorious sunny occasion. Him carrying her over the threshold of their little cottage, talk of children, talk of the future. It was all one big lie, one big deceit, now all a distant dream. She held back more tears as she thought of Peggy. The times they had spent together, laughing, and talking, putting the world to right. Yet, all the time Peggy had been deceiving her as well. Mark had made her understand the predicament of her situation. She stifled back more tears. She'd kissed Mark a couple of times. How she'd worried she was being untrue to Shaun, yet all the time, it was he who was the one not to trust. And then along came Jack…

She'd trusted and loved them all, and had been repaid with what?

He put the phone down, his face red with rage.

He knew something was wrong. If he hadn't persisted in asking, he might never have known. He'd certainly have been one of the last to have found out. He banged his fist on the table and poured himself a whiskey.

'The bastards!', he roared.

FIFTY FIVE

ANGELO and Fraser were enjoying a coffee in the boardroom. Autumn had replaced summer, and the wind was getting up outside. It had been raining all week, on and off.

Business remained good and Jack's replacement, a young man fresh out of Leeds University, David Tatum, was proving a good addition to the firm. The phone rang. Angelo picked it up. 'Ah, nice to hear from you. How are you? Hope all's well.'

But Angelo's cheery mood changed as he listened to the person on the other end. Angelo stood up, pacing round the room, looking at Fraser as he did so. Angelo was nodding his head, said a few 'yes's' and 'no's'. The person on the other end was clearly doing the talking. 'I don't know. If I knew, I would tell you.' Angelo managed to get a word in. 'Okay, of course I will. Absolutely, but he's been gone six weeks or so now. Where, I don't know. Okay, okay, yes, goodbye. And, yes, I promise I will.'

Angelo finished the call and put his mobile on his desk. Fraser looked up. 'Don't ask,' Angelo said. 'But I'm starting to wonder when Jack Bianchi's name will eventually become history in this office?'

Fraser looked at Angelo. 'Now what's he done? And who was that?'

Katie and Mark were huddled under a tree. The pair had met up at a park near to where Katie lived.

The rain had started, the forecast had said it was going ease by lunchtime. Katie had called Mark to say the money from Peggy's estate had dropped into her bank account. Knowing what she did about it now, it felt dirty. She had almost told Mark she didn't want it. But that would just be silly.

'I know a person in London who will sort all this,' Mark said. 'Now the money is there he can transfer it to wherever they want it to go. But it won't all go at once, Katie. And likely separate accounts.'

'I don't care less,' Katie looked solemn. 'I really couldn't give a toss about the money, to be honest. I'm fed up with the whole thing.'

Mark had been doing his best to understand her, but his patience was wearing thin. 'Do you know what, Katie? I think I'll just leave you to sort all this mess that your husband and this Jack Bianchi bloke got you into.' His tone caught her by surprise. 'I know what. I'll contact these people who I've been keeping you away from and who, trust me, you do not want to meet, and I'll tell them that Katie doesn't really give a toss and doesn't want the money. They can have it all. How does that sound? You can sort it with them. Give them the whole lot.'

Katie went to speak, but Mark carried on, his voice raising. 'Sorry, Katie, but I'm up to my eyeballs with all this shit. None of your problems are my doing. I'm helping you out here, I'm caring for you, while all you do is go on about things that I understand have been terrible for you but are nothing I've done. In fact, it seems to me, I'm the only one who has had your back in recent times, yet I'm the one you nag at. Am I the puppet hanging on a string for you to flick and prod when you want, while others drop you, let you down and get you in the mess you're in? It feels that way. I appreciate a lot of things, Katie. I appreciate what you've been through, but you seem bloody ungrateful for the stuff I'm doing to try and help. Sorry, but that's how I feel, because you have no idea, no idea whatsoever how much danger you could have been in, could still be in, if we don't get this sorted.'

Katie stared at him. She'd never heard Mark like this. She went to speak, but nothing came out at first. She faced him. 'I'm sorry. You are right, I am ungrateful. Please, understand though. How I feel. How I'm trying to cope. This is all a nightmare.' She looked away.

He reached out and took hold of her arms, turning her to him. 'Look, I'm sorry. That was out of order, I shouldn't have shouted. I do want to help you. I just feel, I don't know, a bit crap when you go on about other people, all who have let you down, while I'm the one trying to help you.'

'I'm sorry to.' She looked at him, half smiled, leaned forward, and went to kiss him on the cheek. But he turned away. 'No, Katie. No more half hopes, not for me. Let's just get all this sorted.'

Jack had enjoyed a fair amount to drink.

Robert and Ellis' parties at their mansion were known by all on the islands as extravagant, fun nights, and Robert made sure everyone was well catered for, all his employees were invited. Jack had been living on St Kitts and Nevis for three months. He had moved to Nevis, the smaller of the two islands when his money came through from the sale of Peggy's house and the money from her Will. He could have given up his job there and then, but he liked working, and anyhow, there was only so much time you could spend swimming in the Caribbean and drinking Red Stripe. Robert's office was based on St Kitts, but there was easy access across *The Narrows*. Jack worked from home two days a week. It was bliss. He had made many friends and was happy.

'So, Mr Bianchi, how are we doing this month?' Ellis Dartwood slid up alongside Jack, who was standing by the swimming pool. There must have been at least 20 people in the pool, some swimming, most shouting, and things were getting out of hand as the drink flowed, the clock ticking towards midnight, with bikini tops being thrown up in the air as the frivolities continued unabated.

'I've had a bit to drink to be honest, Ellis, so don't take everything I say literally. When you say, 'good month', do you mean workwise or social wise?'

'I mean both.' Ellis smiled at him and took his arm. 'Come on, you tell me all about it. Let's go for a stroll. I'll prop you up.' He smiled at her; she was gorgeous. The pair had got on from the outset.

Ellis was a few years older than both Robert and Jack, she was tall, almost six foot and had long blond hair. She had it all going on, and she knew it, her low-cut dress with a long slit up her leg flowing in the warm breeze. Robert had told Jack during a recent work's trip to Jamaica, Ellis didn't want kids… *'would ruin her figure'*.

'So, are you settling into your pad over on Nevis? Robert has told me it's very nice.'

'It is nice. He came over a few weeks ago to look. I like it, big hammock, little swimming pool. Prefer it that way, I would always rather swing than swim.'

She laughed. 'Would you now. You into swinging?'

Jack smiled. 'Now, Mrs Dartwood, that's more than enough. I may say something I regret, and I don't want to do that to the boss' wife, now do I?'

She smiled and grabbed his arm tighter as they made their way away from the pool and out into the huge gardens that adorned the mansion. The night was warm, the sky was clear, and the stars were bright. It was another stunning Caribbean evening. 'So, Jack, you got a lady friend yet in that wonderful Nevis pad of yours?' They'd been walking for 10 minutes and were still only a third of the way down the garden, but a long way from the pool. It was quiet and still, the sound of the swimmers laughing and cheering now a faint murmur. You could just hear the sea lapping on the shore further ahead. Ellis had stopped the walk as they stood among huge bushes and trees.

'There's no-one. I'm not really into commitment.' He smiled. 'Although that sounds a bit odd, doesn't it? Makes me sound as though I think a lady friend would have to be my wife. What I mean is, I love women, but not to marry them… if you know what I mean?'

Ellis smiled. 'I didn't ask you if you were getting married. Only if there was someone in your life?'

Jack shook his head. 'No, not now. Well, there has been. There was. Could of, maybe should of… that type of thing. But here now, no.'

They were close together. She leaned up against him, pushing her chest forward as she forced him back against a tree. He could smell her perfume; she could smell his aftershave, and the drink on his breath. She looked at him and bit her lip. He knew it was going to happen and he knew he should have stopped. But the drink was too much, his head was spinning, as she moved her lips towards his. They kissed, slowly at first, then more passionately. She pulled away and looked at him but not before biting his lip. She had always found Jack Bianchi sexy from the first day she'd seen him. She loved those dark wavy locks.

'I don't know, Ellis,' Jack said. 'I really don't think this is a great idea.'

She smiled. 'Be quiet. We're in the middle of nowhere.' She kissed him again. 'You think Robert looks after me? Hardly. Bit of a trophy wife, that's the problem.'

Then, standing back, still staring at him, she pulled the strap of her dress down one side, then the other, and moved them down over her shoulders, arms, and hands, she had no bra on. Jack shook his head slowly as she pulled him down burying him into her naked chest. He bent down, kissing her nipples, and fondling her. It went on for a minute, maybe more, until she pulled away and pulled her straps back up and pushed him away. He looked at her. 'Ellis. We shouldn't be doing this.'

'Too right, we shouldn't, Jack… You sexy man.' She smiled broadly; it was all a game. She put her finger to his mouth. He was worse the wear for drink, and she had the power. She pushed him back against the tree again, kissed him, and this time it was her turn. She went down on her knees, wrestling with the belt of his white shorts, unzipping the fly, and pulling them down forcefully with his pants, to his ankles. She looked up and smiled again. 'Not bad,' she said, as she fondled him.

He put his head back and looked up at the stars.

Jordan had been watching. He often patrolled the gardens late at night. It was part of his work for Robert.

He'd seen his boss' wife. He'd watched them both. He'd seen what she had done to him. And now he had the evidence. He was no fan of Jack Bianchi.

Jordan was disgusted, and his loyalty to his boss was absolute.

FIFTY SIX

CHRISTMAS Day in the Caribbean was a different experience for Jack, away from the usual cold weather in England.

A hot, sunny day, swinging on his hammock. He'd turned down the chance to have Christmas lunch with Robert and Ellis. He was happy enough in his own company. He looked at his watch. It was 3pm. He went to the fridge and got out a beer. It was going to be a long day, even with an early night. He sat and pondered. Life was good; his job was going well. He smiled to himself as he thought of Ellis and their encounter at the party. That was a few weeks ago. He'd been worried in the days afterwards how she would react when she saw him. He need not have done. The first time they'd met after 'that night', Ellis had brushed past him in a corridor at work. She was meeting Robert. She'd just smiled and winked.

He looked at his watch again and thought hard. He'd been building up to this for a little while now. No, it had been more than a little while. So, why not on Christmas Day? He picked up his phone and looked at the name... he took a deep breath, hoping it was still the same number.

'Hi! It's Jack' He sent the text and waited.

About ten minutes later... *'What do you want?'*

'How are you? Happy Christmas'.

'How am I? Are you serious?'

Jack swallowed hard.

'Just wanted to say hello. Be honest, I wanted to speak to you. I'm

relaxing with a Red Stripe, thinking of you. I really am thinking of you. I think of you alot.'

'Yes, of course you do. Red Stripe!!! What's that?

'It's a beer. A beer that's popular here'.

'Well, you enjoy it. I suppose you've had a few and thought you'd contact me. Where's here BTW?'

He wondered what he should say. He could sense the rightful sarcasm.

'I know you're angry. Can I call you please?'

'Well, you're right on that. Why should I say yes?'

'Because you deserve an explanation. I understand if you tell me to get lost. I'm sorry. So sorry. I want to talk to you. Please, I can explain. If you just let me explain…'

He sent the text… then sent another straight after… *'I miss you. I've been thinking about you more than you'll ever know. Come and join me. I'm serious.'*

There followed, for Jack, what seemed like an eternity, before his answer came through.

'Call me.'

FIFTY SEVEN

ROBERT looked at the screen.

The video was grainy, but it was clear enough. The anonymous e-mail with the attachment had been sent two hours previous. He nearly hadn't opened it, thinking a subject title *'you must watch this Robert'* was spam. He didn't recognise where it had come from. As he played it back to himself, he took a deep breath and sat back in his chair. He picked up the phone and made a call. Then he made another.

Ellis was cooking jerk chicken for dinner. She knew it was Robert's favourite. With a few potatoes, coleslaw, and batons of bread, accompanied by a good red wine, they would enjoy the evening ahead. She looked up as Robert's car pulled up outside the house. It was 7pm, good timing. 'Guess what we've got for dinner?' she smiled as he walked in. He walked straight past her and into the living room, through the large patio doors that looked out onto the huge garden. 'Surprise me,' he shouted back to her.

'Jerk chicken,' she said as she went out to meet him. 'You want a drink first; it will still be a few minutes.' He turned to look at her. She smiled, but he wasn't smiling.

'You, okay?' She smiled again. 'What's the matter?' She felt his mood odd. He cracked a slight smile and walked up to her. 'That's a good question. How am I?' He smiled at her more this time. 'Aren't I always, okay?'

Ellis had stopped smiling herself now. 'What do you mean?

What's wrong, Robert. Stop messing about. You're worrying me.'

'Am I? Sorry about that, my darling, darling Ellis.'

He wasn't smiling now, neither was Ellis. 'So, what is wrong with me?' He began walking back into the room, Ellis following. 'Come here.' He got hold of her hand and showed her his phone. 'Take a look at this. It arrived in my e-mail box this morning. What is it? Can you see?'

He pulled her close and called up the video. He took hold of her arm as he played it. She went to shrug his grip off, but he wouldn't let her. 'I said, watch this,' he said more menacingly.

Ellis watched the 30-second clip, her heart beating faster as she realised what it was. She felt sick. She said nothing. 'So, my darling Ellis,' he said sarcastically. 'What a good little blow job wife you appear to have become. Just shame it's not me in the video. Ask again, what is wrong with me?'

She went to walk off, but he grabbed hold of her. His mood angry. 'What the fuck do you think you're doing Ellis?' She didn't' reply. 'I said, what have you got to say? I want answers. I deserve an answer. I deserve an explanation if I could possibly even think there was one. You look like a slut, Ellis. You are my wife, acting like a slut.'

She went to break free from him, but his grip was still solid. Robert was a strong man. He dragged her into the room and threw her on the sofa. 'Speak, Ellis. Speak to me.' She had begun to cry. While their relationship had never been perfect, she had never cheated on him. And here it was now, on video. She had no-where to go with it. 'I'm sorry, Robert. I'm sorry.' He stood over her as the tears flowed heavier. 'I don't know what to say. I was drunk, it was all my fault. I don't know why I did it. Please, forgive me. Please. I've never done anything like it before. Please, you must believe me. I'm sorry.'

'Stand up,' he said. She looked up at him. 'I said stand up.' She wiped the tears from her eyes and stood up. They were just inches from each other's faces. He kissed her on the lips. She was shaking as he kissed her again. Then he smiled. 'Show me what you do?' he said.

'What?' Ellis replied. 'I said, show me what you do, Ellis.' He smiled at her and kissed her again. 'You know, what you did to

Jack. That is Jack, isn't it? Even I can see it's Jack Bianchi.'

She looked straight at him. 'I don't understand. Show you what?'

'Oh, Ellis, do I have to make it obvious. Just do what you did to Jack that night. Go on.'

She was shaking more now as he got hold of her head and pushed her down his chest towards his trousers. She began fiddling with his fly, unzipping his trousers and was about to grab hold of him, before he pulled her up by the hair. 'Don't touch me. You're a whore, Ellis,' he smirked in her face as he stared at her again. 'A whore. My wife's a whore and I never knew. I don't want your mouth anywhere near me. I know where it's been.' And with that he backhanded her round the face. She fell to the floor. He picked her up, his face inches from hers, the tears flowing down her cheeks. He grabbed her round the neck. 'Pack your bags and get out of my house and don't come back.'

'No, Robert. No, please. Where do I go?'

'I don't care. You have 10 minutes.'

Jack was watching the television when there was a knock at his door.

He hadn't heard a car come up the drive to his house. He went through the kitchen and turned down the music as he headed for the door, beer in hand. He opened it up…

Bang! Jack's world went dark.

FIFTY EIGHT

HE slowly opened his eyes.

He felt he was in motion and there was a humming noise. He felt sick, then realised he could hardly move. His hands were tied behind his back, his feet were bound. He panicked into life, trying to sit up. He could see more clearly now.

'Ah, Mr Bianchi. Nice you could join us.' The man, sweat pouring from his head, came up to Jack's face grinning. He held a knife in his hand. 'Good to see you. We'd thought you were dead. We're glad you're not. It was a nasty crash. It would have made things, let's say, complicated.'

'What's going on?' Jack's face hurt as he spoke, he had a headache.

'What's going on indeed,' the man replied. 'Well, let's put it this way, shall we, Mr Bianchi. You've messed with the wrong people and now you're going to find out what happens to people who do such a thing. Get my drift?' The man smiled and looked behind him at the pilot, who remained stoically looking forward through the cockpit windscreen as the plane taxied on the uneven grass runway, bouncing precariously.

'What are you talking about?' Jack had shuffled round to sit up.

The man smiled. 'Ah, Jack, you are one lucky guy. You see our boss has a nasty streak and I'm surprised he's letting you off so easily. He's usually worse, he must like you, but I do have a message.' Jack looked at him confused. 'What are you talking about?'

The man took his knife and leaned towards Jack's face, his breath stinking of drink. 'The message is simple. You keep away from our islands. You keep away from Nevis. You keep away from St Kitts, the Caribbean, anywhere within 200 miles. And most importantly, you keep away from Ellis. Our boss is letting you off lightly. If I had my way and you had done that with my woman, you wouldn't be so lucky.'

Jack was silent, the knife was inches from his throat. The man lifted it up and began to gently slice Jack's cheek, drawing blood. He brought the knife down a few centimetres as the blood began to slowly flow down his face. Jack let out a small grimace, but he was helpless with his back against the plane's side. The man was strong. 'A little reminder from Nevis for you to remember us by.' He grinned as he stood back. Then his face contorted. 'I hate men like you,' he growled. 'You think you own everything. You think you are everything. You think you are untouchable.'

He kicked Jack in the sides of his thighs, then he kicked him again. The man took off his jacket to reveal powerful arms. He threw the knife to floor. The pilot looked round; he knew what was coming as the plane taxied, lightning flashing in the distance. He shook his head and closed the door to the cockpit as he heard the kicks and punches fly. As soon as he could after take-off, he turned east, another 20 minutes and the storm would be behind them.

In the back of the plane, Jack's lifeless body rolled from side to side.

FIFTY NINE

KATIE pulled into the car park. It had been another long drive.

For six weeks she had made the same journey to Brighton, two, three, sometimes four times a week. She walked through the hospital grounds and into reception. She knew the place like the back of her hand. Up a flight of steps and along the corridor to Flempton Ward – a specialist neurological unit. She walked through the double doors and looked at the beds ahead, walking down to the furthest one on the right-hand side. Jack smiled as he saw her approach.

'Hi,' she said. 'How are we feeling today?'

He smiled at the only visitor he'd received in the two months he'd been in hospital. The only visitor he had wanted. She leaned over him and kissed him on the head. 'I'm okay,' he tried to smile. 'Managed to eat all my pizza last night, bearing in mind it was veggie. What a result.'

'Well, that's no bad thing. You've lost plenty of weight, a few pizzas won't hurt. And becoming a veggie as well.'

He smiled, held out his hand as she took it. 'Thank you. For all this, for being here.'

'Oh, don't start again. You've said that a million times. Well, probably not a million, but it seems like it. I know how you feel, you've told me, let's just get you on the mend.'

Katie stood up and put some fruit in a bowl beside his bed. Jack still had a long way to go, but he was nowhere near as seriously hurt as when he'd first arrived at a hospital in the

United States. Found near a garage forecourt in Miami in one of the city's roughest neighbourhoods, Jack had been dumped there after the plane he had been bound and gagged in landed at a small airstrip near the city. He'd been driven to the forecourt, beaten again and was barely alive when two girls found him slumped beside a dustbin. He had six broken ribs, a broken arm, both knees, and shoulder. He had a small bleed on the brain, his chances of surviving had been put at less than 20%. He had been placed in an induced coma for two weeks. That was three months ago. His recovery had been nothing short of a miracle since, even though his return to England, and Brighton, had been delayed twice because of concerns over him travelling. But Jack was strong. He'd made good progress. On his return to the UK, he'd asked the hospital in England to contact the solicitors in Banbury he and Katie had dealt with over Peggy's Will. He wanted Katie's number. His phone had long gone. The solicitors had got hold of her. She'd driven to Brighton as soon as one of them had called to tell her Jack had asked for her. She was supposed to have been flying out to the Caribbean to be with him. She'd wondered why he hadn't returned her calls after asking her to join him. She had almost given up on him… again. It had all made sense when she saw him in hospital.

'So, I spoke to the doctor, and he said I could be out of bed next week,' Jack said, gripping Katie's hand tight.

'That would be great,' she replied. 'I don't think I want to be here though when you first try and walk again. It could be a bit scary to watch. Talk about watching a drunk man making strides.'

He smiled at her. He was so glad she was with him. He didn't deserve her after the way he had up and left for Nevis. And yet there had always been something between them. 'You're too good for me,' he said. He gripped her hand tightly once more. She smiled back at him and kissed him on the cheek.

'That's one thing you are right about. I should have told you to get lost. But I couldn't. I suppose it says everything.'

'It does. It says, I'm lucky. Commitment has never been my bag; well, wasn't my bag.'

It was her turn to grip his hand: 'Well, you have probably a few months still to decide if commitment is ever going to be your bag, Jack. Or whether you're getting off on a guilt trip. Because once you are up and walking, they'll let you out of here. And then where will you go?' She raised her eyebrows.

He looked at her. 'At least I have money,' Jack said. 'I've managed to check. It's still all there. I could get a good hotel room for a while. I could even buy a small house – perhaps in the Cotswolds. Do you know anyone who lives there?'

He looked up at her, his eyes watery. He was trying to act brave, but he was scared, she was overwhelming him. No woman had ever done this to him. He'd been given the biggest of beatings, a near-death experience and after all he'd done to her, she'd been there for him. 'I love you, Katie.'

She smiled. 'I love you to.' She leaned over and kissed him again. 'Now, get some rest. I'm going into Brighton to get a few things. I'll be back this afternoon.'

He smiled as she got up. He looked at her, she was so pretty, so easy to understand, so down-to-earth, so everything in a woman he hadn't found up to now. He hated himself for the way he had treated her, and he was going to make sure he loved her like no-one had ever loved her before. She had changed him forever.

For the first time in his life, Jack had a whole heart to give.

SIXTY

THE roses in the garden were in full bloom, summer had arrived. The sun was shining.

Katie was in the kitchen making a coffee, Jack was sitting on a sun lounger in his shorts. A gentle breeze flowed through the garden of their Cotswolds home. Within a few weeks of being able to walk, the hospital had told Jack he could leave. The main concern had always been the slight bleed on the brain, but that had healed, the broken bones were also on the mend. He was still limping and the scar on his cheek was going nowhere. Their relationship had been a whirlwind on their return to Katie's house. The first thing they did was put her cottage on the market, selling it in no time and buying a bigger detached cottage just outside Chipping Norton for the two of them. A house they could call their own. They loved the area. They both loved each other. Every other weekend they would visit Peggy and Cecil's grave and lay flowers. Although the couple hadn't been all they had made out to be, Jack and Katie had much to thank them for, even if the deceit had hurt. Katie had got a part-time job at the local primary school, although she didn't need to work. She enjoyed it, Jack was enjoying the peace and quiet of a different, stress-free lifestyle. He would find work again someday. He thought he might write a book. Mark had been round to see them both, after Katie had called him to discuss her finances, meeting Jack for the first time. It had been a frosty beginning, but had thawed, although Mark made it clear it was a *'nice to meet you, but goodbye'* situation.

As Jack sat in the lounger, he put his hands behind his head and thought of what the last year had brought. It was time to settle down and he knew it. Jack the lad no more.

'Do you want any biscuits?' Katie was walking towards him with two mugs of coffee.

'No, I'm fine. Had three Weetabix for breakfast.'

'Oooh, get you, three Weetabix. Needed it after that performance this morning.' She flicked her eyes. He loved her for it. She had a way of saying the naughtiest of things with such an innocent look. 'Might do it again later,' he smiled as he went to pick his coffee up.

'Will you now? Why wait? She started to undo the buttons on her blouse.

'Stop that. Stop that. I'm only joking. I still have pains in this shoulder.' He smiled as he deliberately pointed to the shoulder that hadn't been broken.

'Didn't think you were quite the man you pretend to be.' They both sipped their coffees.

'By the way, I'm seeing Alice tonight,' Katie said. 'I've got some curtains to drop off to her, so I said I'd stay and have a drink. Be good to catch up.'

'Absolutely. Didn't know we had any curtains spare.'

'Well, that's because you don't look hard enough and certainly don't remember much. We bought two sets from my cottage, and they were in the loft. If you looked in the third room, you would have seen them now on the bed.'

'Ah, those curtains,' Jack said. 'I know the ones.'

'No, you don't you liar.' They laughed.

'Do you miss London?' She moved close to him, fiddling with his hair. He looked at the water fountain in between two large beds of shrubs, water trickling down into a small pond. Their garden was a picture. 'No. Not one bit. I don't miss Nevis either. In saying that about London, on second thoughts, who knows? Maybe we'll live there together one day.'

'Like hell we will,' Katie said. 'I'm no London girl. You'll live there on your own.'

He smiled. 'Knew you'd say that.'

Katie left for Alice's just after dinner.

Jack watched as she drove off and he then headed upstairs towards their bedroom. He picked up his phone and saw he'd a missed call. He thought for a moment, took a deep breath, and decided to return it.

'Well, well, hello stranger. Long time no chat, I knew you would call me back. I hear you've been in a scrape or two. You on the mend? Thought I'd catch up. Perhaps we could meet up… for old time's sake.' Jack paced round the room, phone to his ear, smiling. She was chattering away. 'How are you, Dani? Yes, I'm on the mend. And your beautiful tones still give me a tingle.'

'Oh, shut up. The only thing I've ever given you is a good shag… and you know it.'

Jack laughed. 'Hey, that's enough. How are you? How are things with Angelo?'

'I'm fine. He's gone. We keep in touch, but he knew it was coming. We knew it was coming.'

'Are you sad?'

'Kidding, aren't you? I made a good settlement with him. He's kept the house in the country, I have the apartment in London. He gave me just over a million. I could have taken him to court for more, but what's the point? It's a good deal, we had some good times. He's still working at the firm though. Never did find out who gave him that beating. Remember that? He knows but won't say.'

'Well, there you go,' Jack said. 'Anyway, you called.'

'Yes, I want a favour. I've got all this money and I need to invest it. I could ask Angelo, but he'd likely stitch me up. I could ask Fraser, although he's now a dad with twins, so his head is all over the place. Anyhow, could we meet up and you give me some advice?'

'Yeah, suppose we could.' Dani smiled to herself as she continued to talk, flicking through dresses in her favourite London boutique as she did so. 'And you can tell me what the hell has been going on in your world. Can't imagine it hasn't been interesting. I'm glad you are well again. I did hear it was bad. Then we can head back to my apartment if you like.' She smiled to herself.

Jack looked outside as the sun was getting lower in the beautiful Cotswolds night sky. He loved talking to Dani, but it also made him realise how his life was different now, the way he liked it. 'No, Dani. Not back to yours but give us a call next week. We'll sort something.'

'Spoil sport. What's the matter. All loved up, are we? Don't worry, I've heard. Someone's tied you down at last. I'm happy for you. Lucky her. Okay, enough of that, you know I appreciate it if we can sort this money. Speak soon.' She hung up.

Jack threw the phone on the bed, stood in the bedroom and looked around. He went to the bedroom cabinet on his side of the bed and opened the bottom drawer. He felt to the back and took out the box. He looked at it, before opening it slowly. He looked at the ring. Four diamonds and four emeralds, green was her favourite colour. Even if he said so himself, it looked beautiful.

He was going to ask her tomorrow.

SIXTY ONE

ALICE screamed out loud!

'What? How long gone? Crikey. Katie, you're going to be a mummy.'

Alice hugged her tight as they both embraced, dancing around the living room. Katie had decided to tell her friend as soon as it had been confirmed. She was just over three months pregnant. 'What did Jack say?', Alice said excitedly. 'I bet he's gone crazy. He'll be such a cool dad.'

Katie raised her eyebrows. 'He doesn't know yet.'

'What?' Alice shrieked again. 'He doesn't know. Why doesn't he know? Wow. Don't tell me you've told me before you've told him. That's mad.'

'Well, I have told you before him. I only went to the doctor's yesterday afternoon. I'm going to surprise him tomorrow morning because I'm not working and, well, Jack's never working. I've bought a card today and I'm going to put the picture of the ultra-sound inside it. He'll probably take about 20 minutes to work out what it means, but it will be fun watching him try.'

The girls hugged. 'I'm so happy for you, Katie. You deserve all this. I like Jack. I would say, I'd shag him, but it's not the right thing between friends, is it?' Katie shook her head and laughed. Alice went to the fridge. 'This calls for a celebration. Although with driving and being pregnant, I suppose it's tonic water for you.'

'Tonic water sounds good.'

Alice returned with two glasses, she'd found a half full bottle of wine her and Jeff hadn't finished off. She didn't need a second invitation. She poured Katie the tonic. 'To Katie, Jack and bump,' Alice raised her glass.

They clinked glasses and laughed again.

Jack was flicking through the channels. It was just after 9pm and he wasn't into starting to watch a film at this time of night. Katie would be home soon.

He was out of boxsets to. There was a knock at the door. He looked up and looked out of the living room window. He couldn't see anything. He got up, unsure who could be calling at this time of the evening. There was a knock again, just as Jack reached the door to open it. 'Okay, okay, I'm coming,' he said.

He opened the door and had to look twice at the man standing there. He didn't recognise him to begin with. 'Evening, Jack.'

Jack looked again. 'Toby? Mr Ruskin. Is that you?'

'Correct.'

Jack smiled. 'Hi. What are you doing here at this time of the night? How did you know I lived here?' Toby Ruskin was standing a few feet away from the front door. He had a large scarf draped round a long trench coat. He had a flat cap on. His hands were in his pockets. 'I know a lot about you, my boy. We go back a long way, don't we? You weren't hard to find.'

Jack nodded. 'You want to come in?'

'No, I don't want to come in.' Toby Ruskin moved forward, one foot inside the house. 'I won't stay. It's not a social call.'

Jack continued to look at him, not sure where the conversation was going.

'You see Jack, my darling granddaughter isn't well. She hasn't been well for a year or so now. You remember Olivia.' Now Jack's hackles were up.

'Did you know she'd been sectioned? You know what that is?' Jack nodded. 'Yes, Jack, sectioned, in a secure mental hospital. She hasn't been well since she was attacked in her own apartment. You remember?'

'Okay, Toby, what do you want?' Jack's tone changed. Toby Ruskin smiled at his unease. 'I just wanted to let you know, that's all.'

Jack nodded. 'Okay. Well, you've told me, so I'm happy for you to get lost now.'

'No need to speak to me like that. Don't worry, I'm going.' Toby Ruskin went to turn to leave, then stopped. Jack had his hands on his hips and was looking at him, ready to close the door.

'Before I go though.' Toby Ruskin faced Jack, pulled his right hand out of his pocket, the shiny metal gun appearing from nowhere. He fired three quick shots, as Jack fell backwards onto the floor, cracking his head on the solid surface, blood pouring from his shattered face where the first bullet hit him. The other two ripped through his chest.

Toby Ruskin stood over him. 'You destroyed my family, Jack Bianchi. I'll destroy yours.' He moved forward and fired again into the face of Jack's spread-eagled body. He stood tall over him, before Toby Ruskin put the gun inside his own mouth and fired again, his brain splattering against the walls.

Toby Ruskin fell forward, collapsing on top of Jack.

SIXTY TWO

FOUR YEARS LATER

THERE was a chill in the air and while the sky was blue, it wasn't going to get warm, not today.

Katie had a long black coat on, a purple hat and scarf her mum and dad had bought her for Christmas. She stood and stared at the stone. She stared at the inscription. She laid the flowers. She cried every time she came to the cemetery, she told herself one day she wouldn't cry. But that day wasn't yet. She stood back up after laying the flowers and said the prayer she always had done.

'Don't cry mummy.' Katie knelt beside her daughter – her one bright light – and hugged her. 'Darling, these are tears of happiness.'

'But I thought crying meant sad things, mummy. And you always cry here.'

'Not always, darling.'

Katie looked again at the inscription… *'Jack Bianchi, aged 27, much loved father, son and partner'*. She rubbed her fingers over his name. More tears fell.

'She has your eyes, Jack,' she whispered. She always spoke to him. Katie held her daughter's hand. 'You would have been so proud of her. I'm going to keep telling her all about you. Well, not all the things perhaps,' Katie held back a smile. 'She's growing up so fast. I know you can see her from up there.'

Katie looked across at her as their daughter pulled away and began picking daisies among the headstones nearby. 'Can I put these on daddy please?' She had come back with a handful of the pretty white and yellow flowers.

'Of course, you can, darling. Daddy would love that. So pretty'.

Olivia watched. Her eyes wide open.

She watched the little girl who was with her, the little girl with the pretty white and yellow flowers. It must be her child. It must be their child. The child of that man, the man who she had grown to hate. It was the fourth time Olivia had watched her. Had watched them both. She was glad she was well again. She really was. The people at that place, that place she had been for three years had told her she was well enough now. 'Olivia is better now', they would say.

The voices returned sometimes, but she had never told anyone. That's why they told her she was allowed to leave; go into the outside world. She wasn't crazy. Not anymore. She watched the little girl get back into the car. Olivia knew that car; she knew the house where that car lived. It was the same house where her grandad had been that night. The night he never came back. And she missed him. She had loved him so much. She had been told the story. Oh, how she hated that house and the people inside. But she had been told not to hate people, not after what happened to her. It wasn't good to hate. She started shaking, her eyes wider still. It had been two days since she had taken her medication. She took deep breaths, looked at her cut wrists and hands, then watched the car drive away. And now she had decided. She smiled to herself; it had taken her a long time to reach this point. She pulled out the knife and turned it in her hand. Such a long knife. She sliced it gently through her thumb and drew blood. 'Ouch', she said to herself as she sucked the blood from the cut. She walked towards the stone with the inscription on and took out the knife, scraping at the stone, making marks over his name. She should have done this a long time ago. But they hadn't let her out. And now she was angry. She knew the house where the little girl lived. Where that woman lived. Where that evil man had lived. Where her grandad had gone and never returned. She looked at her knife, turning it in her hand. That was it. She had decided.

Tonight, she would visit the house. Visit them both. Much later tonight.

But she wouldn't knock.

THE END

Printed in Great Britain
by Amazon

38393429R00169